ALL GOD'S CHILDREN

Aaron Gwyn

ALL GOD'S
CHILDREN

Europa
editions

Europa Editions
214 West 29th Street
New York, N.Y. 10001
www.europaeditions.com
info@europaeditions.com

Library of Congress Cataloging in Publication Data is available
ISBN 978-1-60945-618-4

Gwyn, Aaron
All God's Children

Book design by Emanuele Ragnisco
www.mekkanografici.com

Cover image: Pexels

Prepress by Grafica Punto Print – Rome

1827, 1857 and 1844 Maps: Library of Congress,
Geography and Map Division.

Printed in the USA

"There was a day when the sons of God came to present themselves before the Lord. And Satan came also."
—JOB 1:6

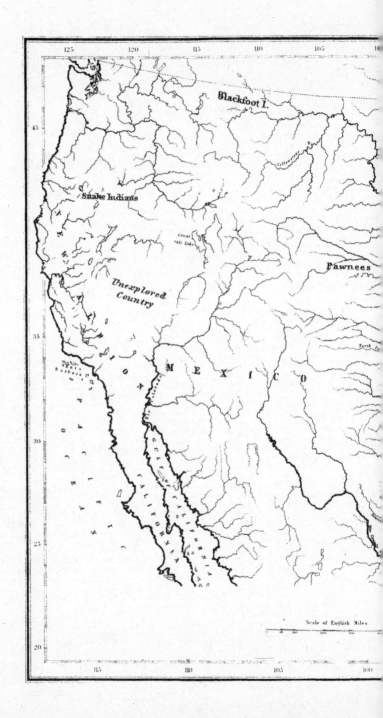

THE
UNITED STATES
1827

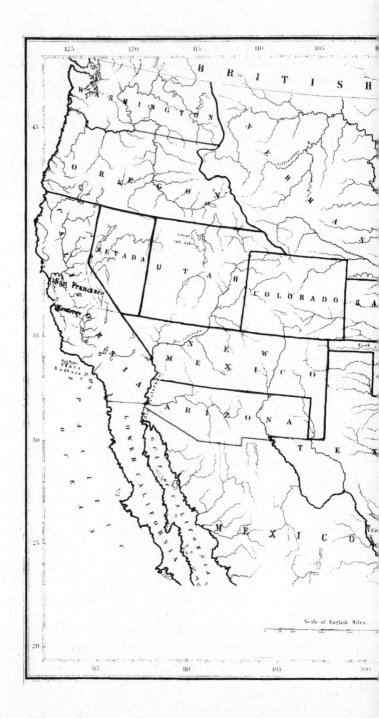

THE
UNITED STATES
1857

MAP OF

TEXAS

AND THE COUNTRIES ADJACENT

1844.

ALL GOD'S
CHILDREN

DUNCAN LAMMONS

—1827—

I came down that winter from Kentucky, travelling the river on a flatboat with two other passengers and a cargo of ice. There were crates and crates of it, packed in sawdust and stacked shoulder-high. Those days, most folks hadn't heard of buying ice; I don't doubt but there were some in the South who'd hardly seen it. If I'd done as Mama taught me and kept up with the papers, I'd have known about Frederic Tudor who was building himself an ice trade out of Boston, cutting blocks from farm ponds and shipping them to Cuba, Charleston, Savannah. He'd just opened a market in New Orleans, which was where me and that barge were headed.

I knew none of this at the time. I figured the crates were full of bug juice or tobacco. I'd just turned twenty, and though my folks had lettered me and hoped I'd take an interest in business or the like, little caught my attention unless it had four legs and passed in front of my rifle.

My second day on the river, curiosity got the better of me and I asked one of the boatmen what they were hauling. He was standing at the edge of the craft, staring into the brown water, keeping an eye out for sawyers. A tree trunk would stave the bottom of a boat quick as you could holler *hickory*.

"It's ice," he told me.

"How's that?"

"Ice," he said.

I figured he was just jobbing me, but he looked serious enough. I asked what they were carrying that for and he told me they sold it.

"Folks give you money for ice?"

"Long as it ain't melted," he said.

Well, I might just've been a tanner's boy from Butler County but I figured I knew a swindle when I heard it. I remember thinking any city that'd pay for ice was liable to slap a tax on well water. God a'mighty. What did they charge for sunshine?

New Orleans was only a way station. The previous year, I'd attended a talk where a man told us that the federal government of Mexico was promising 177 acres of farmland and 4,000 of pasture to families willing to settle between the Sabine and the Nueces. His name was Sterling Robertson. Wasn't much to look at—a squaddy little toad with a fluff of hair tied behind his head—but he could've sold socks to savages. He said that in Texas there was every kind of game: deer and antelope. Turkey and bear. Bee trees and grapes, persimmon trees and cherries. The climate was mild and there were Mexican soldiers to keep the Indians at bay.

Sliding down the river on that flatboat, I thought how Robertson made Texas sound like Eden before the fall.

Or Kentucky. Kentucky back in Boone's day before the slavers came.

I sat watching the country drift past, the fields and farms, the wooding places where steamboats put in to collect fuel for their fireboxes. My heart was homesick and heavy, but every mile south seemed to lift the burden of it. I still thought you could leave America where the planters and plant-managers had everything locked down and laid out. Texas was a free frontier, promising folks like me the chance to start fresh. It's a peculiar sort of man who needs a fresh start by the age of twenty, but I was always peculiar.

I reckon that twenty seemed old to me at the time; now it seems so young. It was certainly too young to understand that America wasn't something you left as much as it was something that you carried, a shape inside yourself—the way stone is shaped by water—all these channels carved inside your soul.

So, while you might've thought you were living in America, all that time it was living in you.

* * *

We reached New Orleans at the end of February. The crew delivered their ice, broke up the flatboat and sold it for lumber. I took a room at a boarding house to wait for a ship that would take me west.

The matron was an ancient woman named Simone—I don't know whether she was a widow or spinster, but if there'd been a husband at some point, she never mentioned him to me.

Upon learning I was bound for Texas, the Madame informed me she'd had a number of boarders over the past several years with the selfsame intentions—one young man was a guest in her house at that very moment; she'd helped him get a job at the Leeds Foundry.

"His name is Smithwick," she said. "Do you know him?"

I told her I didn't know any Smithwicks.

"He's a good boy," she said, "I will introduce you."

But as I had the luxury of lying abed until the sun was up and this youngster rose early to trot off to his foundry job, no such introduction was forthcoming.

During the day, I amused myself by visiting with fellow boarders in the sitting room. At night, I'd go out and walk the gas-lit streets of that strange city. I'd never heard men speak French before.

Or Spanish.

Or whatever it was a young dandy whispered to me in an alley one evening as I was pirooting around the American Quarter.

Come and see, it sounded like. *Come and see.*

I stepped closer to make him out, feeling the old lure in my chest pulling me forward.

I never saw what he hit me with. My knees buckled and the ground came rushing up. I heard a bell in my ears. When the world stopped shimmering, the man was gone and I had blood running into my eyes. I stumbled back down the street, faces floating by, women glancing at me, then quickly looking away.

At the boarding house, Madame Simone tended me and clucked her tongue, brewing a cup of sass tea and seeing to my cuts. Wouldn't show me a mirror, but my face wasn't what concerned me. The footpad had slashed my britches and emptied both pockets.

"Did he get much money?" the matron asked.

I told her the thief had taken every last cent. My eyes were blurry and the Madame's voice sounded as if it came from a long way off.

The Madame dabbed my wounds with witch-hazel. I thought she'd have no choice but to turn me out on the street as I had nothing left to pay for the room but my rifle, shot pouch, and knife, none of which I was prepared to part with.

"Do you know aught of foundry work?" she asked.

"I wouldn't know a foundry from a bull's foot," I told her. "My pap is a tanner."

"Well," she said, "that is no great matter. As long as you have no allergy to a hard day's labor, I can get you employment."

I assured her I had no such allergy and that I appreciated her kindness, but in truth, the proposition did little to raise my spirits. A very low feeling seized hold of me, putting me in mind of my father's warnings before I'd headed south. Pap had agreed I needed to get out of Kentucky, though he didn't think much of my travelling plans.

He said, "You stay clear of New Orleans, Duncan. They shoot cross-eyed men and redheads on sight."

I was neither of these but getting cracked on the head and

liberated of my money had soured me on city-life, and I realized my father had been right—and not just about New Orleans.

Though he never hid his disapproval of my defects of character, he loved me fiercely, always praising my patience for labor and eagerness to learn.

I missed him terribly. Some days I'd pass a man on the street and think I'd smelled Pap on the breeze. A loneliness would come down to crush the breath out of me.

It was then that Mama's voice seemed to whisper in my ear: *You are a good boy, Duncan. You are just and kind.*

Thus, my spirits would be resurrected. I'd remind myself of the proceedings that had sent me running from home. And of the promise I was running toward.

* * *

And so, I took the good Madame up on her offer of employment. The Leeds Foundry hired me on as a finisher—a position I bluffed my way into, figuring if these thieving New Orleans boys could manage it, why couldn't an honest Kentuckian?

The factory forged cast-iron fixtures and steel cotton presses, and at the time of my arrival employed less than thirty mechanics, most a good deal older than myself. They talked a mixture of French and Spanish, and seemed to be friendly enough fellows, but it took me less than a week to wear out my welcome.

I'd never stepped foot in a factory before and had no knowledge of the trade I pretended to possess. For a few days, I carried and fetched for the others—the youngest being the boarder Madame Simone had told me about, an ugly, freckle-faced boy of nineteen—watching the men pour molten iron into molds or pack sand into sections, and though it was noisy, noxious labor, soon I was cutting sprue holes and spouts and even operating the ovens. I went at the job hard as I could, sweating for ten or twelve hours at a stretch.

And yet, for all my effort, I made a very poor impression. I couldn't figure out what it was I'd done. I decided to go the whole figure, thinking maybe newcomers were required to perform double-time to prove they were up to trap. By the end of the next week, I'd worked myself to where I had to auger new holes in my belt to keep my britches cinched around my waist, and still my colleagues bored into me with their murderous looks. I started to wonder if I wouldn't be better off strolling the docks with the cutthroats and bandits.

One morning, when the men's vicious glances were thick as smoke coming off a furnace, that freckled teenager came over and squatted beside me. He was a gangly, stone-faced lad with a severe brow and a big nose that looked to've been broken several times. His ears stuck out. He'd outgrown the sleeves of his shirt by several inches.

"You have got to slow down," he whispered. "These ole boys are about to fix your flint."

Hearing him speak took me aback. His voice was deep and melodious, as out of place in this factory as the meadowlark's song in a brothel.

"Slow down?" I said. "I mean to keep this job till payday."

"There won't be a payday for you if you keep at it like you are. These city-men are crooked as a Virginia fence."

It took me several seconds to understand what he was saying. The problem wasn't that I couldn't keep up with the other workers; it was that I was setting too brisk a pace—the others looked lazy in comparison. This homely young man had saved me a good deal of sweat and, very likely, a thrashing.

I stared at him a moment. Under that stern, unpleasant brow was a pair of good-natured eyes and I believed I saw kindness in them.

"Your name is Smithwick?"

"Smithwick," he said, nodding. "My given name is Noah."

"I'm Duncan," I told him, and after shaking his hand, thanked him for the turn he'd done me.

He said, "The selfsame thing happened to me when I started last month. You see that bald sumbuck yonder?" He nodded toward a hairless mechanic on the other side of the room. "My third day working here, he come up to me and said, 'No sprig of a boy will set the pace for us.' I told him our employer paid me for my time, and didn't I owe him all I was capable of doing in it?

"'No,' he said, 'he pays you for so much work. You get no more for your big day's work than we do for ours, and if you go on like this you'll make trouble for the rest of us.'"

I saw I had thoroughly misjudged young Noah: here was a boy wise beyond his years and warm beyond his looks.

I said, "Where are you from, Master Smithwick?"

"Wellsir," he said, "that all depends on what you mean by *from*. I was born in Martin County, North Carolina, but my pa moved us out to Tennessee when I was just a stripling. Past few years, I been working as a blacksmith in Kentucky."

"I, dad! Whereabouts?"

"Hopkinsville. You know it?"

"I'm from Butler County!" I exclaimed, standing from my crouch, as if being on my feet might prove my place of origin.

Noah stared up at me. "Where's that?"

"Northeast of Hopkinsville, not thirty miles. Madame Simone says you are bound for Texas too."

"I am," he said. "Soon as I make enough to pay the fare."

I'd come to learn that many Tennessee and Kentucky boys had heard that siren call—some, the exact same Siren. It turned out that Noah had attended one of the many talks given by Sterling Robertson, the very man who'd converted me. The apostle of a new faith, Robertson was travelling the western states, extolling the virtues of this *lazy man's paradise*, as he called it. At the time, New Orleans was chock full of young men trying to put together enough kelter to leave the Old States and ship off to this new Jerusalem.

Young Noah had as good a heart as the Maker ever put inside a poor boy's breast, and we took to each other like brothers. While I was able to learn a few passing things about this or that trade, Noah was a master of all things mechanical—by the age of nineteen, he'd been a blacksmith, a gunsmith, and was the best hand at the Leeds Foundry by a furlong. I'd come to find he had courage to boot, and something I didn't have at all: a mind for business, and the ability to put together a little coin.

In the evenings, after our shift had ended, we'd wander down to the wharves and inspect the vessels in port. There were ships of every description—brigs, flats, and barges—everything from the smallest boat to the three-masted behemoth, floating far as the eye could see.

To a couple of landlopers like me and Noah this was indeed a marvelous sight, an ever-changing forest of ship masts, the vessels docking one moment, sailing away the next. And we imagined how we'd be on one of them soon enough ourselves.

Of course, it didn't take long before our nightly recreation was utterly polluted, and we soon got an eyeful of a very different sort of cargo as steamboat after steamboat travelled down the swollen river to dock and drive up coffles of slaves from their fetid underbellies.

My father had strong opinions on the subject of slavery. In addition to running his tannery, he was a deacon of the Radical Methodist church and would even preach, time to time, at brush arbor meetings. In Kentucky, views on the so-called *Negro Question* differed county to county, but Pap was an Emancipationist, and many was the time I'd seen him address a camp meeting, thundering on about the evils of Southern slavers and Northern doughfaces to where half the congregation would be amen-ing him, and the other packing up to leave. Having never seen men manacled and chained together, I couldn't conjure the sights and sounds of their agony, only cobbling together a few notions from Pap's sermons.

Well, my visits to the wharves provided a quick education. I stood there watching as the steamboats put in, threw down their gangplanks, debarked their better sorts from the cabin, and then the middling ones from belowdecks. And once the white folk had alighted and cleared from sight, here came a different kind of passenger. I can close my eyes and see them coming even now. The bridge of a rough wooden beam extends to a door in the hold, the door opens with the sound of a gunshot, and directly, a line of famished black men begin marching across the narrow plank, coming along Indian-file and naked save for a pair of pantaloons, hands cuffed, moving in a kind of shuffle-step, the whole wretched caravan progressing as one clanking machine, heads lowered, each man fitted with an iron collar, padlocks slipped through the latches at the front, a long chain running from neck to neck, the men's white eyes blinking in the twilight.

It either tore your guts out or it didn't—there was no gentle response. The very first time I bore witness to this abomination, I felt sick at the stomach. I could not even speak. Noah was standing there beside me, and I recall thinking if he wasn't disgusted by this ghastly sight, we could not continue our association, however much I enjoyed his company.

"That," I heard him say, "is the vilest thing I ever saw," and my heart swelled with affection for him, just as it filled with hatred for the slavers herding these poor men from the hold.

And yet, we returned. I'll not venture to guess Noah's motives, but as for myself, I couldn't stand knowing all this was happening and turn a blind eye to it, and though there was nothing I could do to prevent these steamboats coming downriver from St. Louis or Memphis, I wanted to sear the image in my mind.

Go on, I'd tell myself. Get an eyeful now. This is why you're leaving your native land. In Texas, such a thing will never be.

Pretty soon, I'd get to thinking of my father and his sermons. So often, I'd thought him too harsh on matters of doctrine, and that had put distance between us—more than 900 miles of it. But I reckoned on the subject of slave-holding he'd been no harsher than what was called for.

Watching those weary souls march up the street toward the auction-houses, I thought his position rather mild.

Cecelia

—Virginia, 1827—

S he was fifteen the first time she ran. She waited until her mistress was asleep, then slipped out the window of the house and made off across the sloping lawn. Down through the beech trees. Down the row of pinewood cabins.

She'd convinced Jubal to come with her. He was a field hand from Mister Wellman's plantation and understood the roots and animals, which ones to eat, which to pass over. Cecelia knew all there was to know about the house, but beyond its walls, she grew uncertain. Her owner, Master Haverford, was a dry goods merchant, and at the parties he held for local planters, he'd have her perform. She'd recite verse she'd memorized, Dante or Ovid. Sometimes, she'd sing. And in the light of the planters' blue, gawking eyes, she discovered something.

It didn't happen all at once. It took her months and years.

It was like waking in the harsh glare of sunlight or waking from an illness to find your fever had broken. All the words her mistress taught her, all these lines of verse. As a child, she thought of it as a kindness, Mistress Anne teaching her to read the secrets.

But here at Haverford's parties, she began to see it wasn't her the planters applauded. Cecelia would finish her recitations, but the crowd wouldn't clap until Anne rose and bowed.

That's mine, she thought. You have taken it from me.

Her affection for the mistress turned to ash.

She began sneaking books from the library the same way

some children snuck sweets; she kept William Cowper's translation of Homer beneath her bed. Day by day, a new Cecelia began to form, and one night, reciting lines from Cowper, she stared out at the watching faces and realized she'd grown smarter than the planters, smarter than Haverford himself. Smarter than her mistress, who'd been like a mother after her actual mother was sold away. Anne's lips moved as she read; Cecelia's hadn't moved since she first learned her letters.

At night, she went back to the poem under her mattress, and he was waiting for her right there: cunning Odysseus. Wily Odysseus. She couldn't read the Greek, but Cowper rendered the hero purely as you please: "for shrewdness famed and genius versatile." Yes, she thought. Not crazy Ajax or pouting Achilles: those men were strong or brutish. Odysseus was a man of tricks. He used deception, a woman's virtue.

Her virtue, she thought.

Just look at these pages: these yellowed pages right here. A moonbeam from the window to light the lines. In this poem, the sea was dark as wine; there were whirlpools and monsters among the rocks. The men were larger than gods, and the gods themselves were petty and murderous. She felt she was more of this world than Virginia. More of this world than these broken hills around her, piled with planters and their slaves. When she watched Odysseus weather the storm inside her brain, she didn't see an olive-skinned Ithacan with black hair and a loincloth.

She saw herself at the prow, staring back.

The vision took root in her, and when she learned there were free negroes in the North, people with neither masters nor mistresses, people with their own lives and property, she decided she'd run away.

Which was something folks did, but she couldn't do it by herself.

So, for an entire year, she spent her evenings with Jubal. She found he had an eye for her, and she liked his nimble hands. She talked and talked, painting a picture of life in the North, using her words for color, giving her portrait shape. She had no idea what life looked like in the North—she'd never been farther than Kingwood—so she made it whatever she wanted. The two of them lived inside it like a dream.

And then Jubal wanted inside her as well.

"First, we must run," she told him, and Jubal needed no more convincing.

He said they could run that night.

* * *

She stopped outside the cabin at the end of the row, crouched and waited for him to appear. She wore shoes inside the house, but she could move more quietly without leather crimping up her toes. She'd begun going barefoot whenever she could.

She watched Jubal exit the cabin, then stand in the yard, glancing around.

She liked that he couldn't see her. She could be so slight and silent.

She stood up and Jubal saw her. He walked over and took her hand.

His touch surprised her. She felt herself go soft. His hand was large and strong, but he held her so carefully, like she was important and rare. She felt it go through her, softening her body, a softness that kept going down.

Then they were walking. They were out among the pines. She'd imagined being frightened, but with Jubal, she didn't feel afraid. Why hadn't she gone sooner? Was she only waiting for him?

He asked if she was tired, and she liked that, but the next time he asked, there seemed to be something behind it.

"I'm doing fine," she told him, and he held her hand a little tighter, and they walked on.

In several miles, they struck the Cheat River, and she felt his hand go slack. There was something hesitant in his touch.

"What is it?" she said.

He stared at the flowing water, at the rocks in the moonlight, jutting up like broken teeth.

Then he raised his hand and pointed, and they were walking along the river's edge.

She'd worried that he'd outpace her; she'd not be able to keep up. Just her being smaller might slow them down. She was determined not to let that happen, and she was proud of her stride. They could keep walking and walking, all the way to—

"Let's sit down," said Jubal.

"I can keep going."

"Let's sit a minute," Jubal said.

He hadn't let go of her hand. They walked over to a clump of catberry and seated themselves on the ground.

She was anxious to start again, but it was nice being close to him. It wasn't just their hands touching: it was their arms, their hips, their legs.

He leaned over and put his lips against her cheek. His lips were soft and damp. She wanted to tell him they should be going, but it felt good what he was doing, and he put his hands on her face and held it like a jewel. His fingers were trembling. She made this big man shake. She was fifteen, barely five feet tall, and look how he was shuddering! It was such a strong feeling, like beating him at a game. She wanted to see if she could make him tremble harder, and she put her lips onto his.

And then the softness went all the way through her. She could hardly think. She was too much for him, just like she was too much for the planters. Her mind was too much, and now she found her body had power as well. Her small, soft body was too much for Jubal's large, strong body. She made him shake and tremble until he cried out.

* * *

They lay there, her head on his chest, a hard pillow that rose and fell. Everything was humming down inside her, and she felt herself falling asleep. She wouldn't let that happen. Soon she'd rouse him, and they would start again.

When she heard the voices, Jubal had just started to snore. She sat up very straight, then placed her palm over Jubal's mouth.

Jubal pushed her hand away, but before he could speak, she shushed him. It wasn't just voices now, but torchlight. Flaming pine knots coming along the river's edge.

She stared out through the leaves. There were three torches, orange and yellow in the dark.

Her heart hammered against the ground. The air smelled of smoke and burning resin. Fear coursed through her, running in her veins like fire. Jubal's presence didn't help at all. She glanced over and saw he'd proned out beside her.

"You just lie there," she whispered. "You lie there real still."

She surprised herself saying this. The words were coming before she even thought to speak.

Because, his eyes in the torchlight were wide open and wet. And the torches were coming closer. It was Haverford and Mister Wellman. There was another man with them that she recognized, though she didn't know his name. She'd sung for him at Haverford's parties. The three men came up. She could've crawled out and touched their boots.

But they walked on past. They passed the shrubs where she and Jubal lay and went walking up the river.

She felt everything inside her lighten. She eased herself into the ground.

Which is when Jubal stood and called out.

"Marse Wellman," he said. "It's me."

It felt like ice water down her back. This man who was so tall and strapping.

You are a coward, she thought.

But in a few moments, Haverford and Wellman were pressed against them with their torches, and she was angry for ever trusting Jubal, for not seeing what he was.

Because now Jubal was trying to make like it was some game that they were playing.

"I had a notion for her," he said. "We just walked out a ways."

Haverford stared. Then Wellman and his companion grabbed Jubal, each taking an arm, and started walking him along the river.

Which left her standing there with Haverford, his face flickering in the light of the torch.

"Answer me truly," he said. "Lie and I will know."

She said nothing, just stared at his chest.

"Did you come of your own volition?"

She nodded.

"He did not force you?"

She said that he didn't.

Haverford sucked his teeth. He was making some decision. He said, "M'lady will never know of this. Do you understand?"

She understood just fine: Haverford was not completely masculine. He subordinated himself to the wishes of his wife.

Then they were walking, following the torches, Jubal walking between the flames. When they reached the outbuildings, she stopped next to Haverford and stood watching as Wellman bound Jubal's hands behind his back, lashed his ankles together, then kicked him onto his stomach.

She realized she'd be forced to watch what was about to happen. That Haverford was instructing her, just as Wellman was punishing Jubal. That this might well be happening to her. If only Haverford willed it.

Because now Wellman had a knife. The other man held the torches, pressing his boot into the small of Jubal's back. Wellman knelt, pinched Jubal's left ear, tugged out on it, then sliced it free of Jubal's skull. He paused a moment, holding it by the lobe. It looked like a sliver of mushroom in the light. He tossed the ear aside and sliced away the other.

Cecelia couldn't breathe. There wasn't enough air, or she couldn't pull it inside her. If she had, she might've screamed.

Jubal hardly made a sound, just lay there huffing. She wondered if he understood what had happened to him. His eyes looked like he'd gone very far away, and she felt she'd done this to him, though her intention was the opposite. She'd wanted to get them to a place where such a thing could never happen, not even in their dreams.

Then Haverford was speaking.

"A man may do as he pleases with his property. It might be, with all m'lady's attentions, you have forgotten this. Do not forget. I'd recommend you have no further truck with field niggers. Do you understand me?"

She nodded. She understood his entire wretched race.

"Very well," said Haverford. "That is very well. Do not mistake my mercy for lenience, or Mr. Wellman's actions for cruelty. You might take it as a lesson."

* * *

She took it as a lesson, and the lesson was this: other people were weak. Trusting them was weakness. If you wanted something, you had to get it by yourself.

And so the next time she ran, she did it all alone.

DUNCAN LAMMONS

—TEXAS, 1827—

Once we'd put together enough money, we boarded a schooner and set sail.

The boat was chartered by Carlysle and Smith. In addition to a few passengers, it carried replenishments for the Mexican army. We had a good wind and put in at Matagorda Bay not three days later, anchoring at the mouth of the Lavaca. But it wasn't until I glimpsed that foreign shore that a question occurred to me.

"What will happen if Mexican troops stumble on us?"

"I've wondered that myself," Noah said.

"Will they arrest us?"

"Well," he said, "we'll be traipsing around their country without a by-your-leave. They might could lock us up as vagrants."

"I'd think the charge would be a sight more serious than vagrancy. They might well brand us spies."

Noah shook his head grimly. "Reckon we should've thought this through before now?"

Of course, the truth was that we hadn't wanted to consider anything that might weaken our resolve.

I said, "How 'bout we don't stumble on any Mexican soldiers?"

"It's a deal," he said.

By and by, a couple settlers saw our schooner, rowed out and took us in to shore. My first step onto Texas soil was planted in dirt the color of coffee grounds. You almost could eat it, I remember thinking, but that night our hosts fed us a supper of venison sopped in honey.

The next morning, Noah and I set out for Colonel DeWitt's colony, farther up the river. As we marched along, we'd pass herds of antelope, droves like I'd never seen.

I began to think, if anything, Sterling Robertson had undersold this fair land.

But when we reached DeWitt's Colony, I had the first inkling our new paradise might be a few apple trees shy of Eden. The settlers we found here lived in constant terror of Indians, housing themselves in rough log cabins with dirt floors and no windows, everything crawling with lice. Colonel DeWitt greeted Noah and myself with warmth, taking us into his home and feeding us at his table. Our first morning, several men invited us on a hunt, which, at the time, we thought rather neighborly. We soon found this was just routine: all day long, the men of the colony stalked the woods, shot game and enjoyed themselves mightily, and all night they lay on the dirt floors of their cabins, shivering.

And there was plenty to make you shiver: shrill owls like I'd never heard, the laughter of coyote and the lonely cry of wolves. In the morning, we rose and drank coffee and shook off our nightly terrors with the pleasures of hunting.

The women had no such recreation. In truth, they had no recreation at all. There was no cotton crop as yet, and so nothing for them to spin. No books or papers, no churches or schools. No garden or dairy or poultry. They spent all their time tending sick children and cleaning the game we brought in, crouching in filthy dresses with their arms slathered in gore while the men laughed and drank off the reserve of whiskey. I'd never seen women treated so, and I thought of my mother and felt guilty about the circumstances that'd caused me to leave her.

But I soon learned this was least of the outrages in DeWitt's

Colony. Our third day with the colonel, he asked Noah and myself to accompany him deer hunting, a gesture any host on the frontier might make to entertain his guests, but I suspected he wanted to recruit us as members of his settlement and rightly assumed wild game would speak loudest to our ears.

Two other men went with us that morning: one named Stephens, the other Reynolds. Stephens seemed a fine enough gentleman, but Mister Reynolds talked too much for my liking. And he kept eyeing my rifle.

Finally, he couldn't help himself any longer.

"Is that a Hawken?" he asked.

I told him it was.

He puckered his lips and I watched his eyes meander down the maple stock to the cheekpiece and on to the iron butt plate.

"That is an awfully lavish gun to cart about," he said. "I'd never go hunting with such as that."

"Is that right?" I said.

He nodded. "I had nothing so fine when I was your age. I carried my brother's old smoothbore until I was nearly thirty."

I didn't see how my rifle was any concern of his, but there is a kind of man who always mocks what he envies, as if by finding fault with it he can cure himself of jealousy.

Of course, I didn't say that. I just wanted him to be quiet. Anything worth shooting would be frightened off by his wabbling.

By noon, we'd taken two young does—the first, my kill; the next, the colonel's—and we were gathered round the second deer, dressing it out, when Stephens went very still and raised a finger to his lips. He pointed through a screen of persimmons where, in the distance, a wild pig was rooting.

It was large enough to make a feast all by itself, dark black with pale streaks on its snout.

I heard Reynolds say, "You'll never get close enough to put a ball through that thing."

"They're skittish," the colonel admitted.

Noah said, "Duncan here can drop it where it stands."

At this, Reynolds gave a snort. "Thomas Plunkett couldn't make such a shot. That must be 300 yards."

"It's a deal farther than that," said Stephens.

"Closer to 350," said the colonel.

"It is 220 yards," I told them. "200 from here to yon gulch and another twenty to the pig there."

Stephens and the colonel turned to look at me, then glanced back at the pig, as if adding the yards one by one.

"Can you really hit it?" DeWitt said.

I shrugged. As much noise as they were making, I was surprised the creature hadn't already bolted.

"If he puts a ball anywhere near it," said Reynolds, "I will eat my hat."

The colonel smiled. "That sounds like a challenge, Master Lammons. Do you accept?"

I didn't say whether I accepted or I didn't. I took up my powder horn from where it hung around my neck and began to measure out a charge, patched a ball, got it started, then rammed it down the barrel.

I got down onto my knees, then proned out on my belly behind the little doe's carcass, using her neck as a rest. Noah and the others watched me, but I shut them out and focused on the pig. We were upwind of the beast and thus far it hadn't shown any signs of spotting us. It would walk a few steps, lower its snout to root, then walk a few more. I made sure my heels were touching the earth, pressed my hips against the ground and started my breathing, watching the pig another moment, watching how the leaves hung motionless from the persimmon trees, then focusing on the blade sight at the front of my rifle until the pig became a dark blotch of color in the distance. At 200 yards, my hold would have to be about three feet above the animal's back, aligned with the pig's right shoulder. I brought my gun up a hair and set my front trigger. Then I drew a final breath, began to release it, and when I got down on a good empty lung I slowly pressed the trigger—I wanted the actual shot to surprise me.

Which it did. The rifle boomed and the men startled and I quickly moved my head to see around the cloud of blue gun smoke. The pig stood rooting. Then it seemed a hard wind had struck it: its legs buckled and it went down on its belly.

No one said a word for several moments. Then the colonel turned to Reynolds.

"It's best to boil it a minute or two," he said. "Then add some salt to the water."

"How's that?" Reynolds said.

"Your hat," the colonel told him. "You'll want to boil it a while to soften the brim, and salt will make it more flavorful."

Stephens started to chuckle and Reynolds' face went red.

"Just don't leave it to cook too long," said DeWitt. "You'll never get it choked down."

* * *

We started back home with our packs full of pig meat. Come eventide, we were close to the settlement, coming down a narrow path Indian-file through the scrub when, up ahead, a clump of lizard's tail began to quiver and then an elderly black man stood up from the cover it'd been providing, pulling his pantaloons up around his waist and securing them with a length of rope. He took a few steps and disappeared into the palms.

I stopped and stood gawking. Colonel DeWitt turned, and seeing the expression on my face, said, "Pay him no mind. That's just Old Charlie."

And so, we continued on our way, branching down another trail until we reached the settlement. DeWitt and Reynolds went to collect their wives to clean the game we'd brought in, but the appearance of Mister Charlie had roused my suspicions and I kept on down the muddy lane past the cabins toward the hamlet's south end. I realized then that my host had failed to offer us a thorough tour of his colony and soon I discovered the reason.

The last cabin fell away behind me as the ground turned marshy and sloped toward the river. I began to hear voices on the evening breeze. I went through a palmetto thicket, rounded a bend, and there in a little glen were half a dozen tents made of old sailcloth, two flickering campfires, and around these, twenty or so black folks, singing in harmony.

I stood there listening to their song. The tune of it was unfamiliar to me—or the words, at least, but the melody was sad and soothing. It called Mama to mind, how, as a boy, I'd lie in bed, listening as she prayed. She was a gracious country woman, restrained in manner and always mindful of the propriety of things. But when she prayed she held nothing back. Her people were what folks called "Shouting Methodists," and when she knelt at night to make her appeals to the Lord, a transformation took place: all the daytime propriety sloughed off like old skin and the soul underneath was red hot. It was something to see this woman who never put herself forward, never fussed nor whispered a cross word, bare herself to her Creator. You wouldn't have known she had such passion squirreled away inside her, such hurt and joy and heartache. She mourned friends who'd passed away, rejoiced over some blessing that had been bestowed on our family, praised God and wept over pains she never mentioned otherwise.

This song I now heard summoned all of that up and a dauncy feeling flooded through me: there is a spirit among black folk hardly to be found among Anglos, a sense of being home, a celebration of the very blood running through the body. It moved something in me.

I blotted my eyes on my shirtsleeve, and having cleared my vision in this way, I was seized by a very different feeling. I saw the threadbare cotton breeches the men wore, the filthy osnaburg shirts—those that had shirts at all. The women were clothed in dresses of plain cloth which had to be about as comfortable to wear as a hair shirt. I realized, of a sudden, that there was nothing cooking over their fires; in fact, I saw no sign of any food at all. I began to notice how thin these people were; many had horrible lesions covering their arms and legs. It struck me at last that these folks were starving.

I turned and went walking back toward the cabins, angry as I'd ever been. I was furious at how these poor people were being treated, and furious that I'd left a slave nation behind me only to find this new land being occupied by slavers as well. DeWitt's colonists hadn't planted their first crop of corn, had hardly sewn a seed, and here they were looking to establish plantations for themselves, sleeping behind their fortress walls and keeping their poor negroes out in tents.

What was it Sterling Robertson had called Texas? A *lazy man's paradise*? And what could be more heavenly to the slothful than a land where slaves performed your labor?

When I made it back to the cabins, there was fresh venison roasting on spits above the cookfires, gobs of the pig I'd killed skewered on mesquite branches and set to sizzle. The residents were milling about, laughing and carrying on. A celebratory air had broken out.

I saw Stephens standing beside one of the fires talking with several other men; they were passing a bottle back and forth. When he saw me, he held out both arms as though he'd embrace me.

"And here is the man himself!" he exclaimed. "Where did you get off to? Were there other unruly swine requiring your attention?" He looked at one of the men beside him. "You've not seen shooting like this, Marcus. The pig dropped like he hit it with a hammer!"

Well, I might have endured such compliments another time, but I was in no mood to discuss hogs or marksmanship. I pointed back toward the river.

"The folks down yonder are in extremis, Mister Stephens."

His brow furrowed and he took a step to look around me to see the people I referenced.

"Who do you speak of?" he said, and the concern in his face was genuine.

"Those Negro men and women," I told him. "Down there by the tents."

Well, that chased the concern from his face as quickly as it had appeared.

"Oh," he said, "their masters find for them."

From the corner of my eye, I saw Reynolds walk up. He stood there with his arms crossed, glaring.

"I don't think they're well at all," I said. "They have nothing whatever over their cookfires and nothing in their mouths but a song. They looked to be starving."

"*Starving?*" Reynolds interjected. "If they are starving, why do they sing?"

"Likely to keep their minds off their bellies," I told him. "Can we not carry some of this meat down to them once it's cooked? I'd say there's more than enough to go around."

Stephens lifted his hands and showed me his palms. "You'd have to take that up with their owners. I myself am poor as Job's turkey: everything I own I brought to this colony in a sack."

Then hoping to put the topic to bed he said, "Tell me: what's the farthest shot you've ever made? Or the *longest* I suppose I mean."

"I'm not sure I know," I said, though I knew very well: I'd once shot a deer through the heart from 340 yards. But I wasn't going to stand and crow about my abilities with families going hungry a half-mile away.

"Well," he said, "that's the finest piece of shooting I ever saw. Perhaps you'll teach Thomas here a thing or two."

"I do just fine," Reynolds said. "I'm not seeking instruction from the Colonel's guest. On marksmanship or slave-feeding either one."

I knew right then that Reynolds himself owned one or more of the families I'd seen down by the river and that he'd taken great offense at my remarks.

"You need a deal of teaching on both," Stephens said, trying to lighten the mood, but I couldn't listen. I went and found Noah and told him everything I'd seen in the sleeping camp, and after he'd heard me out, he agreed that the paradise that had been promised by Robertson was in fact a purgatory. Or, in his words, "A heaven for white men, but a hell for blacks and women."

It seemed so to me, squatting in the muck alongside that muddy river, the live oaks thick with mosquitos and beards of Spanish moss. And the alligators: all day long they floated downstream with their yellow eyes poking above the water, watching for any unlucky thing that came too close to the river's edge. Evenings, you'd hear dogs yelping when the gators walked ashore and grabbed the poor mutts in their sleep.

And a few nights after our hunting trip with Colonel DeWitt, I woke to a more skeersome sound.

It was pitch black inside the cabin. I sat up in my blankets with my heart in my throat.

"What was that?" I asked Noah, who was sitting up beside me.

"I don't know," he said.

Then here it came again, a caterwauling that climbed my backbone joint by joint.

I crawled over, unbarred the cabin door, and peeked out.

Moonlight poured in, then that horrible clamor that'd woken us. I realized it was the voice of a girl.

Then Noah and I were outdoors, running toward the shrieks with our rifles in hand, sprinting through the shafts of silver light. Shaggy limbs blacked out the stars. I heard a dog begin to bark up ahead, and then several dogs were barking, the ruckus intermingled with the girl's shrill screams.

Noah and I came out into a moonlit glen where a sward of grass sloped down to the river. Here the dogs had decided to make a stand, their hackles roached up, howling and carrying on. At first, I didn't see what they were yelping at. Then Noah said, "Good God a'mighty," and I saw very clear.

It was the largest gator that ever crept the earth, long and fat as a canoe, backing down the slope toward the water. In its hideous jaws was a young slave, couldn't have been more than twelve.

The creature had caught the poor child by the arm. She'd screamed herself completely mute; her mouth still moved, but there was no longer any sound. About the same moment I saw her, she seemed to spot me and Noah. Her eyes went wet. A dog moved up and snapped at the gator, and the gator scrambled backward several steps. If he hadn't been so greedy for girl-flesh, he might've taken this brave canine and made his escape.

Up to that second, I'd been frozen in horror, but the mutt's courage stiffened my spine, and I lurched up and clubbed the monster between the eyes with the butt of my rifle. That gator just blinked at me. His eyes shone like a cat's. I fetched him another blow and his great tail swished through the grass like a scythe through sugarcane.

I'd been too unsettled to trust myself to take a shot, fearing I'd hit the girl instead, but my attack on the creature gave Noah some confidence, and he came up, put the muzzle of his gun to the gator's side and pulled the trigger.

Well, the beast didn't like that one bit. He released his hold on the child and went sliding back like a snake. You couldn't tell what was gator and what was grass. In hardly a second, he'd vanished in the water without so much as a plop.

The girl lay there a moment. I feared she might be mortally wounded, but all of a sudden, she sprang to her feet and climbed me as if I were a tree, finding herself a perch atop my shoulders.

We started toward the sleeping camp where the girl had been abducted. Miraculously, she was not even bleeding. The gator must not have wanted to abuse his meal before he had her in the river. As for her part, the child didn't say a word. It might have been shock that sealed her lips, or perhaps her voice hadn't recovered from the screaming. Perhaps she'd been brought up to this foul place from Santo Domingo and spoke no English at all.

We restored her in one of the tents—her howls had failed to rouse her kin, so dead tired they were from the labor their masters put them to—and started back for our lodgings, feeling like knights who'd rescued a damsel from the jaws of a dragon.

But the good feeling of our victory was short-lived. When we arrived at the cabin, we found the menfolk huddled about the doors of their cabins, staring out like frightened children. These settlers who fared forth so valiantly by daytime to snipe deer and turkey were too craven to defend what they liked to call their *property.*

"What was it?" Stephens asked me, but I was too furious to answer.

Noah said, "Did you not hear that girl hollering?"

"We heard her," Stephens said.

"Why didn't you come help?" Noah asked. "It was a gator down there big as a john boat."

All the men just stared like he was speaking gibberish, and

I knew right then I could not live among these cowards—though I had no idea where else to go.

I walked off, squatted beside a sycamore, and had a dark moment to myself, feeling homesick and wishing my life had been altogether different.

It is a judgment on you, I thought. If you weren't such a miserable sinner, you wouldn't be hunkered here among slavers in a frontier far from home.

But directly, I grew ashamed for sinking into despair so easily, and began to give myself a talking to. Or I suppose it was me: it almost seemed like my father's voice, echoing between my ears, saying: *You've spent these past months trying to get yourself to Texas, and now, finding difficulties, you fall into a brown study and pout like a child. DeWitt's Colony is only one among many. This new country is large enough to make your own colony if you must.*

That had never occurred to me—making myself a colony—and I realized how green I'd been. Had I hoped to step off the boat and find this land ready-made?

That was not the way of a world where anything worth living in must be fought for and fashioned, and I glanced back at Noah, watching as he scolded our hosts, thinking we could still have the Texas we'd left our homes to find. Even if we had to build it for ourselves.

CECELIA

—VIRGINIA, 1827—

Running alone was harder in some ways, but easier in others. You wouldn't have any ears on your conscience. Nobody's ears but your own.

It was a matter of preparation. You couldn't leave a single thing to chance.

She began by working her way through her mistress's library. No more poetry, those old Greeks and Romans. Now she devoured geography and medicine, all she could find on poultices. On balms and bandages. On salts and salves. She memorized every map she came across: Preston County, Monongalia County, up to the Pennsylvania line. Beyond that was free country, but she couldn't walk up to the first white man she came across and collapse into his arms. She would have to wise up about the world. She was doing it, book by book.

She grew interested in astronomy, writings on navigation. Some were by trappers, and some by sailors. You could discover north with the Pole Star: the Dipper pointed you to it. As did Cassiopeia, that W in the northern sky. Or Orion over there with his bright shining belt. At night, she stood in front of the house, gazing up into the stars.

Haverford had ordered her to stay clear of Wellman's field hands, but the hands knew things you couldn't find in any book. She talked with them whenever she could. She offered them sweetmeats from her mistress's table.

And there was a girl named Alice she spoke to very freely. Alice was eleven, also the property of Wellman, but she wasn't a field hand. Alice had been purchased two years before from the slave market in Richmond, but she'd been born in Maryland, and Cecelia was interested in all she had to say of that country to the north. Haverford would come home in the evenings, and Cecelia would be sitting on the lawn, braiding Alice's hair. Haverford paid it no mind, and so she continued plying Alice for information. She wanted to know about hounds, especially.

"You can trick them," Alice said.

Cecelia nodded. She conditioned the girl's hair with bacon grease and butter, braiding it into rows, tucking one strand beneath another, tucking away everything Alice said.

* * *

She was seventeen when she made her next attempt. She had a picksack with a kitchen knife she'd stolen. A five-foot length of rope. A loaf of bread, a little salt. A waterskin made from a cow bladder. She was determined not to fill it until she reached the Cheat River.

It was fall again. Everything was dying. She waited until the house was dark, then went out the same window she'd used two years before, inching it up, propping it open, then dropping to quiet grass below.

She was wearing one of Haverford's soiled shirts, and she used the road this time. No slave would do that. No one would think a slave so bold. The sky was clear and the stars were shining. Cassiopeia stood on its edge like an E turned around. She was frightened, but she'd learned to govern her fear like you governed a raging toothache. You pushed down the pain and put your thoughts in your stride.

By dawn, she was north of Kingwood, in country she'd never seen before. She shaded up in the woods, ate a breakfast of bread and salt pork, then buried herself in the leaves.

She slept fitfully. In dreams, the hounds were snuffling through the underbrush to catch her scent. She'd hidden her bedding in the attic; she'd tried to dispose of anything that had her smell. But these nightmare hounds knew every trick. They weren't farm dogs with wet noses and wagging tails. They were enormous beasts the size of horses, fangs like icicles in their massive jaws. And there was Jubal, dragging along behind them with the leashes in his hand, urging them on: *come now. Sniff that nigger out.* She started awake in the midday heat and sat with her back against a cedar, waiting for dusk.

When twilight came, she left her picksack on the ground, walked off a ways and made water, though she didn't void her bladder completely. She bore down, pinched off her stream, walked to the tree line to observe the road, then crossed and made water in the woods on the far side. Then she recrossed the road and finished in a third location.

Doubling back, she slung her picksack, and started out in earnest.

It was evening of the next day when she heard the barking of hounds. Or thought she heard them. Maybe it was the wind. She tried making water, but her stream wouldn't come. She just squatted there, trembling.

She walked down to the road and knelt. She heard the wind in the pines. She heard the birds calling. She went on up the thoroughfare, and she'd made it a quarter mile maybe, when she heard dogs quite clearly. She stopped, and stood there, and tried to think.

You're all right, she told herself, using her mother voice, mothering up her courage. You just keep on.

She went quickly as she could. She was still wearing Haverford's shirt, but she could only use it once. She wasn't certain how well it would work, or if it would work at all. The dusk came on, and the road forked, and when she heard the hounds crying, they sounded very close. She believed she was only a few miles from Pennsylvania and that the left-hand road went to Morgantown. The map was shifting in her head; it was hard to picture with the dogs so close.

There was a stand of spruces just yonder, and she hurried to them, took off Haverford's shirt, and tied it to the highest limb she could reach, standing on her tiptoes, making a knot of the sleeves. She didn't think you could see the garment from the road, and she wondered if that mattered.

Then she climbed down the hill, took the right-hand road, and that night she stepped onto the free soil of Pennsylvania.

Later, she'd claim she had felt it right away, but maybe that was just a trick of memory. She was sleepy all of a sudden. Comfort washed through her like a wave. Why would the fear leave if it wasn't Pennsylvania?

It felt like freedom to her.

* * *

She slept in a grove of cedar, and her dreams were cedar dreams. Her mistress's cedar chest, or gewgaws Anne's father had carved, lined up on her bureau in rows. There was something in the wood that kept bugs away.

She woke to daylight slanting in from the east. Men were standing beside her with their dirty boots and britches. She didn't know how long the men had been there, how long they'd been watching. She had the sense she'd fallen from the sky, and that these men had crawled up from their hovels to see what sort of being had landed.

One of the men was Mister Haverford. She would not think of him as *master*, not here in Pennsylvania. She'd outwitted him and his dogs too. However you sliced it, she had mastered him.

But here he was standing over her, staring hard and cold.

He toed her with his boot.

"Get up," he said.

She laid there. Her pulse slapped at her temples. She had the notion if she ignored him, maybe he'd go away. It was foolish, but he had no authority up here. There was no slavery in Pennsylvania.

Then he reached down, grabbed her by the shoulders, and yanked her to her feet.

His touch woke her all the way. The strength of men always surprised her. Just the unfairness of it made her furious. If you had a rifle, she thought. Or a gun you could hold in your hand. She thought about the knife in her picksack, but it was too late.

Because now Haverford was dragging her from the cedar grove, down the hill to the road. There were horses standing there. There was a buggy. Two hounds sat staring at her with their beaten, brown eyes.

Haverford marched her to the buggy and told her to climb up.

"I will not," she said, but her voice was weak and wavering. She wasn't even sure he'd heard.

All around, men had been speaking to one another. Now they went quiet. She heard a crow begin to squawk. She thought how crows had wings they could use, and that seemed like more unfairness. Who was capturing the crows of Pennsylvania? If anyone needed wings, it was her. She was so frightened it seemed the fear alone would lift her. Terror would suck her into the sky.

Haverford's green eyes were staring. His brow crinkled, like he was thinking of how to pose a question.

But there was no question. He balled his fist and struck her in the stomach. All the air fled her body and she fell forward into his embrace. He caught her by the waist and slung her over his shoulder like a sack of flour, stepping up and depositing her on the buggy's rear seat.

Then they were moving. There was the clop of horses'

hooves and the jingle of tack. She was still trying to inhale. Motes swam before her watering eyes, and her lungs were burning.

She thought how they were always taking away her breath. You needed breath for words, but they didn't want to hear her words. Not in Pennsylvania. They only wanted to hear a song they'd taught her, some poem they'd had her memorize.

You start saying your own words, they closed you up like a box.

We set out from DeWitt's Colony and started up the river. It was rough country, but it beat the beard off living with slavers.

The next few months we went from settlement to settlement. In addition to knowing the farrier's trade, Noah had acquired considerable skill as a gunsmith. There were plenty of old rifles that needed work, but we were hard pressed to find tools, and no one had money to pay us for the labor. We ended up establishing a blacksmith's shop at Bell's Landing where we did a fair business for the budding town of Columbia. For an entire year, we shoed horses, mended tack, and attended every wedding we could find. Such ceremonies were special in those days, where, after the bride and groom had said their vows, the chairs would be cleared away for dancing. Your frontier folk purely loved to dance. We rapped the puncheon floor of many a house and made the splinters fly. A number of us still wore moccasins, and as you couldn't make a satisfactory commotion in such slippers, you'd have to swap shoes with someone and take turns. We didn't mind a bit. We wired, and shuffled, and cut the pigeon's wing, didn't consider the occasion a success unless we'd kicked the floor down to bare dirt by morning.

This was before the land was lousy with Baptists who'd no sooner landed on Texas shores than they went about convincing people that dancing was little better than lying in rut with your neighbor's wife. I can remember the first of these self-proclaimed prophets coming to Bell's Landing to spread libel against our beloved form of recreation. Thomas Pilgrim was his name. Noah heard him missionate one Sunday and asked me about it. His family back in Tennessee had not been as religious as my own, and all this talk about the evils of the dance struck him as rather strange. He reckoned Baptists must be awfully virtuous if they'd pruned their conduct all the way down to dancing.

"Well," I told him, "I'm pretty well acquainted with Baptist virtue. My pap had a saying about them: 'Invite two Baptists over and they won't drink a drop of your whiskey. Invite one, he'll drink all of it.'"

* * *

It seemed the farther I got from Pap, the more I thought about him. He was a hard man in many respects, but he was no hypocrite. He took his approach to everything from King David: *whatever your hand finds to do, do it with all your might.*

He certainly didn't laze about. He worked in his tanning shop and was deacon in his church. In his spare time, he preached the Gospel.

I think he and Mama had wanted a big family, but all they got was me. For a long time, that seemed to be enough.

Then, round my eighteenth birthday, me and Dan Yarborough went on this hunting trip. We were only supposed to be out three days.

We shot a young doe our first morning, and the next, got ourselves a turkey. The game seemed to run right into our barrels. Three days turned into a week, and that week into several more. We hunted and fished and built a little dugout in the side of this cliff. Dan and I shared everything. He was a couple of years older than me, soft-featured and somewhat feminine. We'd been raised together and had always been thick. The longer we lived out there, the thicker we got. It is difficult to explain, but it seemed quite natural to us; I never stopped to ruminate on how it might look from outside. Didn't feel like there was an outside. The wider world seemed to drift away. I lost track of how much time had passed or if time was passing at all. St. Paul says that it is a shame for one man to lie with another, but out there in our wilderness, we felt no shame at all.

When Pap managed to track us down, two months had slipped by. I woke one morning and heard a horse crunching through the leaves, and knew it was my father before I even stepped foot outside. I combed my hands through my hair and hurried to meet him, leaving Dan sleeping in the dirt.

I couldn't see Pap or his horse just yet, though I could hear it crisp and clear. I straightened myself up and tried to count back through the days to when Dan and I had left.

Tell him you been hunting, I thought. Show him all the pelts.

Then there he was, winding through the tall oaks on his gelding, Young Roger. He took one look at me and it was like my skin was made of glass.

"Duncan," he said, and his voice sounded like he was trying to wake himself from a dream.

All of a sudden, the world came rushing back; I felt filthy and wrong.

Pap's eyes were a clean shade of blue. I could see myself reflected in them. It'd never struck me that he was especially proud of who I was, but seeing his cheeks go red with embarrassment—it felt like someone had kicked the wind out of me. How could he know what had transpired 'tween me and Dan? Was I just imagining it?

"Duncan," he said again, and his voice was already different. He started climbing down from Young Roger. I glanced over and saw that Dan had crawled from the dugout to stand there beside me.

"Mister Lammons," he said, nodding. You could tell he was trying to hold his voice steady. For half a second, it was calm enough to convince me everything would be all right.

Pap just stared at him.

He can't know what you've been up to, I decided. It is just your scruples coming awake.

Then, quick as that, he knocked Dan to the ground, seized his throat in both hands, and commenced to throttle him. I'd never seen Pap lose control of himself. I thought he'd kill Dan, sure enough.

If I hadn't pulled him off, he very well might've. Pap and I wrestled around a few moments, and then I felt the heart go out of him. The three of us just sat there, trying to get our wind.

Directly, Pap started to cry.

* * *

That was a very hard time. It never occurred to me I could lose my father's respect, so I had no notion what the loss of it might mean. After a while, he let things lie, and it seemed life might balance back out. I never heard anymore from Dan; it was said he moved out to Virginia.

But it happened again the next year—William Ross, was the man's name—and then it happened a third time with Peter Briggs. Peter was a known nancy, and I'd started to acquire a reputation myself.

Pap could no longer make excuses for me. When I told him I'd asked God's forgiveness, he said, "That's fine, Duncan. That is very fine. But there are things folks won't forgive you for. I pray someday the Lord draws you to Heaven, but the men of this county are liable to elevate you on a rope."

Providence had made me as honest a lad as you could ask for—I was shaped to be truthful in both word and deed. I didn't view matters of right and wrong as goods to be balanced on the scales of men's ambition.

Why then had God seen fit to hollow out this defect at my core that forced me to adopt stealth and secrecy? Feeding this unnatural hunger required me to become a regular Freemason, a citizen of signs and signals, fearing all the while they'd be read by the wrong man—and one wrong man was all that it took.

I hated this thing inside me, resenting the hold it had. How many times had I prayed for God to remove it, this soft, flawed place in my flesh that throbbed and hurt and threatened my being, dividing my attentions and allegiances. I knew if the Lord would only extract this tumor, I would be whole in the eyes of the world. And in my father's eyes.

So, when I attended that talk in Morgantown and heard Sterling Robertson speak about Texas, I thought that maybe I could leave this thing behind. Maybe my heart would be different on the frontier, and those old feelings wouldn't follow me there.

At Bell's Landing, I'd done tolerably well. Noah Smithwick had become a brother to me—I was never afflicted with untoward longings for him—and I felt that I'd begun to make myself anew.

But young Noah began to contemplate schemes for acquiring wealth. He fell in with three recent arrivals to the country—John Webber, Joe McCoy, Jack Cryor—and they pooled their funds, bought 1,000 pounds of leaf tobacco, and decided they'd smuggle it into Mexico and make themselves a killing. I watched the four of them set out one morning with a crew of mules. I warned Noah not to venture south of the Nueces, but yonder he went.

Before departing, he sold me his share of the blacksmith shop, and I made a go of it for a while. But it was not the same without his company, and Bell's Landing seemed drearier by the day. Finally, I unloaded the whole shebang on a man named Furnash and headed for San Felipe on the Brazos.

I saw that Noah and I had gone wrong in settling at Bell's Landing, in ever settling down at all. I suppose another man in my circumstances might have gone courting to find himself a bride, but I was not another man, and having been exiled from the family I'd been born into, I wasn't keen to find another: I did not want to merely remake the thing that had scorned me. I'd started to suspect that the very notion of family was part of our country's problem, yet another way men forfeited their freedom and assumed the yoke of servitude.

I'd developed a rather elaborate philosophy on such matters. What were men meant for? To follow behind a horse and plow and break their backs in the fields? Surely, the Southern masters did not think so, and in their unwillingness to stoop to such labor, enslaved others to do this work in their stead. This was a great evil, but wasn't agriculture itself a wicked practice? And with the tilling of God's soil to produce wheat and corn for the storehouse, other ills followed: the city, for instance, where men lived atop each other and spread all manner of contagion, for, without grain, there could be no city of any size, no throng of folks piled together to suffer.

I did not think it was the Creator's intention for men to be tied to one place. Life was motion and I regarded the owning of land and the responsibilities it entailed as a kind of death— and not a quick, clean one either.

It was in the nature of man to hunt and roam. The thrill I received from stalking game and eating meat I'd killed myself was suggestive of the great joy that awaited anyone willing to untether himself from farms or cities. The promise of Texas was the promise of movement—wild meat enabled such a life—an unsettled land that barely knew the blade of a plow or the curse of an urban boulevard. Out here, a man could ride and hunt at his leisure, and if you could assemble a band of

other like-minded folks and establish a tribe for yourself—
well, this was the only family that interested me, and one of
your own making: not handed down like a poor-fitting shirt.

* * *

I wouldn't see Noah for another five years. In the interim, I
moved from place to place, made money and lost it, made
friends and lost them, made a few enemies which I've kept to
this day. Men are fickle in their affections, but once a man
extends his hatred, he seldom takes it back.

By the fall of 1835, the country was in an uproar of revolution against the Mexicans and that old tyrant Santa Anna. I
threw in with those calling for independence and ended up
mustering into the ragtag army assembling at Gonzales where
the Texians had won their first victory. I rode up through the
rows of makeshift tents and made my way down the mud
street. When I passed a pinewood shop and heard the clank of
a steel, I glanced over and who should be bent over an anvil
hammering at a bayonet but Noah Smithwick himself.

He looked up and saw me, and we commenced to laughing.
The loneliness in my heart vanished like smoke.

"Well, well," I called. "Has the millionaire decided to cast
his lot with us poor Texas rabble?"

"Millionaire, my eye!" he said, and once I'd dismounted
and secured my horse to the snubbing post, he told me how his
entrepreneurial adventure had quickly gone awry, how his
thousand pounds of contraband tobacco had been confiscated
by Mexican authorities, how he'd taken sick with an ague and
would have perished had it not been for the kindness of
women.

We spent the next several days watching men file into
camp. There was no agreement as to uniform; in truth, there
was no uniform. The stragglers were clad in buckskin breeches

or homespun pantaloons. They wore the old tri-corner hat, or caps of animal fur. Here and there, a sombrero. Their outfits were filthy, and if we had a common color to our dress, it was the black of grime.

When we weren't examining the slovenly men we were to fight beside in the coming battles, we busied ourselves making flags, molding bullets and balls, bushing cannon. The best thing these would-be warriors had going for them was the flintlock rifles they carried—good Kentucky long-rifles that put the Mexicans' smoothbores to shame.

Evenings, we all sat around the campfire. Noah had been elected lieutenant, so I made sure to salute him every chance I got. Most of us had yet to see a moment's combat, and the camp had an almost celebratory air. Noah once remarked to me that there was no common cause in those early days: some men were for independence, some for the Constitution of '24, and some for just about anything so long as it ended in a fight.

One night—it was October 12th, I recall; we'd break camp the next day and march for Bexar—we were sitting there making merry when a big bay horse came riding up to the edge of our fire. We went quiet all round, and looking up, saw a square-jawed man in a buckskin jacket with leather leggings gartered up under his knees. He had sapphire-blue eyes that shone in the firelight, long hair the color of wheat, and for a hat, a cap of wild pantherskin. And not just the skin, mind you, but the cat's actual head, its eyes sewn shut and its ears poking up. The teeth hung down from its upper jaw almost touching the stranger's brow. It looked less like a hat, and more as if a panther had leapt on this young man's head and bit into his skull—and him not bothered enough to shoo it away.

Well, I'd seen plenty of coonskin caps and those made of otter, wolf, and beaver, but this was the first mountain lion headgear I'd come across. I daresay, on another man it would've seemed outrageous and provoked laughs and harsh harangues, but on this worthy pioneer it seemed entirely natural.

We were too surprised to greet the rider, so it was him who broke the silence.

"You all riding for San Antonio?" he asked.

"We leave out tomorrow morning," Noah told him. "You looking to enlist?"

The young man gave a nod of his head, then slid from his saddle. Someone passed him a mug of coffee.

"What's your name?" I asked.

"Samuel Fisk," he said. "Or just Sam, if you like."

"Duncan," I told him, and my throat felt tight as a snare. All of a sudden, I had trouble swallowing.

The next day after we'd taken up our line of march, Noah rode beside me and nodded toward Sam who was a few dozen yards ahead of us.

"Keep an eye out for that one," he said.

"Why?" I asked. "He seems brave enough."

"It's not his courage I'm questioning," Noah said.

"I reckon he'll hold up better than some of these others."

"Maybe," he said. "But I don't trust a man till I fought with him."

Noah had been in that first set-to at Gonzales defending the cannon we now pulled behind us with two yokes of longhorn steer—and which ended up proving so worthless we'd bury it at Sandy Creek—and flush with victory and his new rank, seemed to reckon himself quite the soldier.

"Well," I said, "you've yet to fight anything with me except alligators. Do I raise your suspicion?"

"Course not," he told me. "Just mind our new recruit yonder."

We reached the Cibolo and met up with reinforcements led by Colonel Bowie, already quite famous for that knife fight over in Vandalia and all the blades that bore his name, and then here came Colonel Fannin with several dozen men of his own. These luminaries had no sooner begun greeting the troops and shaking hands when I turned to see another contingent drifting down the hill, and at their head, an eagle-eyed gent with side-whiskers and a strong, dimpled chin. He rode a yellow Spanish stallion that looked too small for him and was dressed in dirty buckskin like many of us.

I was informed that this was the great Sam Houston, former governor of Tennessee and soon-to-be general of the Texian army. Most of us didn't know him from Adam, but he had such presence, we all just stopped, and stared, and waited for him to make us a speech.

Which he soon commenced to do in fine fashion. He had a good, deep voice, strong as reverent whiskey, and his words put steel in your backbone; you sat up straighter just to hear them. I can't recall his exact address that day, but the gist was that while we might have come from various settings and circumstances, the cause in which we'd enlisted was of no less importance than the one our fathers had taken up in 1776. Whatever state we once called home, we were sons of Texas now.

When he finished speaking, we fell to clapping and hurrahing him like he was President Jackson himself. He let this go on a while, then lifted his hand and announced we were to follow the competent command of Colonels Fannin and Bowie and continue our march toward Bexar; he himself was bound for the convention at San Felipe to recruit more men. That took some of the sap out of us, as it had seemed he was about to lead us on to San Antonio himself, and seeing the change in our attitude, he told us matters of tremendous consequence were being decided at that very moment. He would raise a larger force and rejoin us soon as possible.

If we'd known that even then he was in a pitched battle

against politicians who were working to undermine both him and our Revolution, we might've marched on these scalawags at San Felipe, but in our ignorance, we watched Houston ride off, feeling dejected we'd have to wait to receive his fine leadership.

* * *

We reached the San Antonio River that evening and made camp a quarter mile from the mission of Concepcion. Colonel Bowie posted pickets and then walked around, apprising everyone of the proximity of Mexican troopers—we were close to their garrison now.

Noah and I made a fire and shared our supper of beans and sowbelly with young Samuel, who seemed a good deal older than he actually was—I'd later learn he was twenty-two at the time. He had a firm martial bearing, and there was something about him that made you feel safe. I couldn't understand Noah's reservations about him, and it occurred to me maybe he was jealous.

We sat there in the chill autumn air with our blankets shucked up around our shoulders, watching the stars appear; the warmth of the fire and the smell of sizzling meat created a very pleasant atmosphere. The notion that we were soldiers seemed ridiculous.

"So," I remember Noah saying, glancing across the fire to where Sam sat with his blue, shining eyes and that panther atop his head, "tell us where—"

A distant boom interrupted him and the entire camp went quiet. I heard a shrieking sound and glanced up to see a speck travelling across the purple sky, moving in between the stars, growing larger, coming our direction.

Is that a cannonball? I wondered.

Indeed, it was. It whistled down and struck the earth a few

dozen yards from camp, landing in the grass with a wet, slapping sound.

I stood up. I didn't know much about artillery. Maybe I expected the ball to explode, but it had already done all it was going to.

"That doesn't seem right," I announced, and I'd no sooner got these words out than there were several more booms, several more specks traversing the sky, then one cannonball after another smacked into the turf, about five or six in total, each going wide of their intended mark—which, I recall thinking, was us.

The men of camp sat watching them land with a queer curiosity. Everything was very quiet.

I turned to Noah.

"Is that it?"

"I reckon we'll see," he told me.

But we saw nothing more that night, and though somewhat more alert, we continued our meals and conversations, and a few hours after nightfall, our march caught up with us, and we fell asleep.

Or most of us did.

I woke to a loud pop that slapped at my ears and echoed across the river. I sat up in my bedding and glanced around. It was gray morning and a thick fog lay over the land. Noah roused himself and sat there rubbing his eyes.

"What was that?" he said.

"Shhh," I told him.

It was then I noticed Sam. He was standing several feet away with his musket in hand, the butt braced on the ground like a walking stick. He stared out into the mist like the statue of a sentry. Noah and I got to our feet, walked over and joined him, but we couldn't see any more standing than we could lying down.

"Was that a gunshot?" I asked.

"Yessir," said Sam.

"Did it wake you?"

"I been awake," he told me.

"Since when?" Noah asked.

"Since night before last," he said.

Which seemed to shame the new lieutenant. His cheeks went red. He and I walked back over to fetch our rifles.

"Thought I told you to keep an eye on him," he whispered.

"Looks like he kept one on us," I said.

The camp was coming awake, dozens of men coughing and clearing their throats—a sound like a sawmill buzzing up. Directly, I saw Colonel Bowie coming toward us, pausing to speak to his troopers along the way. He marched over to Noah and told him our scouts had reported several companies of Mexican infantry approaching with field pieces in tow, and two cavalry units mounted up across the river to block our retreat.

"We best get these men to cover," he said, and ordered us to form a line, sheltering ourselves along the riverbank.

And there we laid in the mud under the pecan trees beside the water. I watched as the men began preparing themselves for a fight, splashing the pans of their muskets with fresh powder, moving their shot pouches close to hand. Noah was on one side of me, Sam on the other, that panther atop his head looking as if it had clenched its eyes up tight, not wishing to see what fate had in store for us. We were outnumbered, and if the Mexicans truly brought artillery with them, outgunned as well.

I gripped my rifle and stared out across the field. The sun was farther up in the sky, and I felt my enthusiasm for warfare begin to vanish. A somber mood fell upon me, and I thought about Mama and Pap, wishing I might say goodbye to them. It occurred to me that it was fairly easy to feel brave while marching along with your compatriots, but lying around waiting for the enemy to shoot you was another matter.

The fog was growing thinner and thinner, then it seemed to lift all at once like a curtain. A few hundred yards out, Mexican soldiers advanced on us in line formation, the men marching up in their single-breasted blue coats and white linen trousers, bayonets winking in the sun. There was a team of mules toward the rear, dragging up an enormous cannon. They unlimbered the piece, got it turned, and commenced to charging it.

The morning was cool, but I broke out in a sweat. My palms were slick as stones.

Colonel Bowie shouted for us to hold our fire.

"What are we holding for?" I asked Noah, but he didn't answer—the sight of the soldados loading that cannon had seized hold of his tongue.

I steadied my rifle and drew a careful bead on the man standing at the rear of the piece. He already had a match in hand. He was only seventy yards away, and I could've made the shot quite easily, but didn't want to get myself in Dutch with the colonel. Also, I thought that if I fired, the Mexicans might charge our position before I was able to reload, so perhaps it *was* better to wait. But then again, maybe it wasn't.

Then one of the artillerymen touched off the piece and the cannon roared. Every thought I had went scattering. I closed my eyes and hunkered. Grape shot peppered the limbs over our head, slicing away branches, sending pecan nuts showering down.

Colonel Bowie yelled: "Keep under cover, boys, and reserve your fire—we ain't got a man to spare!"

I glanced at Noah. His eyes were bulging. The cannon blazed away and tree limbs rattled. Bits of bark sprinkled the back of my neck, and I felt very certain I was about to die. I began muttering a prayer, repenting all my lust and foolishness.

When I peeped back up over the bank, I saw that the Mexicans had us pretty well surrounded.

"We best commence to shooting," I told Noah, but he and his bugging eyes had no response. I turned to ask Sam's opinion on the matter, and that young man looked entirely untroubled by our predicament. He'd gathered up a handful of pecans and was peeling them and popping the nuts in his mouth.

Yes, I thought. He is cool as Presbyterian charity.

Just then, a Mexican in a double-breasted coat with red epaulets lifted a nasty-looking saber and called out something to his men. Then those soldiers raised their muskets and came toward us at a charge.

Well, I reckon we'd seen enough, orders or not, and we let slip with our rifles. The enemy was a rushing blue tide, but when we discharged our volley, that first line of Mexicans went down like they'd been tripped.

It was nothing like I thought it would be: you could not see the hole a rifle ball made at that distance. You sighted your man, pulled the trigger, and down he fell. It did not even seem like something your rifle was the cause of. You knew it in your head, but your heart kicked the notion away. The first soldier I shot went to his knees, then sat down in the grass as though he'd decided to take a rest.

I fumbled up my powder horn and managed to get the snout of it in the muzzle. My hands were shaking and my ears ringing from the thunderous noise. Getting my rifle reloaded was ten times as hard as placing a shot. I'd patched a ball before it occurred to me I'd need to stand up to get it seated and rammed down the barrel, and standing up meant presenting myself to the enemy as a target. I looked at Sam, who'd snuck to the top of the bank and taken a knee. He'd already gotten off three shots to my one and was now reloading a fourth, his hands moving so fast they blurred. It was like watching a card sharp shuffle a deck, everything so quick and perfect—not a single wasted motion.

Out on the field, the Mexicans leveled their own muskets and fired a volley, then came rushing us. Three times they charged our line, and three times we threw them back. The pecan trees and that river bank gave good cover, but it also prevented some of our boys from shooting as much as they would've liked. A man named Dick Andrews grew so excited by our displays of marksmanship he stood up and stepped forward to get a better shot. He'd no sooner raised his rifle than the Mexicans touched off that cannon and peppered the poor man with grape. He collapsed on the ground, clutching his stomach.

Andrews just lay there groaning. Noah leapt up, grabbed the man by the ankles and started tugging him back toward the river.

"Talk to me," I heard him say. "Is it bad?"

"Yes," Andrews told him. "I'm killed. Lay me down."

Noah yanked up Dick's shirt and began searching for his wound. There it was: a thumb-size hole pumping blood and bile. Dick's face had gone bone-white and I knew there was no way he'd live.

Then I couldn't watch any longer. I glanced over and tried to concentrate on Sam charging his rifle. He seemed to sense it, turned his blue eyes on me, and just like that, I felt safe again. It was the strangest thing. He was shorter than Noah and myself, but broader through the shoulders, more thickly muscled, his neck round as a tree.

"That cannon," I told him, "is like a blunderbuss."

"I don't enjoy it," he said, as though speaking about cream in his coffee and not an artillery-piece that'd just split our comrade's belly.

Then a curious expression came over his face. He mumbled something to himself, turned, and went up the riverbank, disappearing over the lip of it.

I was too startled to call him back. I crawled up a ways and peeked out. Yonder he went, sprinting off across the field, right into the mouth of that cannon.

Well, the Texians had been waiting for the opportunity to get more intimate with their foe and seeing Samuel in his frontier dress and crazy cap seemed to set something off in them. Our entire line gave a cheer.

Then, they stood and went surging forward as well—or *we*, I should say, for I was with them too—looking to give our enemy the bayonet. This sight was too much for the Mexicans and they began to fall back. Even the gunners operating the cannon gave up. All three of them mounted a mule that had pulled the caisson, one behind the other on the poor beast's back. Sam slid to a knee, and shouldering his rifle, fired. Two of the Mexicans fell from the mule, one sliding left, the other right, the rider in front leaning down onto the animal's neck and snapping the reins.

Then Sam had reached the deserted cannon, throwing down his rifle and shouting for us to help him turn the piece. We came rushing up, got it wheeled around, and one of our men who knew something of artillery charged it and lit the fuse. When the gun went off, a swath of soldados collapsed like a great wind had blown them down.

* * *

It was a grand victory. We'd routed an army of superior strength, and searching the bodies of those Mexican soldiers, we soon discovered why. The smoothbores they carried couldn't match our rifles for range or accuracy, and the powder in their cartridges was little better than charcoal. It was not even worth collecting to replenish our stores.

My first taste of combat had a powerful effect on me. I felt like I'd run a dozen miles. Back home in Kentucky, I'd seen men seized by the madness of buck fever: you bring down an animal with antlers the size of a hat rack and the thrill of it is like leaping out of your own skin.

Well, what I'd just experienced was ten times the sensation. It wasn't just the killing that brought it on—let me say that right out—but rather some mixture of shooting and being shot at and emerging from the affair unscathed. I didn't want another battle right away, but I knew the whole episode had set the hook in me. My hands were shaking from the flush of it. I went over and sat beside Noah. We looked at each other and I went to laughing. He shook his head, but directly he was chuckling too. It felt very good to be alive, having just seen what we had, and there was also this sense we'd taken part in something that might outlive us, long as there were men to tell the story.

It didn't occur to me that the Mexicans we'd trounced must have felt as miserable as we were grand. It would take more than a decade for such a thought to come knocking at my door, and when it did, it battered down door, house, and all.

But at just that moment, I was young and victorious and in the company of friends.

"What are we laughing about?" Noah said.

"I don't rightly know. Not an hour ago, I was pretty certain we'd be killed ever one of us."

"I was too," he said.

At some point, Sam had disappeared into a throng of militiamen, all of them slapping his back and congratulating him on leading the charge.

"Where has our comrade got to?" I asked.

Noah stood up and glanced around. Then he lifted his chin and gestured with it. "Yonder he is."

I looked and saw Sam walking back down by the river, picking nuts from the ground and stowing them in his possibles bag. He didn't look like a man who'd just led an army to victory. He seemed unbothered by the trial, neither jovial nor gloomy.

Noah and I walked down to join him and we took our dinner in the shade of those pecan trees that had screened us from Mexican fire. Sam's actions had raised him considerably in Noah's eyes; he sat studying this brave warrior with a much different attitude than what he'd had the day before.

"Where'd you learn to fight like that?" he asked.

Sam slurped at the coffee we'd made him.

"Fight like what?" he said.

"Clearly, you've seen a good deal of battle," said Noah.

Sam took off his pantherskin hat and set it there on the ground beside him. His hair gleamed like spun gold.

"I never said nothing bout battles," he said.

"How many fights have you been in?" Noah asked.

"Fights or battles?"

"Battles then," said Noah.

"That was my first," Sam said.

CECELIA

—VIRGINIA, MISSISSIPPI, LOUISIANA, 1829–1837—

There were no more poems; there was no more singing. Haverford said he would take her to market the first chance he got.

Mistress Anne was inconsolable. She wept for the better part of a week, begged her husband to show mercy, but Haverford said he was fresh out. Cecelia watched them fuss and argue, watched her mistress slump from room to room; you'd have thought she was the one getting sold.

The stupidity, Cecelia thought. She felt that she should be owning *them*.

In years to come, she'd think of this as a time of falling. She was falling from the tobacco soil of Virginia to the cotton lands of the south. In the slave port of Wheeling, Haverford sold her to a planter named Greer. Cecelia spent the next three weeks on a steamboat, drifting down the rivers to Mississippi.

She was sold once more in Natchez and confined to a house along the river: six years in a house where everything smelled of mold. From the window, she'd watch field hands pass, knowing they'd have traded places with her in an instant. But Cecelia had stepped foot onto free soil in Pennsylvania and now she was a runner. Now it was in her blood. She slipped out of the house one night and was stopped at the river.

That was the end of her house days, they said. She'd spend the rest of her life in the fields.

She was carted to a plantation in the back of a wagon: a new plantation, not far from the one she'd just escaped. She saw the big house and the bare, flat fields, and the buyer drove her down a narrow dirt lane. They pulled up alongside a row of warped pinewood huts, each identical to the other: pitched roofs and windowless walls. Black folks sat on the sloping porches or stood in the doorways staring out, the men in long, threadbare shirts, no trousers or shoes, their naked legs just bones with a loose covering of brown, sagging skin. The women were skeletal, and many of them walked about bare-breasted, nothing but filthy skirts to hide their nethers. Cecelia felt ashamed for them, and then she was worried about her own calico dress: how long would it last? How long before it frayed and fell away?

The white man stopped the wagon and ordered her down. She had no sooner stepped to the ground than the buyer popped the reins and was moving again, rolling down the lane until he passed into a grove of cedar.

Cecelia stood there. The slaves studied her, motionless, mute. Their skin had a strange red tint; their hair had grown out and faded in the sun. A bird called. From somewhere, an infant screamed.

Then the men and women were off the porches, out of the huts, swarming Cecelia, surrounding her. Voices spoke in all accents, from all sides:

"Have you seen my Johnny, about thirteen year: he stands yay high?"

"My husband—name of Walter Johnson: he from Alabama. Got a birthmark on his cheek looks just like the moon."

"You seen Sissy? Sweet little Sissy? She's skinny as a bean pole. She's missing this tooth."

Cecelia shook her head. She hadn't seen Sissy; she hadn't seen Walter or John.

She hadn't seen Thomas, Toby, or Rachel.

Hadn't seen Hyppolite or Harriett.

Never heard of Big Tim from Hawk's Nest.

She hadn't seen her own kin since she was a child. What made them think she'd seen theirs?

* * *

It rained. The weeks passed in a gray downpour. The rain fell straight down, descending in sheets, screening off the world, closing them into their cramped cabins. Cecelia was only waiting for an opportunity.

She looked out one day and saw there was fur on the branches. The next, bugs hovered and crawled. After a shower, the ground would steam, mist rising from the earth as if it were about to burst into flame. She fell asleep on the thin pallet she'd been given, smelling springtime in the air.

And woke to the noise of a horn blaring, lying in the dark with her skin prickling from the sound. Bodies moved in the hut, though she couldn't quite make them out. The brass squawk of the horn died away, and she lay there listening to the hum inside her head. She'd been dreaming of something pleasant, but the horn had blasted it from her brain, and she tried to think what it was, caught an image of a green sward sloping up, but the horn sounded again, a single raw note rising. The hairs stood on her arms. She rolled off the pallet and got to her feet.

She filed outside and stood on the bare dirt with the others assembling around her in the predawn light, watching the overseer approach on his swaybacked mare. They called him Mister Timothy, a large white man who kept his hat pulled down to his eyebrows. He wore a pistol on his right hip, and tucked in his belt on the other side was a rawhide whip with a handle made of wood.

The sky in the east was a band of red running flat across the horizon. The overseer began calling the names of those who would serve as captains, nine names, ten. These men stepped forward. Then Mister Timothy was reading names from a tablet he held, assigning each to a captain. Cecelia heard her name, and she walked over to stand beside Okah, a tall slave with Delaware in his blood: calm-faced and kind.

Okah's crew assembled around him, and then they followed him over to a shed where he began to distribute hoes. He had a dozen charges this morning: man, woman, and child.

They'd spend the next several weeks planting. She thought she'd get the chance to slip off into the trees, but the overseer watched them all day long. In the meantime, she worked and waited.

Okah would hold a bag of cotton seed, and women filed past, filling their apron-pockets. They'd line up at the end of a row, some with hoes, some with seed. One would pull the blade across the earth and another would follow, bending to settle each seed in the trench the hoe made, then covering it with soil, stepping on it gently with the ball of a bare foot—day after day until the planting was done, and there was nothing but to wait until the seeds became green shoots; the shoots, stems. Then those stems grew tiny leaves, small as the ears of squirrels.

The rains continued and there was still no opportunity to run.

It was April.

It was May.

June came, and they were back in the dark in front of the cabins, watching the overseer ride up on his mare. She followed Okah over to the shed and was given a hoe. The crew shouldered their tools like rifles, and went trekking toward the darkened fields.

There was the slightest breeze, spiced with cedar, though Cecelia hadn't seen any cedar these months: just oaks and acres of cotton. The plants looked black now in the half-light. The crew walked out along an earthen dike, passed an enormous live oak bearded with moss. She studied every leaf and blade of grass, memorizing everything she could.

Then they were in the field among the cotton. The plants came just to her waist. They were following a row east, marching single-file, when the sun breached the horizon, and they went squinting along in the shine of it, wading in that sea of green leaves, the white flowers turning red in the glare.

At the far end of the field, they staggered out in a line, each of them taking a row, the boy and girl in their crew working one together. Cecelia had the calluses for it now, but the first week had been blisters and bleeding palms.

Okah turned his head to either side, and gave each of them a look.

"Yes," he said. "Stay with me. Let's not give Marse Timothy cause."

All bent and began hoeing, chopping the weeds between the plants, cutting them up, turning the black earth.

The captain set the pace, and Okah was an excellent captain: he didn't set a pace no one could keep up with, but he didn't set one slow enough to get the overseer's attention. She glanced up and saw Mister Timothy walking his mare across the dike, hat pulled low. You felt his eyes on you like the sun.

After an hour, they stopped to receive a breakfast of cornbread, a cold lump of it about the size of your fist. Then it was back to the hoe, chopping earth, a dead sound that shushed to you, the squad of them working in tandem, an occasional clink of steel when someone struck a rock. Once every hour, you were allowed to walk over to the wagon, stretching your muscles as you went—it was the bending that got you, the bending and being bent—and the child in the wagon bed would hand you a ladle-full of water. Cecelia thought she'd never tasted anything like it: sweet and flavored with oak.

And then the hoe was back in your hands, but your hands

were numb. You wouldn't feel them until later, after a supper of the same cornbread you'd eaten for breakfast and lunch— a little salt pork, two radishes apiece—lying there on the corn shuck mattress, and finally your hands could feel again, and what they felt was the hoe: there was no hoe now, but that's what you felt. Everything had tightened inside, but somehow you were loose. She would lie there and after a while there was that floating sensation they called sleep, and you might see their faces in dreams—Jubal, Alice, your mother— and when the pleasure of it started to come and they were about to speak, it wasn't the sound of their voice you heard, but the corkscrewing blare of the horn.

* * *

She was good with the hoe. It was punishing labor, but her hands understood it, her arms knew the motions. She never lagged behind the captain; she was quicker than most of the men, coming down the row, chopping weeds, careful of the cotton: she never so much as nicked a plant. You progressed by inches, turning the earth, light to dark, brown to black. There sat the overseer up on his horse, watching, but you might take a second, a brief moment, to turn and examine your work: the line of tilled dirt stretching back down the row. You made one thing into another, weeds into perfectly turned soil, baking in the sun.

But by day's end, headed toward the cabins with the hoe on her shoulder, she'd glance back to see row after row of cultivated earth, and couldn't tell which were hers, which were Okah's or Margaret's or Isaiah's, walking along with a sting in her breast, needing to know which rows she'd done and which she hadn't, what belonged to her and what didn't, and then she couldn't think of it anymore, could only think about that handful of cold cornbread, her stomach straining for it, and the sting in her breast was a mosquito on her sternum, sucking out a meal of its own.

A small skeletal girl trailed behind her. Her name was Ruby. She shared a hut with Cecelia and she had a baby she carried in a burlap sling. Ruby hoed the fields with that baby; Cecelia didn't see how. The infant slept, or cried, or stared out at the passing plants. Sometimes Ruby worked with Cecelia's crew, sometimes she didn't. Often, she lagged behind her captain.

The overseer didn't seem to care about the baby; it was the lagging he wouldn't have: you kept pace with your captain, infant or no.

Cecelia thought she might offer to carry the child herself. Mister Timothy was watching Ruby closer and closer.

And there was something else, something less generous. The baby seemed to call to her, begging to be held. She thought if she could just nuzzle it, that might give her strength. Maybe she'd take the child with her when she ran.

She rose from the pallet one night, stole across the room to where Ruby lay with her child. Ruby would coo and speak to the baby boy, but Cecelia had never heard her say his name, as though the name was some secret between them.

Cecelia knelt there and touched Ruby's shoulder—hard and sharp, no muscle or flesh to it, just bone.

"Miss Ruby," she whispered.

Ruby looked up at Cecelia out of her hollowed eyes.

"That man is watching you," Cecelia said. "Timothy."

"Yessum," said Ruby.

"It worries me. It worries me for you and your babe."

"Yessum," Ruby said.

Cecelia watched her a moment, watched the infant dozing beside her. She thought about the absolute blessing of this child, the company he provided, even if he couldn't yet speak a word. The touch of someone who needed you, who gave off love like a stove did heat.

She said, "I could carry him some of the time. Out in the field. I could carry him for you, now and then."

Ruby stared at Cecelia. Her lips did nothing. Her eyes did nothing. But somehow, her face began to close. She cupped her baby with one hand and pulled him close against her, and Cecelia knew this girl was in trouble.

She patted Ruby's hard shoulder and started to rise.

"Cotton coming," Ruby said.

Cecelia looked at her. "How's that?"

"Cotton coming," said Ruby. "Be different when we pick."

Cecelia knelt there. She didn't see how picking cotton would improve Ruby's situation, how the girl would be better off when she had both a baby and a cotton sack weighing her down.

"Yes," Cecelia said, trying to think of something to comfort the girl, something to reassure her, but nothing came to mind.

Then a strange thought passed through her head. There'd been a note in Ruby's voice, almost as if Ruby wasn't asking for reassurance, but was trying to warn her of something, and Cecelia rose and returned to her pallet.

I'll get away from them, she thought. Nothing frightened her so much as weakness.

Come the next day, Ruby lagged behind, and all day long, the overseer watched. It was July now, and heat came pressing down from the sky, the blue like a great blanket to smother them. Mister Timothy had begun to carry an umbrella, shading himself, his face impassive. Cecelia saw Ruby in the field, hoeing down the row all by herself, and then Cecelia saw the overseer studying Ruby. He won't have it, she thought. There was something in the man's posture. He never said a word, but Cecelia could tell by the way he sat his horse what was coming.

At sunset, up by the cabins, the overseer called roll, eyes glancing up from his tablet to the answering faces. It wasn't until he called Ruby's name that Cecelia realized the girl was absent.

Crickets chirped from the bushes. Folks stared at the ground. Then the crickets died away and it was very quiet. Cecelia could hear her heart beat in her ears.

Then she heard a shuffling sound, and here came Ruby, hoe on her shoulder, baby on her back in its burlap sling. The girl walked up and joined the crowd there in front of the cabins.

It was twilight under the oak trees, in the shadows of the pineboard huts. Everything was in suspension. Then the crickets started pulsing back up, screeching and scraping out a song.

The overseer examined Ruby several seconds, and then he climbed down from his horse. Cecelia watched him make his way through the crowd of black bodies, men and women parting as he came. Then he stood there in front of Ruby. The girl said nothing, looked at nothing. Her chest rose and fell. What was she, thought Cecelia: fourteen? Fifteen?

You were fifteen the first time you ran.

"On your belly," Timothy said.

Ruby blinked a few times. She tugged the sling around so that her child was against her chest, then, cradling the infant, removed the sling: carefully, soundlessly, didn't want to wake the babe. She handed him over to a woman whose name Cecelia didn't know, went down on her hands and knees, and then proned out as the overseer had commanded her.

Timothy bent and set his tablet in the dirt with the same care Ruby used passing her child to the woman, then reached and took the hem of Ruby's skirt, flipping the garment up to reveal her thighs, her buttocks, her back. There was a lattice-work of scars, black and blue and purple, and Cecelia turned away.

You must look, she told herself, though she didn't want to. She felt it was important to see what happened. Not looking would be a cruelty to the girl; it broke faith with Ruby, betrayed her. So Cecelia made herself turn back and watch, but it was a different kind of watching. It was the kind of watching you did in dreams: you weren't fully inside yourself; you weren't fully behind your eyes.

The overseer was straight again. He'd pulled that whip from his belt, long as a king snake. There was nothing at all in his face: no anger, or arrogance, or irritation, and Cecelia knew he'd done this thousands of times, he had no more hatred for Ruby than the carpenter had for the head of a nail as he brought down the hammer.

And Cecelia thought that this was worse, watching it all from that strange place where she'd gone. It would have been better if he'd hated the girl he was about to savage; it would even have been better if he'd enjoyed it. But Timothy was only working; it was only what he did. He'd done it a thousand times; he'd do it a thousand more. He wasted no energy, no emotion. He pulled back his arm, and the whip hissed through the dirt, and Cecelia could see that he controlled every inch of that plaited rawhide lash. It came slicing through the air, but Cecelia had turned again and shut her eyes. She heard the loud crack and the scream that followed like an echo, then a second crack and scream, and she thought, though God had made men and women, He'd not made them very well. There'd been two cracks, two screams, and now there was the sound of the girl vomiting, and God, thought Cecelia, had gotten it wrong. Your eyes closed at such moments, but there was no closing up your ears—there were no lids to them—and there were no lids at all to your thoughts. You couldn't turn away from them, could never turn away, and Cecelia was quite sure of it, God had gotten them completely wrong.

* * *

The cotton was laid by, tall enough that the weeds were drowned in shadow. The hoeing came to an end. The plants were shoulder-high, and then they were taller than the men who'd tended them, large and leafed out. Buds appeared, growing fatter all through August, the branches drooping under the weight.

Late one night, Cecelia was lying on her pallet, putting the day out of herself before she dropped down into sleep, and she felt a shift in the air, a kind of opening, and she woke the next morning to find that the bolls had exploded: everywhere you looked, the fields were snowed with white fluff. Fibers drifted on the breeze. Just as Ruby told her, the cotton had come.

And why haven't you run yet? she thought.

It has to be perfect. I'll only get one chance.

Her first day picking, Cecelia was assigned again to Okah, but there was concern in the man's face when he handed her the sack. Something passed across his features like a cloud across the sun.

"Keep close to me," he said. "It'll take you time to get the sleight of it."

Cecelia had felt relieved the picking was about to start, no more chopping, no more stooping over the hoe.

"I'll keep up," she told him, irritated he seemed to think she couldn't. Ruby had been assigned to their crew today. He ought to be worrying about her.

Okah nodded, but she could tell he didn't believe her. He held a hand up, closing his thumb, index, and ring fingers into a claw.

"You're using these three to pick with," he said. "Just these three. Don't use your pinky or your mid finger; you'll stab it on a boll."

Cecelia looked at her right hand. She touched the tips of her ring and forefinger to her thumb. It felt wrong. Wasn't natural. She glanced up at Okah and saw him reading her thoughts.

"You want to *pinch* that cotton," he said. "Don't leave a speck of it behind."

"I won't," said Cecelia, and her words had a raw edge to them. She'd already shown what kind of hand she was, out-stripping the men, hoeing out ahead of them, nearly as fast as Okah himself.

"I'll try not to push too hard," he said, "but I can't let Mister Timothy see us dawdle, neither."

"Don't hold back on my account," said Cecelia, and now she was mad. She'd get away from all these people—poor Ruby and this man who questioned her strength. *I'll leave all of them behind.*

The cotton went running to the pink horizon. Okah and his crew formed up at one end of the field, each hand choosing a row. Ruby had the one right next to Cecelia, that baby slung on her back, her skirt dragging with the weight of the dew.

Cecelia couldn't think about the girl right now. She stooped and started picking.

Straightaway, she could see what the problem was going to be. She was right-handed as you could be, but you had to pick the left side of the row as well as the right, one side and then the other. She had the picksack slung over her right shoulder, the mouth of it on her left hip. She reached for the first puff of cotton, gripped it with those three digits Okah thought were so important, pinched and pulled away. She pinched too hard, and some stem came off with the actual cotton, and she had to remove it with her left hand before slipping the fluff in her sack. When she reached for the next handful, her middle fin-ger got in the way, and she felt a sharp prick.

She jerked her hand back and stuck the finger in her mouth, sucking it. Then pulled the finger from between her lips and studied the tip: a bright bead of blood swelled like a baneberry. Her eyes shot to Okah and he was looking back at her. He lifted a hand and slapped his ring and forefinger against his thumb. She nodded to him and bent back to work.

Within half an hour, she was wishing for the hoe. You had

to use that odd grip, and you had to do it perfectly every time. She couldn't do it perfectly even once. She picked away the stem and fibers, or she caught only a piece of cotton and came away with strands. All four fingers of her right hand were bleeding, and the little cotton in her sack was blotched with red. And her palms that were always sweaty, slick on the handle of the hoe, were dry as a bone. The cotton sucked all the moisture out of them, such an odd feeling, your hands like a buzzard's talons.

She stopped and studied them a moment. She didn't want to look up, knowing she'd fallen behind the others. Then she remembered Ruby. She'd forgotten the girl for the last hour, but now Cecelia needed her, needed to watch Ruby struggle. It was cruel to enjoy someone else's misery, but Cecelia couldn't help herself. She stood up straight and looked around.

Ruby was no longer there beside Cecelia. The girl had picked out ahead of the crew, out ahead of Okah. There she went, picking with her right hand and her left, both hands at once, fingers dancing among the bolls like a fiddler's upon the strings, right and left, right and left, both hands going, pulling white. Cecelia had never seen anything like it, and she started suddenly to cry, though she couldn't afford tears, couldn't spare the water. She reached out and touched the cotton with her claw.

* * *

Evening, when it was too dark to tell bolls from leaves, they emptied their last sacks into the baskets, and carried the baskets up to weigh. Mister Timothy was in the shed with his tablet and pen. He'd call out each picker's name as the captains hung the baskets on the steelyard and weighed them up.

"Little Stephen," he said. "Hunnerd forty-pounds."

Or, "Jim Hawkins. Hunnerd seventy-one."

Or Ruby. The girl had picked two hundred and thirty-six pounds, the most of anyone that day.

The overseer wrote each hand's weight next to his name in the ledger. Then he nodded for the captains to remove the wicker basket from the scale, and hang up the next.

That was Cecelia's. Okah carried her basket, hung it on the steelyard, then stood there eyeing the dirt.

"Twenty-eight pounds," Mister Timothy said, then looked at Cecelia over his tablet.

Cecelia swallowed. Or tried to swallow. Her throat felt like fur.

"You know what that means?" Timothy asked.

She had no idea.

"Twenty-eight is your bottom," he told her. "We'll say thirty, starting tomorrow. It's a lash for every pound you're short."

Cecelia nodded, and then she was walking toward the cabins. From behind her, she could hear Timothy calling out the next hand's name.

Then Okah was there at her side.

"You done all right," he said. "You'll get better." He held up both hands, thumbs and forefingers and ring fingers. "Practice it."

She lay on the pallet after her supper of cornbread and salt pork—no radishes tonight—practicing her claw. There was a sharp pain across the back of her right hand, and she couldn't make the ring finger of her left hand hook in correctly: it brought the middle finger with it. She thought she should slip out and make her attempt right then, but her brain was so fogged she could barely think. She drifted off at some point and woke to the noise of the blaring horn. Her right hand was crusted with blood from the day before. She couldn't make it into a fist.

They were out in the fields come sunrise, twelve of them lined up with picksacks on their hips. Cecelia thought, Thirty pounds. It does not have to be but thirty. Her captain today was a small, quiet man named Whitmore. His tattered shirt hardly covered his hams. He stepped into a row, stopped and began picking. Cecelia stepped forward too. The sun was coming up behind her, and the field of cotton was purple and pink. A scraggly shadow stretched out from her feet and angled down her row. She squeezed her right hand, massaged it, but it wasn't working. She'd have to get by with her left.

She went along, clawing up the cotton, pricking herself on the bolls, but she couldn't think about any of that. She had to think about those thirty pounds.

In an hour, she'd sweated her dress completely through. It was September, but hot as ever. The sun was a great lidless eye. She ate her cornbread breakfast and emptied cotton from her sack into the wicker basket at the head of the row. She drank a ladle of water and felt her body soak up every drop.

Noon, she was in the middle of the field, picking with her one good hand, wiping blood on her dress. Her fingers were so sticky with it she couldn't get the cotton to fall into the sack, had to scrape it from her fingers with the blade of her right hand. Children were coming down the rows with buckets balanced on their heads, bringing it out to the pickers from the wagons. Like little angels, she thought. They brought it out, then bore the empty buckets back to the wagon, and Cecelia saw that several had hairless circles atop their heads where the buckets rested, little boys of six and seven with bald spots like old men.

She stood in front of the shed that evening, swaying in the twilight.

Mister Timothy was calling names, calling weights. The captains hung the baskets on the scale. The overseer made marks in his ledger.

She was drifting inside herself when she heard her own name being called. The fatigue bled away, and she was alert as the overseer's expressionless face. Okah and Whitmore lifted her basket and hung it on the steelyard. Mister Timothy studied the scale.

"Twenty-nine pounds," said Timothy, and then motioned the captains to bring up the next basket.

She stood there thinking, Twenty-nine. He said twenty-nine. And she was still thinking that number when everyone was weighed up and had started for the cabins. It was dark now, and the shed was lit by two pine knot torches stuck in the ground. The overseer was writing in his ledger. She'd turned to walk away when she heard the man say, "You owe me a pound."

Cecelia didn't know how to answer. She didn't know if she was supposed to.

"On your belly," Timothy said.

He spoke so matter-of-factly, it didn't even seem that this was what she was supposed to do. Perhaps she'd imagined it.

"Get on your belly," the man said.

Her legs wouldn't hold her. She dropped to a squat and looked up at the man. He nodded for her to continue, pulling the whip from his belt.

Lord Jesus, she prayed, and terror chased the rest of it from her brain. She lay breathing against the earth. Maybe the man wouldn't strike her. Maybe it was just a threat.

Then she felt him flip her dress up, exposing her bare legs and nethers. The shame of it took the fear away. He tugged the dress up to her armpits.

"Mister Timothy," she said, "I would—"

The lash knocked the wind from her, and she lay there gasping. She felt her bladder go from the shock of it, and then she felt the white-hot pain across the middle of her back. She would've cried out, but she didn't have the breath to do it. She was fighting for air, on her side now, lying in the mud she'd made.

Her breath came back all at once, burning her lungs. It hurt so bad you couldn't even cry. The muscles in her back were in spasm, and she didn't know how she'd stand.

She saw the overseer from the corner of her eye, coiling his whip, then tucking it back in his belt, his calm face flickering in the light of the torches.

"Thirty pounds," he told her, then stepped off into the night.

* * *

She was lying face down on her pallet when she felt that someone was kneeling there beside her, and she opened her eyes.

It was Ruby, the skeleton girl, the girl of the dancing hands.

They stared at one another several moments, and Cecelia thought that Ruby might have been pretty if she'd had food enough to be pretty on, if she didn't have a child taking what little flesh she had, nursing that baby and picking cotton, three meals of cornbread a day.

Ruby reached out and put her bony hand on Cecelia's arm. There was an urgency in the girl's eyes that Cecelia hadn't seen before.

"He hit me," Cecelia said, still surprised, still couldn't believe it had happened.

"You can't think like you do," Ruby said.

"Okah says I need to use my hands, but I can't use either one."

"You can either pick or think," said Ruby. "You can't do them both. How short were you this evening?"

"A pound," Cecelia said.

Ruby nodded. "You get that short again, put a clod of dirt in your sack. Just a clod will do it. It'll break up so's Mister Timothy won't find it, and it'll almost always get you a pound."

"Could you always pick like you do?"

"No'um," said Ruby.

"Who taught you?"

Ruby stared a moment. There was a cleverness in her eyes, and Cecelia felt guilty for the impression she had formed, for ever thinking this girl was weak.

"The whip taught me," Ruby said.

* * *

She'd never say she learned to pick. She'd say her body learned, a second Cecelia who'd lived all these years inside her marrow, waiting to come to the surface. Was it the lash that called this stranger up or was it only shame? The feel of her dress flipped onto her back, her buttocks bared to all the world.

Whatever it was, the Stranger had emerged, and Lord could this Stranger pick! She went down the rows, almost as fast as Ruby: right hand and left hand, right and left at once.

Dancing, Cecelia thought. I have become a dance.

Stooping and picking, both claws at work. The picksack full, dump it in the basket. Water and cornbread under the sun. Water and cornbread in the torchlight by the shed, her basket hanging from the steelyard by its handles.

"Cecelia," said Mister Timothy. "One hunnerd sixty pounds."

Day after day, she followed her captain out across the dike. Each hand took a row, bent and started picking, and as soon as Cecelia made her fingers into a claw, she seemed to retreat inside her skull, shine and shade spreading around her, this shadow stretching away from her feet. She watched as the ragged specter pinched cotton from the bolls, and it was the Stranger picking.

Cecelia perched up there in her head over the coming

weeks, out upon the ledge of herself. What was this thing that took her over? Was there more than one of her inside?

She could think like this for a time. She could sit up there on the ledge of her skull while the Stranger did her work. Using both hands: that's what brought the Stranger on. Right Hand Cecelia, Left Hand Cecelia. Her body and the shadow that it cast.

And then she woke one morning and couldn't think at all. She could feel the knots in her back, the dirt cool against her calf. She could hear the others coming awake in the cabin, smell them as they passed the pallet and made their way outside.

It was very odd. She got to her feet and went out the door, forming up with the others to wait for Timothy. The sky was dark and there were no stars in it. A drop of water touched her nose. Then rain was falling all around them, coming down in sheets. The overseer rode up in the black sunrise, and sat his horse, holding the umbrella in one hand to keep his ledger dry. He called out crews and captains, and then Cecelia was following Okah to the shed. The rain began to let up, and then it stopped entirely. Okah gave each of them a picksack, but when he passed Cecelia hers, he stopped and stared.

"Miss Suss," he said.

Cecelia just looked at him.

"You all right?" he asked.

Cecelia didn't know. It was so hard to weave a thought. She'd make the scrap of one, and then it would unravel.

Time seemed to pass. They were walking. She had the picksack on her hip and she was stooping there in a row. Her claws were moving, closing on cotton, and then a voice spoke loudly in her ear.

Nothing, it said.

She turned to look behind her, but no one was there. She'd worked out ahead of the others; she was a good forty feet from the nearest hand.

She stood a moment, listening, smelling the earth.

She'd stooped to pick again, and here came the voice, inside and outside all at once.

Nothing, it said.

She turned and looked behind her. The sun breached the horizon, and threw its light upon her face.

Lying on the pallet at night, her hands opening and closing, thoughts would come to her, loose as gauze. She'd try to lace them all together, but before she could get the warp of them, she was drifting off to sleep. No thoughts in her dreams, just impressions.

Back in the field at dawn, that voice would hiss at her, harrying her down the rows. She felt it was familiar, had a face to it, a name. But names were so hard these days. They'd been syllabled inside her, but right and left hand pulled them apart.

She picked faster, trying to stay ahead of the voice, keep out in front of it, move so quickly it couldn't catch up. Stooping and picking, placing cotton in the sack, glancing back over her shoulder, then hurrying forward, the world coming to her in flashes and specks, and then the voice coming, chasing her along, a hot hiss scalding her brain: *Nothing, nothing, nothing, nothing.*

* * *

When harvest time was finished, the Stranger receded and she could think again. She was herself.

Or almost herself. The picking had changed her. Murder had grown in her breast like a brand-new organ. She imagined killing Timothy. She mused on it the way she used to long for food: prying his eyes from their sockets or sinking the blade of her hoe in his throat. She felt the most pleasurable thing in the world would be to watch him bleed.

This was a painful desire. White men were the murderous beings, not her. She was better than them. She'd always thought so.

Maybe there's a murderer in me too. I will have to chase it out. In order to be better than them again. In order to hate them as I should.

She'd learned several things as well, things she wished she didn't know. She had never dreamed that her body could fail her, that she could become estranged from her own mind. She understood why these poor people didn't run, why they could not. The labor carved you into pieces. It whittled you down to nothing and then became your life.

One harvest had taught her all this. What would several harvests do? Years and years of them?

And now that she could think again, she realized something else: there were no elderly hands on this plantation, no old men or women. Far as she could tell, no one over the age of forty.

She lay on her pallet, considering that. So strange it had never occurred to her, and the next thought was *where did they go?*

The answer came like a slap: she knew exactly where they went. She sat with it for a day, and then she took it to Okah.

The man was quartered in the cabin next to hers. Cecelia found him sitting at the rear of the little hut, his long legs spread out, something on the dirt between his knees.

She walked up and squatted beside him, placing a hand on his shoulder to announce herself.

Okah glanced over at her, then looked back at the ground. There on the dirt were rows of little stones, all shapes, all sizes, dark stones and light.

"What is it?" she asked.

Okah reached down and took a clear white stone and placed it beside several dark ones.

"Is it a game?" she asked.

"Just my rocks," Okah said.

"What are they for?"

"I like them," he said.

Cecelia had never given much attention to rocks. She'd studied trees and flowers all her life, but never stones.

"Is it something special about them?"

"No," said Okah. "They're mine, is all."

This scared her. Why did it scare her so?

She said, "This place is going to kill me, isn't it?"

Okah didn't look at her.

"It'll kill all of us," he said.

"How old are you?" she asked.

"I'm twenty-eight in February."

She nodded. "I was seventeen when they sent me down from Wheeling. I'll be twenty-four this fall. I thought I'd live to have babies, but that's just something I told myself. I won't ever have a family. Not if I stay."

Now Okah looked at her.

"You want to be real careful," he said, "about the way you talk. It's some in these cabins would sell you for a loaf of bread."

"I've been careful," she told him. "If I keep being careful, I'll end up in a grave."

Okah looked at his rocks.

She said, "I used to think I could do it by myself. That I didn't need anybody at all. I thought I'd find the perfect moment, but there isn't such a moment, and I need all the help I can get."

Evening was coming on. It was dusk beneath the naked branches.

"I enjoy you, Miss Suss. I'd hate to see something bad happen."

"You're seeing it," she said.

"There's things," said Okah, "a heap worse than dying."

"Yes," she told him, "isn't it so?"

* * *

She left that night. She took the food that Okah gave her, rolled it in a picksack, and snuck into the trees.

She found that getting away wasn't the problem. Furtiveness was in her bones.

It wasn't until she was several miles from the plantation that she understood the real obstacle she faced: she was alone in an unfamiliar land of cypress swamps and every trail led her to a marsh.

Within a week, she'd taken sick from drinking bog-water and the hounds sniffed her out. The slave-catchers must have thought she would die; they were surprisingly gentle. They carried her to Natchez and locked her in a room.

She lay on a cot with a raging fever. She was so thirsty. She couldn't stop shivering.

A doctor named Cartwright came to tend her. He was a bald, portly man with red sideburns, and she knew he was only healing her so she could be sent to market.

"What is wrong with me?" she asked.

"You are a drapetomaniac," he said.

"I'm what?"

"It means your owner has been indulgent. It means you like to run. Your womb is narrow and you will never carry a child to term." He put a cup to her lips and told her to drink.

She thought she would pass away and see her mother, but it was only the fever that passed. She was able to eat again, sleep again. They fed her very well and in several weeks she could stand.

As soon as she was walking, they escorted her to an intersection called Forks of the Road.

Here she was purchased by a grocer from Natchitoches and taken to Louisiana. Falling. Always falling. And at her new owner's home she didn't make it through the night. She waited until dark and walked out the front door.

That was a mistake. She knew it the moment her feet touched the grass, but she hadn't recovered from her time in Mississippi; she wasn't thinking clear.

Two slave-hunters caught her on the bayou. These men were as rough as the others were tender. They bound her wrists, snugged a rope around her neck, and dragged her into Natchitoches.

It was bright noon, a cloudless spring day. Seemed everyone in town had turned out just to see her leashed up like a dog. Couples walked the streets; buggies went clacking past. No one would look directly at her; they all turned their heads.

She decided to stare at every single person she passed. She wouldn't let them ignore her. She'd force them all to see.

Look at me, she thought, but the man she was eyeing didn't dare.

"Look at me," she whispered, and two white women began to examine something in a store window.

She stared down drovers, and clerks, and a boy selling newspapers from a booth on the corner: the year was 1837. She stared down men with canes, men with mules, men with aprons and spectacles on their faces. The slave catchers tugged her down the thoroughfare, and a man rode past on a big bay horse, and she glanced up to stare at him too.

But as soon as she did, the man drew his reins, stopped in the street and looked right down at her.

He was a young man, blond and bearded, shining blue eyes and buckskin clothes, a pistol and a knife in his belt. Her captors jerked her forward, and she glared up at the rider, daring him to look away.

He wouldn't look away, just sat there watching, and suddenly, she felt ashamed. She didn't want him seeing her after all. The men led her up onto a pineboard walkway and through the open door of a building.

Here, they stripped her naked, wetted her down with lukewarm water from wooden pails, and lathered her up with soap. It was the first time she'd washed in close to a week, and she watched the water trickle down her legs, black as ink. After she'd rinsed and dried herself, the men gave her a clean calico dress and a head scarf with a floral print—the fabric rough as gravel.

When the three of them came back out onto the street, the blond man was sitting in front of the building, as if waiting just for her. The slave catchers led her down the boardwalk and into the city's jail, the blond man following the whole way.

They kept her in a cell awaiting auction. The constable was a fat man with a lisp. He said she was in for it. She'd be bound for cane country, sure enough. Her beauty couldn't keep her from it.

"You know what they do to cane niggers?" he asked.

"I bet you're going to tell me," she said.

"Don't take a tongue," said the constable, and his face had gone bright red.

He studied her several moments.

"Crazy, ain't you?"

"No," she said.

"Yes, you are. I'm about half-crazy for talking to you."

"Then don't," she told him.

She saw it in his eyes, weighing up the cost of doing her violence. This man had power, but he didn't own her body. Anything he did to her he did to the pockets of men who paid his salary.

"Let's see how smart you are tomorrow," he said. "Let's see how your tongue works then."

She leaned against the brick wall of the cell. She was afraid. This fat constable was right. She could not drift any lower than Louisiana. They would hack at her body like they'd hacked off Jubal's ears. They'd cut her and cut her until she had nothing left.

DUNCAN LAMMONS

—TEXAS, 1835–1836—

With our victory over the Mexicans at Concepcion, we were on the high ropes: every man was for marching on Bexar the next day. Or every man but Colonel Bowie who thought we needed cannon for a serious siege. Austin disagreed. As did Ben Smith. An argument ensued, and once officers begin to speechify, their soldiers lose all interest in fighting.

Without battle to occupy us, we took up the bottle. Coming from temperance folk, I'd received no education in spirituous liquors. But the rowdy boys of camp said they would be my Princeton and Harvard. Day after day, as our commanders held their councils of war, the rest of us drank till we were shot in the neck. Soon, we'd forgotten all about our Revolution. Even the trouncing of the Mexicans seemed a distant memory. Fights broke out. Men challenged each other to duels. One cold November night, having tied on the bear, I decided it might be a good idea to go for a swim in the river. Had Noah not come to my rescue, I'd have surely drowned.

I recovered from the incident with nothing more than a powerful headache, but Noah took sick with a fever. He got so bad off, he put in for a furlough and headed out for Bastrop.

Sam was now my chief companion. But wild as he looked in his panther cap and wamus, he wouldn't drink a drop of fool's water and had no desire to learn.

"Did you not ever try it?" I asked him.

"I tried it," he said. "It gave me a rash."

"You got a rash from whiskey?"

"Yessir," he said. "Made me break out in leg irons."

To busy himself while the troops carried on their celebrations, he began to go out looking for game. Worried that hanging around with the revelers might lead to another midnight dip in the San Antonio—and without Noah to fetch me out—I sobered myself up and accompanied Sam on his hunts.

Taken all round, he was a study. It was not just that he had courage: he was more wild than brave, ignorant of fear and courage both, like a perfect beast.

But he was a beast with history, though it came out of him in the oddest ways.

One morning, we were stalking a drove of turkey, trying to catch them in the open, when all at once he plopped down in the grass like a flustered boy and propped his rifle across his knees.

"It's no use doing this on foot," he said.

I didn't know what he meant. I stood staring down at him.

"We ought to be on horses," he explained.

"You can't hunt turkey from horseback."

"You surely can," he said. "You can lasso them from the saddle."

"Lasso?" I said, and he went on to tell me how he and his pap would ride after a flock of turkey, keeping them on the wing and away from timber until the birds tired out and dropped to the ground. Then they just rode up and roped them.

"Where was this," I asked, "that you were lassoing turkeys?"

"Arkansas," he said. "Just south of the little rock."

"That's how they catch birds in Arkansas Territory?"

"It's how Pa did it," he said.

I thought there'd be more to the tale, but for the moment, that was it.

Then, a few nights later, we were sitting around the fire,

listening to the boys belt out their songs when Sam turned to me and said, "What do you have against Arkansas?"

I sat there trying to figure out what he meant, then recalled our conversation from the morning before.

"Don't have nothing against it," I said.

"Where are you from?" he asked.

"Kentucky," I told him. "Butler County."

He stared into the fire, mulling this for a bit. I thought he was about to inquire what had brought me so far from home and that I'd be forced to fabricate a story.

Instead he said, "Where's that?"

Thinking he meant Butler County, I set about trying to situate it in relation to other parts of the state, but he interrupted me.

"No," he said: "Kentucky."

Well, that took me aback. A few of the boys around us left off singing and started to listen in.

Not wanting to embarrass him, I dropped my voice to a whisper: "You've never heard of Kentucky?"

"I heard of it. Where's it at?"

"It's on top of Tennessee."

I watched that information sink in. Or fail to sink.

"You don't know where that is either," I said.

"No," he said.

"Have you seen a map?"

"I don't know," he told me.

I wasn't sure what to say to that, just stared at him until he said, "I can't read."

"Well," I told him, "that's nothing to be ashamed of."

"I'm not," he said, shrugging.

And it was no lie: he wasn't. He didn't even know that there were men who'd be embarrassed to admit their ignorance of the written word, and suddenly, I felt very protective of him— a strange sensation given it was he who'd strengthened my resolve when the bullets were flying and that Mexican cannon was blazing away.

Later that night, I lay there with the men dozing all round. My heart was going very fast and my brain would not be quiet. I began to think about Dan Yarbrough all those years ago, about the time we'd spent on our hunt. My skin began to hum, and I sat up and looked over at Sam sleeping just a few feet away, watching his chest swell and collapse.

I lay back down, shut my eyes up tight, and began to give myself a talking to.

All that is behind you, I thought. *Do not tarnish yourself like you did back home.*

I wanted my past to be wiped clean from the slate of memory. Or like Sam's understanding of geography, hazy and blank.

Or even better, to never have existed at all.

* * *

Toward the middle of November, our army was reinforced by a pack of men calling themselves the New Orleans Greys, and we commenced our siege of San Antonio de Bexar, moving up on the garrison and fighting our way forward, house by house.

But when the new year rolled round, the character of our campaign changed rather drastically. Noah rejoined our ranks, having recovered from the fever that afflicted him, and as the three of us were experienced riders, we were mustered into a ranging company under the command of Captain Tumlinson. Sixty horsemen assembled at Reuben Hornsby's station there on the Colorado. Our mission was to protect colonists from the depredations of Indians, who, finding themselves ignored for several months while we carried our fight to the Mexicans, began to court our attention, confiscating Texian livestock and anything else they happened across.

I've heard it said that old Stephen Austin had called for mounted companies of rangers during the early days of his colony, but Tumlinson's was the first I ever saw, and I was proud to count myself a member. Some of the captain's men were salty and others rather green. A boy of barely seventeen years joined our ranks—Levi English, a skinny lad with a long angular face. Like Sam, he was from Arkansas Territory, and like Sam he was on the prod, enjoying a fight the way most folks enjoy dinner.

We busied ourselves building a headquarters up on Brushy Creek, but we'd no sooner completed our blockhouse than Santa Anna crossed the Rio, making a fast march for Bexar and the famed Alamo garrison. Tumlinson's company was called east to Bastrop to cover the evacuation of Texian families fleeing the tyrant.

It was early March and the trees were leafing out. We'd started one morning with the intention of guarding the old San Antonio road, when a courier named John Lunsford came loping up and caught us. There was hardly a drop of blood in the man's face. He sat his horse and stared at his hands.

"What is it?" Noah asked.

Lunsford cleared his throat. He mumbled something.

"Speak up," said Noah.

"They're dead," Lunsford said.

"Who?" Noah asked.

"All of them," said Lunsford, and I thought he might air his paunch.

But he steadied himself and informed us of the Alamo's fall, of the deaths of Colonel Bowie and Travis. Of the execution of David Crockett. He said General Houston's army was now retreating east.

"East to where?" I asked, but Lunsford didn't know.

We went quiet all round. I thought if the hard hand of war could take great luminaries like Bowie and Crockett, what chance did a no-account like Duncan Lammons have? I glanced over at Noah who, during his absence from Texas, had lived for a time with Bowie and his brother on their claim in Louisiana. His eyes were wet. I looked back at Lunsford.

"What's Houston expect us to do?"

"The General needs ever man he can get," he told me. "It's all hands and the cook."

"He's going to want scouts on this road," I said. "Unless he means for Santa Anna to steal a march on him."

"Well," he told me, "I'll not volunteer you for the duty, but if you want it, pick you one of these men and get to scouting."

"One?" said Noah, startled out of his grief. "Gad, John: why not just shoot him yourself? There's an army of Mexicans marching on us and you want to send a single man?"

"It's a war," Lunsford replied, shrugging.

Noah looked at me. "Don't you do it, Duncan."

"Someone's going to have to," I said.

"He's right," said Lunsford.

"Shut your mouth," Noah told him.

And still no one raised his hand. They were stout lads, all of them, but they had no desire to throw their lives away.

Neither did I, for that matter, but as the oldest member of the group—I'd turn twenty-nine that year—I wouldn't let the task fall on a younger man.

"I'll go," I told them. "Does anyone care to ride with me?"

"Craziness," said Noah.

"It's all right to be scared," Lunsford said.

"Scared, hell!" said Noah. "We're all of us scared. What we're not is suicidal."

It seemed like there'd be further bickering, but Sam spoke up.

"I ain't scared," he said, then turned his blue eyes on me. "I'll ride with you."

Well, he might as well have told me my sins were forgiven. We said our goodbyes, shook hands with Noah, and went trotting out to look for an enemy that'd just taken four hundred of our friends and fellow soldiers and put every man of them to the sword.

* * *

There was no wind and the morning was quiet, just the creak of our saddles and the chirp of blue jays as we passed.

We were supposed to be on the lookout for the Mexican army, but it soon struck us that Indians were a far greater threat, being only a party of two. Our horses were fresh, and I didn't doubt we'd have much trouble outrunning Santa Anna's cavalry if we happened upon them. Comanche ponies were another matter.

By evening, we'd passed Plum Creek and hadn't seen sign of Indians or Mexicans either one. We made camp on a rise that looked out over the road, loosened our saddles and slipped the horses' bits so we could feed them palmfuls of corn. I didn't want to risk a fire up on that ridge and announce our presence for miles around, so we ate a supper of cold biscuits and sowbelly and then sat staring at the stars.

Directly, Sam took off his panther cap, laid it carefully on the blanket beside him, and commenced to rub his eyes.

"You sleepy?" I asked.

"I'm all right."

"Go ahead," I told him. "I'll let you spell me in the morning."

It seemed as though he might protest a bit more, but he laid down and pillowed his head in the crook of an arm. His breath went shallow and his face slackened.

Then he opened an eye and looked at me.

"Quit watching," he said.

That embarrassed me some and I didn't say anything.

"I cain't sleep when it's somebody watching."

"Sorry," I said. I glanced back up at the sky and right away he was snoring.

He slept all that night and all the next morning. I was anxious over the Mexicans said to be making for our position and couldn't have gotten a minute's rest even if I'd had a regiment with me.

It was afternoon when he woke. He sat up with the sun in his eyes and locks of blond hair matted to the side of his face.

"What o'clock is it?" he said.

"Why?" I asked. "You got some place to be?"

We mounted up and rode until we hit Cedar Creek. The colonists having fled, the entire country was empty and quiet, no smoke from the chimneys, no candlelight in the windows of the cabins. It put me in a skeersome sort of mood, and I was thankful for Sam's company, though I might've wished him a bit more talkative. Chickens squawked around the yards, and having eaten nothing but a few hard biscuits, I was savage as a meat-axe.

I glanced over at Sam. "You hungry?"

"Always hungry," he said.

"What's say we get a fire going and help ourselves to some of this poultry?"

"You're not worried about Mexicans seeing us?"

"I don't think they're coming this way. Our reconnoiter was likely for nothing."

He shrugged. "I'll see to a fire then."

"I reckon that puts me on chicken duty."

While Sam foraged for kindling, I gathered a mess of eggs, killed two pullets, then sat and started to pluck them.

Sam carried in an armload of firewood, feathered a few mesquite branches with his knife, stacked all the kindlers just the way he wanted them and then went over and started rummaging round in his traps.

"I've got my flint and striker right here," I told him, but he shook his head.

When he came back, he had a buckskin bag over one shoulder, a long stalk of yucca and a hearth board with six or seven holes bored along its edge.

I wiped a feather from between my fingers and watched him.

He knelt on the ground, anchored the board under his moccasined foot and slid a wood chip under one of the holes. I realized what he was about to try, but I didn't quite believe it.

"What're you doing?" I asked.

He looked up at me. "Building this fire," he said.

"You're welcome to my tinderbox."

"I'm all right."

"Are you?" I said. I'd heard of producing a coal with a spindle and fireboard, but I'd never seen it done. I'd never even known anyone who'd tried it. The Lord gave us flint and steel for a reason.

"Do you want a fire or not?"

"Surely," I told him, "but I was kind of hoping for one tonight."

"I'll have it for you in about a minute if you quit hollering at me."

"Don't let me stop you," I said.

He pulled a nest of dry grass from his bag and set it to one side of the hearth board. Then he took the yucca stalk and fit its tip into one of the blackened holes.

Well, I hadn't been expecting any entertainment with my supper. I put down the chicken and leaned forward to watch.

He began rubbing the yucca stalk between his hands, working his palms down its length and then working them back up again, leaning into the spindle, giving it his weight. The stalk spun back and forth. After a minute, a thin trail of smoke started to rise. His hands went faster and faster. Fine black dust was filling the notch he'd cut in the side of board, piling up on the woodchip underneath it. Then he tossed the spindle, bent down and tilted the board very gently.

He lifted the chip of wood; you could see the little coal smoking atop it, glowing faintly in the dusk. He tipped this into the nest of grass, grabbed the nest in both hands and began to blow into it from underneath, closing the bundle into a smoldering ball.

Thick smoke poured out of it. Then it burst into yellow flame.

Sam glanced at me and smiled.

"I will be damned," I said.

* * *

We skewered the chickens on mesquite branches and set them to roast, so giddy at the prospect of a hot meal we commenced to giggling. I went into one of the deserted cabins and emerged with a cast iron skillet. It was well-seasoned and I thought eggs would be very flavorful in it.

But when I got back to the fire, Sam stared at the skillet like it was a bugbear.

"Where'd you get that?" he said.

"Yonder cabin," I told him.

"Put it back."

I wondered for half a second if he mightn't be jobbing me, but his cheeks had drained of their color and his ears were bright red.

"How are we going to fry up these eggs?" I asked.

"I don't know," he said, "but I ain't cooking in a woman's skillet without her leave."

"I doubt the good matrons of Texas would begrudge a couple patriots using their cookery."

"Maybe so," he said. "But you ain't asked them."

I took the skillet and hung it back on the nail inside the

cabin. When I returned to the fire, Sam looked as if all was right with the world.

"What do you propose we do about these eggs?" I asked. "Put them back too?"

"Pa used to eat them straight from the shell," he told me.

"Well, that was him. And this ain't Arkansas."

"Fair enough," he said.

Roasted chicken and hot coffee was our feast that night, and it proved an excellent combination. We lay beside the fire, eating and slurping from our mugs.

"I say we ride for Bastrop come morning," I told him.

"I say we do too."

The fire crackled and the stars were bright. I thought about the ruckus over the skillet and something occurred to me.

"Were you close with your mammy?" I said.

"Yessir," he said. "She was the best woman I ever knew. And braver than any man by a furlong. I cared for her after she got the milk sick."

"What about your pap?"

"He was stabbed by Simon Crabtree in '24."

"He was stabbed?" I said.

"Yessir. Crabtree was robbing our traps—or Pa thought he was; we could never catch him at it—and this one day we were at the trading post, and Crabtree come up the steps, and Pa told him to cut it out, stealing from us that way, and when he turned, Crabtree put a knife in his kidney and Pa bled on out."

"Lord God," I said. "You saw this?"

"I was standing right there."

"What happened to the rascal?"

"Nothing," he said, and his face seemed to tighten. "Nothing happened to him. He just walked off in the trees and I never heard tell of him again."

"I'm very sorry," I told him, but my condolences seemed awful thin.

I said, "And your mammy got the milk sickness?"

"It burned right through her," he said.

"Was it just you?"

"Me and my brother. He's younger than me. Pa's sister came and got us—she and her husband—and they brung us down to Robertson's Colony."

"Where are they now?"

"I don't know," he said. "I got tired of Uncle Joel whipping on me and I run off."

"What about your brother?"

"Uncle Joel never whipped him."

I lay there. It was such a sad tale, unbearably so to my thinking.

I said, "What did you do between the time you left out and when you rode into Gonzales last fall?"

"Various things," he said. "You always ask so many questions?"

"No," I said. "Not generally. I had better manners fore I came to Texas."

"From Kentucky," he said. "On top of Tennessee."

We lay there a few moments.

Then he said, "It's all right, Mister Lammons. I'm just not used to talking about it, is all."

"Well, anytime you feel like it, I'd be pleased to listen."

"Yessir," he said. "I thank you."

But he never spoke another word on the subject, and I recovered enough of my manners not to bring it up.

* * *

We rode back into Bastrop the next evening. Since Sam and I had been out on reconnaissance, the town had emptied itself of all but twenty-two members of our ranger company. Tumlinson had gone to fetch his family out of harm's way and several dozen of the boys left in search of General Houston's army. The band of remaining riders now called Noah *captain*.

"Well, well," I told him, "this war is turning out rather well for you."

"Oh, yes," he said, "it's been a meteoric rise. A few months ago, I returned from the Redlands with gold in my pocket thinking I might court myself a helpmeet. Now, my money has gone for this swaybacked plug, and instead of a perfumed young maid for company, I've got you unwashed vagrants."

"That is some way for a captain to talk about his troops."

"What did you and Samuel find on your reconnoiter?"

"A skillet," I said. "But I put it back."

"You saw no Mexicans?"

"We saw nothing but grass and chickens," I said. "They seemed very glad we paid them a visit. Even the two we ate."

"But the road is clear?"

"If Santa Anna is marching on us, he's not coming that way."

He paused to think about all of this. Then he said, "What do you think we ought to do?"

"If the Mexicans are truly coming, I'd hate for the fine residents of Bastrop to lose stock to them. Let Santa Anna furnish his own beef."

He agreed. He ordered us to sink the boats on this side of the river, and we started down the Colorado.

A few mornings later, we were trying to herd our countrymen's cattle, when Sam drew rein and sat his horse, squinting off into the distance. That caught my attention, and I rode up beside him and asked what he saw.

"I believe the Mexicans have joined us," he said.

"What?" I said. "Where?"

He gestured with his chin, but all I could see across the river was the green haze of cedar.

Noah had noticed us conversing, and he came up and asked what we were looking at.

"Sam says he sees Mexicans over there."

Noah shaded his eyes with a hand. "I don't see any."

"There are at least six hundred," Sam said.

"Six hundred?" said Noah. He looked as if he thought Sam was only pulling his leg, but I knew Sam well enough to know he didn't tease.

By now, several more men had ridden up beside us. Levi English was among them, and his young eyes saw what mine and Noah's couldn't.

"Jesus!" he said. "Is that the Mexican army?"

"Apparently," said Noah, and he ordered us to forget the cattle and jump up some dust.

We rode all day long. If the Mexicans had seen us, they hadn't sent cavalry in pursuit. But now we knew they were out there, marching us down.

We steered for Cole's settlement at Brenham and about midday started passing deserted cabins. They were the very picture of panic. Doors stood open to whatever livestock decided to wander in. There was bedding and plates spread around the yards, cups and silverware and tools of various kinds. The settlers, in their terror, hadn't known what to leave and what to take. We rode through abandoned hamlets followed by packs of starving dogs, and at one farm, chickens came clucking down the hill and formed up along the side of the road like generals attending a review of their troops.

That evening, we started passing the first of the refugees, old men driving wagons piled with belongings and their eyes full of fear. We told them to pull for Brenham, trying to speak an encouraging word where we could. Sam studied these evacuees out of his calm blue eyes—hard to say what he made of it all.

Just around sundown, we came down a rough wagon trace and saw a sturdy pioneer woman up ahead of us, pulling a handcart that likely held her every last possession. It was a pitiful sight, and one I didn't care to linger on—it seemed very private to me, very personal. I turned to look away and noticed the other men doing the same, Noah and young Levi. But as soon as Sam set eyes on the woman, he snapped his reins, rode up alongside her and dismounted.

"What's he doing?" asked Noah, and I shushed him, trying to figure that out myself.

A peculiar scene began to play out before us as Sam approached this woman like she was a long-lost relation. I can recall the exact look of her stern, determined face. She had hair the color of Sam's big bay horse and her eyes were rather widely positioned. She set the yoke of her handcart on the ground, placed the heels of both hands in the small of her back and stretched. The hem of her homespun dress was in muddy tatters.

What must Sam have looked like to her in his greasy buckskin? And yet, his face was shot through with kindness. It stirred something in me.

"Madam," he said, touching his panther cap with a knuckle as though he'd doff it to her.

She stood there eyeing him with suspicion, reluctant to return his greeting.

"State your business," she finally said.

"Just wanted to ask if you needed help."

"That depends," she said. "Who are you?"

"I'm Samuel," he told her, then nodded over to us. "I'm with Smithwick's Rangers."

"Are you all Houston's army?"

"Not just yet," he told her. "We're trying to find it."

This seemed to reassure her somehow, and she told him that all day men had been riding up to panicked colonists, claiming to be from General Houston himself, informing the refugees that Santa Anna was less than a mile away and it was time to throw down their traps and run. She said this lie had worked rather remarkably: the self-proclaimed soldiers waited until the settlers had cleared the area, then gathered up whatever possessions they'd left behind.

The woman's tale made Sam furious, and his face went a deep shade of red. He said, "General Houston's army is many miles from here; the men you've seen claiming to be his soldiers are liars. If I come across these yacks, I'll wear the ground out with them."

"Oh," said the woman, "I wasn't born in the woods to be scared by an owl. Their story never worked on me."

"Where are your menfolk?" Sam asked.

"My father is old and poorly. I sent him out in the bed of a wagon day before last. I believe those he left with are making for Matagorda Bay."

"What will you do?"

"I reckon I'll pull for Matagorda as well."

Sam nodded. He asked her to bear with him a moment, then walked over to us and addressed Noah in a whisper.

"Captain," he said, "this woman requires assistance."

By that time, other evacuees had come up on our rear, passing us left and right with their broken-down oxen and mules—as sad a sample of humanity as I'd ever seen.

Noah said, "Gad, Samuel, look at them: they all require assistance. We're not teamsters. We have an army to join."

"But, Cap," said Sam, "what will she do?"

I was eager to hear the answer to this myself.

Noah sat there staring at the woman and her handcart. He shook his head.

"She's in good company," he said. "And it seems she's held her own so far."

Sam said, "We must take her with us."

"Absolutely not," Noah said.

"Captain," Sam protested, but Noah raised a hand to cut him off.

"She's not a soldier," he said, "and in case you haven't noticed, she has no mount."

"She can ride mine," said Sam.

"No," said Noah. "Get on your horse."

I watched rage flash like lightning in Sam's eyes, and if I told you it didn't scare me, the Lord might strike me down as a fibber. I felt something very bad was about to happen.

But once again, Sam surprised me. He drew a long breath and marched over to his horse. He didn't mount up, though. Not yet. He pulled several biscuits from a saddlebag, walked over and handed them to the woman.

"Keep on for Matagorda," he said. "Do you have a weapon?"

The woman nodded. She bent down, rummaged in her cart, and drew out a bowie knife the size of a short sword.

I smiled at this, but Sam's brows were knit in concern. There was a chivalrous impulse in him, and that troubled me. Other than his lack of schooling, I'd seen no vulnerability in him whatever.

And there was something else about it, something I wouldn't admit to myself. I watched him walk back to his horse and climb aboard. He looked over at Noah and gave him a nod.

Then our company began riding, moving along the dark under the trees.

* * *

Two days later, we were crossing a pasture when we heard the noise of gunfire rolling out to meet us. We all stopped as though we'd struck a wall, then sat our horses, listening. Presently, there was a loud crack like thunder, then the ground trembled.

"That is cannon," Noah said.

Night and day, we had pursued General Houston without a

great deal of assurance that we'd find him, but now every man of us knew we'd located him. We went down a cow path, live oaks towering on either side, then hit a massive trail that went over the lush green fields. Only an army could have left it, the grass flattened and the earth chewed up, a swath several acres wide. The farther we went along it, the louder the gunfire got—and not just the rumble of cannon now, but the constant crackling of muskets. It lasted half an hour, then cut off into silence.

We'd ridden very hard, and not wanting to blow our horses before taking them into battle, paused to recruit them. Noah sat his mare, gripping the reins so tightly his knuckles were white.

"They'll be dead and gone before we reach them," he said.

I had the selfsame fear: that we'd arrive on the battlefield only to find Sam Houston butchered and his men put to the sword.

"Rider coming," said Sam. "Look yonder."

A white man was approaching on a painted pony, seeming in no great hurry to reach us. He came trotting up, hailed us and asked who was in command.

"I am," Noah said.

"Are you Bob Haskins?" the rider asked.

"I'm Captain Smithwick."

The rider nodded his approval. He said: "The general had intelligence you were en route. He's sent me to notify the ranging companies of our victory: we've annihilated the Mexican army."

We just sat there staring.

"Annihilated?" Noah said.

"What happened?" I asked.

The rider said, "What happened is they'd nearly pushed us into yon river, but then they lay down behind their breastworks and took a nap. General Houston ordered a charge and we rode right over them."

Young Levi English said, "Mexicans took a nap?"

"They did," said the rider. "*Siesta*, it's called. Best taken round noontime, but I'd imagine it's even better when you ain't got an angry bunch of Texians moving on you. We charged up and beat out their brains with our rifles."

"Son of a bitch!" said Noah, one of the rare occasions I have heard him swear. Knowing Houston personally, he was embarrassed not to've been able to get our company into the fight.

I understood the sentiment, though I'd already experienced a mess of fighting. I figured that once you'd seen a body blown apart by rifle balls and cannon, you'd seen them all.

So, I was unprepared for the scene the rider led us to, escorting us over the beveled pastures, through the piney woods to the field where we found the Texians in celebration, drinking and carrying on. The dead Mexicans had been stacked like fence rails; there were so many of them. Buzzards circled the sky, but they'd only drift down to light on the poor bodies of horses. They showed no interest in the Mexican soldiers at all.

Cattle had no such scruples, a great many of which had wandered up now that the shooting had stopped and begun feasting on the corpses. If I ever had regard for those animals, I lost it that day. The sight of them chewing on folks put beef off my menu for years to come.

* * *

General Houston's horse had been shot out from under him, and he'd shattered his ankle in the fall. He was placed in a wagon and carried off to Matagorda. Command of the army now devolved upon General Rusk, who proceeded to move his force to Victoria.

We rangers were tasked with guarding the baggage left

behind, an added insult for those of us who'd missed out on the closing battle for Texian Independence. And when we were finally allowed to join the others outside Victoria, General Rusk put out a call for blacksmiths to head into town and serve as an armorer's corps, repairing rifles and refitting wagons. Noah and I were daft enough to admit our expertise in these matters. I shook hands with Sam and told him I'd see him in a week or two.

There in Victoria, we spent our days working on guns and bushing cannon. It was like old times in Bell's Landing, and I felt a great optimism for what my life might become.

For ten days, Noah and I labored there in the blacksmith's shop, and every night I rehearsed what I'd say to Sam when next I saw him. The battle of Concepcion and the siege of Bexar had given me a taste of combat, and while some men found it repugnant, my palate had awoken to strange new flavors. When it was boiled down, warfare was a kind of hunting, but as the risks were much higher, so were the rewards. At Bexar, my marksmanship had been in high demand and throughout the whole of the campaign I'd felt necessary in a way I never had before. The men you fought beside needed you, depended on you; together, you were like a single creature. The loneliness that used to visit me so often had vanished.

Now, our ranging company would be asked to protect settlers as they returned to their homes and I imagined that Sam and I would ride together for years to come. A great closeness developed in such circumstances and I thought that this was what I'd been searching for since I was very young.

The higher hurdle was that I didn't know Sam's thinking on these matters, and having time to reflect, I thought about his exchange with the pioneer woman; I thought about the chivalry he'd shown insisting I restore that skillet to its place—in all this I detected a fierce need for women and their company. I hoped I was misreading the signs, but desire can so scramble up your thinking, you cannot figure north from south nor up from down.

Then I thought, you are getting ahead of yourself, Mister Lammons. There will be time.

It was a fine spring morning when Noah and I rode back to the encampment of rawhide shelters. We went up the mud trail and presented ourselves to General Rusk.

He told us we were to be placed in a company that would ride against the Comanche, who were said to be harassing the settlers as they returned to their homes. The detail suited us better than slaving away at the anvil, and we went to collect Sam.

But he was nowhere to be found. We stalked from campfire to campfire, asking after him. All knew his name and exploits—his panther cap was memorable to every man—but no one had any idea where he'd gotten to. Here and there, men passed a bottle, far too casual about Sam's disappearance for my taste, but I'd come near getting myself in a panic. Seeing my growing distemper, Noah said he'd go ask General Rusk. I stood there, trying to get a handle on myself.

Half an hour later, Noah came walking back down the little lane. He had a curious expression on his face and my heart dropped into my stomach.

"What is it?" I asked. "Did something happen?"

"They sent him out as a courier."

"Courier?" I said. "He can't even read."

"So much the better. They won't need to worry about their correspondence being pilfered."

"Where did they send him? Columbia?"

"Matagorda," he said. "To General Houston."

This calmed me some.

I said, "So, he's in Matagorda?"

"He was in Matagorda. Now he's on his way to Natchitoches."

"That's 300 miles!" I said.

Noah shrugged. "Closer to 350."

It felt as if my legs had the bones yanked out of them. My mouth didn't work. I listened to Noah explain what General Rusk had told him: how our Revolution had been financed by bankers and merchants in Louisiana, how, now that victory had been won, Houston would have to negotiate the debt we'd incurred. Stout-hearted souls had been selected from our ranks to make their way back and forth from . . .

I couldn't listen any longer. There were a thousand things that could befall a man between here and Louisiana; I knew because of the thousand things that had befallen Noah and myself.

I walked over to a cook fire where men were boiling coffee. Two of them passed a bottle back and forth.

"What will you take for that?" I asked.

I didn't know their names, or they mine, but we recognized each other from the campaign. One of the men offered the bottle right up.

"Don't need to give us nothing," he said. "You're welcome to a sip."

"No," I said. "All of it."

An hour later, I sat against a live oak, and the spring morning was a bright green blur. I wondered what beast it was that gave you something one day and took it from you the next. I don't know as I'd been one to imbibe the liquor of self-pity, but at that moment, not knowing when I'd see Sam again or ever, I drank fairly deep.

CECELIA

—LOUISIANA, 1837—

S he stood on a tree stump, surrounded by staring faces, the white faces of men. Women did not attend slave sales unless they were being sold themselves, and she was the only negress at auction this day. The auctioneer stood in the grass beside her, saying: "Bidding starts at five hundred, boys. Who'll give me five, got five, now five and a quarter, five and a quarter, now half, half, got half—it's a fancy gal, this one—now five-seventy-five, seventy-five. Yessir, now six, six, who'll give me six . . ."

It was hard to look at men who wanted to buy you. They were a gaudy bunch, canes and silk cravats—planters, most of them, the county's upper crust. She stared down into the green carpet of grass, searching for a word. She'd been defiant. That was the word. And for her defiance, they'd flushed her half the length of the nation. She thought of the past ten years, a decade of falling, and a wave of sadness swelled up in her so high she thought she'd drown.

When she glanced back up, she saw a man standing toward the rear of the crowd, apart from all the rest. It was the rider she'd encountered several days before, the one who'd followed her all the way to her cell. He was closer now, and she was able to study him. He had sandy blond hair, bright blue eyes, and you could tell he was some kind of soldier, though he wasn't dressed like it. He wore a buckskin jacket, leather leggings, and he was staring at Cecelia like she was familiar to him. She stared back as if he might be familiar too. He was a young man, but even so, he seemed unimpressed by all these planters and their finery. His expression said he held them in contempt, and she'd never seen men such as these looked down on, not even by other whites. He'd so captured her attention, she didn't hear the auctioneer say, "Sold," and when the auctioneer's aide stepped over and took her hand, she started and jerked away.

She hadn't seen the man who'd purchased her. The aide led her back to a tent where she'd wait for her new owner. Money would change hands; deeds would be signed. Cecelia knew this happened, but she'd never witnessed it.

She sat on the floor of the tent cross-legged, singing softly to herself. She was anxious to see what sort of man had acquired her, but she tried to keep her voice clear and calm.

And who're you keeping calm for? You don't have a soul to sway, one way or the other.

I have myself, she thought.

Do you? the voice inside her asked. Are you sure?

Directly, the auctioneer's aide came striding toward the tent. There was a tall man on his right, dressed like the other planters—silk hat and cane—but on the aide's left was the blond man in his rough clothes, a long knife in a leather scabbard, a pistol tucked in his belt. He walked alongside the aide, but he was addressing the tall planter, making some appeal. The planter just shook his head. He seemed to think the blond man would go away, but Cecelia could see he wasn't going anywhere. The three of them stepped up to the tent's entrance.

"If you wished to acquire her," said the tall man, studying Cecelia, "you ought to have offered a bid."

"I'm offering it," the blond man said.

"Mr. Fisk," said the aide, "we have other negroes for sale. You may find one that suits you even better."

The man named Fisk ignored this. He looked past the aide at Cecelia's new owner.

"A thousand," he said. "That's a hunnerd and fifty profit, and you don't have to lift a finger."

He spat in his palm and extended it, but Cecelia's new owner didn't even turn his head. His eyes cut sideways to study Fisk's hand, and Cecelia knew he wouldn't touch it.

Which disappointed her for some reason. She'd already taken a dislike to this planter. He had a lazy eye and there was something cold in his face.

"Sir," he said, "I've done all the nigger-trading I care to this day. Mr. Camden is correct: there are others being sold as we stand here, chattering. And for considerably less than you offer me."

Fisk watched the man a moment. His eyes were bright, and his face was sunburned, as if rarely out of the weather.

"Eleven hunnerd," he said.

"I'm sorry," said Cecelia's new owner. "No."

"You won't taken eleven hunnerd dollars?"

"I will not."

"Twelve hunnerd," Fisk said.

"Sir," said Cecelia's owner, "I don't believe you are in earnest."

Fisk stood there with his hand still out. He lowered it and hooked the thumb inside his belt.

"Do what?" he said.

"I suspect you are not entirely serious," said the tall man. "In your offer of twelve."

Fisk stared at the planter, his brow furrowed.

"You're saying I'm a liar," he said.

"I did *not* say that, Mr. Fisk. Don't presume to take offense where none is given."

"Pre-sume," said Fisk, trying out the word. He looked at Cecelia, and she thought there was something about his face. He didn't seem like the type she'd encountered at slave sales.

He glanced back at Cecelia's new owner.

"You're not interested in my money, you're saying."

"That's exactly what I'm saying," the planter told him.

Fisk's eyes narrowed.

Then turning, he walked away.

* * *

She sat beside the lazy-eyed planter on the front seat of his buggy, trotting along a narrow lane. Every mile they put behind them made her more nervous. She'd never had a man force himself on her, though she certainly knew it happened. And this man would try her at his first opportunity.

They made their way down the deserted road, winding through the bearded oaks, the trees hemming them in. They passed down a flat stretch where she could see bare cotton fields through the trees, then the road turned and went into a stand of cedars.

They'd hardly gone fifty feet when they rounded a bend and there sat Fisk on his beautiful bay horse. He had a chestnut mare just behind him, and he'd positioned these animals in the very center of the road.

And what was it he wore on his head? she wondered. The skin of some cat?

The planter began slowing the buggy and brought it to a stop. She thought that Fisk looked older than he actually was. Something about his manner. He sat his horse very straight. His neck was thick with muscle and his hands were large.

"Afternoon," he said.

The planter climbed down from the buggy and Fisk dismounted his horse as well. The two of them squared up in the road, Cecelia on the buggy-seat, watching.

The planter said, "You are obstructing the thoroughfare."

Fisk said, "You're sure you won't sell to me?"

"I'm quite certain."

"You're definite on that?"

"Remove yourself," the planter said.

Fisk's blond beard was scruffy. He lifted his hand to stroke it.

"Because you think I ain't serious," he said. "You think that I pre-*sume*."

Cecelia felt a shift in the air. It went strange, and there was an unmistakable scent of savagery on the breeze, just like there'd been in those moments before they'd hacked off Jubal's ears. She leaned forward on the seat, got her feet planted, and hunched there, waiting.

"What's your name?" Fisk asked.

"Childers," the man said.

Fisk nodded. He stroked his beard with his forefinger and thumb. He said: "Might think better of it when you get home."

"Better of what?" said Childers.

"Selling to me."

"I don't believe I will," Childers told him.

"Might," said Fisk. "We could ride back and talk about it."

"Ride where?" Childers said.

"Your house," said Fisk. "A man thinks different in his house. Reflects on all the mistakes he's made."

"Sir," said Childers, but Fisk was still speaking.

"You a married man?"

"I am," Childers said.

"We'll ask your wife her opinion," said Fisk. "I don't doubt but what Mrs. Childers is a educated woman. How you reckon she'll feel about you turning down twelve hunnerd dollars? Buy a mess of waistcoats, I'd think."

Childers's mouth opened. He stared at Fisk—the pistol, the knife in its leather scabbard.

"Do you mean to threaten me?" he said.

Fisk said nothing. He stopped stroking his beard and began to scratch the back of his neck.

"Because," continued Childers, growing more confident, "I can promise you: I'll not be browbeaten by some bounder who's—"

Fisk slapped Childers very hard across the mouth. It happened so quickly, Cecelia barely saw. Fisk's hand had been behind his head, scratching, and then it'd leapt out and struck Childers's astonished face.

Fast, thought Cecelia. He is very fast.

Childers staggered backward several steps. His cheek was dark red. Cecelia could tell he'd never been touched in anger. He went down onto a knee, working his jaw back and forth. He kept blinking his eyes open, shaking his head.

Fisk's expression hadn't changed at all, though a vein bulged out on his bull's neck like a rope.

He said: "Anyone ever tell you you're hard to do business with?"

Childers made a low, moaning sound.

"Well, you are," said Fisk. "And it's nobody trying to browbeat you. I meant to make you some money."

Childers fingered his jaw. He seemed to be testing it for something. When he looked back up at Fisk, he extended his hand.

"Twelve hundred?" he said.

Fisk shook his head. "That offer's been rescinded."

"*Rescinded*," Childers said.

"Means it's been withdrawn."

"What offer do you make?" Childers asked.

"I'd maybe give you five."

"Five hundred?"

"Five dollars," said Fisk, and glancing up at Cecelia, he winked.

"I paid eight-fifty!" Childers told him. "Not two hours ago, you offered me twelve!"

"And you decided it'd be more profitable to be a horse's ass."

"Suppose I involve the constable?" Childers said, though there wasn't any force behind it, and Cecelia knew wherever this blond man was headed, she was going with him.

Fisk turned and looked over one shoulder, and then he turned and looked over the other.

"I don't see one," he said. "Tell you what: you go get him, we'll stay here and wait. Just don't take too long. I been known to get impatient."

* * *

They took a winding way across the countryside, Cecelia on the chestnut mare named Honey, Samuel on his big bay horse.

That was the man's name: *Samuel*. That's what he said to call him.

Cecelia had never addressed a white man familiar. You were expected to master and marse your way around, like a roach scurrying for cover. But this man seemed different, like he didn't know the rules, or didn't care about rules, or was making new rules of his own. He was an exception, and exceptions ended badly for her. She sat the horse behind Samuel, peeking up at him, then looking down at her hands. She didn't know what to do with them, never been on a horse in her life. She held onto the saddle horn, but that didn't seem right: it wasn't shaped for hands. Samuel had her horse's lead line tethered to his own tack, and all she had to worry about was staying in the saddle. She liked it, riding and watching the country pass. A good little mare, was Honey. Cecelia reached down to pet her.

They made camp in the woods beside the road. Samuel built a fire, boiled up a bag of beans, and set a kettle on the coals.

She sat there watching. She was wondering when the pain would come. Would he hit her or would he kick her? Would she wake to find him on top of her, pressing down?

"You take coffee?" Samuel said.

"Tea," she said. She'd never had coffee. She'd never been offered it. What was it to him if she had coffee? Her hands were shaking and she clasped them together to try and steady herself. She'd done fine while they were moving, but now there was nothing between the two of them but the crackling fire.

Samuel said: "I've only got the one cup, but you're welcome to swap with me, you want some of this."

She stared into the fire. She watched the spout of the kettle steam.

Samuel removed it from the coals, took off the lid and poured in a handful of coffee grounds, then set it to one side. He rose, walked over to his horse, took a skillet from his saddle bag, came back over, squatted and began cutting slices from a slab of salt pork.

"Take a while on the beans," he said, slicing with his knife. "I've got a loaf of bread. Half a loaf, anyway."

She hadn't noticed just how young he was. In Natchitoches, in the presence of Childers, or sitting up on his horse, Samuel had seemed a good deal older. Just the way he carried himself, as if he hadn't come across anything he couldn't walk over like a bridge.

He looked at her with his dark blue eyes. He really was much younger than she'd thought. It gave her an edge, but she wasn't sure exactly how. She was taking in everything about him, searching for the weakness. There was always weakness. Finding it was like finding a lever: you could move something heavier than yourself.

Dusk was coming on. She thought she saw bats flitting through the air, but they might have been birds. She was very alert. She heard everything there was to hear, smelled every scent on the breeze.

Samuel left the beans to simmer, rose and walked back over to his horse. He drew another pistol out of a saddle bag. So, he has two guns, she thought, but then he pulled out a third. He walked back over and sat by the fire, placing a pistol on either side of him, removing the pistol from his belt on his right hip, and tucking it in his belt on the other side, butt forward.

Yes, she thought. One gun isn't enough for him: he wants to shoot you with three.

She sat there, studying him. She thought she might be able to kick coals into his face before he pointed one of the pistols at her, but she pictured him slapping Childers.

You'll need to distract him, she thought.

She said: "Are we in any trouble?"

Samuel had been paying attention to the beans. Maybe he was planning to eat before he shot her.

"Trouble with who?" Samuel said.

"Anybody," she said, nodding at his guns.

"Not as far as I know," he said.

She stared at him. The pistols had her spooked, but she realized they had nothing to do with her. He'd gone to the trouble of stealing her; he wouldn't up and shoot her full of holes. He didn't have that air about him, but his air was very strange. There was nothing in her experience to prepare her for it.

"What are you scared of?" she asked.

Samuel had his long knife in hand. His pistols shone in the firelight. He cocked his head and looked at her.

"Scared?" he said.

Yes, she wondered. What would that be like? Not to be scared. Then she thought she might use this to her advantage. Because, perhaps he ought to be scared and didn't know it.

They sat listening to the fire. She couldn't stop looking at the guns, wondering what they felt like. She'd never been this curious about anything in all her life.

"Can I hold it?" she said, and then thought, No. You shouldn't have said that.

Samuel was stirring the beans with the blade of his knife. He glanced at her, then nodded to one of the pistols there on the blanket beside him. Was that what she wanted to hold?

"Yes," she said, and then thought, He is different. He is a different kind of man. That was good, but it also made her nervous. She didn't know how he was different. The guns weren't allowing her to think.

Samuel switched his knife to his left hand, wiped his fingers on the underside of his thigh, took up the pistol and handed it across.

She reached out and took hold of it. The gun was heavy, much heavier than she'd have thought. Smooth to the touch, the steel a little cool. She could feel the danger in it, and she liked the possibilities of all that it could do.

She sat there, feeling its weight. She could sense his eyes on her. She handed the pistol back across, and Samuel took it and laid it on the blanket.

She was instantly ravenous. Maybe it was the smell of the beans and frying pork, or maybe it was holding the gun. She looked at Samuel.

"How'd you know I wouldn't shoot you?" she said.

"You ain't shot anybody," said Samuel, grinning.

"How do you know?"

Now Samuel laughed, and she felt cross with him. Had she said something funny? Did he think she was that ignorant, couldn't figure out how to work a gun?

She must have made a face, because he stifled his laughter, and started pinching at his nose.

"I wouldn't hand a gun to somebody who'd shoot me with it," he said.

"You've been around a lot of shooting?"

Samuel just shrugged, as if it was no great matter, and she wasn't irritated with him anymore because maybe he would teach her.

She said, "You've killed people, haven't you?"

"Mexicans," he said.

"Why did you kill Mexicans?"

"They went to oppressing us."

She watched him a moment. She asked how the Mexicans had done that.

"Done what?"

"Oppress you," she said.

"I don't know. It's what the men told me."

"What men?"

"The ones who said the Mexicans were oppressing us."

She didn't say anything. Everything about this man was foreign to her. But there was something familiar too. She couldn't put her finger on it.

They sat there eating quietly; the food was very good. She could feel herself liking this man, and it had been a long time since she'd liked anyone but Okah. It had been years. She'd taken those things out of herself and placed them in a jar. Her mind was shelves and shelves of all the things she was storing. This was the love she'd bottled up after they'd sold away her mother, and this was that close feeling she'd bottled up after Jubal lost his ears. This was her hope of reaching Philadelphia; this was her hope of being free, not surrounded by people who were slower: being around them was like walking through molasses. All the slow people of the world; let's cover Cecelia with moss.

Samuel wasn't smart like her, or not smart in the same way. But his mind was quick and agile. There was no fear in him at all.

And he sat right there and let you hold his gun.

If he hadn't been so young, perhaps he'd have known there were plenty of things in this world to be scared of.

He might've even realized she was one of them.

Duncan Lammons

—Texas, 1836–1839—

1836 was a bad Indian year, the worst then on record. Our ranging company spent all winter riding against the various bands niggling the Republic.

But come springtime, Noah was for trying a different approach. Under flag of truce, he ingratiated himself to a Comanche chieftain by the name of Muguara, and the chief invited Noah to live in their camp for a spell.

"Don't tell me you're considering it," I said.

"I'm absolutely considering it."

"What the devil for?"

"Because I'm tired of roosting in this saddle. I've got blisters on my backside and my feet feel like rocks."

"You're blind as a snubbing post," I said. "You traipse out there with those howlers, you'll lose yourself a mess of hair."

He thought about that for several minutes.

Then he said, "No, Duncan, I think you're wrong. We need to establish commerce with these people, and I believe this might could be a start."

"People?" I said. "Is that what we're calling them?"

"Well," he said, "what name would you give?"

"I've been too inconvenienced to give much thought to the matter, Noah. Most of the Indians I've encountered have tried to pop an arrow through me."

Noah shook his head. "There are an awful lot of Indians in these parts to have to go to war with all of them. Would you not rather have some as friends?"

Levi English, who was lying on his bedroll several feet away, had been listening to our conversation and now couldn't help but enter it.

"*Friends*?" he said. "Begging your pardon, Cap, but you're ignorant as a mule-eared rabbit."

I feared Noah might sharpen the young ranger's hoe for such saucy words, but apparently Captain Smithwick was in a diplomatic mood.

"Why haven't I got sense, Levi? Tell me something."

"You cannot be friends with horse Indians. My pap was killed by the Pawnee in Arkansas. They killed him and left him lay."

"I am sorry about that," Noah said. "But these tribes are different one from another. I don't think we can lay your paw's murder on the Comanche."

Levi mumbled something, rolled over and showed us his back. Noah and I sat there with the fire crackling. I wished that Sam was with us; he'd have been able to convince Noah of his error.

I cleared my throat.

"He has a point," I said. "At the very least, you might consider it."

Noah said, "It cannot be that all of these *people*"—and here he gave the word special stress—"mean to do us violence. As I see it, a man is a man. If we can learn what it is they want, there is no reason why we can't have relations."

I supposed he was right, but still didn't like this talk about men-being-men as I suspected I'd be forced to kill a mess of them before it was all said and done. I tried to think about Levi's murdered pap, but now Noah's newfound Quakerism was rattling around in my head like a handful of gravel.

"It is a fine notion," I told him. "Are you willing to go to hell for it? What if you're wrong?"

"Then I guess you will have to do without me," he said. "But I am determined to try."

We continued to argue most the night, but I was barking at a knot. When he left out at dawn, I told myself I'd never see him again.

But he returned that summer just as plump as you please. He wore buckskin breeches, a necklace of glass beads, and his hair was down on his shoulders.

"Well," I said, "I knew you for a heathen when I first clapped eyes on you. Here is the proof."

All that day, he regaled us with stories of buffalo hunts and life in a Comanche camp. In three months' time, he'd picked up a fair amount of their lingo, and had acquired the name *Juaqua*. Old Muguara promised him that his band would not trouble us so long as their hunting grounds were respected.

"You impress me," I said. "Now, if every tribe would have you as their houseguest, we might get somewhere in about a hundred years."

"We might," Noah said.

* * *

There was still no word from Sam. I asked after him everywhere we went, but folks didn't know what I was talking about.

"He wears a panther skin," I told one wall-eyed patriarch outside Gonzales. "He's made a cap of it."

The man nodded at me.

"Good for him," he said.

That spring, our second term of enlistment was drawing to an end. Noah asked what I planned to do.

"What do you mean?" I said. "I'm signing on again. How about yourself?"

He said that he was done with rangering, and it was no idle threat. When his term of service was finished, he set out to open a shop in Bastrop. I dithered about a few days, then put my name on the roster. They gave me a captaincy and a good company formed under me: Calvin Barker. Jimmie Curtice. The Mexican Joel Ramírez, who wanted above all things to be counted a true Texan—and was so in my book.

Levi English was still with us; I'd watched him become a full-grown man. There was Oliver Buckman and Hugh Childers. Ganey Crosby who used the name "Choctaw Tom." John Berry. John Williams. Isaac Casner.

New recruits straggled in every year: vagabond boys with a hankering for blood or men who'd exhausted the other meager prospects our Republic had to offer and concluded it was either ride or starve. If these troopers had one thing in common besides their gift for violence, it was the dire circumstances of their youths. I began keeping a tally of how many rangers told me they'd seen their fathers burn up with fever or get stretched by a hangman's noose. They recounted tales of terrible accidents: falls from horseback, wagons swept away by swollen rivers, attacks by mountain lions or panthers—Choctaw Tom told me his pap had been savaged by a billy goat. The animal pushed the poor farmer into a corner of his barn and butted him so fiercely his organs ruptured.

My men had been raised by uncles or stepfathers, brutes who lashed them for imagined offenses or because it gave them pleasure. Noah and myself were the only rangers I ever knew who could not recite you some juvenile misfortune. I often thought about that. Does every talent have its seed in calamity?

But be assured, it made no odds how terrible their fortunes had been up to the time of their enlistment: you'd have been hard pressed to find a more spirited bunch. We sang songs round the fire or played elaborate jokes on each other. It was a brotherhood for all of us, a second childhood for many. As captain, I became their father.

I can recall when Felix McClusky mustered in—he was an Irishman who'd come over from the old country and spent exactly one week in Boston before deciding to drift west. How he ended up in Texas I'll never know. He had a shock of bright red hair and his brogue was so thick he'd have to repeat himself to be understood.

Some talked very low of the Irish in those days, but I was inclined to have special sympathy for them—my own dear mother was a Gillespie by birth; her father had come to Kentucky from the Emerald Isle in much the same way our new recruit had travelled to Texas.

But McClusky—he stretched the seams of sympathy to bursting.

He stood five foot five and a more aggressive man I've never met. He imagined slights everywhere, mostly against the Irish, always against him. He'd fight a man at the drop of a hat and he'd drop it himself. He fought big Isaac Casner this one time and, I swear to you, it was like watching a mouse whip a wildcat. McClusky could hardly reach high enough to punch poor Ike in the face; he'd jump up in the air to strike him, land and then leap up to hit him again. After he'd walloped Ike five or six times, Ike turned to me and said, "Captain, will you get this snorter off me? This is starting to hurt."

The boys all liked McClusky, but they decided he needed some gentling. This one day we were headed down into a field of grama when we spied a polecat ambling along. We reined up, meaning to keep our distance.

Well, being untutored in the ways of wilderness creatures, McClusky didn't know a skunk from a barn door.

"What a lovely little cat," he said.

A scheme occurred to Levi English; I saw the look pass over his face.

"Oh yes," he said, "and they are easily tamed."

The wild Irishman needed no more encouragement. He slid right off his saddle and made a run for the startled critter, thinking to make a pet of it, no doubt. He wasn't six feet away when the skunk lifted its tail and doused him in scent. It looked like McClusky had struck a wall. He fell backwards and began scrambling and screaming for help.

Of course, we were near falling off our horses with laughter.

"What's wrong?" Levi called. "Can you not catch it?"

But the joke turned on us rather quickly when we realized we couldn't get the scent off McClusky or abandon him either one, and after the second night of trying to sleep with him in camp, I walked over to Levi and booted him in the leg.

"Why in tarnation did you set him on that thing?" I asked. "I can barely stand to eat."

Levi looked up at me out of his watering eyes. The odor was so pungent it was like something had crawled inside your head.

"Captain," he said, "I wish I hadn't done it."

"I wish you hadn't either. The amusement we got was hardly worth the penalty we're paying."

Young Levi was always one to look on the bright sight.

"Maybe it'll keep the Indians off us a few days," he said.

Which proved to be the case: we encountered no Indian for nearly a month. By the time McClusky aired out, he was no less vicious, but his lack of aroma improved his personality for us considerably.

CECELIA

—TEXAS, 1837—

They crossed the Sabine at Gaines Ferry and went riding along the King's Highway into the Republic of Texas. The country was flat as a coffin lid and the horizon leveled out into a light blue haze. There was so much sky Cecelia wanted to cower. At night, she'd lie on her blanket, staring up and gripping the ground on either side of her, thinking she might slide off into the stars.

But after a week, her body seemed to settle. I have stopped falling, she thought. I've stopped that for now. She reached and smoothed her hand along Honey's neck. Samuel had taught her to use the reins, to shift her weight back or forward. To push up to a lope. Riding was new to her, but she suspected she might be good at it.

"Don't you think?" she asked Honey. "Don't I ride you good?"

They made camp that evening in a ring of live oaks. Samuel started a fire by spinning a stick between his hands—rubbing it faster and faster until smoke rose from his kindling—and she sat there studying him as he prepared their supper, watching his face above the flames. She couldn't decide what on earth he was after. He didn't seem to want a servant. Didn't want to beat or bed her.

She cleared her throat and he glanced over at her.

"Can I ask you something?" she said.

He nodded for her to go ahead.

"What made you take me from that man?"

"Childers?" he said.

"Yes."

He sat a few moments. Then he said, "I never seen a woman treated that way—led down the road on a rope."

"You'd never seen slaves before?"

"Not till I came to Texas, I hadn't. It wasn't any slaves where I was raised."

"And where is that?"

"Arkansas Territory. Or, that's what they used to call it. Suppose it belongs to the Cherokee now."

"And that's why you had a mind to steal me: you'd never seen women on a rope?"

"I reckon so," he said. "It riled me, is all."

"Is that why you wouldn't pay him?"

"Pay who?"

"Childers," she said.

He gave an exasperated laugh. "Twelve hundred dollars! I ain't got that kind of money!"

She wondered why he'd offered it, then—*was he only feeling the planter out*—but she didn't ask. Another question had occurred to her instead. She pulled her legs to her chest, wrapped her arms around them and rested her chin atop her knees.

"What do you mean to do with me?" she said.

Samuel's brow crinkled. "*Do* with you?"

She nodded.

"Don't mean to do nothing."

"You don't consider yourself my owner?"

He snorted. "I ain't owned anybody yet."

"You're saying that I'm free?"

He shrugged as if it was no great matter. "Free as any of us."

Yes, she thought. And yet you took a deed off Childers. Slipped it in your saddle bag.

"So," she said, "I can just ride off whenever I have a mind?"

"Well," he told her, "not *ride*, I don't reckon—that pony don't belong to me. I'm headed to see the man it does belong to, but far as being free, you're welcome to go wherever you like whenever you like it. I might try and convince you to pick a better spot than here, though."

He was right about that; she had no idea where she was.

But there was something in all this more pressing than their whereabouts and now was her chance to confirm it.

She said, "You're being straight with me? I can really go wherever?"

"I ain't going to stop you," he said.

That next morning, they traveled through a valley, hills on both sides, a low mist hanging in the air. It parted to let them pass, then closed swirling up behind.

The sun was slanting in, coloring the mist a bright copper. She reached out to touch it and felt something open inside her chest. For years, there were no possibilities. For years, everything was locked down tight. Now, there were all sorts of prospects, things she never considered. She certainly never considered crossing paths with a man like this.

Samuel slowed his horse and stopped. He sat there, staring at the hillside to the north.

She followed his gaze. High on the hill, a man sat astride a magnificent paint.

That is an Indian, she thought.

She didn't know how she knew that, but her heart was pattering. The man was bare-chested and slender with long blue-black hair; he wore a feather in it, and there were glass beads around his neck. No saddle on his horse. No weapons she could see.

"What's he doing?" she whispered.

"Watching us," Samuel said.

She sat there. Samuel's hands were on his pommel, though

he wasn't relaxed. Not tensed, either. He's just alert, she thought: very alert. She wanted to say something, but her mouth was too dry. Samuel's blue eyes were bright. He lifted his head slightly and his nostrils flared. Did he smell something? He seemed older to her again, like he'd seemed at the auction: he was younger when it was just the two of them, but older in the presence of other men.

She looked back at the man on the ridge. He was an Indian, all right. She didn't know anything about Indians, though she'd heard about Indian attacks all her life. She'd heard this from white people, who were the only ones she'd ever seen attack anything. She thought there were all these gears grinding, like a gristmill at work, gears you couldn't see, but they linked her to Samuel, linked both of them to the Indian on the hillside. They were all caught up, grinding together.

The man followed them the rest of the day. They'd lose sight of him for an hour as the road wound down into the rocks, and then the trail would crest out, and there he'd be on another hill: silent, motionless. She'd not seen him move so much as a finger. The breeze stirred his hair, but that was all the motion there was.

"He's making me nervous," she told Samuel.

"They're good at it," Samuel said.

When they stopped at dusk, she couldn't see the Indian anymore. They made a fireless camp in a sandstone basin, and Samuel took all his pistols out of their bags and lined them up on the blanket beside him, sitting up against a rock. She was very tired, very frightened. She lay down on her blanket and closed her eyes.

Then she opened them.

"I can't sleep knowing he's out there," she said.

"Try to," Samuel said.

She shut her eyes again, and then thought about offering to wake and watch with him or let him sleep while she watched;

they could take turns. She wondered if he'd trust her to do that, and she was thinking probably not. Her mind began to wander, and she remembered all the books in Mistress Anne's library, how she'd worked her way through the shelves, volume by volume. She was imagining all the words that had passed before her eyes, all the letters, and then the print began to blur, and she drifted off to sleep.

* * *

She woke with a start. It was dark, but the eastern sky was paling. Samuel was sitting exactly as he'd been when she'd closed her eyes, and she felt embarrassed that she'd been able to fall asleep. It was like she'd admitted to something shameful.

Samuel was quiet and sullen all day. Ever since they'd been travelling, he'd started his morning with coffee, but this morning there'd been no fire to make coffee on. She didn't even know if it was the coffee he was sulled up about.

Perhaps he was just tired. He'd sat up all night, watching for Indians who hadn't appeared.

Then she realized she was preoccupied with his moods, whether or not he was angry or tired—Lord knew he wasn't preoccupied over hers. If he'd just deal with her fairly, she might be able to help him, but he didn't want to deal fairly. He was another man who thought he held all the cards, thought she was incapable of holding anything at all. He'd deny her talents just like all the others, and she was furious with him. She was furious with herself for ever thinking he was different.

She glanced at him.

"You're not a bit different," she said.

Samuel looked at her.

"What's that?" he said, and she said, "Never mind."

Later that afternoon, they were winding through a thick

forest of juniper when she heard a sharp, snorting sound and then four Indians on painted ponies started out from the trees and passed just in front of them in a gust of horseflesh and the musk of their lean bodies. It happened so suddenly, she didn't have time to blink or breathe. Samuel booted his gelding forward, and then they were in a clearing surrounded by oak trees and ash. Samuel reined up and stopped. He had her horse's lead line in hand, and he turned it around his saddle horn three times very fast, then pulled a pistol from his belt and cocked the hammer. His chin was tucked, and he was watching the Indians who were now circling them—hair and horses and feathers, two of them with clubs in hand, though she didn't know if these were implements for riding or weapons of war. Samuel had the pistol cradled to his chest, barrel pointed at the sky. He was turning very slowly, trying to keep her behind him, himself in front, but the Indians were circling so quickly he might just as well have kept still. She had the sense Samuel was trying to defend her and that was a strange feeling indeed.

Then she felt a hand reach out and tug at her dress, but Samuel was turning them again. One of the men made a yipping sound—a high chirping noise, playful and threatening all at once—and an awful corkscrew feeling climbed her backbone.

And still Samuel hadn't pointed his gun. It occurred to her that there might be other Indians in the woods. So, maybe Samuel was hesitant. And things were not yet hostile, or not entirely hostile—there was the sense of a game about it—though she wished the Indian hadn't touched her. He shouldn't have done that. She felt these men were testing Samuel, that they wanted him to fire his pistol: if he fired, maybe they could do more than just touch. There seemed to be rules to this encounter and she knew nothing about them. Samuel was doing very well, she thought. Didn't seem to be afraid, just responsive, waiting for the moment to point his gun.

He hadn't said a word. He made a clucking sound with his tongue to direct his horse. Everything was getting close and tight—the Indians were riding closer, their circle was getting tighter—and then one of the Indians broke off and went riding for the trees, making the yipping noise as he went. One broke off, then they all broke off. They were not fleeing, just trotting toward the tree-line. And then they all disappeared in a shimmer of leaves and quivering branches. Dust rose in the air like smoke.

Samuel glanced at her, and she saw a tremor of nerves pass across his face.

"Can you ride?" he asked. "If I give you the lead, can you keep up?"

"I'll keep up," she said.

Samuel uncoiled her lead line from his saddle horn and handed it across.

Then they were pounding down the wagon trail, both horses at a gallop. She had never ridden this fast, and she had no idea the toll it took on you. She broke out in a sweat and gave the horse its head. The wind stung her eyes. The tree limbs were blurring by. She was scared, but there was a thrill to it. She almost felt like yelling. Then she did. She released a yip, an imitation of the Indians who'd grabbed at her, and she was surprised to hear Samuel yip back. The two of them were galloping along the trail, yipping, and then the woods fell away and they slowed their horses and went trotting out onto the wide pastureland.

Samuel reined up, and they stopped. They were looking at each other, their horses blowing. Something had changed, but she wasn't sure exactly what.

"Yip," she said, and they started laughing.

They made camp that evening among some live oaks beside a stream, and when Samuel climbed down from his horse, he was limping.

She watched him several moments.

"What's wrong with your leg?" she asked.

"I think I mashed it," Samuel said.

"With those Indians?"

"When our horses bunched up."

She stood there while he limped around gathering brush for the fire.

"Let me look at it," she said.

He didn't answer, just kept limping around. She watched him hobble, pretending he wasn't hurt.

By the time he'd got a fire going, and the guns lined up on his blanket, his ankle was so swollen he couldn't get his boot off. He lay there tugging on it. He'd broken out in a sweat and the boot seemed to be some opponent he was grappling.

And still he wouldn't ask for help.

She walked over, squatted beside him and put her hand on his shin. He stopped pulling on his boot and looked up at her.

"It won't come off," he said, and suddenly, he was like a little boy. Young and old at the same time.

He allowed her to take his boot heel in one hand and the toe in the other. She pulled very gently and his blue eyes came welling up out of their sockets.

"Does it hurt?" she said.

He shook his head. He was biting down on his lip and trying to keep the pain out of his face.

Which was silly, she thought: it hurt or it didn't, and it was plainly hurting him something fierce.

"I'm going to pull harder," she said.

He stared at her like he didn't know what she was waiting on. She wondered who he was pretending for? If he wanted to show someone his brave face, he could ride back and show the Indians.

She used the force of her annoyance to yank the boot harder, but the boot wouldn't come, and the muscles were flexing along Samuel's jaw, blue veins standing out on his neck.

He wouldn't say anything. He'd sit there clenched up till he cracked a tooth.

"We might have to cut it," she said.

Samuel reached over, drew his knife from its scabbard, and handed it across.

She squatted there with the blade. Samuel was leaning back onto his elbows, his eyes glazed over. She began to cut along the seam where the leather was stitched together, up the shaft of the boot toward his trousers' leg.

The pale flesh of his ankle looked like it might burst; there was blood underneath the skin. She sat there examining it in the firelight.

The first thing he said was, "I just bought those in New Orleans. Cost me twenty dollars."

She folded her saddle blanket and made a pillow, then slipped it under the crook of his knee. The ankle seemed to be swelling even bigger as she watched, but it was likely just the way the firelight was flickering.

Samuel said: "Heat me up some water to pour on it."

"Why?"

"I feel like I want some, is all."

"No, you don't," she told him. "You don't want any heat. If it was colder, we could skim ice from that creek and wrap it in a bandage. Hot water will swell it worse."

She was touching his shinbone very lightly, working her way toward his ankle. When she looked back down at him, he was staring up at her curiously.

"Is that true?" he said.

"Yes," she told him.

"How do you know?"

"I read it," she said. She realized she still had the knife beside her. If he didn't like that she could read, maybe he'd like the point of the blade. She watched the knowledge that she was lettered sink down into his eyes, waiting for it to catch.

"Where?" he said.

"Where what?"

"Did you read it?"

"In a book," she told him. "In Virginia."

She watched him take in this information; it went right down inside him, and he nodded. He lay there with light and shadow on his face.

"Did you read anything about boot-making?" he asked.

"We didn't have any books on boots."

"Figures," he said, and he looked so disappointed. Like a disheartened child. She felt something happen in her chest, like there were ropes attached to different bones inside her, and all her life, the world had been pulling them tighter. But the disappointment on Samuel's face made them loosen, and she felt like she could breathe. Her eyes welled up. She turned her head so he wouldn't see.

But, strangest thing, he felt it. He felt it right away. The very moment the ropes went slack, Samuel said, "What is it?"

She didn't answer. She stared into the dusk.

He said, "I'm not going to let them get you."

The Indians, she thought. She wasn't scared about Indians, but it was just as well to let him think so.

Because now he was old again. He was leaning up on his elbows, telling her not to be afraid, why he kept two of the pistols on his right side, and the other on his left, and she couldn't listen to his big talk anymore. The ropes had gone loose. Everything felt loose inside her. She'd been pushed and pulled so much today: the Indians, the boot, the books. Pour hot water on my ankle. She put her hand on his chest, pressed her cheek to his forehead, closed her eyes and held him still. She was saying, "Shhhhhhhhhh, now. Shhhhhhhhhh," and he wasn't speaking anymore. He was lying very quiet, his heart beating so violently she could feel it in her palm. She knew right then he'd never been with a woman, and there was something about this that softened her even more. There was the riding softness, and the yipping softness, his disappointment over boots. The rope-slack softness, the softness of her knowledge. She had him here with his leg propped up, forehead against her cheek and his heart slamming against her hand—bee-*dum*, bee-*dum*, bee-*dum*—and she'd never felt softer in all her life.

Duncan Lammons

—Texas, 1840—

Come springtime, I received word that Noah had established a gunsmith's shop up on Webber's Prairie and taken himself a bride. I put in for a furlough and went to pay the newlyweds a visit.

Being mechanically gifted as ever, Noah had constructed a marvelous cabin, the joinery so fine it looked to've been done by freemasons. I tied my horse and halloed the house. A dog started barking behind the cabin. Then the front door opened and Noah walked onto the porch.

This life will change you if you let it, though I suppose it'll change you even more if you don't. My old friend bore little resemblance to the ugly, freckle-faced boy I'd first met in New Orleans, back in the winter of '27. His beard now was long and thick, and the hair atop his head had started thinning. Married life seemed to agree with him: his belly poked out over his belt and there was the unmistakable glint of happiness in his eye.

He came down the steps, seized my hand and started to shake it.

"Ole Duncan," he said. "You are looking well."

I reached down and patted his stomach. "You don't seem to've missed any meals yourself."

"Come meet my Thurza," he said, then turned and called toward the door. "Thurza! Mister Lammons is here."

"Captain Lammons," I informed him.

"Oh, yes," he said. "That's right, isn't it?"

Mrs. Smithwick appeared and beckoned us inside. She had

supper steaming on the table, and when a woman fixed a hot meal in those days, you didn't do her the injury of letting it cool.

She was precisely what I would've wanted for Noah if I'd selected her from a store: sturdy and broad-shouldered, with a plain faultless face and a wise pair of eyes. Thick wrists. Callouses on her palms. There were no dainty women on our frontier, I assure you.

Noah kept up a steady stream of chatter while Thurza and I smiled and traded glances. Yes. They were a good match, though I failed to understand why a man would muster out of a ranging company and resort to family life. Perhaps I'd set so little store by family, it would've been mysterious to me whatever the pairing. I'd long since determined that no woman would master me. Of course, there was no danger of that; my dear mama excluded, I felt nothing for women but a mechanical curiosity. They were such different creatures from us.

Noah was still talking. He'd asked a question I hadn't heard.

"Beg pardon," I said. "I've grown rather deaf in my declining years."

He said, "I asked if you've considered taking your land payment."

"No," I told him, expecting I was about to be subjected to a lecture on how I ought to find a bride, take my headrights and stumble into my dotage like a respectable citizen.

But that wasn't his tack at all.

"It's likely for the best," he said. "Let Thurza tell you what happened to her mother."

"You tell it," she said.

"No," he told her, "go ahead."

Thurza started to do so, but then Noah interrupted her.

"Mother Blakey," he began.

"My mother," Thurza interjected.

"Her mother," Noah said. "A widow, mind you, who gave two sons and a husband to our revolution—"

"Daddy died before the war," she said.

Noah waved away this fact, inconvenient as it was to the tale he was unfolding.

"Do you remember T.J. Chambers?"

"Judge Chambers?" I asked.

"Yes," he said. "Judge Chambers. Well, your honor laid claim to four leagues of land on yonder side of the Colorado."

"Good for him," I said.

"Oh, there was nothing good in it," he said. "It was the self-same acreage where Mother Blakey had installed herself. She'd been given those headrights back in '36. Not to mention the Hemphills, Colonel Knight, and several other families. Chambers said they would have to buy back the land from him or lose it and their improvements as well."

"How could he do that?" I said. "Did Mrs. Blakey and the others have proper title?"

"They did indeed," said Noah, "but titles are being contested left and right. I hired Judge Webb to represent Mother Blakey, and Chambers agreed to write out a deed for half her headrights, 4,400 acres further up the Colorado. She was able to relocate, at least."

"So, he stole half her land," I said.

"It's better than what happened to the others. The Hemphills and Colonel Knight lost all their property."

"I don't see how he could do that," I said.

"He did it. So, when you decide to take your own payment, be certain there are no flaws in the title. Or hope no one invents a flaw, as I suspect His Highness did to Mother Blakey. Folks won't say so, but this Republic needs some sorting."

"I suspect so," I said, "but who will do it?"

Noah pushed his plate away and leaned against the table conspiratorially.

"I've exchanged letters with President Houston on the subject. He wants the United States to annex us as a state."

Well, this was as bad a bit of news as I'd heard since they'd told me Sam had been sent out as a courier.

I said, "I left Kentucky to get out of the States."

Noah laughed. "Is that not something? Man runs away from his nation only to find he didn't run far enough?"

Thurza giggled at this, but I didn't see the humor. I hadn't fled a thousand miles risking life and limb only to see America plant its flag on soil I'd fought to free.

"*Far enough*," I repeated. "Just how far does a body have to go?"

"Oh, I don't know," said Noah. "The moon?"

* * *

When I got back to camp, Felix McClusky was waiting for me at the edge of the grove where we picketed our horses: arms crossed, his lean, bearded face a bright red.

"And are we taking in every foreign nigger that comes calling?" the Irishman asked me. "Is that the way of things?"

"What do you mean?"

"I've no complaint against Ramírez, now. But isn't one greaser enough?"

"Felix," I said, "I don't have a clue what you're talking about."

"So, it's not your doing, you say? Then maybe you should tell him, Cap'n. Or maybe I will. Maybe I'll—"

And before I could figure out what had touched him off, he stomped away into the trees.

I gathered my traps and followed, curious as to what could get him in such a lather.

When I reached the little glade where the men were camped, I discovered a new rider had joined our ranks, a tall, broad-shouldered Spaniard with a head of thick black hair which he wore in a long, braided queue—a style fashionable among our colonial forefathers and perhaps still in vogue across the sea. He was talking and laughing with the other men while McClusky looked on, fuming.

His name was Juan Juarez and from the moment I shook his hand, I knew he was first-swath: here was a man with a square, dimpled chin and a calm, soldierly bearing.

"It is good to meet you, Master Juarez."

He performed an elegant little bow, dipping his head and placing his palms along thighs. His skin was the color of silt.

"Pleasure," he said.

"Did you come to us direct from Spain?"

"Galveston," he told me. "I am in New Orleans before this, sailing from France, the port Le Havre."

I choked down the urge to ask a thousand questions, contenting myself with the most important of them.

"Have you scrimmaged with the aborigines?" I asked.

He stared at me a moment. "Your Indians?"

"Our Indians," I said.

"My experience as soldado is from the Canut revueltas." He lifted a hand and rubbed his thumb against his forefinger, trying to produce a word. "The sublevacion. The rebeliones."

"Rebellion," I said.

"Exactly so. We are led by Marshal Jean-de-Dieu Soult. But in this country, I have seen no combate. I did luchar one of your Tonkawa in Galveston. I have heard the Comanche are very different."

"For a fact," I said. "I hope you didn't muster in for the sport."

He shook his head. "No. No deporte. They said this service is pay in land. I have wanted to own land for many years."

I nodded, thinking about what Noah had said regarding the problems with our titles, deciding not to mention it lest I discourage our new recruit.

Then something he'd said struck me: it took several

moments for Spanish words to sift their way into English. *Luchar* meant *wrestle*: had he really luchar-ed a Tonk?

I asked him and a grin spread over his face. He had dark brown eyes, almost black, like polished stones beneath his brows.

"Yes," he said. "Tonkawa Joe, he is called. Men luchar him for money. Or they tell me you may. No one was excited to do this. His teeth are filed to points."

"You know why they do that, don't you?"

He nodded. "They say, 'Juan, he is caníbal—his teeth are sharp to eat the flesh of men.' Maybe this is so. But I only see Tonkawa Joe eat griddlecakes or bacon. He is three trescientas libras."

"What caused you to mix it up with him?"

Juan smiled. "Myself and the other stevedores are speaking after work and this Tonkawa Joe comes to the docks with the man who collects his monies. He calls to us, this man, and says that we are all cobardes: none will luchar Señor Joe.

"I tell him I am no cobarde at all. And I have gold to say so."

He stopped and looked around where the men of the company had begun to gather to hear the story of this great Tonk wrestling bout.

"Go on," I told Juan. "They're eager for entertainment, is all."

"I was speaking of the wager?" he asked.

Which is when McClusky said, "You were spinning a yarn about how you whipped a Tonk."

Juan said, "I made no claim of whips, senor. We luchamos. He is so greased with lard I could not get a hold."

"Well," said McClusky, "this company don't luchamos an Indian. We knock his brains out with our rifles."

"Felix," I said, "why don't you let the man say his piece."

McClusky shrugged. "I'm not amused by lies, Cap'n."

The men had been snickering; now they went quiet. I could hear the fires crackling.

Our new recruit didn't seem to be a man whose honor you'd want to insult, but he was still unknown to me, as he was to the rest of the company. McClusky was testing him. And not for no reason: a ranger is only as good as his ability to inflict violence; a man who is just talk is dangerous.

Juan looked confused. He glanced at me and said, "¿Él me desafía?"

"What'd he say?" McClusky asked.

"He wants to know if you're challenging him," I said.

"Challenge?" McClusky guffawed. "Challenge to what? I wrestle a deal better than a greased-up Indian."

"Bueno," said Juan. "It was a poor match."

The men all laughed at that. McClusky's ears turned bright red and before I could stop or steer it, we went from hearing the tale of a wrestling bout to witnessing one in person.

And so, the would-be combatants walked out beyond the light of the cook fires to a bare space of dirt and we all gathered to form a ring. Juan was the taller of the two by a head, but the Irishman was mean as a snake. He stood there eyeing Juan for several moments.

Then he said, "First man to call quits?"

Juan shook his head. "I do not quit, señor."

McClusky said, "How're we deciding a winner, then?"

"It will be no mystery," Juan told him, and a vicious look came into McClusky's eyes. He lowered his chin and lunged for Juan with both arms extended like a man diving into a creek.

Juan didn't flinch or falter. He sidestepped McClusky and latched onto him from behind, snaking an arm under the Irishman's chin and putting some kind of hold on him. You could see he'd done it before. Many times, perhaps.

McClusky's entire head went purple and he commenced to make a gurgling sound. In a few seconds, his legs went wobbly and his eyes rolled back into his head. When Juan let go of him, McClusky hit the dirt like a sack of flour.

Everyone was quiet for a heartbeat or two.

"Shit on a snake," said Levi English. "Is he dead?"

Juan shook his head. He wasn't even breathing hard, and I was reminded of Sam that day at the Battle of Concepcion, loading his rifle and firing on the Mexicans as their cannon blazed away.

"Roll him," he said. "Lift his legs."

Which the men did, and directly, McClusky sputtered, sat up and eyed everything like a newborn calf.

"Did I whip him?" he said, and everyone began to snigger.

Or everyone but me. McClusky had gotten the humbling he deserved, but I have never enjoyed to see men embarrassed. I knelt beside him and patted his shoulder.

"You whipped him good, Felix. Why don't you celebrate by resting yourself, now? I don't think our new recruit can take another beating like that."

* * *

We sat up late into the night, Juan and myself, visiting while the men around us dozed. In addition to being a wizard in a wrestling match, he was a bit of a scholar, much better educated than myself, which was no high hurdle.

Thing was, I'd become so accustomed to dealing with the unschooled men who populated our companies, I'd nearly forgotten what it was like to conversate with someone who'd mastered the written word. Not that I held myself superior to those under my command, but there is a close feeling that comes to you from the pages of a book—and in fellowship with someone initiate in its mysteries. Talking with Juan was like a lamp inside my brain. I felt myself lighting back up.

He put me in mind of Sam, though the two of them shared little but physical courage. All told, I'd spent less than six months with young Samuel, but still he loomed large in my memory and affections. Why should that be? Who are these people who, at a moment's meeting, seem as if you've known them forever, while others you live with daily feel lifeless as faces in a cracked painting?

If Sam possessed a natural intelligence for friendship and fighting, Juan had a mind that appreciated the literary arts too—things I'd paid so little attention to over the past several years that I'd nearly forgotten their existence. At the blab school my folks sent me to where the whole room of pupils recited their lessons all together like Catholics taking Mass, we hardly touched on poetry, and I thought of my dear mother who had tried in vain to supplement my education with the poets of antiquity—Virgil and Dante, Shakespeare and Milton. But I was an anxious child, eager to please my father, and I wondered if I'd become a hand at hunting and marksmanship because I was truly drawn to such things, or if it was only Pap's affection I was trying to earn. It is hard to figure why we choose what we do, and perhaps the real detriment in all of it is that we feel we have to choose at all, for why shouldn't a boy love verse and the rifle too?

Juan seemed to have no problem planting his seed in both soils. On his third night with us, I came on him propped with his back to the fire, studying a little volume he held so close to his face he could've licked it—a strange occurrence all round as I'd never seen a ranger read anything round the campfire. There were men who carried the Good Book in their traps, but I hadn't known them to crack its covers.

I stood there taking in the sight of this grappler studying his book like he was in a library and not camped in the wilderness on the Colorado.

"What you reading?" I said.

"Wordsworth," he said, not yet looking up.

"Beg pardon?"

"William Wordsworth. A poet of Inglaterra. You haven't heard of him, Captain?"

"Well," I said, "there's just not a whole lot of interest in

English poetry among men in this line. Though I daresay I'd welcome it."

He gestured for me to sit, then thumbed back and forth and a few pages and cleared his throat.

"Our birth is but a sleep and a forgetting," he read. "The soul that rises with us, our life's star, hath elsewhere its setting, and cometh from afar: not in entire forgetfulness, and not in utter nakedness, but trailing clouds of glory do we come from God, who is our home: heaven lies about us in our infancy. Shades of the prison house began to close upon the growing boy, but he beholds the light, and whence it flows, he sees it in his joy."

He stopped and looked up at me.

"Now that is something," I said. "Read that last part again."

As he began to do so, the men rose and gathered round, and soon he had quite an audience. I'd scant hope that Juan would make lovers of poetry of this rough band, but the longer he read, the more mouths I watched open and gape in child-like wonder. He must have read for a good ten minutes, and when his voice began to falter and he stopped, I saw that Felix McClusky was standing at the edge of the group, listening.

He nodded toward Juan and I thought he was about to deliver some slight or insult, but instead he said, "Is that the end of it?"

Juan nodded. "Would you hear another?"

In the firelight, McClusky's face looked bashful and boyish.

"If you'd not mind," he said.

The other men agreed. Then they began commenting on this or that phrase they'd caught, how nicely it was turned, how true.

I shook my head. I thought I'd been riding with men I knew. Ruffians and reprobates. And yet, in a few minutes' time, Juan had revealed them to be poetry-lovers in buckskin.

Yes. Our new recruit was indeed a Godsend.

Not least of all, for me.

CECELIA

—TEXAS, 1837—

They stopped in the town of Washington on the muddy Brazos River. Samuel tied their horses to the post outside a cedar-log building, then stood there rummaging in his saddle bags.

She glanced up the dirt street of the little hamlet: to that mule over yonder with the dejected look on its face; to the chickens wandering from yard to yard, pecking at the mud. She heard a door open, and a red-haired man emerged from a dilapidated hut and slumped against his porch railing, staring.

She turned and looked back at Sam.

Your wilderness manners are one thing, she thought. Let's see how you treat me among your own.

He'd produced a small leather satchel, but was still searching his bag, lips pursed, digging through his traps.

"Did you lose something?" she asked.

"I reckon," he said. He glanced up at her and lifted the satchel. "I got to take this in to Captain Barker. Won't be but a minute."

Then he turned, went hobbling up the steps, and disappeared inside.

When he came back out, the satchel was gone and he had a sheaf of papers in hand. He hoisted himself into the saddle, and they started back down the lane.

He seemed very pleased with himself. He'd begun whistling a melody that meandered up and down.

Any other time, this might've annoyed her, but she couldn't

stop looking at the papers he carried, and the more she stared at them, the more nervous she got. She knew the bill of sale he'd taken off Childers was in his far-side saddlebag, but she couldn't help thinking these new documents added something to it.

When they were a mile or so out of town, she couldn't stand it any longer. She chucked her horse up alongside him and nodded at the papers.

"What are they?" she asked.

He didn't say anything, didn't stop his whistling, just handed them across.

She slowed her horse and stopped there in the road, unfolding the documents, reading through the pages. She was surprised to find they didn't mention her. In fact, they had nothing to do with her at all.

The first page was just a note that read:

This is to certify that the name of Samuel Fisk appears on the muster roll of Capt. John Tumlinson's Volunteer Company who was under the command of Major Williamson in the expedition against Santa Anna.
—John Tumlinson, Captain of Rangers

The next page was in two parts and written in a different hand:

On the application of Samuel Fisk in pay for services in the war of Independence between the Republic of Texas and Mexico in 1835:
I am well acquainted with Samuel Fisk the applicant here personally present—he is the identical Samuel Fisk who served in Capt. Smithwick's Company. I was a member of the same company and have received pay for my services and was also paid for the use of my horse.

Private Fisk has received no pay for his service.
Sworn to this day of 16 April 1837
—Josiah Barker

Underneath this was another message, reading:

Personally appearing before me the undersigned Samuel Fisk
who upon oath says:
I served under Capt. Smithwick in 1836. I was in service 18
months, I never receiving any pay for my services or the use of
my horse to which I was entitled the same as other members of
the company. I never hitherto applied for my pay or authorized
any person to apply for me.
X
Subscribing to and sworn before me
this 16 April 1837
—Josiah Barker

"You didn't sign it," she said, and the words were hardly
out of her mouth before she realized why.

He could not write his name, probably couldn't read these
pages.

"You were in a war?" she said.

"That's an awful proud name for it."

"It says *for services in the war of Independence*."

"Well, if it's wrote down, it's got to be true then, hadn't it?"

"What's the pay they're talking about?"

"Land," he said. "My land payment. Government's short of
gold, so they pay us all in property."

"All of who?"

"Rangers," he said. "Our ranger company."

"Is that an army?"

"It's a sort of one," he said.

"Are you still in it?"

"As of right this minute, I'm not in nothing. My term expired in Louisiana, but I was supposed to bring that satchel to Captain Barker, so that's what I done."

"What was in the satchel?"

"I don't have no idea," he said.

"And you're finished? With your rangers?"

"Captain wanted me to sign on for another go, but I told him I was tired of people telling me what to do."

She felt herself relaxing, her heart beating slower, and as it did, she saw once again what a striking man he was. He really did have a rough beauty to him. It was just that you didn't expect it, so it took you unaware.

Folding the papers, she walked her horse over and handed them back to Samuel. She asked where they were going.

"Well," he told her, "they say I have to ride to the land office in Austin. I show them these papers and then I can pick out some property and hire a surveyor."

"Then what?"

"I don't know then what," he said. "What about you?"

"What do you mean?"

"Where do you want to go?"

She'd been waiting all her life for someone to ask her this. Of course, she had no answer. No practice at answers. It flummoxed her so badly that she kneed Honey into a walk, got out ahead of Samuel, then pushed the horse to a trot.

She wouldn't have him looking at her, seeing the baffled expression on her face.

Where *did* she want to go?

The only place she'd ever considered was *away*.

Duncan Lammons

—Texas, 1840–1841—

T hat summer, we were deployed along the Brazos, scouting for any sign of Comanche. In those days, it was not unheard of for them to venture so far east. Later that year, Chief Buffalo Hump would lead his Penateka braves to the Port of Linnville and raze it to the ground.

But that catastrophe was still some weeks away and we'd seen no Indians of any stripe for months. In the eventide, I'd allow the men to light as many cookfires as they wished and often a bottle would be passed around.

One night, after partaking of a particularly stancheous jar of mash, we began to question Juan Juarez about his birth and homeland, how he'd crossed the great ocean and ended up with the likes of us.

Juan didn't consume spiritous liquors. He sat with his back to the fire, studying us, as if trying to determine just how drunk we were.

"Who would want such stories?" he asked. "Why not rather a poem?" He retrieved his Wordsworth from his blankets and began to thumb the pages.

Levi English said, "You can read to us any night. We're asking about your kinfolk. Your raising."

Juan's brow knit. He glanced at me.

"Tu familia," I told him. "Su crianza."

He shook his head. He lifted his book.

"But this is a very great poet, no?"

"For a fact," I told him.

"And you would rather some story of myself?"

"The men are partial to you, Master Juarez. Take it as a compliment. Un cumplido."

He looked at me, then at the faces flickering in the firelight. He closed his book and set it there beside him.

"Very well," he said. "What would you know?"

"Where were you born?" Levi said.

"On Tenerife in the Islas Canarias. You would say the *Isle of Dogs.*"

"I thought that you were Spanish."

"Si. Castellano. El español. Tenerife is a colony of España."

"It's an island?" Levi said.

"An island," Juan told him, nodding. "But an island of coast, mountain, forest, all three. There is desert as well. You walk out of foothills into the sea."

I said, "Did you live in a town?"

"Si, a village," he said. "A village near the shore. Mamá and Papá. Mi hermanos. Mi abuela."

It sounded like quite a life; I couldn't imagine him wanting to leave it.

Nor could McClusky. The Irishman said, "If you were so happy, what brought you to us?"

"I cannot say we were happy all the time, but we were often happy."

Then something in his face changed. He seemed to grow more thoughtful.

"Mamá, when she carries me inside her, has a strong premonición I will be a girl. So, being a boy, I am much surprise to her. Maybe too much surprise.

"Mi hermanos are older than myself. They tease and call me *Juanita.* Mamá takes their part; only Abuela takes mine. Papá is a fisherman and has no time to take any part at all. His hands are fat with the scars of his nets."

"Who's Abuela?" Levi said.

"His grandmother," I told him, then looking at Juan, "Your mother's mother?"

"No," he said. "She is Papá's. Mamá does not like that she is come to live with us. She is old and tells us stories. The Witches of Anaga. The Lumia who wanders the night and sinks her tooth into whichever child she finds. The Dip, a dog who takes the children's blood as well. These are the stories Abuela enjoys to tell."

"Did it scare you?" Levi said.

"No. Both mi hermanos are frighten of her, but I am not frighten. I like her stories very much. We have only three beds in our home and some one must share with Abuela. I say that I will share and Abuela tells me many more stories than mi hermanos.

"Mamá is pray all the time, thinking some bad thing will befall her hijos. 'Do not go down to the shore,' she says. 'Do not go up to the mountain.' She is sure this bad thing will happen, but Abuela thinks Mamá has a weakness.

"'Your mamá has put her fear inside your hermanos,' she tells me. 'How will they be men?'

"'They will not,' I say.

"'No,' she says. 'They are cobardes. But you are brave already. These is why Lumia will pass you by. The blood of a brave boy dries Lumia up like wind. Your hermanos? Why not sink a tooth into the heart of a cobarde? If I had a tooth left to me, I would do this myself.'

"It is the corsarios especially that worry Mamá. Piratas of Barbary. They take anyone they can find and they find many. There is a blacksmith of our village named Juan also, a big man, very strong. But one day he is gone. No one knows to where. People say the piratas take him. Mi papá says it is foolish to think the piratas take this man.

"'He drinks too much,' Papá says. 'He drinks and is fallen into the sea and drown. What would piratas want with such a man?'"

"*Pirata?*" McClusky asked.

"Pirates," I told him.

"Si," said Juan. "Corsario."

"Why did they take your people?" I asked.

"Not just my people, Captain. The Frances, los italianos. Old, young, it is no difference. It is for esclavos that the piratas take these people. Or for rescate. Or as rehén."

"English," McClusky demanded.

"Hostages," I told him. "For ransom."

Juan nodded. "Abuela thinks my mother fears the corsarios too much.

"'You see,' she tells me. 'Your mamá does not like that I should speak of Lumia, but she will talk of the piratas until she turn your hermanos into cobardes. I ask you: which is worse?'

"Better than stories, Abuela loves to eat bananas. Bananas all the time. Papá brings her these when he can think to do so, but his mind is with the fish. Mamá makes soup for Abuela to eat, but Abuela cares nothing for soup.

"When I bring her back bananas, you should see her eyes.

"'You are like Rodrigo Diaz de Vivar,' she says. 'You are ten of your hermanos.' She peels the banana with her fingers. Her face shines. 'Not ten,' she says: '*cien*.'

"'Why do you bring her plantanos?' mi hermano Miguel asks.

"'He must bring her these,' says mi hermano Gabriel, 'or he cannot share her bed.' He sucks his lips over his teeth like they are Abuela's gums.

"'You are afraid of shadows, Gabriel. You could not fetch a potato from the ground.'

"Gabriel takes one of the bananas and puts it obscenely between his lips, a gesto I will not understand until much later, when I am un esclavo in the pasha's palace.

"But I tell Abuela and she understand very well. At supper, she takes one of the bananas, staring at mi hermanos all the while. She does not peel it. She says, 'They say that the tooth of Lumia is a similar size. She is silent as a mouse in all her movements, but her tooth she cannot quiet.' She holds the banana like a great fang. 'It clicks against the open windows she will slip inside. It scratches the floors as she crawl on hands and feet.' She places the tip of the banana on the table and drags it. Miguel looks down at his lap and Gabriel puts out his chin to show he is not frighten, but both their faces are as pale as if the Lumia has drain their blood already.

"'I myself saw her when I was just a child,' says Abuela, 'and I—'

"'This is enough,' Mamá says. She turns to Papá in her anger, but Papá is hiding a smile.

"'I suppose you enjoy these pagano lies,' Mamá says.

"'I suppose,' says Papá.

"That night, lying with Abuela in the dark, I can hear mi hermanos cry. Abuela hears them also. She begins to laugh."

* * *

Juan told us that the next year some manner of blight was visited on the banana trees of his island. Before this, he'd only had to walk a mile or so to find fruit for his granny; now he had to go five miles or more.

He'd become quite expert as a climber; he could clamber up a trunk quick as a squirrel.

On a scout one morning, roosted up in a banana tree, he looked out between the leafy stalks to see a number of boats pulled up on the beach, small boats such as the fishermen of his little island used, but unfamiliar in their design. He felt a tremor of fear, but his granny had taught him the shame of such cowardice, so he gathered the bunch of bananas he'd come for and slid to the ground. He now saw that farther out from the coast, a great ship was anchored. He knew right away who it belonged to and he started off into the trees, taking a footpath that would lead him into his village by a secret route.

He was moving along at a good clip when he heard voices, and crouching behind a palm, saw a party of rough-looking men moving up this trail ahead of him. This path was out of the way; no foreigner could've known about it. And these men were certainly foreign; they wore tunics of exotic color and carried damascene scimitars in their hands. At their head walked a hunched, filthy man in sailcloth, leading the corsarios to his village.

He said, "The man is very familar to me. I am thinking now that Mamá is not so foolish as mi abuela has said. I am thinking I am the foolish one."

But still, he didn't panic. He kept himself hunkered behind cover and watched the party out of sight.

"I am trying to decide if it is better to carry the bananas I have gathered, or whether to do so is not so good, and it is then I notice a very strange smell—like fruit and smoke have mixed. I do not yet know how different one man's scent is from another, one people's from another. My nose has no experiencia. The scents I know are Mamá and Papá, mi hermanos, mi abuela—who always smells to me of bread."

He was catching wind of another band of pirates coming up the trail behind him. Likely, these Berbers' diet was a good deal richer that the fish and fruit Juan was familiar with. Up to then, I daresay his palate hadn't known much spice at all.

So now, he had pirates up ahead and pirates back behind. He lowered himself to the ground and lay there on his belly. He started saying a prayer his mama taught him, a Catholic prayer to Mary—though perhaps there are few others in those climes. Having no real defense against the raiders but church bells to warn villagers, folks put their faith in the protection of Heaven as poor people are wont to do the world over.

But Juan's prayers helped about as much as mine ever have.

The second band of Berbers had come up and started to pass. He watched their boots and sandals and stockinged feet trample along, footwear from all across Europe, taken in their many raids. And then a pair of bare feet stopped beside him. A deep voice spoke in an unfamiliar tongue, and though Juan hadn't the least notion what the words meant, he knew they were addressed to him.

He lay there with his heart fluttering in his chest, as was my own heart to hear him tell it. I looked at the faces of the men around that campfire and there was genuine fear in their features—not least of all in McClusky's. It seemed to me I must be looking at the same expression of terror that was on Juan's face all those years ago.

He said: "I feel mi cuero cabelludo on fire and my hair goes very tight. There is a hand pulling me, yanking me to my feet. And here I am staring into the eye of a corsario from mi mamá's stories. I have heard her stories since I am very small and still never believe until this moment. I had believed in Lumia more than any pirata, and I feel I have betrayed Jesucristo by trusting mi abuela's tales."

"They take and set me in this boat. Maybe an hour passes. Maybe it is more. I am hoping, perhaps, the men of our village have beaten the corsarios. Then I am thinking of Mamá's stories of being a girl on La Gomera. The men of her isle built towers on the shore to keep watch always and when a strange ship was sighted, the bells of the church would ring and the villagers would flee into the hills. I am thinking that if the men of my village are fighting or fleeing these piratas, where is the bell now? Why doesn't it ring? Perhaps I am too far, I think. Perhaps it rings and I cannot hear and all the piratas lie bleeding in the soil already and our village is safe.

"Then birds come bursting from the trees all around— chiffchaff, and stonechat, and the blue chaffinch that I most love to watch. They scatter up from the branches into the sky and then the corsairos come, hurrying toward the boats where we wait.

"They are not just the two bands I have seen, but many more. Ten or eleven or maybe twelve. Hundreds of piratas. They have taken women from the village and several of the fishermen and a great number of boys: some are tied together and some stumble along with their hands bound before them and then I see that they have Father Linares as well. He is the priest who performed mi bautismo; I know him all the time I can remember.

"Then I see the band of piratas that I first notice on the hidden trail, led by the filthy man in sailcloth. And seeing his face, I know why he is familiar to me: it is the blacksmith who mi papá said had drank and drown himself, and I feel a hatred in my heart I have never known. But still, this is not the worst."

Levi shook his head. "Cousin," he said, "I hate to hear what's worse than that."

Juan shrugged. "You will," he said. "But I will tell you. The worst is that I see four corsarios come down from the trees, the last of all the piratas. They are carrying the brazen bell of our church—I have never seen it but up in its campanario—and now I know why I have not heard it ring. I do not wonder then what they could want with it, but I know if they have manage to take this bell from where it has been all my life, there is nothing these piratas cannot take, and nothing they cannot do."

* * *

"I do not know how long we are at sea," Juan told us. "It is perhaps a week. Perhaps it is longer. Pressed together in the dark, you cannot always tell. The others cried out to God, but I did not. I knew I had betrayed Him, so how could I call on him like this? In my heart, I asked His forgiveness, but I knew, having listened too long to mi abuela's stories, I had committed a very great sin. What may redeem such betrayal? I suffered this in my soul, but I could not give it voice."

They put in at Algiers one morning, the port of Algiers. Juan said to feel the ship stop moving was a kind of pleasure. To rest without motion. And then, led up onto the docks, he felt the sun on his face and began to weep. He'd never considered the great comfort of sunlight, the blessing of it.

Sad to say, these fine feelings did not last. He and the other captives were herded down a street where all the citizens of Algiers had turned out to greet them. Or so it seemed to him at the time. Juan had never seen such a crowd. Their Berber captors paraded them into the heart of the city and every street was lined with men and women, young and old alike. They threw refuse and rotten vegetables at the prisoners. Juan said that a boy of maybe five came toddling up to him only to spit in his face.

"They are shouting all manner of insult," he said. "One word in particular I hear over and over: *kalb*. This is 'dog' in their speech. Not even knowing the word, I am soon feeling like one. I feel such shame with all the peoples mocking and laughing. I am ashame to be seen by them."

"Why were you ashamed?" Levi asked. "They're the ones ought to've been ashamed for treating you so."

Juan puffed at his pipe. He said: "There are many more of them than us, and all of them taunting and yelling. It makes a difference how many there are."

Levi shook his head. "That don't figure for me," he said. "Begging your pardon."

Well, it might not've made much sense to Levi, but it certainly did to me. Hadn't I tucked tail myself and run for Texas once my own defects of character were trumpeted about Butler County? *Kalb* indeed.

Juan seemed to feel no need to explain himself, just continued his story, telling how they were taken to the palace of one of the city's wealthy lords. Here, they were kept in much better quarters than he'd expected and given much better food. They weren't whipped or given chores of any kind. In fact, they had little to do but worry and wait.

After a few weeks of such seasoning, they were shaved, he said. Head, body, and beard.

"Shaved?" I said. "Whyever for?"

He puffed his pipe and for the first time in the telling of his story, I thought I saw something come into his eyes, some reflection of the misery he'd endured, like a mountain peak mirrored in a pool.

He said, "It is to show all the world that we are bonded. We have a master now."

He went on to tell us how grown men he'd traveled with in the corsairs' galley now broke down weeping as their beards were razored away. It was the last thing they had of themselves, I reckon. The last thing to show that they were men.

I looked at Juan's hair gathered in that queue behind his head, thinking, *Yes. Now I see.* If the misfortunes he described had been visited upon me, I would not scissor away a single strand.

"Then," he said, "after all this is done, we are taken to the badestan for sale."

The badestan was a market similar to the ones Noah and I had seen in New Orleans, it sounded like. And once a price was decided, a man walked over to that captive and painted a number on his naked chest.

"What for?" Levi asked.

"It is our price," Juan said. "The price that is decided."

"But you'd already been bought," Levi said. "Why write it on you?"

"No, no," said Juan. "It is only our first price. "Our precio estándar. *Guideline*, you may say. So the pasha knows our worth."

The pasha represented the Sultan of Istanbul in much the same way that a priest represents the Pope in Rome.

"We are taken to his palace and now he can have—" He paused, trying to formulate the phrase in English.

"First pick?" I said.

"Si," he said. "First pick."

And so they were traipsed before the pasha and here he comes in, with a retinue of advisors and hangers-on, a large man in silk finery, turbaned and with a great black beard, inspecting each man and the price they'd hung on him.

McClusky snorted. "What'd you go for, laddie?"

"I do not know," Juan said. "The number is here"—he touched himself in the flat space between his collarbones. "I cannot look down to see."

He told us the pasha was beginning to select those men he would buy for himself when the priest stepped forward.

"Your Excellency," the padre said, "I have come to see my religion is a false one. These many years, I have lived as an infidel. I wish to confess and embrace the true faith of Allah."

Well, the pasha eyed Father Linares a moment, then turned, waved one of his counselors forward, and spoke something in the man's ear. This man nodded, bowed to the pasha, then left the hall in a great hurryment. Pasha smiled at the priest. He told the padre to come closer and when Father Linares stepped up beside him, the pasha threw his arms open and embraced the priest, who, I reckon, was a priest no longer. When Father Linares turned back around, he would not look the other captives in the eye.

The pasha began picking those he'd purchase for the bargain price scribbled on their chests, the choicest and cheapest. He cast an eye on Juan.

"And you," the pasha said. "You will be mine as well."

Juan told us he did not know if this was good fortune or bad. "I am still angry with Father Linares. The men who are not seleccionado are taken away—I will never hear what is to become of them—and the four of us who belong now to the pasha are standing in the quiet hall: it is we, the pasha, his asistentes, and the priest."

It was then that counselor reappeared and with him were two turbaned men with curved daggers in their sashes—like guards, said Juan, but just not exactly.

The pasha turned to Father Linares and asked if he was indeed in earnest about swapping out religions. The padre nodded that he was.

"Good," the pasha said. "This is very good. Remove your gandora."

"Pardon?" the priest said, but the pasha did not answer questions and he did not give orders more than once. The pasha merely whispered a word to the two guards and one stepped forward, seized the priest, and stripped his tunic off him, yanking it up and over his head.

"Lie down," the pasha told him.

The priest glanced around the room. His entire head was the color of a ripe, red apple. The sweat shone on his skin like blisters. In his rush to emancipate himself, he hadn't exactly considered what his freedom might tax him.

"Where?" he asked the pasha, still not understanding who asked questions in the palace and who it was that answered them. The other guard came up behind him and swept him off his feet, slammed him to the stone floor. He'd begun to howl rather loudly.

"Do not move," the pasha told him. "It is worse if you move."

The larger of the two guards was holding Father Linares, pinning him down, and the other squatted, drew the dagger from the golden scabbard in his sash, and taking hold of the priest's shrunken pizzle, began to cut away the foreskin.

Well, McClusky didn't like this one bit.

"They hacked off the poor man's bod?"

"No," said Juan. "The prepucio. To circumscribe him."

"Circumcize," I said.

"Yes," said Juan. "Very much."

"Savages!" said McClusky.

"Well," I told him, "I daresay that's rather gentle compared to what these slavers get up to on these big plantations, Felix. Cane slavers and such. They brand the poor folks like cattle."

McClusky shook his head. "That's a good deal different now, Captain."

"Is it?" I said. "Tell me how."

He was so flustered he couldn't seem to make a sentence, just sat there fuming.

Levi spoke up. He said, "Well, most Southern men don't have any slaves at all, Cap. Sounds to me like all these Moslems do."

Juan removed the pipe stem from his mouth. He said, "This is not true."

"They take you prisoner and you're going to sit there speaking up for them?" McClusky said.

"I am not speaking up," said Juan. "I am telling you—most Musulmanes have never seen an esclavo and many who have have never owned one themself. It is only a particular kind of man."

"And what kind would that be?" McClusky said.

"The rich kind," I said.

"Yes," said Juan. "The very rich."

Levi leaned over and spat into the grass beside him. "It's still not the same as what folks do over here," he said. "Not even similiar."

"No?" said Juan.

"Not by a long chalk," Levi said.

McClusky said, "And there's a deal of difference between putting a few niggers to work picking cotton and stealing Christian men from their homes, cutting off their pizzles."

"Not off," Juan reminded him. "Just the prepucio."

"That's no great distinction," Levi said.

"I might say the same to you about the poor negroes our slavers keep," I said. "Fact, I see no difference at all between what these Berbers once did and what the good Christians of the South continue doing. And it is not just a few, Felix. It is untold thousands. And didn't they once have homes in their native lands before being stolen away themselves?"

"It's as I've told you," McClusky said. "Niggers are one thing; white men are something else."

"They're all God's children," I said.

At this, McClusky stood, swatted the dust from the backside of his pantaloons, and strode off into the dark. "I'll not listen to any more of this," he mumbled.

We sat watching him recede from the light of the campfire, then sat listening to coals snap and sizzle.

Then Levi said, "And what about these Indians we skrimmage with?"

"The Comanche have slaves too," I told him.

Levi nodded. "That's what Captain Smithwick told us. But are Indians the same as white men?"

"They are people," I said, though the words felt strange in my mouth and my throat tightened up.

"Why are we hunting them then? Tell me that, Cap."

"We're paid to fight them, Levi."

"That's no kind of answer," he said.

And I knew he was right. It wasn't.

CECELIA

—TEXAS, 1837—

She was astonished at how she enjoyed riding, being able to sit up and see the country scroll by, a new vision from one moment to the next.

Only problem was the thinking that it brought, the horse's hooves striking old memories from the earth or jostling them from the soil of your brain.

It was her mother who came to her in these thoughts, spreading through her like Victoria creeper. The memory of her grandam was very close, but she'd shut out her mother ages ago.

The womenfolk of her family had been with the Haverfords for generations. Her grandam had tended Master Haverford when he was just a boy, working in the kitchen at the old plantation house in Randolph County. So it was with Cecelia's mother. So it was to be with her.

But Charles Haverford had been married ten years and Anne had yet to give him a child. You could see just how badly the mistress wanted to mother. When she took to Cecelia, no one was surprised.

She was only four when Anne began teaching her the alphabet. She could remember sitting on the woman's lap, turning the rich-smelling pages of the primer, logs crackling beside them in the stone fireplace, the creak of the old oak rocker. Her mistress's finger moving down the page:

Apple-Pie.
Bit it.

Cut it.
Divided it.
Eat it.
Fought for it.
Got it.
Had it.
It'd it.
Joined for it.
Kept it.
Longed for it.
Mourned for it.
Nodded at it.
Opened it.
Peeped in it.
Quartered it.
Ran for it.
Snatched it.
Turned it.
Used it.
Viewed it.
Wanted it.
Excited it.
You'd it.
Zoned it.

Her mother didn't care for all this book learning. Neither she nor her own mother were lettered and she could already feel Cecelia growing different. She said it was their mistress's ambition to take the girl for her own.

The three of them shared a room in the servant's quarters and one night, Cecelia lay there, listening to them argue the subject.

"Only trouble can come of it," her mother said, and there was such anger in her voice. Cecelia could never summon the same feeling for the woman that rose so naturally in her for

174 · AARON GWYN

Grandam or Mistress Anne. There was a meanness in her mother; there was something hard.

"Listen, now," her grandam said, "anything gets them folks to take a better interest in her is all to the good. And don't you go getting crossways over it."

Her mother said, "And how will it be for her among her own? This attention will set her apart. Just you watch."

"Shoo," said her grandam, "you don't know."

"Mark it," her mother said.

"You mark this here, missy: somebody or other's jealous."

She waited for her mother to say that she wasn't, but instead the woman rose and left the room.

Her grandam muttered to herself a while. Cecelia stood from her pallet, crept over and climbed into bed beside her.

"Yes," her grandam said, "you come here, baby," and Cecelia laid her head on the woman's shoulder, her grandam's arm around her. She bent to kiss Cecelia's brow.

"You are a clever-loving girl. You're my little augur."

When her grandam passed that spring, Cecelia cried and cried. She was losing her only friend. Her grandam had always spoken right at her like the two of them were girls.

And there was that close feeling, that great soft sweetness. Her grandam's freckled cheeks. Her brown, shining eyes.

Anne comforted Cecelia and held her as she wept. She said she'd always loved Cecelia's grandmother—a fine woman who served the Haverfords without flutter or fuss.

Her mother was no comfort at all. She seemed relieved Grandam was finally gone.

"There'll be changes now," she told Cecelia. "It's a considerable amount of suffering in this world. Hear me, girl: this ain't the last of it."

She lectured Cecelia about the dangers of these books she worshipped. They weren't natural. They took us away from each other.

"Why you want to sit round staring at scribbles? You think that is life?"

Cecelia couldn't explain. It was like going to a place inside yourself where another life sparked. You dreamed, but weren't sleeping. Voices talked, but there wasn't any sound.

One morning, she met Anne in the parlor for her daily lesson and found the woman searching the room, overturning pillows on the settee.

Anne turned and saw her. She said, "Do you remember where we put your book, honey?"

"No'um," she said.

"Did you take it to your mama's room?"

"No'um. It's always on yon table."

Anne stood for several minutes with her brow furrowed. Then she walked over to the bookcase, ran a finger along the spines and took down a slender book with a blue cover.

"We'll let Mr. Webster instruct us," she said.

This new volume was called *The American Spelling Book* and in addition to the alphabet it had tables with words of one syllable—*big, dig, fig, pig, wig*—and words of two syllables—*glo ry, gi ant, gra vy, gru el*—along with verse for children, teaching them to know their duty:

A bad life will make a bad end.
He must live well that will die well.
He doth live ill that doth not mend.
In time to come we must do no ill.

One day, this book too was gone. Anne looked and looked, but it was no great disappointment to Cecelia as she'd already learned its lessons and committed a good deal of the pages to memory.

She was too big to sit on Anne's lap anymore. Now they sat side by side, Cecelia reading to her mistress from Aesop's

Fables, pausing only when she happened on a word she didn't know. At which point Anne would hold the book at arm's length to tell her the meaning of *quantity* or *obstruction* or *transgress.*

But when this volume went missing, Master Haverford became involved: the book had been a gift from his grandfather and he suspected Cecelia had stolen it. He sat her down and questioned her at length.

"And you will swear you did not take it?"

"She didn't," Anne said, who seemed upset that her husband would even accuse her.

Haverford gave his wife a look.

"Am I thrashing the child?" he asked. "Let her answer."

"I swear," Cecelia told him. "I touch nothing without Mistress's leave."

Haverford said that was very well. But until the book turned up, there'd be no more lessons.

She would've rather he'd beaten her. The lessons were the best part of the day—not just the learning, but showing her mistress how well she'd learned, that she was just as clever as Grandam always said.

But the mystery was soon solved: Aesop was discovered under a head of rotting cabbage in the refuse pile. A further excavation unearthed Webster's blue-backed speller, then the first primer that had disappeared. All three books were badly damaged and Haverford put his servants under such threat of lashing that the story came out: how Cecelia's mother had been seeing digging through the garbage heap, depositing items in it.

When asked if this was true, her mother offered no defense. She said she'd accept her stripes without complaint.

Only, there wouldn't be any stripes. Cecelia met Anne the next morning, hoping to resume her lessons, but her mistress was sitting there very quiet. Her face was streaked by tears.

She glanced up and saw Cecelia standing in the doorway.

She stretched a hand towards her and said, "Come to me, sweet girl."

The woman told her that some day she would have a man of her own. She'd see how they got peculiar notions wedged in their brains, and once they did, there was no dislodging them.

She said Cecelia's mother was on her way to Richmond. She would serve another family now.

Then she said something else, but Cecelia didn't hear. The world started to shimmer. There was a glow at the edges of things.

I have caused this, she thought, panic climbing the back of her throat.

That night she lay in the room she'd shared all her life with Grandam and her mother—still on the pallet; she couldn't bear the thought of being in the bed by herself—her eyes open as the room went dark, then darker. It had never occurred to her how much she'd relied on her mother's spirit, the presence of her. The woman was hard, but it was the hardness of bedrock, and now Cecelia felt her own foundation crumbling. She had never been afraid before. She'd never been alone.

It went on like that for some time. It seemed that anything she touched might molder beneath her hand. This chair. The arm of it right here. There hardly seemed to be any substance to it at all.

Sta bil i ty.

Firm ness.

Which was the only thing that seemed to help: finding a word to contain the shape of her thoughts or fears or feelings. This *des pair*—case it in a box of six sides. This *horr or*.

And then she met her mistress in the parlor one morning and Anne was holding the thickest book she'd ever seen.

It was a poem called *The Odyssey*—that meant journey, Anne said—and it was the story of a man stranded far from home. He had to undergo trials while returning to his family, terrible trials with monsters and witches and strange transformations. Men turned into beasts and back again. A woman wove her fate and unloomed it every night.

And there was such courage in this strange, glorious tale. Odysseus was courageous and clever, and when you read his exploits, so were you. You feared with him, loved with him, passing through danger and joy. After a while, the Poem seemed to live inside you.

She wondered if the opposite could happen. And then it did.

It wasn't your mother you missed, but *Pen el o pe*.

It wasn't Haverford you kept an eye on, but *Pol y phem us*.

You weren't a slave girl of nine years, but a king who journeyed far and wide, a Wand'rer in lands remote.

That was useful, wasn't it? A life you could endure.

Take it in bits as short as syllables—the fear and panic, the loneliness and hurt— wrapping each second in poetry, line by line by line.

Duncan Lammons

—Texas, 1841—

Juan had a smoothbore British musket which he carried in a scabbard made from an old pant leg. While this might have been a lethal instrument in the Old World where men formed up in ranks to mass their fire and hurl volleys, in a company where you had to aim a weapon rather than merely level it, he might as well've carried a mesquite branch. I decided he ought to make friends with our Kentucky rifle.

I procured him a good cap-lock—John Hall's patent—and zeroed the gun myself, filing down the front sight until it would shoot palm-sized groups at 100 yards.

A few mornings after he'd related the tale of his abduction by the Berbers, I shook him awake before the other men had risen and the two of us walked down from camp to where I'd set up several slabs of limestone against a grassy hill, the white rock standing out against the green—a brighter target than any Indian would present, I assure you.

I spent some time instructing him on how to judge distance, read the wind, measure charges and patch balls, and when at last we got down to shooting, Juan impressed me yet again—not for any special talent he had for marksmanship, but for his ability to take in everything I told him without question or argument. I knew from long, frustrated experience that if a man has ever touched a firearm, you can hardly teach him a thing. Or if you do manage it, you'd best prepare to listen to all he thinks he knows on the subject.

And so, simply by virtue of being able to receive instruction,

Juan proved almost a prodigy. I told him to lie on his belly and he lay on his belly. I told him to get his heels down and down they went. If I'd tried to improve McClusky's marksmanship, or even Levi's, I'd have had to argue like a senator. But in a few hours, Juan was shooting very well indeed, and I knew with several more sessions, he'd be a dependable rifleman, though you could never guarantee how a man would hold up under fire. You didn't really know how you'd react yourself.

* * *

Of course, we were all eager for Juan to resume his story of his time among the Berbers. Or all except McClusky, who regarded our new trooper with a combination of curiosity and disdain.

And yet, it was the Irishman himself who bid Juan to continue his tale, glancing over at him as we sat round the fire after supper.

"So," McClusky said, "you were in the clutches of pirates and pashas and the rest. What then, Spaniard? How'd you come to cross an ocean and grace us with your presence?"

Juan smoked his pipe.

He said, "It is another story, how I traveled the sea."

"Aye," said McClusky. "I'm asking you to tell it. Or do you need more time to cook it up?"

I shook my head.

"Nevermind him," I told Juan. "It's some men have a peculiar way of showing interest."

Juan stared into the fire. The men were all watching him. When we'd just about decided no sequel was forthcoming, Juan said: "I was made woodcutter."

"How's that?" McClusky said.

"A woodcutter," Juan told him. "For the pasha. He sends

me to work in the hills behind the city. To cut timber for the ships. To mend what is broken."

"You built ships?" Levi said.

Juan shook his head. "I gather the wood that builds them."

He puffed at his pipe a few moments, then began to unfold a tale of labor so backbreaking I could feel it in my joints. Lacking any rivers to raft the lumber they cut to the shipyards, they were forced to drag tree trunks over hill and dale, working under threat of the driver's whip.

"And I am realizing," he said, "why the pasha has chosen me, that it is for the strength I have built climbing trees, gathering bananas for mi abuela. All the climbing has make me very strong. And so, I am unsure again of my path: mi abuela or Mamá? Both have brought great troubles." He stopped and looked around at us. "What is the way a man must live his life? The Christian or pagano? Is it the devil who threatens our soul or the Lumia mi abuela talks of? I am between these two and cannot decide."

I cleared my throat. "Did you ever consider doing like your priest and swapping out?"

"To become a musulmán?"

"Jesus, Cap," said Levi. "Are you forgetting how he said they confirmed the padre?"

Juan said, "I tell myself whatever is the case, I will not take up the ways of the Musulmanes. It will be Mamá's or mi abuela's. But never the man who have made an esclavo of me."

"Fair enough," I said.

Juan nodded. He told us how he labored from the age of twelve to fifteen, hauling trees from the hills around Algiers. And then how the pasha had him brought to the palace one day.

"I am to be a gift," he said. "To the divan in Istanbul. I will board a ship that very day."

"And what's a *divan*?" Levi asked. "Is that a lord?"

"He is un agente. In the Sultan's gobierno. The pasha smiles at me and says my life is becoming better now."

And so young Juan was sent to Istanbul.

He painted us quite the picture of that faraway city, a great forest of spires and turrets, sloping down to the ship masts of the harbors where an orange sun sank into bright blue water. The domed temples where the muezzins called worshippers from their minarets. And at night, candles in the tower windows like a hundred thousand stars.

He was taken to the divan's home—a kind man, Juan said, but he barely got to know him. His second week in the city, the divan hired him out to a consul from Sweden.

"Hired you out?" I asked.

"Yes. The divan tells me I am to be a servant for this man and his wife. And so I am."

"He paid the divan for your time?"

"Si."

"But not you, I don't reckon."

"No," he said. "Not me."

"Did the Swede speak Spanish?" Levi asked.

"He speaks everything," Juan said. "Ingles, frances, persa. His own language, of course. It is his job to do so."

"Like an ambassador?" I said.

"Very much."

"Well," said Levi, "least you weren't strictly in the hands of Moslems anymore. Or not as much, I suppose."

Juan drew on his pipe. He looked into the fire. Two tongues of flame flickered in his eyes.

"Not at much," he said. "Though I will wish it."

"Why'd you wish that?" Levi said. "Had to be some kind of improvement for you. Swedes are white, ain't they?"

"Si," said Juan. "The embajador William Nilsson; his wife is called Saga. For fifteen years I am their servant. But it is not improved. It is a time of hell."

He told us how he lived in the same residence as the Swede and his wife. Here, everything had to come up to the standard of the big bugs: the fixings served at their table, all the silverware and crockery, the pillows and cushions and furniture.

And their servants as well. He brought in a tutor for young Juan, a scholar named Ahmed—a small, spectacled man, gentle in his speech and graceful in comportment. It was Ahmed who expanded Juan's rudimentary grasp of the written word to encompass the Latin Bible, English poetry, the French and Turkish tongues. He taught Juan his lovely manners and instructed him how to wait at table, even schooled him in the art of grease wrestling, the Turk's form of grappling. Juan developed great affection for the man and he proved a fine pupil.

And as Juan was describing his education and the clerical duties he performed for the consul, McClusky stopped him.

"You said this was a hell, Spaniard."

Juan smoked his pipe and studied the Irishman a moment. "It is the worst time of my life."

"I don't see it," McClusky said.

"What don't you see?"

McClusky shook his head. "You tell us you were taken from your home by Moslem pirates, branded and sold like a mule and set to work dragging trees. You watched your priest's bod peeled by Saracen daggers. And here now you're clerking for an ambassador and studying poetry like a monk. Where's the hell in that?"

Well, for once McClusky had a point. Juan's fortune seemed to've changed in every respect.

"There are very many hells," Juan said.

McClusky snorted.

"And is this one of them?" he said, gesturing at us. "Lounging here with the lads telling stretchers? Do these embers conjure the eternal bonfire for you as well? Or might you be level-full of shite?"

I thought the Irishman had gone a bit far with his needling, but McClusky knew no other way to go. He purely loved to goad a fellow.

But Juan was a hard one to rattle and instead of explaining these many hell fires he'd referenced, he skipped his story forward fifteen years to tell us how he was released from bondage and came to sojourn with us in our Republic.

And here again he difficulted us, for after hearing the horrible tale of his abduction, we all expected that the account of his escape from the hands of his tormentors would make our hair stand on end.

But the story of his deliverance was simply this: "In the year 1830, the Sultan issues a firman freeing esclavos europeos throughout the Empire, and I am allowed to take a ship to the port of Nice."

"Then what?" Levi said.

"Then I am free," Juan told him.

We all just sat staring at him.

"That's no kind of ending," Levi said.

Juan shrugged. "It is what happens."

The men began to mumble all round. This conclusion didn't suit them either. They commenced telling him so.

Isaac Casner said, "That won't do at all, Mister Juan."

"No," said Juan. "It is not a story Texans enjoy to hear. I must rather tell that I am wrapped in a kafan and taken for burial to rise and swim to freedom. Something of this kind. Some historia salvaje. If it is a law that releases me, the Texan is not interest."

McClusky had been shaking his head to where I thought it'd come off his shoulders.

"You must take these men for fools," he said.

"No," said Juan. "Not fools. They are Texans."

I said, "I think we expected something else, is all. Being how you were snatched up. I think we'd imagined you'd absquatulate a little more . . ." I trailed off, hunting a word.

"Dramatic-like," Levi said.

Again, Juan smiled. He began to refill his pipe and I knew that his story was over. Or, at least, this was all the story we would get.

* * *

I couldn't get to sleep that night. I tossed and turned Juan's tale in my mind. I felt that if McClusky hadn't started to interrupt and insult him, Juan might have told us about the torments of Istanbul. Perhaps not doing so was his way of punishing the Irishman. Perhaps, if it was just the two of us talking, he'd tell me.

Around midnight, I stole across camp and knelt there beside him. Was I really going to wake him just so he could finish his story?

He said, "Captain."

Soon as his eyes opened, I lost my nerve. I wasn't going to pester him about the hell he'd referenced—the *many hells*, I think he'd said. There was a darker pain in him than what came from being taken from his home and family, darker even than the torturous labor they'd set him to. I couldn't bring myself to prod it.

So, instead I whispered, "Would you mind telling me why you settled on Texas?"

"Settled?" he said.

"Why you came here," I explained. "I reckon you might've gone anyplace you liked."

He raised up on his elbow. "I came for the property," he said.

"The land payment?"

He nodded. "I hear that your Republic pays its men in land."

"It was that important to you? Owning some land?"

"Very much," he said. "For twenty years I have nothing of my own, nothing whatsoever. All the time I am thinking about a house that is mine. I lie at night and fantasear it: a little property, a little home. I think to have this one day might be to have myself again. It is hard to explique, but it seems to me the reverse of being un esclavo. If esclavos own nothing at all, to own a thing is to be free." His head canted to one side. "Do you understand?"

"Yes," I said, and my throat thickened with regard for him, thinking of how it must have been for him all those years. He didn't have to go any further into describing the hell he'd endured.

I felt understood quite well.

CECELIA

—TEXAS, 1837–1840—

The land Samuel surveyed was beautiful: lush and very green. The mesquites were flowered out, all the branches drooping. Thick pasture grass for the horses, the soil black as ink.

Something had shifted between the two of them. She thought the shift had started that day the Indians encircled them. Or maybe even earlier. Maybe the shift started when Samuel let her hold the gun. Perhaps something was already shifting when Samuel took her from the planter, or in that moment she stood on the stump, staring at him toward the back of the crowd.

They lived in a dugout the first several weeks, then started building a jacal. The two of them would work all day, cutting trees for timber, gathering sandstone for the walls. She liked searching for rocks, seeing how they fit together, the grain so rough your palms cracked and bled. It felt good, solving the puzzle of it, watching the shanty rise out of the earth.

At night, they slept on pallets. Two pallets on opposite sides of the room, though they were never more than ten feet apart. He never tried to touch her; he never raised his voice. They worked in the daytime and cooked together at dusk, woke the next day and had their coffee. A comfort rose up between them. That's how she thought of it: comfort like a warm, rising tide.

You need to enjoy this, she thought. You've come so far.

And that was true. She marveled at how far she'd travelled. Texas was a dream, but the rest of the earth a nightmare.

She started having those too, which she thought was strange, because, even in the worst of times, even in Mississippi, she'd never had bad dreams. Maybe if your life was a nightmare, you didn't need them when you slept. Maybe if your days were a fantasy, the nights paid you back with terror.

In the early morning, Samuel would hunt and fish, carry back game for their meals. Around the middle of May, he cleared ten acres and started planting corn. He said they could have squash the following year, maybe a little cotton, a couple dozen rows. She could be in charge of that if she liked.

"Be nice to spin some cloth, wouldn't it?"

"You spin some cloth," she told him. Just the mention of cotton made her furious, and she refused to speak to him the rest of the day. She felt that old panic pumping in her veins. She didn't say a single word until suppertime when he looked over at her and said, "I can plant the cotton."

"That's good," she told him. "Because I won't touch another cotton seed long as I live. I won't hoe or pick or clean."

He stared at her several moments, head tilted to one side.

"Well," he said. "You don't have to."

* * *

What was she to this man? What would she become?

Lying there one night, she raised up on her elbow and glanced over at him sleeping on his pallet. Moonlight turned his blond hair to silver. He still had something of the boy about him, though he was more powerfully built than any man she'd seen.

There is no one like him, she thought. Not in all the earth.

Her throat went tight and she swallowed to loosen it. She lay back down and closed her eyes.

When she woke the next morning, the smell of autumn was in the air, and Samuel commenced talking about the cabin he'd

build them, a good log cabin with puncheon floors, better than
bare dirt by a mile.

He began cutting trees on the hill, hacking down cedars
and stripping away their limbs. Clearing ground, levelling it.
One day he rode into the town of Bastrop, and when he
returned a few hours later, there was a tall black man riding
beside him on a chestnut mare. The two of them spent the
afternoon hefting the logs Sam had cut, moving them into
place. Over the coming weeks, the cabin went up like a spell
had raised it. The black man's name was Jonas. He and Samuel
would ride off in the mornings and return around noontime,
pulling the trunks of pine trees behind their horses. They
hewed these into boards for roof and siding.

She watched very closely, trying to learn the method of it,
but Jonas was so skilled at the labor, it was difficult to see what
he was doing. She'd fetch them water from the stream or take
up kettles of coffee. Jonas would smile and thank her. His manner was very familiar to her, like the hands she'd known in
Virginia: courteous, deferential.

And then one afternoon, when Sam walked into the woods
to retrieve the axe he'd mislaid, Jonas turned to her and all the
deference left his face like a mask slipping.

He cleared his throat, coughing into his hand.

"There's a colony across the Rio," he said. "A whole heap
of runaways."

"Pardon me?" she said.

"North of the Sierra Madre," he said, the slave bleeding
from his voice. "Near the town Monclova. In Coahuila, there.
Thousands of us living free."

"I don't understand."

"Yes, you do."

She stood there a moment. She couldn't see Sam anymore,
but she could hear him crunching through the woods.

"Is it very far?" she whispered.

190 - AARON GWYN

"It's six hundred miles," he said.

"That might as well be a million," she told him. "And I don't know this country."

"I'd take you," he said. "They's folks do it all the time."

"Then why are you here to tell me this? Why haven't you gone yourself?"

His eyes roved down from her face, to her chest, her hips, then roved their way back up.

"I been waiting," he said.

She shook her head. He was making her awfully nervous.

"Mister Whipple's place," he said. "Not three mile from here. Last farm fore you come to Bastrop. If it's a night you can get away, you come to the quarters. Whipple don't keep a watch on us."

"You are dangerous," she said.

"Last farm fore the town of Bastrop. Not three mile. You come get me anytime."

Then Sam emerged from the woods with his axe in hand, walked over to where they stood, and Jonas's mask slid back in place. When he spoke again, his speech had darkened. The entire conversation they'd just had was like a bubble drifting off, vanishing in the air.

* * *

They finished the cabin a few weeks later. She was alone with Jonas twice more, and he brought up the colony both times. She didn't doubt the truth of what he said at all; it was the six hundred miles that bothered her.

And Jonas himself, who'd likely be the same as Jubal if she gave him half a chance.

Black or white, she thought. If they have that mess dangling between their legs, their brains are pure corruption. They can't see any farther than getting you on your back.

And yet, that didn't account for Sam. If all their hearts were selfish, why hadn't he tried her?

He's waiting, she thought. Lying for his chance.

But hadn't he had chance aplenty? He could overpower her if he took a mind.

He cannot outthink you, though. He knows that you are smarter.

Oh, I am smart, all right. Sit around and argue myself into a stupor. I am the smartest one in all the world. Run five times, caught five times. Just so smart I can hardly stand it.

And why was she caught? It was not just lack of knowledge that did her in. It was that she'd run from white to white—this white place to that white place. She'd never had a destination outside the States, never had the chance of reaching another country.

And here is this woodsman to teach you things you didn't know. Here are opportunities you never had.

Here was Jonas with his stories of a runaway colony.

She didn't trust Jonas, but she didn't have to trust him.

Use him, she thought. Use his dangling brain. Use Samuel with his lack of fear and his know-how for a thousand things.

But you are free now. For the very first time.

Am I? she wondered. What if it's just a story to keep me here.

She woke one morning on her pallet and sat there chewing all of this. Samuel was already on a hunt, the cabin quiet except for the creak of joists when a breeze blew through. The smell of cedar was overpowering. You grew used to it throughout the day, then went to sleep, and woke with the scent in your nostrils like something had crawled inside your skull.

She crossed the room to fill the kettle and saw he'd left water in it for her. He had stoked the fire before he stepped out, and there was a handful of beans that he'd pounded to dust with the coffee stone; all she had to do was put the kettle on the grate.

She stood there looking at it for several moments. She felt irritated with him, though he'd done nothing to warrant this frustration.

If he was just like the others, it would be no problem. She could have scraped him into that bucket with everyone else she despised. The bucket made sense. You didn't have to waste thought on the bucket-people anymore.

But this man wouldn't fit in the bucket.

He steals you, then asks what you want to do. Carries you off to Texas, then lets you set up house. He's white and free, has never known the hand of slavery, and here he sets out coffee fixings, tiptoeing about to let you sleep.

You must use him, she thought. Learn his fearlessness till you can wear it like a skin.

* * *

That winter, she had him teach her a host of things. How to load and shoot the rifle. How to judge distance and read the wind.

"What does wind have to do with it?" she asked.

"It pushes the ball," he said. "Shoves it wide."

This seemed unlikely, that wind could catch a rifle ball in flight, but a lot of what she learned from him was different from the world she knew. You tanned deer hides with the animal's own brains. You knew where a bear was feeding from its scat. When you got lost in the piney woods of that country, you could discover your trail by circling back on it, searching for the smallest signs: change of color, needles kicked out of place, the scars your shoes left on bare dirt or fallen branches. Always keeping the sun between yourself and your footprints. He was so good at it. He read tracks like a sentence across the page.

It occurred to her that the things they knew and didn't know fit together quite perfectly, and this understanding unsettled her even more. His patience was unnerving, the fact that he was willing to teach her to hunt, and shoot, and track. That when it came down to it he was teaching her how to run.

Who is he? she'd wonder, lying there on her pallet those winter nights, having learned yet another skill that showed her how doomed her previous attempts had been.

She thought, Maybe I have become used to such poor treatment that anything else undoes me.

She felt guilty about this, and that made her furious.

He was toying with her; he was driving her mad. He saw what other white men hadn't: the way to truly destroy her was with generosity and care.

She lay there and turned that over in her mind. She drew a deep breath and blew it toward the ceiling.

No, Cecelia. You are toying with yourself.

Spring put buds on the tree limbs and the days grew warm. One morning, Sam was teaching her to fire the pistol. She held it just like he showed her, planting her feet exactly as he said. But when she pulled the trigger and the gun went off, a stinging grit flew into her eyes.

She dropped the pistol and began to claw at her face. There was a feeling like ants beneath her eyelids, burrowing back into her skull.

Sam's voice was in her ear, saying, "Don't paw at it, now. Don't scratch." He got hold of her wrists and held them very tight.

"Try and look at me," he said.

She couldn't do that, couldn't get her eyelids open. She tried to pull away from him, but he was so strong.

"Easy now," he said. "Open up for me."

She growled at him, the ants digging farther in. She felt his beard brush up against her face, then something warm and wet swiping her left eye, working between the lids. It certainly wasn't pleasant, but he was taking the sting away, bit by bit.

When she blinked, her vision was blurry. Sam had let go of her wrists and was holding her head in both hands. He leaned closer and went to work on her other eye. She'd thought he had a damp cloth, but there was no cloth. He'd used his tongue to lick out the grit, and here he started doing it again.

It was a ridiculous thing for someone to do to you, but as it was helping, she let him lick away. He went from one eye to the other, back and forth, lapping her eyes with his tongue.

She started to cry. It wasn't fear, but relief. She realized she was going to be all right, and she realized that she couldn't take this anymore. The closeness, the confusion. She wouldn't lie awake wondering what she was to this man. She wouldn't do it.

Tonight, she thought. Last farm before the town of Bastrop. I'll wait until he falls asleep.

And so, she lay on her pallet that night, watching the fire-light flicker over his face. It did not seem real there could be someone like this. You won't last, she thought. The world won't let you. That stirred something inside her and she knew that it was time.

She moved about the cabin silent as smoke, eased the door open, stepped outside, started easing the door back into place. The hinges creaked, and she stopped and stood there, her heart like a fist, forcing herself to breathe.

Out in the cedarwood stable, she bridled Honey, draped the saddle blanket over her, and then the saddle. She wrapped the latigo, drew the cinch tight, fit the hole over the tongue, then pulled back-slack to lock everything into place.

She was aboard the horse, about a dozen yards from the stable, when she stopped and looked back at the cabin. There was a soft breeze coming through the trees, a little cool.

Don't, she thought.

She sat there. She felt like she was making a mistake.

But wasn't it a mistake to stay?

Last farm before Bastrop, she told herself. Turn around and ride.

He'll wonder about me.

Then let him wonder. You didn't ask for this.

No, she thought. I didn't know it was something you could ask for. I didn't even know it existed.

And here she was running.

Riding, the voice corrected her. You are *riding*.

But she wasn't riding. She was sitting there staring back.

* * *

He was still asleep when she opened the cabin door and stepped inside. Still asleep when she crossed the room and pulled his knife from its sheath. She stepped up beside the pallet. Her heart was going like mad.

Cut him, she thought. If you cut him, he won't have power over you.

He doesn't have power over me now.

Then why is your heart galloping? Why do you tremble?

Do it, the voice inside her wheezed. Cut him quick and deep.

She tightened her grip on the knife handle, angled the blade along her thigh. Should she stab him or should she slash him? She watched the light flicker across his pulsing throat, arguing with herself.

When he spoke, it startled her so badly she nearly dropped the knife.

"What is it?" he said.

She stood there. She didn't think he could see the knife, but she tucked the blade farther behind her leg.

"Did you hear something?" he asked, though he didn't

196 - AARON GWYN

make any attempt to get up. His eyes were like pools of blue light. She could stop them from ever shining again.

"What do you want with me?" she said.

He didn't say anything, just lay there staring up.

"Must you own my body to become someone? Am I the start of this for you?"

He blinked a few times. The firelight flickered.

He began speaking in a low voice, almost a whisper. It was never his intention to own anyone.

"It was not your intention, but what did you take me for? Why did you steal me from that man?"

"I never planned it," he said.

Her frustration with his answer felt like it would split her skull.

"Here I am, Samuel, whatever you intended. You say I'm free, but where is the proof of it? I won't be someone's property. I won't live that way again."

He closed his eyes and said: "I saw you that day, being pulled down the street. I didn't know what I was going to do about it, but I couldn't let it be. I asked a man, and he told me where you'd be offered for sale. I loitered around, and then a few days later, there you stood."

He'd said all of this before. She was getting nowhere. She'd end up opening his throat just to keep him from talking.

He told her how sad and lovely she'd looked. He started to nudge his way through the crowd, but by then they'd led her away.

"I asked someone what'd happened to you, and this one man pointed to that dandy and said, 'He's what happened, mister.'"

So, Samuel had approached this man—Childers, she reminded him.

"Childers," Sam said. "And I asked the same question you put to me."

"Which?" she said.

"What he meant to do with you. He looked at me like he didn't know what I was talking about. By the time we got back to where they had you, it was all picking up speed, didn't seem like there was any price—"

"And then you took me," she said. "You say I can go anywhere I like, but here I am with you. It doesn't matter if you paid twelve hundred dollars or no dollars at all. Don't you see that?"

He stared up at her. He had no idea how close he was to getting murdered.

Then he rolled off the pallet, stepped over to the table, pulled out the little drawer in it, and removed a folded sheet of paper. He walked back to the pallet, handed it to her, then lay back down.

"There," he said, as if this settled everything.

She didn't need to unfold it. She knew what it was.

It was such an odd thing, holding the deed to yourself. She'd never seen such a thing before, much less held it, and she had the sense that reading it would only make it more powerful.

"What do you mean for me to do with this?" she said.

"You can do whatever," he said, and there was a despair in his voice. "You want me to chaperon you into Mexico, I'll chaperon you into Mexico."

"You'd do that?" she said.

"I'll take you anywhere you want. Lord took everbody ever meant anything to me, so why wouldn't He take you too?"

She shook her head. It is always the Lord with these people. They can't see they are the ones.

She was about to tell him this when a thought presented itself. It made her feel very strange.

But then she was moving, inching toward the fire, watching Samuel all the while. The light flickered in his eyes, and she

198 · AARON GWYN

bent over and set her bill of sale on the coals. It caught instantly, tongues of orange flame curling up the corners—like a spider shriveling—but still he lay there, his eyes sad or hopeful, she couldn't quite decide. Her hands were still shaking. She'd forgotten she still held the knife, and now Sam nodded to it.

"Did you feel like you needed to kill me?" he said.

"I don't know," she told him. "I don't know what I thought. If I am to live here, it will be because I truly choose it."

"Yes," he told her. "Because you choose."

Duncan Lammons

—Texas, 1844—

'44 was another bad Indian year, though the next one would be even worse. I'd been hearing of Captain Jack Hays for a while now, and that winter I finally met the gentleman, a short, spare man who looked more like the barrister he'd been than the fearsome Indian fighter folks remember.

I have heard it said that the Rangers never had much difficulty dealing with the Comanche, but I am here to tell you that we had quite a lot. The ranger companies were bested by them again and again. A good deal of the credit goes to the courage and horsemanship of that tribe, but there is a share that can rightly be attributed to the sheer idiocy of our tactics. The Texians had defeated the Mexican army by relying on the rifled musket, so when it came time for us to fight horse Indians, we fell back on that trusted weapon.

And that was our mistake. You cannot fire a long rifle from horseback, and you certainly can't reload one in the saddle. Early scrimmages all had a murderous similarity. The rangers would encounter a war band on the plains, dismount, stake their horses, and then prone out on the ground with their rifles. Putting a ball through a target you don't know the exact distance of is no easy thing but doing so on a moving target is nigh unto impossible. And the Comanches were a target that did not just *move*: they swung and zagged about at a gallop, nimble as dancers, sometimes shifting to the offside of their painted ponies and using them for cover.

The Texans would fire a volley with the Indians wheeling out of range, and then, as they set about reloading, the Comanches would close the distance quicker than any white man ever dreamed, and ride right over the anxious Anglos. Entire companies were rubbed out this way, with bow and lance and club. On seeing a band of Comanche on the prairie, I used to turn and tell my troopers, "Any man dismounts, I will shoot him myself."

All of that changed in '43 when a peculiar piece of weaponry fell into the hands of Jack Hays. A northern ne'er-do-well by the name of Samuel Colt had managed to produce a five-shot revolver at his factory in Paterson, New Jersey. These days, it is all *Sam Colt this* and *Sam Colt that*, but I'd remind such talkers that when the man manufactured that first batch of pistols, he could scarcely give them away. I don't think he made more than a thousand. Somehow, he gulled the United States army into buying these, but the army considered the weapons too temperamental for service, could not contrive a use for them, and they in turn unloaded the bulk of the guns on the short-lived Texas Navy, thinking they'd rooked our Republic into buying so many paper weights.

When General Houston disbanded the Navy, those pistols found their way to Jack Hays and his rangers, and that shrewd man saw what others hadn't—here was the weapon that would end the threat.

And so, we began to hear how Captain Jack took the fight to the enemy. Each of his troopers were armed with two Colt pistols, and whenever they encountered a Comanche war band, the brave captain would order his rangers to charge. If the men in his company thought better of it, they kept it to themselves, though there were surely some who reckoned that anyone who'd charge mounted Comanches on the open prairie was a fool.

But they were too afraid of Hays to say so, and the captain led them toward the Indians at a gallop, telling them not to discharge their pistols until they were riding among their foe. The Comanche, expecting they were about to collect a fine crop of vouchers from these white fools, rode right into the Texans, whereupon ole Jack issued his famous orders, "Powder burn'em, boys!"

Well, the Indians had never seen firearms that did not have to be reloaded after every shot, and each ranger let loose five rounds quick as he could cock the hammers and squeeze. Those braves rode into a curtain of death, the rangers not losing a single man in that engagement, and thus the tactics of the ranging companies were changed forever, and the course of our Republic's history as well.

Two of these Colt Patersons came into my possession, and as I was the captain with the most terms of service at the time, I was able to procure a pistol for each of my troopers. I was seldom sober in those days, and with a courage born of corn liquor, we rode against the Comanche, and Apache, and the Caddo, and any other poor devils we happened across. My entire impulse in those days was to ride and shoot and drink. I told myself I was doing service to the Republic I'd fought to establish. Encountering the hot swarm of our pistol balls, the Indians moved west, and the line of settlement with them. New territory opened, land that months earlier no one dared venture into, as the ranging companies pushed the Indians toward the sunset.

* * *

We were camped one starless night just north of Austin, when our scout, Isaac Casner, came trotting in, circled the main fire and began calling for help. Uncle Isaac was a plump man who tipped the beam at two hundred pounds and was not easily spooked. Up to just that moment, I'd hadn't seen him spook at all.

I'd been sitting on my bedroll, visiting with Juan as had become my custom of an evening. I stood up and cleared my throat.

"Over here, Isaac. What's the trouble?"

He walked his horse over and when he got close I saw an arrow protruding from the animal's flank.

"Captain," he said, "I think we're fixing to get ambushed."

Hearing this intelligence, I ordered the fires doused and the horses brought in. The troopers began to rouse and see to their weapons and soon we were gathered in an enormous ring, ready to fight or flee, whatever was required.

"What happened?" I asked Isaac.

Isaac said, "I was out on yon ridge when I seen shadows moving in the grass and then that arrow hits Little Billy."

McClusky, who had begun to consider himself an expert on the Indian, said, "What kind were they, Ike? Waco? Comanche?"

"I don't know," Isaac said. "I never stopped to ask. I took off riding and here I am."

It wasn't like the Comanche to loose an arrow before they had stampeded your mounts and it wasn't like them to miss a rider and hit his horse. Horses were a currency for them, and to some bands they were outright family.

We spent the night waiting for our camp to be overrun and by the time morning rolled round, our nerves were frayed and we were jumpy as cats.

Or most of us, anyway. When the sky paled, I looked over and saw that Juan had lain down at some point and gone to sleep.

I walked over and toed him with my boot.

"You get a good rest?" I said.

"Muy bien," he told me, smiling.

"That's good. You feel up to a little Indian fighting this morning, or would you rather sleep a little more?"

"I am at your service, Captain. What would you have of me?"

Well, I wasn't entirely sure. I wondered whether we ought to just let the previous night's attack go unanswered. A certain type of man might have thought Uncle Isaac had gotten off rather cheaply. But as the purpose of our company was to stop depredations before they occurred, I decided we'd best go take a look.

And so, I made one of the worst decisions of my cap- taincy—perhaps of my life. Which is saying something: it is a long, lurid list.

"What do you think?" McClusky asked.

"Well," I said, "I reckon we ought at least ride out and see how the cat jumps."

Which suited the Irishman just fine. Course, he didn't need a reason to hunt Indians, would've killed any one of them for a fid of tobacco.

We debouched along a cattle trail that led up through the scrub. The ground was wet and you could see the narrow prints of prairie wolves, but the Indians we were looking for knew better than to ride over bare dirt when they didn't have to and it took us the better part of the morning to cut their sign.

It was Juan who smoked them, finding the tracks of unshod ponies at the bottom of a gulch, then a twig stuck in the dirt with one of its forks pointing west—a sign the Comanche used to guide members of their band who'd fallen behind. We gath- ered round for a council of war. All agreed we were looking at Indians, but as to whether they were the same Indians who'd attacked Isaac, we were divided.

"It's them," said McClusky. "I've no doubt of it, Cap'n."

Juan knelt in the grass, inspecting the tracks more closely. He looked up at me. "I do not know," he said.

"I do," said McClusky.

Juan shook his head. "They might belong to many riders."

"But white ones," said McClusky. "What Christian rides a barefoot horse?"

"Could it not be Apache?" Juan asked.

McClusky snorted. "You've no more sense than a little nigger with a big navel. There's not an Apache north of the Colorado. The Comanche cleared them out ages ago."

I stood listening to them bicker, staring at the ground. I was unsettled for reasons that were mysterious to me, then and now, and should have broke off and led everyone back to camp. But in those days my greatest fear was not showing my troopers courage and a willingness to pursue the enemy.

So, whoever the tracks belonged to, we followed them the rest of the day.

It was long about the shank of the afternoon when we saw two riders sitting their horses in a cedar grove, two hundred yards out. I fetched up and the men stopped on either side of me. The Indians—for Indians they were—sat there studying us. We studied them right back.

I looked over at Isaac. "You see anyone you recognize?"

"I don't know, Captain. I never got a look at the man. Those are likely his cousins, though."

"Doesn't seem to me like these boys are on the prod," Levi said.

As he spoke, eight more Indians emerged from the woods, their painted ponies blending with the trees behind them so that their riders seemed to hover above the earth.

"Not on the prod, my arse," McClusky said. His sneer would've cut through marble.

"Cap," said Levi, "What are they doing?"

"Making me nervous," I said. "Hush and let me think."

But the Indians did nothing else, and as they'd yet to make a hostile demonstration, I was reluctant to initiate one myself. I was about to suggest we move to higher ground when all ten riders turned their horses and, slick as a whistle, began walking back to the tree line. And once they'd done so, I saw what I'd been unable to see before: each horse bore two riders on its back. Our foe had doubled right in front of our eyes and I was suddenly very proud of my indecision; we'd been outnumbered and hadn't known it.

"We're just going to let them mizzle on us?" Levi said.

"You bet we are," I said. "In case you hadn't noticed—"

I was interrupted by the sound of a gunshot. My horse started and when I got control of her, I looked over and saw McClusky lying in the grass with his rifle to his shoulder, a blue cloud drifting over him. I glanced back toward the Indians and saw several of the men had dismounted and were kneeling round a brave that McClusky had blown down.

The Irishman stood and began measuring out powder, just as casual as could be.

My hat felt too tight for my head. I was so angry I was shaking. I booted my horse over and stared down at him.

"You fool!" I barked. "Those men offered us no threat."

He just shrugged. "We'll be fighting them sooner or later, Cap'n. And I for one vote for sooner."

"You have no vote," I told him. "I ought to have you whipped."

"For what?" he said.

I started to tell him exactly what for, but then Levi got my attention.

"Cap," he said, "look yonder."

I looked. Nine of the Indians were approaching at a lope, and following behind them, seven braves on foot bearing lances. There had been a few hundred yards between us, but quick as you could blink, the riders covered half that distance. I thought if these weren't Comanches they were doing an awful fine impersonation.

"Be Jaysus," McClusky said, and the smug warrior from several moments before had vanished like smoke.

I had been in enough fights over the years to know the

advantage an attacker had. Once I knew a snarl was unavoidable, I had one rule and that was to *be first*: first to fire a volley, first to order a charge. You wanted to avoid a posture of defense at all costs.

These types of scrimmages were won or lost in a heartbeat, and in the time it took for my heart to kick the wall of my chest I saw our whole strategy go completely to blazes. The men grabbed their rifles and began to dismount—they seemed to have forgotten the new revolvers stuck in their belts. Besides me, the only man still in his saddle was Juan, all the others were already on their knees drawing aim with their muskets. One gun went off. Then several more. They'd failed to lead their targets, of course, and they'd missed them, of course, and Indians went wheeling around our flanks, four riders one way, five the other, and in a matter of seconds we were in a ring of shouting enemies. There was no immediate danger from those circling to our right—they were merely cutting off the possibility of our escape and couldn't use their bows from that side—but the four Indians moving left of us began popping arrows into our little band, holding their bows level with the horizon, calm as saints in a cemetery.

I yelled for the men to mount their horses, but they didn't hear. Jimmy Elkin dropped to his knees with an arrow jutting from his throat. Then Tom Cunningham went down.

The men had formed a line about a dozen feet in front of me and, having discharged their weapons, were standing now to load, fumbling with shot pouches or struggling to fit their ramrods into muzzles. I had no doubt a few had already dry-balled their rifles: when a trooper's blood is up, he will often forget to charge his gun. Many a gunsmith working on a dead soldier's musket has found four or five balls rammed down the barrel and not a grain of powder to drive them.

"Lanceros!" Juan shouted, pointing toward the Indians rushing up with their long, feathered spears.

Well, I had no intention of letting my boys get butchered like Christmas pigs. I booted my horse forward, shucked my right foot out of the stirrup and kicked young Levi in the back of the head, knocking his hat off and sending him staggering.

He said, "Hell-far, Cap!" but I kept on down the line. I caught Bob Thomas in the temple and Dick Wagner between the shoulders. I was aiming at Uncle Ike's shoulder when he turned around to catch my boot on the bridge of his nose.

"Mount up!" I yelled. "Mount up if you want to live!"

They began to do so. Ike's nose was badly broken, his beard sopped in bright blood. I heard him say, "We make it back to camp, you'll wish you hadn't done that, Captain," but I reckoned if we lived to see evening I'd shout and sing hosannas.

I pushed my horse to a gallop and made for the ring of Indians. I had it in contemplation to force a gap in our enemy's ranks, though I feared my horse had better sense than her rider and might very well throw me.

But a breach opened up as we approached, the Indians' horses swerving to avoid colliding with ours, and here we came bursting through—first me, then Juan, then Levi. I looked over my shoulder and saw Wagner, McClusky, and Bob Thomas make it as well. Dean Oden had just cleared the ring when his mount was shot from under him. It seemed to happen quite slowly: the horse's forelegs buckled and then the animal's body struck the earth, Dean pinned underneath it—one second he was on top of his horse, the next it was on top of him. And then it was like a dam had burst and Indians washed over Oden and I lost sight of him forever.

We went pounding out over the prairie at a gallop, the six of us leaning low over our horses' necks. Soon, the poor beasts were snorting; we were baking them, but there was no other remedy. As our mounts began to bush, the Comanches began catching up. To rights, they were riding among us, firing arrows.

208 - AARON GWYN

Here it is, I remember thinking. This is your death. I felt I had unfinished business to conduct, having failed to find Sam and speak my mind. I'd feared that such a confession would prove disastrous, but at just that moment, it seemed a greater catastrophe that I would take my burdened heart to the grave.

This might seem a rather reflective moment to indulge in the midst of an Indian fight, but it all transpired in the *twinkling of an eye*, as the scripture has it. One of the braves had pulled level with me, not twenty feet away. I felt my thumb cock the hammer of the revolver in my right hand, and I felt the trigger flip out against the pad of my forefinger. I pointed the pistol and fired.

A black hole appeared on the Indian's cheek just beneath his eye and his head whipped back as if I'd struck him a blow. He slid from the saddle, hit the ground and went tumbling. I heard the braves ululate their high-pitched screams, a sound that raised the hairs on my neck.

They harried us across a pasture of scrub and prickly pear. I knew if we kept up the pace we were riding at, we'd jigger our horses for sure. But my pistol shot had reminded the others of the Colts in their belts and several shucked them and began to fire.

The Indians were baffled by these magical weapons that could shoot more than once without being reloaded. I saw Juan put two balls in one of our attackers' ponies. I watched McClusky draw his pistol and level it at an Indian riding alongside him.

But when he pulled the trigger, his horse fetched up short and launched Felix into the air. He hit the ground and our pursuers dropped back to encircle him. You could hear him shouting curses.

Just four of us had escaped from the fray: me and Juan, Levi English and Uncle Ike. We drew rein and bunched there for a moment, staring back at the Comanches swarming around the

Irishman. The Indians rode paints, all except a tall, balding buck who sat astride a magnificent palomilla stallion, a cream-colored horse with a snow-white tail.

Juan looked over at me. "We cannot leave him," he said.

I shook my head, figuring McClusky's suffering would be fairly short, but before I could say it, Juan snapped the reins, booted his horse forward, and went rushing back toward the six Comanches who were about to collect the Irishman's pelt.

Well, if I live to be a hundred, I'll not witness such a sight again—Juan whipping his horse to a gallop and charging right into the teeth of our enemy, his Colt Patersons in either hand.

What could the braves have made of it? A man riding down on them like that? It put me in mind of Sam charging that field piece, back at Concepcion. The Indians had just turned to offer some sort of defense when Juan opened up with both pistols.

I thought his horse would throw him like McClusky's had, but the beast only galloped faster. Two of the Comanches' mounts reared and the gent on the palomilla—he must have been their warchief—raised his bow.

Or he started to. One of Juan's pistol balls struck him and he lurched out of the saddle, stumbled off a ways, went to a knee. The remaining Indians scattered like quail from a bush, one rider pausing beside his unhorsed chief, reaching down and pulling the injured man up behind him.

Juan wheeled round and started to make another pass— heaven knows how many chambers he'd shot through—but the Comanches had had enough of this man and his strange artillery. They drew back fifty, sixty yards, then turned and loosed a volley of arrows.

Juan rode up beside McClusky, who lay there wheezing on the ground. The two of them exchanged words I couldn't hear. When I reached them, Juan had dismounted and was trying to help the Irishman to his feet. One of McClusky's legs wouldn't straighten far enough to touch the ground, and his right arm seemed to've been yanked out of socket and hung uselessly.

I slid from the saddle, tucked my horses' reins in my belt, and set about helping Juan lift McClusky and get him situated on Juan's horse.

The sky was purpled over in the east and stars were winking down. The Indians were still bunched together, howling.

I looked at Juan, pointing to McClusky's injured leg.

"Can he even fork a horse?" I said.

"I'll fork any horse you please," said McClusky. "Just get me aboard him, by Christ."

We managed to get him boosted into the saddle. Something hissed past my ear and I realized the Indians had loosed another flight of arrows at us. They came raining down out of the lavender sky, one snapping against the pommel of my saddle, another finding a home inches from my moccasined feet, and I knew if we didn't make an evacuation our lives would be worthless. I'd turned to tell Juan this when his head whipped forward and he pitched into my arms. I heard the Comanches scream in triumph.

I lowered Juan to the ground, expecting to see an arrow sticking out from between his shoulders, but the missile had struck the back of his skull and glanced off. I felt my heart climb up the back of my throat, and I began yelling for help.

The arrow tip had opened a nasty cut on Juan's scalp; it bled freely, but that didn't worry me as scalp cuts always seem worse than they are. What frightened me more was the thought that the arrow had snapped Juan's neck; he lay limp as a doll in the grass. I squatted over him, feeling for a pulse on either side of his throat. I glanced across the prairie at the four Indian horsemen backlit against the western sky. They launched a final volley, and then their chief lifted an arm and called out in a loud voice. The Comanches turned their horses and in a few seconds they were gone.

By then Levi English and Uncle Ike had joined us. Levi sat his horse, staring down at Juan.

"Is he killed, Cap?"

"No," I said. "I don't think so."

I glanced up and saw the horrified expression of McClusky's face.

"Why did he do that?" he said.

"He was trying to save you, Felix—what do you think?"

McClusky shook his head.

"Jaysus," he said, "will he not come round?"

It was midnight before we got him back to camp. He still just lay there, insensible, and I figured the likelihood of his ever rousing was poor indeed.

But as distressed as I was, my heartache didn't hold a candle to McClusky's. He begged us to fetch a doctor that night.

"I'm scared to move him," I said. "And those Indians we scrimmaged with might still be about. We'll send for Chalmers at dawn."

"Dawn?" he said. "I'll ride to Austin right now."

"That leg is likely broke, Felix. Maybe your arm too."

"Damn my arm," he said.

Then he began to weep. He had no trouble killing a man. But the thought that Juan had laid down his life for him was unbearable. I'd never seen someone so undone by an act of compassion, so thoroughly unmanned.

* * *

Come sunup, we rode into Austin, borrowed a wagon, loaded Juan in its bed, and carted him into town, leading his horse behind us.

Doctor Chalmers came out onto the dirt street and examined Juan in the early light, lifting the lid of one eye, then lifting and staring into the other.

212 - AARON GWYN

"Here," he said, and his voice was too resigned for my liking, "bring him on in."

We hauled Juan into the doctor's house and laid him out on a low bed. The room was lit by an east-facing window, the warped panes magnifying the sunlight. The doctor cut his new patient's shirt down the middle and stood pressing around on his belly.

McClusky cleared his throat. "Ain't his gut that's afflicted," he said.

The doctor didn't raise his eyes to acknowledge this. I hushed McClusky and stood watching Juan's chest rise and fall. His breath seemed to come very shallow.

Chalmers moved on to examine Juan's head wound which leaked a thin serum, and once he'd thoroughly inspected the scalp, he looked up and said, "Did anyone see how he received the injury?"

"It was an Indian arrow," I said. "The bone seemed to turn the tip of it. He went right out like you see and hasn't woke since."

"No," said the doctor, "I wouldn't imagine."

"Can you not tell what ails him?" McClusky asked.

The sound of Felix's brogue seemed to irritate the old sawbones. He answered the question but looked at me when he did.

"His skull is fractured," he said, waving me over. Bending down, staring close at the patch of scalp between the doctor's fingers, I saw that the flesh was bruised soot black, branching out from the cut in a nasty-looking web.

"When will he come back round?" I asked.

"He might not," Chalmers whispered.

"Speak up," McClusky said from the other side of the room, and now the doctor looked at him. He turned to me and said, "I have no problem treating your man, but I will not do it with this bogtrotter barking in my ear."

Murder came into McClusky's eyes.

"You dare threaten me?" he said. "I've just the thing for you." He drew his belt knife and started for the old man, but I caught him around the waist and with Uncle Isaac's help, muscled him outside.

Once we'd subdued McClusky, I went back in and told the doctor I'd pay whatever it took to get Juan back on his feet.

"We're salaried in land," I said, "but I can transfer title to you if—"

Chalmers raised a hand and stopped me.

"We can discuss compensation another time, captain. For the nonce, you may leave your man with me. If he passes, I'll see to his internment."

I swallowed hard.

"I'll be back through in a month," I said. "I'll leave his horse as collateral."

We shook hands and I went back out and stood in the street. I figured the next time I met up with Juan, I'd be staring down at his grave. I walked to where his horse was tied and began rummaging through his saddlebags until I found his volume of Wordsworth. I took the book, went over, and climbed up on the wagon seat. McClusky was sitting there, his eyes wet and red.

"What did he say, Cap? Will he be all right?"

I reached and put a hand on his shoulder, but no words of consolation came to me. The two of us just sat, a hot wind blowing in our face and a hawk gliding high above, drawing a hunter's circle in the silent sky.

CECELIA

—TEXAS, 1840–1843—

They shared a pallet that night, and come morning, Sam went to work constructing a corn-shuck mattress and a cedarwood frame. They never talked about it, and they didn't need to talk—the days of separate beds were over.

Sleeping with someone was strange. Sharing space, sharing covers. Not that she needed covers. He put out heat like a pot-belly stove.

They slept side by side in that bed for two more months before anything happened. It wasn't like she would've thought; there was no great to-do. She woke one night to find he'd rolled over onto her arm. She tried pulling out from underneath him, but she was pinned.

"Sam," she whispered.

He snored. He swallowed and smacked his lips.

"Samuel," she said.

"What?" he said. "What is it?"

"You're on my arm."

He apologized. She drew her numb arm to her breast and began massaging it back to life. Then she glanced at him. He lay there on his side, blue eyes open. He leaned closer and nuzzled her shoulder with his nose.

It reminded her of a dog and she couldn't help but laugh.

"You're a peculiar white man," she said. "Did anyone ever tell you?"

"They told me," he said.

She rubbed her arm, smiling. She started to get a soft

feeling. She scooted up against him, pressed her forehead to his chest, and lay there very still.

"Do you know how?" she whispered.

She could hear his heart all of a sudden, thumping against her head. She ran her hand along his arm, back and forth to calm him.

"It's all right," she said. "You don't have to know."

"I don't want you thinking small of me."

"No," she told him. "It's all right."

She pressed against him until he rolled onto his back, and then climbed on top of his stomach. He felt so good, like he'd been carved out of hickory. You wouldn't think a body could be that solid.

When she reached down and slipped him inside her, his eyes went big.

She worked her hips. She kissed the hollow of his throat.

There was an ache to pleasure that was almost getting what you wanted, almost getting it, and almost getting it, and then the warm rush of getting too much.

That was new to her—the too-muchness of life. The seasons unspooled themselves and she felt like the bounty would break her heart.

Sometimes their closeness frightened her. She'd spent so much time with just herself. Being close with him wound her up, and, time to time, she'd get irritated or cross. But then he'd stand some way, or the light would catch his boy's cheeks, and the irritation turned to fear. He would leave her. He would die. Indians would start out from the trees and club him into an imbecile.

And then she woke one morning to find her stomach was upside down. She didn't even make it to her feet. Threw up right there beside the blankets.

For the next several weeks, she could hardly eat. Just a whiff of food made her stomach rise. The cedars were spinning. She put a hand out to make them stop.

She directed Samuel to make her a tea from ginger, but the tea did nothing. He rode into Bastrop, came back with two freshly killed chickens and cooked up a stew. She could drink the broth, but not much else.

Then, just like that, the sickness went away, and she was hungry for everything. She glanced down one afternoon in the fan of winter sunlight and saw how far her belly had swollen. She'd noticed before but had put it down to how she was eating.

Or maybe I've ignored it, she thought. Maybe I haven't wanted to see.

There was no looking around it now. She tried to remember where she was in her moons, but she couldn't recall the last time she'd bled, and a panic went off inside her.

And then she got very calm and her voices were discussing it, like two people trading slaps inside a room.

Do I tell him?

You do *not* tell him.

I'll have to tell him. I don't have a choice.

But here came the panic again and the voices snuffed out like candles. Because, there was no telling what he would do. He'd lived with her in this place, and that was something, but a child was quite another. It would not be white. Or not exactly.

If he recognized the half of it that was like him, would he love that half? Half-love would be fine with her, she thought. She could make up the rest.

But it will be half-hate, she thought. Half-suspicion.

Then she was angry. She went inside the cabin and slammed the door behind her.

And sat there on the bed, plotting. She'd take one of the horses and leave. She'd do it before the child came and she was restricted further. But that wasn't right; it wouldn't take the child coming. She'd be stricken before then. She had another month? Two months, maybe? Then she would be unable to run or ride. She wondered if this was his plan the whole time: to get her to submit to him and hobble her up with children.

Samuel came in. He was saying something to her, but the blood was loud in her ears, and she was deep inside her plans.

"Are you poorly?" he asked.

"I have your child in me," she said.

There, she thought. See how that suits him.

He stood staring down at her. Had he been ignoring it too? The two of them, walking blind inside this dream?

He put a hand across his mouth, thumb on one cheek, fingers on the other, cupping his face.

She started crying. She wanted him to understand it was her anger causing it, but she was too blubbery to talk.

And it wasn't just anger. It was grief. She was already grieving this life they'd made, all of it crushed up inside her, swelling.

Then he was kneeling there beside the bed. He didn't say anything. His face was white and warm. He reached and put his hand against her body, fingertips on her sternum, palm just below her ribs. Too high. She moved his hand down to show him where, and it upset her all over. It was being able to run that had always comforted her. No place they could put you you couldn't flee. Not if you were willing to do what it took. And she'd been willing to do anything at all. Or thought she was willing. Now there was this. It was trust him or nothing, and she began to shake.

And here was Samuel kneeling with his hand on her stomach. Very ginger, very careful with his touch.

"I swear," she told him, "you had best do right. I swear to God Almighty."

Still, he didn't say anything. She didn't know if this was Samuel the man or Samuel the boy she was looking at. Then he removed his hand, leaned in and placed his ear against her stomach, and she stopped crying that instant. She wanted to tell him there wasn't anything to hear, but he had his head pressed to her belly, and he was the father of whatever was inside her. This might have been boy-Samuel kneeling between her legs, but when he pulled back and looked up at her, he was smiling.

* * *

Her water broke in September. Samuel saddled up and rode into Bastrop.

She leaned against the wall, fighting this lightning inside her. She couldn't stand to lie down for the pressure.

But several hours later, Samuel came up the road with an ancient black woman behind him on his horse. The woman's name was Sadie and she'd midwifed since she was a girl. She wanted Cecelia to squat and bear down.

"I'm squatting," Cecelia said, and then the lightning arced through her belly, and her breath caught in her throat.

The midwife's skin was like a slice of apple left to dry in the sun—the same color of brown, that same texture—her hair white as cotton. She had small eyes set back in her skull, but there was fire in them.

She knelt between Cecelia's knees.

"Got a head showing," she said. "Breathe for me, now."

Cecelia didn't want to breathe. She'd hold onto her wind till she passed out, and deal with having babies when she woke.

"No," said the midwife after several moments, "that won't do." Then she reached up and took Cecelia's left ear between her thumb and finger and twisted it very hard.

The room went bright; Cecelia cried out. She was breathing and pushing down.

Everything came gushing: the lump in her belly, her water and bowels; it was all rushing out.

When she opened her eyes, she was sitting on her heels, panting. Sadie held a bloody mass of flesh in her hands, wiping, giving Samuel orders. He handed her his knife. He handed her clean rags and a bowl of water.

The boy the midwife offered Cecelia was very small. Skin like a cup of tea. Strands of straight black hair.

She didn't know the name until she saw his scrunched little face, and the face produced the name in a flash: he was *Robert*.

When the cord was cut and tied, and Sadie had swabbed him clean, they swaddled the boy and laid him against Cecelia's breast.

Then here was Samuel, nosing in like a dog.

"Give him here," he said.

"Mind his head," she told him.

"I'll mind it," Samuel said.

He stood there with Robert wrapped in his arms, rocking from side to side. So proud, thought Cecelia. His face was pure joy. He couldn't take his eyes off the child. He was laughing and crying all at once, his eyes like wet stars.

* * *

Those days were another dream of life, another dispensation. She nursed the babe every few hours. The boy was very quiet. He watched everything out of his tiny eyes.

You are mine, she thought. My own body.

Robert squinted at her. He seemed to be trying to focus. He had very long lashes for an infant, very dark and thick.

"You are beautiful," she told him. "Yes, you are."

The fear and worry left her; she no longer had room. There was this babe feeding off her; there were the bare branches in the sky. A soothing feeling took over, and love welled up inside her. She knew that's what it was, love like a warm rising tide.

Had she ever felt it? It took in Robert and Samuel in its flow; it took in her own body, all three of them, floating.

She had refused to admit she loved this man. What was different now? It wasn't that he was out there hunting and making rifle balls. He was out there circling. She and Robert were the center, and he was willing to circle around, bringing in deer meat and the rabbits that he killed. One evening, he came in toting a small, black bear. She didn't know what bear would taste like, but it must have fattened itself off berries, because it was the sweetest meat she ever had. She wanted him to get another, but that was the only bear he could find.

There was snow on the ground in January. Wolves howled at the stars. She lay there with Robert between them, the bear skin at the foot of their bed.

I have a family, she thought.

That is what they are.

F all of that year, I took another furlough and rode down
to visit Noah. We'd hardly clasped hands and greeted
each other before he said, "Did you hear about Sam?"
"Hear what about Sam?"

"I was in Bastrop a few weeks back," he said. "Going up
the steps of Alexander's store, I look over and yonder he stood,
talking with John Berry. Seems he's taken his land payment and
established himself a spread."

I felt the air go thick. The sunlight looked like it was
strained through muslin.

"What kind of spread?" I asked. "Whereabouts?"

"I didn't see the place," he told me. "But there in Bastrop
County."

I can't recollect what happened next. I must've lumbered
up the steps and gone to sit at Mrs. Smithwick's table. Perhaps
I even took a meal with the couple, though I have no idea what
we ate or spoke about. How did I excuse myself? Did I pre-
tend sickness or fabricate a lie? I couldn't tell you. I can't even
remember taking my leave.

The next thing I recall is being in the saddle again, riding.
The past seven years seemed a dream. I could hardly tell you a
thing I'd done. There were faces; the places I'd ridden
through; the wind and rain and sunshine—my skin told the
tale. My father would likely have laid the blame for this at
liquor's door, but that is an easy culprit. All told, I'd spent
barely six months with Sam, but those six months were worth

a lifetime. Taken together, they were more life than all my other months combined.

Heading down to Bastrop, I felt the fog of the past several years lift and light came flooding in. I was as happy and hopeful as I'd been in my boyhood before everything got so thundering confused. The little appaloosa I rode was a good all-day horse, and as we went along, I told her what I'd say to Sam, rehearsing all the things I hadn't had the chance or courage to tell him during that revolutionary springtime long ago.

I hit town round sundown and found John Berry's house, tucked in behind his gunsmith shop on the road to Nacogdoches. Old John and his missus were at the supper table, and nothing would suit them but that I pull up a chair and load my plate. They were courteous folk, but once John had told me where he believed Sam was located, I lost my appetite. They offered me to spend the night, and as I was somewhat unfamiliar with the country, I allowed it'd be better manners to ride out come daylight and might save me a bad accident if Sam mistook me for an intruder. Missus Berry fixed me up a pallet, and I lay there staring at the ceiling, listening to my heart strumming in my ears.

I was saddled up and riding before daybreak. It was a fine, bright morning, a little cool, the leaves starting to turn, the smell of cedar on the breeze.

I expected the homestead might be difficult to find. I went down a cow path through the turning trees, and midmorning, smelling smoke, came out from a grove of loblolly pines and saw a cabin up on the hill. If it didn't belong to Sam, I figured the occupant could provide further directions. I rode up to the front yard and hallooed the house.

The door opened and a lovely Negro woman stepped out, a baby swaddled up in her arms. She was small and petite with light brown skin and hazel eyes.

I removed my hat and told her good morning.

"Good morning," she said, an eastern lilt in her voice.

"I am looking for a friend of mine who has property in these parts. I am sorry to trouble you."

"It isn't any trouble," she said. "Samuel will know."

The name did not even register, partly because he was always *Sam* to me, partly because a mother and child wasn't something I associated with him at all.

She stepped back into the house, the door opened wider, and then, there he stood.

He looked older, a little thicker through the shoulders and chest. He'd grown himself a beard to mask his face, but I could've picked out those blue eyes in a sea of dragon treasure.

"Duncan," he said, and his smile of recognition was worth a thousand bottles of bourbon.

I slid down from the saddle and let the reins hang. *Ground-picketing* we called it, which either meant you possessed a horse you trusted like your own body or you were too lazy to tie up.

Or too distracted. How long had I practiced this moment in my imagination? Now I was struck mute as a stone. I walked over and extended my hand, but he ignored it, stepping forward to embrace me.

There is something that happens to men of a certain age, to bachelors such as myself who never feel the touch of women. My mother had been very affectionate, and my father kissed me until I was a full-grown man. But then I'd gone decades with nothing more than a handshake here and there. Your body can forget the touch of others. It yearns for a while, demanding to be handled, but like anything you don't feed, after a time, it starts to dwindle down and die.

But it can be woken. It can wake on you right quick.

Sam let go, stepped back and studied me.

He said, "Come in. Come and meet my Cecelia."

My skin was still buzzing, so what he'd said didn't quite

sink, my whole body flushing, the hair standing up on my arms.

I followed him inside the cabin. It was well-constructed, and though the craftsmanship fell short of Noah's work, everything was in apple-pie order: a fireplace at one end of the room, little shelves on the west wall—sugar, coffee, and other staples in store-bought jars.

"You've got it fixed up considerable homely," I said, giving the puncheon floor a few stomps with a boot heel. "Did you build it by yourself?"

"Pretty near," he said, motioning me to a clapboard table and pulling back an oak wood stool. "Will you take a cup of the brown gargle?"

"I would enjoy one," I told him, taking a seat and hanging my hat on my knee.

He took the kettle down from a shelf, dipped it in the water pail and set it to boil on a grate in the fireplace. The woman had seated herself at the head of the table, still cradling her child.

A very young child, I thought, though I was seldom around infants and had no idea of the babe's age, or if it was a he or she.

"Duncan," I said to her, smiling, and she nodded to me and said, "Cecelia."

"I am pleased to meet you, Miss Cecelia. How old is your little one?"

"Just under a year," she said, and then she angled the child toward me. "His name is Robert."

It struck me as rather odd that Samuel had acquired himself a Negro maid, but the press of everything had been too much for me to get my bearings, and out of courtesy, I leaned forward, wiped my paw along my trouser leg, and reached out to pull the blanket back from the boy's face.

He was a beauty like his mother, his skin a little lighter, his hair soft and black as a raven. He mumbled the buds of his tiny lips, and I was about to tell Cecelia what a handsome child he was when his lids opened and he looked up at me with his jewel green eyes, Sam's eyes in that miniature face—not the color, mind you, but the sheer blaze of them—and I jerked my hand away as though I'd been bitten.

Sam had come over from the fireplace to stand beside us. My heart began bucking like a stallion and I looked at Cecelia, then up at Sam, the proud father beaming down at his boy, his face full of love. Everything went dim. For seven years, I'd hunted this man the length and breadth of our Republic, and now I stood up, putting a hand on the table top to steady myself, knocking over my stool in the process.

"Are you poorly?" Sam asked. He nodded at the far side of the room to a sunken bed—likely the very bed where he and Cecelia had conceived this baby boy—and said, "Lie down a minute."

Well, that was the last feather. I turned and stumbled out the door.

Outside, the autumn sun was blinding. My mare grazed in a patch of grass, and I walked her down and mounted up. I felt old of a sudden, very old. Sam was in the doorway now and he called something to me. I wouldn't look at him, wouldn't show my pitiful face. I walked my horse back along the cow path and pushed up to a trot.

Directly, we commenced to burn the breeze, the leaves blurring by. I did not feel betrayed: let me say that right out. Rather, I felt that the hard hand of the Lord had swung down to swat me a final blow. And I deserved it. I'd done everything to beg Him for such a slap—all my lust and foolishness—and for some strange reason, I began to laugh.

Or, it was laughter that came out of me. It didn't seem to be me who was doing it—certainly, there was nothing amusing. I felt like He had borrowed my mouth, just like He'd borrowed that of Balaam's ass, that the Lord Himself was laughing, and I thought of my father all those years ago, riding Young Roger through the Kentucky forest to find me and Tom Yarbrough bached up together. The laughter died away, and I began weeping as my father had wept decades before, and now I understood. It hadn't been out of shame as I'd supposed, but rather, my father had seen this very moment coming for me. He'd known if I pursued my heart's desire, I'd find myself galloping through a wilderness in an unfamiliar land, an old man without home or family, learning at long last how all things end in judgment.

* * *

There'd been a time when all I wanted was to be of use. I'm sure the sound of that might drip with honey, but it is true.

Now, I'd ride into towns with my company, feeling like a vicious beast. These new settlements had sprung up after the Rangers had cleared the countryside of Indians—tribes who'd occupied those lands for as long as their fathers and grandfathers could remember. We'd come riding up the mud streets of Mustang Branch, or Chambers Creek, or Cibolo Pit, and the residents would stare at us from the porches of their homes or the galleries of their stores, eyeing us with disdain. We'd liberated these very places of Pawnee, Lipan, and Wichita. Of Kickapoo, Caddo, and Apache. We'd spilled the blood of a noble enemy, had our own blood spilled, only to be gawked at by people who'd stumbled in from the Old States after all the fighting was finished, folks who hadn't won the land with human currency; they couldn't understand why butchers such as ourselves were needed.

I began to consider the notion that someday we wouldn't be.

In the spring of '45, we rode back through Austin to pay

Doctor Chalmers a visit. I'd put this off too long, not wanting to deal with the sadness of standing over Juan's grave. Between losing him and meeting Sam's son and paramour, I'd been drained. I'd never claimed to be an especially hardy man and the past year would've curled up a stouter soul than mine.

So, conceive my dismay when I found the good doctor had withdrawn his shingle and his home was now occupied by a tanner named Birch. He told me Doctor Chalmers could be found at the little hotel on Bleaker street.

I located him at the Cole's saloon instead. He was seated at a table behind a plate of steaming bacon with a bottle of sour mash to wash it down. He hadn't looked like a soaker when I met him the previous year, but some men hide that infirmity rather well.

He glanced up and chewed for several seconds.

"Captain Lemmons," he said.

I didn't care to correct him. I asked what I owed him for seeing to Juan's internment.

"Internment?" he said. "We don't generally bury the living around these parts."

"Meaning what?"

"Meaning your man rose, took up his bed and walked, as the scripture says."

"He's all right? He just up and left?"

"Well," said the doctor, "I never said he was all right. But he left, irregardless. You only missed him by a few weeks." He sipped his whiskey and set it down. "Or a month, maybe."

"I don't expect he mentioned where he was going."

"Not to me, he didn't."

I stood there thinking that now I'd spend another decade tracking down Juan as I'd spent the previous one hunting Sam.

Chalmers cleared his throat. "That Paddy still riding with you?"

"McClusky," I said. "He's with us."

"Watch yourself around that man."

I told him there was no need to watch myself.

"You say that," he said. "I think you know better."

"I've no ambition against the Irish, doctor. I'm half Irish myself."

"You were born in this country?"

"Kentucky," I said.

Chalmers nodded. "Then you're about as Irish as a mesquite."

All this drunken palaver was wearing thin. I gave the doctor two gold eagles and a shiny Liberty Head half eagle and turned to leave.

"Captain," he said.

I looked back at him.

"A man hurt like Juan—just because he's walking around and talking doesn't mean he's like he used to be. You meet up with him, you'll see what I mean."

* * *

We were bivouacked on the Colorado when he found us. I recognized the moro gelding from a quarter mile away; as did the other men. They all stood and gave a hurrah. But when the rider came closer, the cheers quieted. Soon, all you could hear was the crackling of the camp fires.

Juan got down from his horse and came forward. His hair was cropped very short, and since I'd last seen him, it had gone white. As had his whiskers and his beard.

"Juan," I said, and we shook hands.

We stood there a moment. I was about to say how good it was to see him—which would've been halftrue; it was good to see him alive and walking—when I heard McClusky voice from back behind me saying, "Where is he now? Where is our Lazarus?" Apparently, the Irishman had been down to the latrine when Juan rode up; now he pushed his way through the press of bodies and stood gaping at Juan as if he had indeed risen from the dead.

And well he might've.

He glanced over at McClusky.

You could not tell whether he recognized McClusky or not, whether he gave any thought to the price he'd paid for rescuing this man. He simply nodded at the Irishman.

At which point McClusky doubled over and went to blubbering.

Though somewhat theatrical, it was a genuine display, and none of us was unmoved. What must that have been like: to know a man you'd once despised had liberated you from the clutches of the enemy at such cost to his person? I never wanted to labor under such a debt.

* * *

I couldn't sleep that night: something gnawed at my spirit. I rolled it back and forth in my brain. I ought to've accepted Juan's return as the miracle it was. But it unsettled me. Perhaps it was seeing this once healthy man in such reduced capacity. Perhaps it was the outpouring of emotion I'd witnessed. Around first light, I gave up my attempts at slumber and walked to the river to wash.

When I walked back into camp, the eastern sky had paled. I was the only thing up and moving. I passed Dan Bannon in his bedroll and Uncle Ike in his, working my way around the sleeping bodies in their blankets.

And here was Juan, lying on his back with both eyes closed, his chest rising and falling. He was thinner than before, his body loose inside his clothes. I stood there watching him, the sky growing lighter, and I noticed something I hadn't been able to the previous night. I'd made out the silver stubble on his scalp and the silver moustache hiding his upper lip, twisted to sharp points the same as ever. Now I saw that his skin had a gray tint to it as well. At first, I thought it was just the morning light, but when the sun breached the horizon and the rest of the world blushed pink, Juan's flesh was still the color of ash. That feeling of desolation swept through me; I couldn't decide the source of it. I thought about Sam, his frontier wife and child. A panic was moving in my blood.

Then I saw McClusky. The Irishman had spread his blankets crossways at Juan's feet so that their two bedrolls made a T. The image of a pet lying at the foot of its master's bed flashed through my brain and I turned and went back to the river.

* * *

It was long about this time that I noticed my eyesight starting to flag. Though never as eagle-eyed as Sam, my vision carried farther than most men and a good deal of what I was able to accomplish with a rifle depended on it. I could still count the leaves on a limb at half a furlong, but my knack for telling an "h" from an "n" had flatted out.

I discovered this flipping through Juan's Wordsworth. I'd been planning to reunite book and owner at some opportune moment, and removing the volume from possibles one morning I performed a little gesture I'd seen my father execute a thousand times with his Bible: opening the book and then holding it at arm's length to bring the words into focus.

Levi was sitting there beside me at the fire, molding rifle balls, and he turned to give me a look.

"You need spectacles?" he said.

"Mind your business," I snapped, feeling my cheeks color.

Levi shrugged. "Lots of folks require spectacles, Cap. I didn't mean to rile you."

It didn't matter to me that he was right: vanity cares nothing for the truth, and I was sour over it the rest of the week. I'd wake in the morning before the others were up, take the slim volume and walk out a ways from camp, standing with my back to the east, waiting for sunlight. Something in me hoped my eyes might recover; maybe they were only tired. But when I saw the text was no clearer on day seven than it'd been on day one, I decided it was time to acknowledge the corn: these eyes God gave me were wearing out and it would not be long before other things began to wear as well.

It put me in a frail frame of mind. Perhaps it called up Pap for me; perhaps it was just my pride. But over the coming months all this touched off some strange alchemy in my brain: my weakening eyesight caused me to question a dozen other faculties, and finding them less robust than they'd once been I began to question my place as the head of a ranger company. These men had become my brothers, the only ones I'd ever have. Of what use would I be to them if I continued to decline?

Of course, the decay was mostly in my noggin. It was only that I'd never given much thought to my mortality before now, and cast in a new light, the path I'd chosen to ride seemed thick with obstacles, and my prospects rather grim. I woke one autumn morning smelling decay on the breeze and knew I would return to visit Sam. Forget my embarrassment, my jealousy.

There is so little time, I thought. If I am forced to leave this family of rangers, I will need to find another.

I did not stop to consider that acquiring this family would mean separating Sam from his.

How is that the heart refuses to tally such costs?

CECELIA

—TEXAS, 1845–1846—

Samuel spent his days hunting and trapping, gathering pelts, riding into Bastrop to sell the surplus. The country was settling up, which seemed to disgust him, but there were always new men to purchase his meat and skins, so he was of two minds.

Cecelia was of one mind and one mind only. That was new for her. For years she'd been divided. She'd separated herself into parts that could take pain, absorb loneliness, soak the hurt up like cotton. And there were parts of her to minister to these parts, to build them up again.

Then there was Samuel. There was little Robert. Wasn't it strange how other people could unite you, collapse your halves into a whole? She thought it was strange, but the more she dwelled on it, the more she suspected it wasn't strange at all. This was how folks ought to function. It was Virginia that was strange, Mississippi and Louisiana: no wonder she'd been a stranger there.

* * *

With an infant, her life was food and sleep. She could hardly tell one day from another: bright sunshine one moment, moon and stars the next. It was fall, then winter, then here came spring again. She didn't know where the time got to, but she was content like she'd never been.

Robert was walking by eighteen months. He was a graceful

child, agile in his movements. His hair black and soft as down. The green eyes in his beautiful face. His father's eyes, she thought. Never mind the color: it was Samuel's vigor, Samuel's fire.

These days, Sam was burning with it. He rode back and forth to Bastrop, fretful as a cat. More and more, he worried about this Republic he'd fought for; folks said it would be annexed by the States. The frontier would vanish. According to Samuel, it was already vanishing. Game was still plentiful, the soil still black. But make no mistake, he told her: the Americans were coming. Men were buying up headrights, plowing and clearing land.

Samuel shook his head. "Fore too long, you won't be able to turn around."

She believed him, but it was hard to feature. The country they'd passed through eight years ago was wilderness. They'd moved onto this acreage, and she hadn't stepped foot off the property since. She'd seen all of the nation she wanted to, thank you kindly. On this property, she was a queen.

That fall, their visitor came calling again—Duncan Lammons, one of Samuel's compatriots from the Revolution. He was a tall, gray-eyed man with thick dark hair and a coal-black moustache that reminded Cecelia of a brush. He had a low, gravelly voice that sounded like he was constantly clearing his throat. He had eyebrows that needed trimming. He was a courteous man, but there was something about him she didn't trust.

He'd paid them a visit the year before, riding up out of the woods one morning on his appaloosa. The two of them had sat at the table, talking, making over Robert, but then he started looking poorly. He stood up, staggered out the door, and then she heard his horse pounding along the trail. Sam had followed him outside, trying to call him back.

"Is he all right?" she asked when Sam came back inside, but

234 - AARON GWYN

Sam wouldn't talk about it. She figured that was the last she'd ever see of him.

Now she saw him all the time. Twice a week, he'd ride in to take supper with them; he and Sam would sit up trading stories: fights against the Caddo, fights against the Apache. She wasn't thrilled about hosting the man, but his presence seemed to please Samuel.

Sitting at the table one evening, she turned to him and said: "Were you ever married, Mister Lammons?"

He looked over at Samuel. "Why's she call me *mister*?"

"Cause she hadn't seen you with a jug in hand, rooting around like a hog. You ain't shattered your respectability."

"Yet," Lammons said.

She said: "Do you drink whiskey, Mister Lammons?"

"Does he drink whiskey," said Samuel. He looked up at the ceiling and shook his head. "Good Lord Almighty."

"Duncan," Lammons told her. "Call me Duncan."

"Duncan," she said.

Lammons ignored the remarks about his drinking and went back to the topic of marriage. He said, "The ladies never much took to me."

"I'm sure," she said, "there are plenty of women who'd have you."

"Supposed to be a leper colony out by Bexar," Sam told him. "Maybe you'll get lucky and find a blind one."

Yes. The two of them put on quite a show.

In bed that night, after she'd gotten Robert down, she said, "Do you think Duncan is lonesome?"

Samuel didn't answer for several moments.

Then he said, "How's that?"

"Duncan. The way he looks at you. He seems lonely to me."

"Could be," Samuel said.

They lay there for a time.

"What's on your mind?" she said.

"I just get to thinking."

"About what?"

"These settlers," he said.

"Is it as bad as all that?"

He said it was. The men coming their way were a different breed entirely. They didn't have frontier values.

"What do they value?"

"Cotton," he told her. "Much as they can plant."

She thought it couldn't possibly be so dire.

But it went just as he said: Texas became a state that December, and February of the next year relinquished its sovereignty.

Sam had been expecting this, but he didn't expect the Mexican cavalry who crossed the border in April to rout U.S. troops; he didn't expect Congress's declaration of war on May 13th.

Sundays, he rode into Bastrop. He'd come back and report the news: how Santa Anna had returned to Mexico. How, once he was at the head of an army, he pronounced himself president and vowed revenge on Texas.

"Wasn't ten years ago, we had him prisoner. Some of the boys were for stringing him up right there, but the aristocrats shouted them down. I could've walked over and stuck him with my knife."

"Santa Anna?"

Samuel held his palms a few feet apart. "I wasn't that far away."

One cold January night, we were bivouacked in the belt of loblolly pines there in Bastrop County. I'd dozed off by the fire in a pleasant, drowsy mood and when I woke to high, hideous shrieks my first thought was that the band of Comanche who'd wrought such destruction on our company had somehow located us and determined to finish us off. I grabbed my pistols and began shouting for the boys to rouse themselves and offer a defense.

Which was when McClusky sprinted from the trees into the light of our campfires, the Irishman shielding his head with both hands and caterwauling like he was being pursued by Furies.

"Where are they?" Levi English yelled. "I can't see them, Cap!"

Nor could I. It took us several minutes to realize there were no Indians at all. McClusky had been attacked by an old hoot owl protecting his brood.

Which might sound rather comical, but I assure you, there was no humor in it. McClusky had woken in the night and stalked off into the trees to relieve himself. He was standing there, doing his business, when there came a great blow from above and hot blood ran down his face. He said it felt like knives carving his scalp. Then here it came again. Wings slapped his cheeks, his shoulders; he ducked and raised his hands to fend off the assault and the tip of a talon pierced his left eye.

We tended him the rest of the night, offering whiskey to calm him, and by first light he was drunk as a fiddler.

He might well have wished it had been Indians who'd beset

him: he was a bloody, mutilated mess. Patches of hair had been torn out and they'd never grow back: the hideous gashes the owl made would turn to slick, red scars.

At just that moment, it wasn't his appearance, but his vision, that concerned me. I knelt there in front of him and tried to examine the wound, which seemed to bleed whenever he blinked.

"What can you see out of that eye, Felix?"

"I can't see nutting," he told me. "Nutting a' tall."

Over the coming weeks, the iris faded from brown to cloudy white. Men who'd been disfigured in this way often wore a patch—out of respect for others more than anything. But McClusky wouldn't hear of it. He seemed almost proud of the deformity.

He figured that if the world was unfair enough to allow such horrors to befall a man, he would remind every person he spoke with of that grim fact. To his thinking, there was no reason why misery was visited on one and blessing bestowed on another. Good and bad deeds didn't enter into what Providence parceled out for us.

And so, he would not trouble himself with questions of right and wrong.

I didn't bother to remind him that he'd never done so.

* * *

Of course, it was not just McClusky who'd been inconvenienced by the tides of fortune. Surely, Juan had much greater cause for bitterness.

And I suspected that he was bitter. He just didn't trumpet it like his Irish friend.

The previous year, after Juan had returned to us from his sojourn with the doctor, I walked over and sat beside him, resting my saddle bags on the ground beside my knee.

"Juan," I said, "it is mighty good to have you back."

"Yes," he said, nodding, and the corners of mouth twisted up in a smile. But there was no smile in his eyes.

Reaching down in my saddle bag, I pulled out Juan's book of poems and handed it to him.

I assumed he'd thought it was lost forever, along with the rest of his traps, and that being reunited with the volume would surely raise his spirits.

He took the book and stared at it a moment, then opened the cover and began thumbing pages. I thought he was looking for a particular passage, but he closed the volume and set it on the ground.

"I thank you," he said, and I realized in that moment he did not recall my name. He knew me, remembered me as his captain, but the name itself wouldn't come to him.

It was uncomfortable to sit any longer, so I bid him good evening and made my way back to my bedroll.

A few nights later, Juan came across camp and sat beside me, returning the visit, I suppose. He had his volume of Wordsworth in hand and my name was on his lips again—he'd likely had McClusky refresh his memory.

We sat in silence several moments. Then he turned and said, "Captain Lammons"—very formal, and this tore at my heart as he'd become light on ceremony when speaking with me.

"Captain Lammons," he said, nodding at the book of poems, "did I used to read this book?"

The question frightened me in a way I didn't understand.

"It's your book," I told him, then wished there'd been a more delicate way to phrase it. But I was too startled.

He nodded and I watched as his eyes welled with tears and spilled onto his cheeks. Not tears of sorrow, mind you, but of rage. He wiped them away.

"I have read it cover to cover," he said. "I cannot recall a single word."

"You've been through a deal of suffering. It will come back to you by and by."

He shook his head, turned and looked at me.

"Did I enjoy it very much?"

"Did you enjoy what?" I asked.

He lifted the book in answer.

"You used to read it every night," I told him. "You'd read it to the company pretty regular."

He nodded.

"It is a strange thing, Captain. I can tell it ought be familiar to me."

"It'll come back to you," I said.

"I do not know. I can make nothing of it. If I had a gusto for it, it has gone."

To this I had no response. And I could see his concern: to lose memory of having read a book is one thing. But to be unable to appreciate a thing that once gave you such pleasure is quite another. Your memory of something can change, but what you love, you love.

Unless you become a stranger to yourself.

* * *

Word came that we would go to war with Santa Anna for a second time—only now, instead of the Republic of Texas against that foul tyrant it would be the Republic of these United States.

From the time I heard that President Polk had ordered General Zachary Taylor to build a fort down on the Rio, I knew the wire-pullers back in Washington were looking to honey-fogle us into a fight.

The sticking point was the border. While Texas claimed the Rio as our boundary marker, Mexico put the border farther north at the Nueces. The papers said President Polk wanted to extend his country coast to coast and was seeking some way to acquire New Mexico, California, and other territories in the west. And so, looking to force the issue, he had General Taylor move his army and occupy the mouth of the Rio Grande. Naturally, the Mexicans took this unkindly, sending their own troops to probe American defenses which led to the ambush of Captain Seth Thornton, who the Mexicans took prisoner, a number of his soldiers being killed in the skirmish.

And so President Polk had his war, but when I heard that the Rangers were being mustered into Federal service to act as scouts for the Army, it didn't set right at all. There was no doubting Santa Anna was a despot, but what of that? Were we in the business of deposing these? During our Revolution, we'd fought to lift his boot from our throat, but what was the governance of another nation to me? I did not care to see the U.S. plant its flag in California. Would the men in my company benefit from this expansion? No—they'd bleed for it.

The Texans acted as though they'd won the war already. Men who'd ridden with ranger companies over the past ten years were encouraged to swell our ranks. Many of them would die on foreign soil in a fight that was not theirs.

As the days passed and we prepared to head south, I began to take a different tack. I thought of those early days with Captain Tumlinson's company, riding with Sam and Noah; it seemed that life had never been so sweet. I felt that if only Sam would muster in and join us, it would be old times again.

Thus, my prejudice against the enterprise took wings, and I was all for riding on Mexico forthwith—provided, of course, I had Sam to ride with me. Perhaps we could even manage to drag Noah out of his retirement.

This should tell you the quality of my thinking at the time, and it wouldn't be wide of the mark to guess that liquor played a good part in my fantasies.

The problem, as I saw it, was that if I mentioned all of this to Sam, Cecelia would smother the idea straightaway. The woman did not like me; you could see that very plainly. If there was any hope of recruiting Sam for the venture, the proposal could not come from my lips.

So, I went to Juan and spoke with him over supper, told him of Sam and the asset I believed he'd be for our company.

"Take some of the others and go talk with him in the morning. It's no need to mention me. Just say you've heard of his service during the Revolution and that his country could use him once again. Or don't say *country*. Say, *Texas*, rather."

"Texas?" Juan said.

I nodded. "Will you do this for me?"

"I will," he said, then paused. "But you say you are friends of this man?"

I could tell where he was headed with the question—*why not communicate the message myself?*—and I began to grow cross.

"If you aim to do it, do it. I'd rather not talk it to death."

His brow knit and he studied me a moment. He shrugged. "We do not have to talk at all. I will go when it is light."

* * *

And he did, taking Levi, Uncle Ike, and John Douglass to make the case. And Felix, of course, which was something I hadn't reckoned on when I brought the matter to him. I ought to've told him to leave the Irishman in camp. Lord knew McClusky didn't put the best face on the things.

Well, it was too late now. I milled around, awaiting their return, restless as a gypsy. I busied myself tidying up, scouring pots and pans, distributing kindlers to the firepits around camp.

When I passed by the fire Juan had been using the past several days, I saw something in the ashes that hadn't quite burned, a wedge of paper, it looked like. I bent and lifted it from the cinders.

It was his volume of Wordsworth. Or what remained of the book—a length of the spine and a chock of a blackened pages.

I stood there holding it in my palm and a feeling of dread blew through me. I felt like I'd committed some terrible crime, though I couldn't think of what that might be, and after a while, I laid the charred book back among the ashes and went to see to my horse.

CECELIA

—TEXAS, 1846—

She was sitting out in front of the cabin, drawing in the dirt with Robert, when a pack of rough-looking men came loping up the trail. They seemed to be soldiers of some kind, but they had no uniforms to speak of. They wore bob-tailed black coats, or long-tailed blue coats, felt hats, leather caps, all kinds of trousers.

The man at the head of the band rode an apron-face sorrel with four white stockings. He reined up and sat glancing around.

He was a hard, little man, a tight little man. He had a shock of red hair, and freckles across his nose like flakes of rust. He didn't seem to notice Cecelia. Then he did. He turned and stared down at her, and she saw he was blind in one eye. It looked like someone had dropped milk in it: the pupil was wide and white.

"Samuel Fisk," he said, and his voice was a thick Irish brogue.

She didn't say anything. She picked up Robert and set him on her lap.

Then the door opened behind her; Sam stepped out.

The man's good eye went from Sam to Cecelia, Cecelia to Robert, back to Sam again. You could see him calculating.

"You're Samuel Fisk?"

"Maybe," Sam said.

"I'm Felix McClusky."

"All right," said Samuel.

A tall man next to Felix said, "Señor Fisk, I am Juan Juarez. Could we speak to you?"

"Speak," Sam told him.

"Could we speak inside, perhaps?"

Samuel shrugged. He stood to one side of the door and made a motion with his hand.

The men dismounted and lumbered in. Samuel glanced at her. He shook his head, stepped inside and shut the door.

She sat there, holding Robert.

He said, "Pawpaw's friends."

"No," she told him. "Definitely not."

After several minutes, the Irishman came out. She was glad this man was no longer in her home, but there was also an insult to it, as if he couldn't stand to be inside the cabin.

It's fine, she thought. The quicker they're gone the better.

She glanced down and saw the boy was staring up at McClusky. She squeezed his arms, and Robert looked down and studied the ground.

Then he glanced back up.

"Your eye," he said.

The man turned and regarded Robert a moment.

"Yes," he said, pointing to the clouded pupil, "it is my dirty eye."

The hair stood up on her arms. She opened her mouth to speak, but McClusky was talking again: "All's it sees is dirt."

"Dirt," Robert repeated.

McClusky nodded. He palmed his knees and bent over until he was nearly nose to nose with the boy.

"Aye, lad. But just this minute, it is seeing *you*."

* * *

"What were they after?" she asked once the men had left.

Sam said, "Wanted me to sign on for this commotion down in Mexico."

"The war?"

"I guess that's what it is."

"And what did you tell them?"

"Told them I wasn't interested."

She shook her head. "I don't like it."

He said not to let it worry her; he'd told them flat out his rangering days were over.

"And how'd they take it," she asked, "your not joining up?"

"They weren't just real happy, but it's not a whole lot they can do. They're riding for Mexico next week. And it's some of them won't come back, neither."

She debated whether to tell him of the Irishman's exchange with Robert, then decided to leave it alone.

But she couldn't get shed of the feeling McClusky had given her. She hadn't felt like that since Louisiana. For the past nine years, she'd been shielded by live oak and cedar, acres of green pasture: sage grass, wild rye. She'd grown into motherhood. And something else besides.

Then one day five filthy men appeared and she was this other person again. The trees and prairie didn't protect her. The glare of a one-eyed Irishman brought it all rushing back.

* * *

The next morning Duncan Lammons paid them a visit; it seemed he was headed for Mexico as well.

He sat at the table with Sam, drinking coffee. She pulled a chair back and sat between them, watching Lammons very closely, watching how he looked at Sam.

Lammons smiled. "Best go with me," he said.

"To Mexico?" said Sam.

"Absolutely. We could sure use your rifle. It might could be rather enjoyable."

"Might could be we've got different notions about enjoyment, Duncan."

246 - AARON GWYN

Lammons chuckled. He sipped his coffee. "They say that—"

She interrupted him, couldn't hold it any longer. "And what am I to do while the two of you are traipsing about Mexico?"

Lammons's smile faded. He said, "We won't be that long, Miss Suss. You might manage without him for a bit, couldn't you?"

"And what if he's killed? How will I manage then?"

Lammons blushed.

"Just an idea," he said. "Course, it's his decision entirely."

"Yes," she told him. "It is his decision." She looked at Sam. "And he's made it."

Sam said, "I told them I wasn't interested. Fact, I'm a little surprised you're going, Duncan."

Lammons said, "Well, I reckon I've got a fight or two left in me," but by the look on his face, he didn't seem to believe it. There was a sadness in him, and something in her couldn't help but reach for him. She'd been angry just a moment ago, and now she had her hand on this sad man's arm.

"You be careful," she said. "You'll come visit us when you're back?"

Lammons nodded, seemed about to say something, then just sat there, staring down at his coffee, and it occurred to her she might never see him again.

There was a relief in that thought. She was of two minds about him. He seemed to be a threat and then not. She was jealous of the time he'd spent with Sam and she was saddened by his loneliness.

You are strange, she thought. A strange kind of man.

And that was the problem, for she was strange as well.

Duncan Lammons

—Texas, 1846—

The summer of '46 was a thick, hot summer. Ten years had gone by since my previous war. It might as well have been a hundred, so changed was the country and the men I'd ridden with. In truth, it seemed everything was altered but my loyal, lustful heart. I'd turn forty the following spring. I had no home other than my own busted saddle; I was a perpetual bachelor; my hopes for a union with Sam were beyond recovery. Which didn't diminish my affection, but on that journey to Mexico, I took myself to do.

Mister Lammons, I thought, *if you are to have association with Sam you must cast out any last notion that this fantasy you've pursued these years will ever come to be. It is time you woke from your dreams. You may yet be of some use to him. Accept what fellowship he's offered; rid yourself of your jealousy. If you are to wring any joy from the years that remain to you, you must receive this truth.*

This lecture—and others of a similar nature—occupied me as we rode down into the dust of Mexico, and on this journey, I had occasion to see Juan with fresh eyes. So much had transpired between the time he returned to us and our leaving out to rendezvous with General Taylor's army that I hadn't realized what a different man he was. The good-natured lover of poetry who cheered the men and lifted the burden of my loneliness had vanished.

How much of what we believe about our companions is what we must believe in order to keep from falling into black despair? I'd spent the balance of my life searching for a kind of family—not the usual sort with wife and children, but a family nonetheless. What I hadn't been particularly eager to find was the truth about folks, and I began to see how my desire that people be a certain way had polluted all my thinking. This was yet another thing I'd have to tend to. The farther south we rode, the more I saw the size of the tasks that lay before me. Why was I traipsing off to war? There were battles aplenty to be fought within the thin walls of my skull, enough to keep the armies of my spirit occupied for years.

One night, once the men were asleep, I walked off some little ways from camp, found myself a flat shelf of sandstone, inspected it for snakes, then took a seat and uncorked a bottle I'd hidden away in my traps. Soon, I'd be in the company of Federal troops and might not be able to take a nip of whiskey when I pleased, and when I began to ruminate on that, I saw how reliant on strong drink I'd become.

And why? The first thirty years of my life I'd not taken so much as a sip. Was it Sam that sent me to the bottle? No. I couldn't lay that at his door. I thought about the past decade. It'd been at the Battle of Concepcion that I'd first taken up with liquor and was it some great coincidence that this was where I'd first shot a man? Mind you: it was not the killing itself that caused me to seek the aid of stimulants, but rather the come-down from killing. The fighting had frightened and thrilled me—in many ways, I'd never felt more alive than when the bullets were whizzing—but there was a sadness after battle was done, a melancholy waiting for me like a lost companion. I'd taken this for a kind of weakness. Whiskey helped push the blue devils away, or so I'd thought, but now I considered the possibility that it merely numbed me to things. It made little difference I considered our cause just: there is a heaviness that descends on you after a fight, and I'd sought to lift this heaviness with drink.

But the fog that puts you in must itself be lifted. To feel some life again, you must seek another fight; then another drink; and thus it had been for over a decade now.

And even so, reflecting on all this, I neither put down the bottle I was sipping from nor saddled my horse to ride north. I required both liquor and combat, and yet I had begun to despise them both.

I was startled out of my musings by footsteps approaching. I stowed the bottle under the ledge of sandstone and tried to determine just how slewed I was.

Presently, the figure came closer and I saw that it was Juan. He stopped and stood there a moment, trying to make me out.

"Captain?" he said.

"It's me," I said.

He came up and seated himself on the rock beside me. I offered him the bottle, but as always he waved it away.

"Can't sleep?" I said.

He shook his head. "For all I sleep, Captain, it is not worth the lying down."

"Didn't used to have any trouble in that regard, did you?"

"No," he said, "I did not."

We sat a moment. The Jerusalem crickets drummed around us.

"I am change," he said. "Very much change. It is not some secret. I cannot even recordar how I felt beforehand. I just know I am different then."

"It takes time."

In the starlight, I could just make out the bulge of his jaw. You could feel rage coming off him like heat from a stove. He was like that now: cool one moment, hot as a poker the next. And for no particular reason that I saw.

"He tells me it might be this way. El médico."

"Chalmers," I told him.

"You see?" he said, tapping his temple with a finger. "Was I this bird-witted beforehand?"

I exhaled a long breath.

"No," I said. "If I am honest, I would say you were not. You could recite your poems from heart like you read them off a page."

He was silent for several minutes.

Then he said, "You ought have let me go, Captain."

"Let you go where?"

"You should not have taken me to Chalmers."

"Just let you die, you're saying."

"Yes. That is what I say."

I stared at him for a time.

"You need to get some sleep," I told him. "You'll feel different after a good night's rest."

"It has nothing at all to do with sueño. You know it does not."

And he was right: I did know. But if really he thought I'd have let him die without trying to get him seen to, that arrow had hit him harder than he realized.

"Have you given any consideration to what you'd have done in my place? If you were captain and I'd have fallen?"

"I have thought and thought about it," he told me, his voice grim, precise. "Sometimes it is all I think."

I said, "Juan, I hate what happened bad as anyone. But I still don't think this is the end of things for you. I can't believe the good Lord brought you back from the brink just for the torment of it."

"Por qué no?" he said.

"Beg pardon?"

"Why would He not? And why would *you* believe He would not, Captain." He shook his head. "Especially you."

I did not like the path our conversation was turning down, but there was nothing about the conversation to like.

"What's that supposed to mean?" I said. "*Especially me.*"

He sat there, staring into the dark. After a while he said, "I know men like you before, Captain. This not new to me. No es asunto mío. The consul has a similar anhelo. A similar deseo."

I didn't quite catch his meaning and didn't exactly want to. What desire did he speak of? And what consul?

Then I recalled the story of his time among the Turks.

"The Swede?" I said. "In Istanbul?"

"Si. Señor Nilsson. From the time of mi llegada he will come to me in the night, in the room he has for me. I am fifteen and he is very large. A very large man. Night after night after night. How will I fight a man this size? I am just a boy, Captain."

Well, his meaning was pretty hard to miss now.

"You offend me, Juan. I am not some pederast to lie with children. I have never in all my—"

"No," he said, holding his palms up in surrender. "Not a pederasta. It is the deseo itself I speak of—to lie with another man. Do you not think it is a cruel God who put this deseo in you and place you among those who will kill you for it?"

My hands started shaking. I stood up.

"Good night to you, Juan. We can talk tomorrow. And when we do, you won't mention any of this to me. Nor anyone else. Tomorrow or ever."

"Yes, Captain," he said, resignedly. "Of course."

"Night," I told him, and taking up my bottle, left him sitting there on that shelf of sandstone with the crickets and his cruel God for company.

* * *

We caught up with Ben McCullough and his men at Matamoros on May 23rd. Of the various ranger captains under the command of Jack Hays, McCullough was accounted the most accomplished—some would give that prize to Sam Walker, and I suppose they would make a respectable case.

Truth be told, every ranger thought his captain the wisest and most gallant, and whether McCullough was any braver than Walker or Bigfoot Wallace, I cannot say.

McCullough was about as cool a head as I ever saw in a scrape. The man's blue eyes regarded the heat of battle the way most men look at a feather bed: he was utterly at home with rifle balls whistling by and the sound of booming cannon. We camped there at Matamoros for several weeks and then on June 12th General Taylor ordered McCullough to pick forty men and ride out to reconnoiter the area between Fort Brown and Monterrey—a Mexican town Taylor had decided to capture, his confidence bolstered by his victories at Palo Alto and the Resaca de la Palma the previous month.

On Saturday, September 20th we hove up before the white-walled city of Monterrey. I noted the date in the little journal I'd started keeping, thinking I would document our trip south of the border. All my life, I'd dreamed of participating in some big adventure in a faraway land and now, nearing the age of forty, my eyes beginning to falter, fresh aches in some different joint each morning, I knew this campaign would be the last I'd see and Mexico the farthest land I'd ever get myself to. I meant to set down everything that happened to us. Of course, I've yet to meet the trooper who didn't daydream about writing up his experiences for folks to read—I've known some who weren't even lettered and indulged the fantasy.

Ben McCullough's rangers formed up on the broad plain in front of the fortress town we aimed to sack, its high walls backed by blue mountains. I sat my horse and stared up at the city; it looked like a castle out of some legend. I was proud to count myself a member of McCullough's company and I wished that father might've seen me. I wondered if all the things I'd done would've changed his opinion. But look at me—nearly forty years old and whenever I thought of Pap I felt like a sniveling boy. It made me ashamed and angry. I hated

Pap and I loved him; I did not give a fig for what he thought and still desired his approval; I wished the old man dead and lay awake some nights, fearing he might be.

A great commotion started me from my reverie: General Taylor and his army were approaching and each of the rangers sat his horse a little straighter, knowing we would be Old Rough and Ready's cavalry.

Directly, the men began to remark a ball streaking across the sky. Then came the boom of the cannon that'd launched it. It was like the Battle of Concepcion, more than twenty years before. The cannon ball struck the earth well wide of its mark and once we realized no more accurate missiles were in route, we gave a great cheer. A feeling we would take the city with very little resistance blew through us like a breeze and then another hurrah went up; men pointed and clapped. One of the rangers had spurred his horse forward and was galloping toward the city, daring its sharpshooters and cannon, taunting the Mexicans. He leaned low against the neck of his blue gelding. I realized it was Juan.

He rode in an arc, travelling close under the very walls of the city. We saw puffs of smoke atop the battlements as the Mexican rifleman touched off their pieces, then the crackling of gunfire reached us. Juan kept charging and I saw there was no way he'd be touched. It was a brave display, but also very foolish, and one by one other rangers began to follow suit, each riding a little closer, daring the Mexican guns. Puffs of smoke would rise, the crack of rifles rang out, and then the rider would complete his circuit and make it back to the company where his comrades greeted him as if he'd just won a battle.

It was high entertainment for the boys and General Taylor let it go on a while—far too long for my liking. When Juan came trotting back down the line, men leaned out to slap his back and congratulate his courage. I thought about the day he'd charged those Comanche to rescue McClusky, but that was very different from this spectacle, and I felt fairly certain he'd never make it back to Texas alive.

That evening, we made our encampment beside a spring at Walnut Grove, a picnic ground for the nearby city. Taylor summoned Colonel Hays and General Worth to his tent for a counsel of war while the rest of us—rangers and U.S. Army regulars—made campfires and swapped stories. Against the general's orders, McClusky set out in search of liquor. I ought to have reprimanded him, but as my own tendency to drink would've made me hypocrite on the subject, I just sat and watched as he and Juan stalked off past the flickering fires where soldiers saw to their weapons, expecting to see some sport in the morning.

I realized as I sat there that a young Army lieutenant with brown hair and calm blue eyes was watching McClusky as well. The lieutenant stood about a dozen feet away from me and I wondered if he'd divined McClusky's intentions and was contemplating whether or not to report him.

I glanced over at the young man in his blue uniform at the same moment he glanced at me. He nodded rather shyly.

"Evening," I said. Though rangers had been mustered into Federal service, we wore no uniform and were not expected to behave as regular soldiers with the salutes and ceremony, but out of respect, I stood, walked over, and offered the young officer my hand.

"Duncan Lammons," I said as we shook.

"Lieutenant Grant," he said.

He gestured toward McClusky. The Irishman had made his way to the other side of camp and was conversing with a group of men around their fire.

"Are you that man's superior?"

"I was," I told him. "He's been in my ranging company for several years now. I suppose the only superior officer that really matters among us Texans is Colonel Hays."

We talked for a while. He was soft-spoken, and despite the epaulets on either side of his jacket—ornaments that made many men strut about like bantam roosters—carried himself with great humility. And yet, I sensed a tremendous reserve of strength in him, the nature of which was beyond my experience.

We shook hands again, and then he went off to see to his duties—I'd later learn he was quartermaster for General Taylor's army. I bedded down and tried to put thoughts of the coming combat from my mind.

* * *

They say Monterrey is a beautiful city—the gem of northern Mexico—but on the September afternoon that General Worth ordered us inside its walls, the air was choked by dark clouds of rifle-smoke and the breeze smelled like a rotting sewer—the townspeople had been cooped up inside the city, unable to make forays to the river or provision their commissary. Rangers dismounted their horses and filed in with U.S. regulars, Juan, McClusky, and myself among the ranks, waiting for word to move inside the walls.

I noticed a lost-looking boy making his way down the ranks. The young soldier couldn't have been more than nineteen or twenty: a slender, handsome youth with a thatch of blond hair and bright gray eyes. You could tell he'd barely begun to shave yet; there was a pale fur on his ruddy cheeks.

Something in him reached out to you. Even to McClusky, who when the boy passed us, turned and called to him: "You there, lad!"

The young man walked over. His name was Ned Hirsh, a Pennsylvania boy. He told us that he'd fallen out of step with his troop and was looking for a company to join.

"You can go with us," McClusky said. Then he glanced me. "That all right, Cap'n?"

I nodded at the Mississippi rifle young Ned carried.

"Can you use that piece? Do you have ball and powder?"

Ned touched the horn hanging on its leather strap around his neck and then the shot pouch on his hip.

"Have you taken fire?" I asked.

"No, sir."

"It's no need to sir me," I said, though, in truth, I appreciated his manners. He was a fine young man, if he was a little green. Of course, I must've looked mighty green myself to Colonel DeWitt when I'd strolled into his colony at a similar age.

I told him he could join us for the time being, but when we met with his company, I couldn't promise his officers wouldn't discipline him for falling out of the column.

"We're in the Federal service," I explained, "but we have no say over regulars."

"You all are the Texans," he said, and I saw the light in his eyes. U.S. troops held the Rangers in high regard and I'd be lying to say it didn't thrill me to see it.

McClusky said, "When we tell you to do something, laddie, we mean for you to do it."

"I'll not hold you back," the boy said. "That's my word on it."

The ranks were now moving once again and we began to file toward the city gates, passing under the arch and into Monterrey.

The streets were deserted, the windows boarded up or shuttered. Our boots echoed down the cobblestone alleys.

"Have they abandoned it then?" McClusky said.

"I reckon it's a possibility," I said, but a few minutes later we heard the crack of rifles several streets over and I told the men to look lively, we'd see some sport directly. I felt my mouth going dry as it always did before a fight. I pulled my pistol from my belt and checked to see the nipples were capped. Juan and McClusky were doing the same.

Ned watched us. He gave a soft whistle.

"Those are a sight," he said. "Can you get good range with them?"

"Fifty yards," I said. "Enough at these quarters. We depend on rifles any farther out."

He was still eyeing the pistol.

"Could I hold it?" he said.

That tickled me some. I'd become so used to the guns, I forgot their rarity. I put the hammer at half-cock and handed it to Ned.

He received it like it was Arthur's sword—the forefinger of one hand under the barrel, his other palm cradling the grips. He studied the cylinder and the long octagonal barrel. He handed it back to me, shaking his head and smiling.

"Five shots?" he said.

"Five," I told him.

He opened his mouth to say something else and the adobe wall behind him went wet and red and he collapsed to the cobblestones, a hole beneath his right eye, white smoke curling out of it. The sound of the rifle shot followed close.

"Jaysus!" McClusky said.

Juan had been crouched just to one side of the boy and there were bright drops of blood spattering his face. My heart was in my throat. I glanced up at the rooftop opposite our position and thought I saw the man who'd shot poor Ned, but he disappeared before I could point my pistol.

There were rifle shots from roofs of other buildings, and I realized we were in a bad way; the Mexican soldiers had gulled us into a turkey shoot. Juan realized this too. He stood up and glanced around, then told us to follow him. I hadn't the least notion what he was about, but with bullets sparking off the streets, I wasn't about to argue.

There is a murderous hatred that boils up inside your breast the instant an enemy discharges a gun at you. It's surprising how quickly the feeling comes, how powerfully it seizes your faculties. I'd experienced the same sensation numerous times in our campaigns against the Indians.

But I found this day that such loathing is compounded when the person firing at you is a sharpshooter operating from cover. The unfairness of it turns your stomach.

McClusky and I followed Juan as rifle balls cracked the air, the three of us moving toward the door of an adobe house—it doesn't quite seem accurate to call them houses as the city was so closely populated that the citizens' homes shared walls with each other; one family's bedroom abutted another family's kitchen. I saw now that Juan intended to get us off the streets and out of the sights of Mexican marksmen. As we neared the residence, Juan sped up, battering the door with his shoulder and sending it flying back on its hinges. He disappeared inside with McClusky and myself following.

We found ourselves in a low-ceilinged room that smelled of spoiled flowers—a vase of withered dahlias sat on a three-legged stool. I closed the door behind me and we stood there several moments recovering our wind. The muffled sounds of gunshots came from outside. I saw there were no windows in the room, no windows in the other room where two cowhide bedframes sat against either wall, no mattresses or bedding, the former residents having taken these, likely, when they fled the city.

There was the noise of men shouting, American voices, and the three of us seemed to share a common thought: there was no way we could hide out in the safety while our comrades were fighting in the streets.

Juan squinted at the walls, seeming to examine them for something. He walked over, placed his palms against the adobe, then turned his head and put his ear to it.

"What do you hear?" McClusky asked.

Juan shushed him. He listened a moment more, then looked at me.

"An axe," he said.

"A what?" I asked, but McClusky was already overturning tables and rifling through the meager belongings. I watched the Irishman a minute, then turned back to Juan.

"We don't get ourselves back in the fight, we're liable to get hauled up in front of General Worth. Or Jack Hays will hang us for cowards."

"Juan," called McClusky, holding up a little hatchet.

"Give it," Juan said. He tucked his pistol in his belt, took the hatchet, and walked over to the wall across from the doorway. Then he reared back and buried the hatchet in the wall.

"Juan," I said, but he'd already worked the hand-axe free of the crumbling adobe and given the wall another chop.

I stood there watching. In a minute or so he'd made a gap you could stick your head through—it gave onto a chamber on the other side of the wall much like the one in which we stood. He paused in his labor and turned to look at me and McClusky.

"Be ready," he told us, then started back at it with the hatchet. In several more minutes, he carved out a rough doorway, just wide enough for him to squeeze through.

And squeeze through it he did, McClusky and myself following, emerging into the room on the far side, also a residence, also deserted, but this one had a pane-less window, covered with heavy white oak shutters. Juan and I took up a post on either end of it and he unlatched a little bar and pulled the shutter back. He gave a quick peek and then moved back to cover. Several gunshots rang out, none directed at our position. I stepped over and peeked out myself.

The window looked onto a broad avenue where the bodies

of U.S. soldiers in their blue uniforms lay sprawled. Clouds of black smoke drifted in the air.

A guilty feeling overtook me for being forted up indoors while our countrymen were being butchered. I glanced at the roof across from us and saw a number of Mexican soldiers in a nest built of sand bags; most were presently occupied with recharging muskets that seemed to be some version of the old Brown Bess that British redcoats had carried in the Revolution.

Then I looked toward the square off to my right where companies of American troops were hunkered a few blocks from the central plaza. They had a few furlongs to go before claiming the very heart of the city, but here Mexican resistance was stiffest and a constant chattering of gun-fire crackled. Our boys looked to've found decent cover, but they couldn't take a step without exposing themselves to a shower of musket balls or grapeshot from the soldados on the roofs, a hail of lethal hickory nuts sparking off the cobblestones.

Then a magnificent steel-gray horse trotted round the corner and came down the street at a gallop, coming our direction. It wore an American saddle on its back and my first thought was that the animal had gotten free of its owner and bolted for safety. But as the horse came closer, I saw it carried a rider in blue uniform, though I suppose *rider* misses the mark. The soldier had only one boot in the stirrup, squatting alongside the horse with his arm draped over its neck and his other leg wrapped round and wedged under the cantle. He was pushing the gray full-chisel, using it for both carriage and cover, and whenever they came to a cross street where the Mexicans had their fortifications, the soldados would open fire. I expected the daring horseman and his beautiful mount to be shot down any moment, but the Mexican sharpshooters could hardly discharge their weapons before the rider had blown past and was screened by buildings once again.

The man traversed block after block in this fashion until he was no more than thirty yards from the window where I watched and then I saw his face. It was the young officer I'd spoken with several days before at Walnut Grove. I couldn't stand to crouch there gawking while such a courageous man was gunned down and I couldn't look away. The Mexicans on the roof across from me were watching too. They stood and leaned out over their sand bags to take aim, but before they could fire on him, the lieutenant and his gray horse passed below us and went pounding up the street, toward the outskirts of the city. I craned my neck to see him, but a building blocked my view. A cascade of rifle-fire broke out in that direction and I prayed the officer's luck would hold; he'd exposed himself so bravely and here I was cowering.

I glanced over to the Mexicans on the rooftop, cocked my pistol and felt the trigger spring out against the pad of my forefinger. I braced both forearms on the window sill and sighted down the barrel, putting the blade of the front sight on the bottom brass button of the Mexican's double-breasted coat. I judged the distance to be about thirty yards. I thought about that and the fact I'd be firing at an upward angle and moved my front sight onto the top, left-side button of my target's jacket. When I squeezed the trigger, the man toppled back and disappeared. The soldier standing beside him began looking around to see where the gunfire had come from and he'd just glanced down at our window when I cocked the hammer and shot him too. Then I ducked down and scrambled back again the wall. My heart was galloping in my chest and my ears were ringing. I'd never fired a pistol indoors before; the sound had nowhere to go and I might as well have fired a cannon.

I looked at Juan and held up two fingers. He nodded. The room was so thick with gun smoke I could barely make him out. I heard McClusky start coughing. Juan cocked his pistol and stepped to the window and as soon he did so a spray of dust erupted and he dropped to the floor.

262 · AARON GWYN

"Juan!" I yelled, thinking he'd been shot, but he just motioned for me to get down. I sprawled onto my belly as a thunder of musket-fire rang out from the rooftops and pieces of adobe began raining down.

I don't know how many Mexicans were shooting, but at that moment it felt like Santa Anna's whole army. The walls were coming completely apart, musket-balls ricocheting around the room. I glanced over to tell McClusky to get low, but he was already on his stomach with his fingers in his ears. He was saying something I couldn't make out.

In the meantime, Juan had belly-crawled over to the wall at our right and was hacking out another passageway with his hatchet. It took him a little longer, working from the ground like that, but pretty soon he'd opened a moon-shaped gap like a little arch, and started beckoning us toward it. McClusky and I didn't need much coaxing; we went clambering through like lizards.

This new chamber was different from the first two we'd invaded—long and low-slung with a walnut table that ran the length of the room. A banquet hall, I reckoned. Or some kind of hall, anyway—certainly no residence. A Mexican flag was presented along one wall and there were displays of Spanish armor such as the conquistadors must have worn. We seemed to've hacked our way into some sort of martial gallery: the weapons mounted on the walls ought to have been signal enough that our luck had taken a miserable turn. But we were so relieved to be out of that room the Mexican sharpshooters were firing into that we were slow to comprehend our predicament. I still had three shots left in the pistol I held, and five more in the one stuck in my belt. I can't recall how Juan was situated. I don't think McClusky had fired his guns at all.

There was a passage at the far end of the hall where the building dog-legged to the right, and the three of us moved toward it rather carelessly. My concern was for finding our way outside to rendezvous with our company—moving through a hostile city cut off from your fellow troopers will put a skeersome sensation in your belly. I thought of Sam and how, when the bullets were flying, he made you feel safe. I'd once had a similar feeling about Juan.

We reached the passage, turned the corner and stepped into what looked to be a canteen. Here, there were a number of small wooden tables, and at these tables, six or seven Mexican troops taking their midday meal. The nearest one wasn't ten feet from me. The men must've been so absorbed by their repast that they'd not heard us coming down the passageway. Perhaps the cascade of gunfire outside the little refectory had masked our footsteps.

Juan, McClusky, and I froze like statues and the Mexicans froze as well. I seemed to notice a thousand things all at once: a row of escopetas leaning up against the far wall; one of the soldados knifing through the bloody meat on his plate; the drone of flies buzzing about the tables; the startled eyes of a boy soldier of perhaps fifteen years; the perfectly spotless baked clay floor, swept so clean it looked to've been painted; the smell of hot wax and the flickering of candle-flames sawing back and forth.

The man seated nearest had his back turned to us, and noticing the expression of his comrades' astonished faces, turned to glance over his shoulder. We'd all been caught up in a breathless moment, sharing the shock and surprise. This man's movement seemed to shatter it. McClusky cocked his pistol and placed it to the soldier's head.

When the gun discharged, the Mexican's teeth scattered across the floor like a handful of gravel; the man collapsed onto the table, McClusky already pointing his weapon at another soldado, firing again and again and again, dropping his weapon and reaching for the other in his belt; Juan shooting too, the Mexicans just reaching their feet before being blown down, several already sprawled on the floor as blue gun smoke drifted through the room. It happened very fast, yet seemed remarkably slow, as any man who's ever been in a gun-fight can attest. The Mexicans seemed to fall like ash, McClusky firing into them, Juan firing, sparks leaping from the muzzles of their guns. My ears rang so loudly I no longer heard the shots, just a high, steady whine. When the hammer of McClusky's pistol snapped on a spent cap, the sound was like a hand slapping a bolt of cloth.

The dead and dying men lay all over, some wailing, one crawling toward a Brown Bess leaning against the wall. It had a rusted bayonet attached. Juan stepped over and seized it, then started around the room, spearing the survivors. I stood there watching. I hadn't fired a shot.

McClusky had noticed the soldado belly-crawling toward the row of weapons; he tracked through the blood the man had left behind him, his boots leaving pale prints in the wet, red smear. He stepped on the Mexican's back, tucked his pistol back in his belt and drew his Bowie knife.

Well, that was the last feather. The room smelled like feces and iron. I turned, stumbled back down the passageway and into the room with the long table and aired my paunch on the floor. I'd seen every foul sight a battle could present, but it seemed a fresh kind of slaughter had entered the world, some brand-new viciousness. I retched again. It felt like someone had shoved a fistful of cotton down my gullet.

When I righted myself and got my breath, I went back to join my comrades. Juan was moving around the room, search-ing the dead men for anything of value. Which might seem unusual, but is as common in warfare as udders on a milch cow. The oddity was that I'd never seen him do something so covetous. Then my eye fell on McClusky.

The Irishman was on the ground beside the Mexican whose throat he'd just cut. He'd rolled the man onto his back. The soldado's blinking eyes watched his killer, lingering just at the edge of life. McClusky bent down and got very close to the man's face. I thought he was about to kiss the Mexican, but that wasn't it at all.

The soldier was panting. Then he drew a long breath that would be the last he'd ever take and when he started to exhale, McClusky got so close that their lips nearly touched. As the Mexican released his final breath, McClusky began to suck it in, inhaling it the way a cook breathes in the steam off a pot of beans.

A ghastly wet rattle came from deep in the Mexican soldier's chest and his eyes opened even wider.

Then the man was gone. McClusky leaned back and sat on his heels. His face was relaxed. He seemed to be anywhere but a city where two armies were caught in a murderous clash. His good eye glanced up and took me in, but I was fixed on the other: the pupil large and black as the bore of his pistol.

* * *

We ventured out into the street on the other side of the building and fell in with a company of U.S. volunteers who'd been fighting house to house. I talked with a grizzled old sergeant and learned that our indoor engagements with Mexican troops was the Battle of Monterrey in miniature: all through the city, rangers had been tunneling through walls to get at sharpshooters on the rooftops, fighting them hand to hand.

We made our way into the heart of the city and the last pocket of Mexican resistance, and by evening, General Taylor had negotiated an armistice that would last for six weeks. In the celebration that commenced when we heard Monterrey was ours, I was separated from McClusky and Juan. Which was fine by me: after witnessing the set-to in that dining room, I decided I needed a break from my comrades. As dark drifted through the bloody streets, I happened upon the young lieutenant who'd ridden so bravely past the enemy marksmen, a feat that would've made a Comanche jealous.

We met in a stone plaza and clasped hands. His face was blackened with gun soot, but his blue eyes were clean and bright.

"Lieutenant," I said, "I spied that maneuver you performed earlier. That's as canny a bit of horsemanship as I've ever seen."

His face blushed so powerfully you could see a flush of dark red beneath the layer of dirt and grime.

"I'm thankful," he said, "that Nellie wasn't injured. It isn't Christian to use an animal so."

The cobbled streets were sticky with blood. You could hear the screams of dying men like barbarous birds.

"Well," I told him, "I've not seen a great deal of Christian behavior since we crossed the Rio."

The lieutenant's mouth tightened and he shook his head.

"No, Captain Lammons. Taken altogether, this has been a wicked affair. I don't think the Mexicans were equipped for such a fight. Today's battle was simply murder."

* * *

Still, the Rangers had acquitted themselves valiantly and I heard tell General Taylor was proud he'd mustered us into service. Yet he only had us on loan, and I would've loved to have seen Old Rough and Ready's face when Jack Hays went to inform him that many of the Texas boys had already overstayed their enlistment. A ranger's term of service was generally a year, and most men in ranging companies had signed on the previous fall. No doubt, General Taylor made all manner of entreaties to Colonel Hays as the Texans were the best cavalry he could've hoped for, but Jack was true to his word, honoring his rangers over the demands of the nation we'd just joined. The colonel would lead the Rangers north on the second day of October.

I took this as excellent news. The whole campaign had soured something in me. My term of enlistment had expired some months ago, but I didn't know exactly when; as I'd had no intention of ever mustering out of the service.

Those final days in Monterrey, I'd wake in the cool autumn mornings and feel a chill in my bones. What did I have to show for my years of service? The Republic I'd fought for no longer existed.

A more sobering thought would hit me when I considered taking my land payment and mustering out of the company: where could I possibly go? There was Noah, of course. But if I took my headrights around Webber's Prairie, would my jealousy let me live so close to Sam, seeing him week to week with his frontier wife and son?

There had been a time when Juan might have factored into my plans, but that had passed. I hadn't seen him since the evening we were separated, during the merrymaking that accompanied our taking the city. I reckoned this was likely for the best; I did not want to know what all McClusky had done. Colonel Hays was allowing his men to indulge in spirits, but he'd issued three general orders that might as well've been carved in stone: no ranger was to plunder the homes of Monterrey; no ranger was to harm the citizens' livestock; no ranger was to lay a hand on any woman or child.

I suppose I oughtn't have been surprised when Isaac Casner came knocking on the door of the little house where I was quartered. It was the evening before our departure for Texas and something anxious had been brewing in me all week. When I opened the door and saw Ike standing there, I knew it was about Juan and Felix before he'd spoken a word.

"Cap," he said, "you're going to want to see this."

I put on my hat and followed Uncle Isaac through the winding streets.

By the time we reached Hays's quarters, a crowd had formed around the building, Texans crowding the doorway and bunched around the open windows, leaning against the sills. Ike made a path for us, and I nudged in between the dirty troopers, stepped up through the doorway and entered a hall that was ringed about by rangers, most of whom I knew, a number of which I'd ridden with over the past decade.

Jack Hays stood at the far end of the room, the short man with his pale eyes blazing; in front of him, two men stood with their backs to me, one short, one tall. I stopped and stood there. I'd never attended a court martial before. How do you court-martial men who were kept in service by little more than the promise of land titles that were likely to be contested?

The colonel had turned to confer with a man whose face I recognized, but whose name I didn't know. Then he turned back to Juan and McClusky.

"Well," he said, "if either of you have ought to say in your defense, now's the time to do it."

They stood there a silent moment, Juan staring at his feet, McClusky in a posture that was far too casual for the taste of Jack Hays.

"Colonel," said McClusky, "I'll not be made a catspaw of."

"*Catspaw*," said Hays, his brow rumpling. "What are you talking about?"

I saw the problem right away: Felix was absolutely snapped. You could hear it in his voice and see it in the way he swayed on his feet.

McClusky said, "I mean to say that you ordered us to take the city. Private Juarez and myself shot as many Mexicans as any regular, I'd wager. More than most, mind you."

"The problem," said Hays, "isn't how many Mexicans you shot. The problem is the two of you were reported robbing houses, and then the lieutenant here finds the plunder among your belongings. Explain yourself."

McClusky said, "None of that coin belonged to us, Colonel."

"Yes," said Hays. "That is why you're standing here."

He studied both of them.

"I've no objection to you men tying on the bear, but we're answerable as to how we conduct ourselves in this city. Do you wish the honor of Texas to be stained and her best men branded sneak thieves?"

I realized then that Hays felt guilty about the savagery of the fighting he'd ordered his men into, about the rangers he'd lost. He had no reason to explain himself to a couple of privates, and for their part, they were lucky not to've already been the guests of honor at a string party. He was giving them every opportunity to exonerate themselves.

Juan, I thought. Say something.

And then, as if in answer to my prayer, Juan coughed into his fist and said, "I myself have no concern over what a Mexican brands me." He eyed Hays for a moment before adding, "Colonel."

A hush passed through the room. Several men cleared their throats.

And still the colonel showed restraint; he'd no desire to bring down the hard hand of punishment on men who'd fought so bravely for him, and he certainly didn't want other rangers to see him doing so. Perhaps he was wondering how he'd ever recruit another company if word got out that he'd executed a couple of Texas boys for taking a little kelter off people who'd sniped at them from rooftops.

"Private," he said, "who is your captain?"

Juan didn't answer; nor did McClusky. I realized they were showing loyalty, thinking their refusing to say my name might protect me somehow. A number of sights passed through my head: Juan reading his poetry; Juan rescuing McClusky; Juan lying on Doctor Chalmers' table like a corpse.

I stepped forward.

"Colonel Hays," I said. "I'm these men's captain. Duncan Lammons."

Hays nodded and motioned me up. I walked over and stood beside Juan, feeling every eye in the room on me, the back of my neck hot as an iron. I suddenly felt that I was guilty of something I couldn't name.

Maybe I was.

"Captain Lammons," said Hays, "these are your rangers?"

"Yessir," I said.

"They stand accused of a serious offense."

"Yessir. I understand that."

"Did you have knowledge of it?"

"None at all. Not until Private Casner came and got me in my quarters about half an hour ago."

"Are you willing to stand for them?"

"Sir?"

He said, "I asked if you're willing to stand for them, Captain. To vouch for their service. What is your opinion of these men?"

I glanced beside me, catching the sheen of gray stubble from Juan's face, the red tuft of McClusky's filthy beard. I thought about Felix bending over the soldado, sucking his last breath away. I thought about the conversation I'd had with Juan en route to Mexico, that he known what I was the whole time. I swallowed very hard and looked back at Hays.

"Colonel," I said, "they've always acquitted themselves well. I've never known them to steal. I don't know what they've been up to the last few days, but if they've disobeyed an order, I'd say it's out of character."

Hays nodded. His eyes wandered around the room. He'd been a lawyer before coming west. Perhaps he'd be one again.

"Captain," he said, "let's you and me speak in private."

* * *

When I stepped back into the hall, all the rangers were gone except for Juan, McClusky, and the grizzled man assigned to guard them.

I walked over, dismissed this gentleman, and waited for him to get out of earshot. I turned and looked at Juan.

"The colonel is discharging you from service," I said. "You and Felix both. He wants you out of Monterrey pronto and on the trail north. You can keep your arms and horses."

"Tonight?" said McClusky.

"Tonight," I said.

McClusky said, "We'll rendezvous in Bastrop then?"

I looked at him. "What rendezvous?"

"Our company," he said. "Where do you want us to reform? If we head out tonight and you all light out tomorrow, we'll lose track of one another for a few weeks, at least."

I shook my head. "There's no more company. Not for you and him. You're discharged from service altogether. If you try and muster into another troop back home, your life won't be worth dog's meat."

"They'd keep us from signing on, Cap'n?"

"They'll hang you," I said.

Juan just stared at me. I couldn't tell how much of what I said was registering.

"How do they expect us to find for ourselves?" McClusky said. "Are we supposed to go live with the savages?"

"I don't know," I told him. "But for the nonce, you and him need to saddle your horses and jump up some dust. The time for palaver is done."

Juan had already turned away, but McClusky just stood there.

272 · AARON GWYN

"Cap'n," he said, "this ain't right."

"I understand you feel that way. But ever since you've been down here, the two of you have been standing in your own light. You have to know that."

Of course, you could take one look at him and see he didn't know it. By his way of thinking, he'd conducted himself as cleanly as you could ask for and it occurred to me that perhaps he and Juan would ignore Hays's new order like they'd ignored his previous ones and I'd have to stand by and watch as they were executed.

But then he turned and started for the door. The sadness of the whole affair finally hit me and I knew I would be seeking a bottle that night. There just wasn't any way around it.

So far, it had been McClusky who'd protested; Juan hadn't spoken a word. The two of them reached the doorway and were starting through, when Juan turned back and said, "What about our headrights, Captain?"

It was a question I'd have expected McClusky to ask.

"There's not going to be any land payment, Juan. You defied the colonel and wouldn't speak a word to defend your-selves. Jesus—headrights? You're lucky to have a head."

He glared several moments at me out of his dark, brown eyes. I found myself wishing I hadn't dismissed the guard.

Then he turned and walked out the door and the two of them went off into the night.

CECELIA

—TEXAS, 1846—

And so, Lammons went to Mexico and left her Sam alone. She knew the man might die down there, but the more she thought about it, she wasn't sure she cared.

"Can you not see it?" she asked him one day. "The way he looks at you?"

Sam was working on the cabin. It'd been several weeks since Lammons left and Sam was fidgety as a spider. He was convinced the Kiowa would ride against them. Or that the Comanche would launch raids into Bastrop County. They rarely ventured east of the Balcones Escarpment anymore, but now that the ranging companies had headed south to join the army there was nothing between the settlers and Indians but cedar logs and chinking. Sam seemed bent on turning their little cabin into a fortress. He'd taken the door off its frame and fixed it to swing outwards so no one could kick it in.

"Course," he said, "they could always just fire the dratted thing. This cedar burns up awful quick."

He'd ignored her question. She walked outside and sat with Robert on her lap, watching Sam work. He was opening the door back and forth on its hinges, shaking his head doubtfully.

"Are you listening to me?" she asked.

"I'm listening."

"What did I say?"

"You were talking about Duncan."

"Yes. About the way he stares at you."

"That's just the way he is," Sam said.

"I know it's how he is. That is my point."

He began stomping at the dirt until he'd kicked loose a stone the door was catching on its new path.

"Well," he said, "he's not staring at me now." He turned and made his wolf face at Robert, snarling his nose up and curling his fingers into claws.

"Woooooooooooooolf," he growled.

Robert began to squeal with delight.

"Wus!" he shrieked, and Sam reached down, grabbed the boy, tickling him and howling.

Sam wouldn't hear a single word against Lammons.

And why not? She understood the man had been his captain, but Sam had no captain now.

"Do you not know that?" she asked him the following day.

"I know that," he said.

"And he's not your family either."

"I never said he was."

"We are your family," she said.

* * *

Sam could hardly sit still. It was one thing after another: first the door, then a new bullet mold, then he went into Bastrop and returned with a second rifle.

One morning, she woke to find him out in the yard, splitting lumber to cover up her window.

She stood in the door watching him a while.

"Samuel," she finally said, "I enjoy to see the sunrise."

He turned and looked up at her like she was speaking Dutch. "You can come out to see the sunrise."

"I like to see it as I cook. And we'll have to burn our lamp or candles during the day to even see by. What'll that tax us?"

He stood there very still. He always got still when he was thinking. His eyes went unfocused.

Then he said, "Fair enough."

He contented himself with building shutters on the inside of the window that could be closed up and barred. She was glad she'd be able to watch the world while she cooked, but she really wished he'd settle down; he was making her nervous. Ten years they'd lived here and no Comanches had attacked. Two summers ago, fetching water from the creek one morning, she'd been kneeling on a shelf of sandstone, filling the bucket, when she glanced over and saw an Indian watching her from the trees. She didn't know if he'd been there the whole time or if he'd just crept up, but he was motionless as a statue, studying her out of his calm, curious eyes. She felt her heart speed up, but she wasn't exactly frightened.

"Hello," she said.

He said nothing back. His eyes blinked. She took the pail by its rope handle and began walking up the hill, thinking, Do not run. It is bad if you run. And when she reached the hilltop, she looked back and the man was gone.

She never saw him again and she never mentioned the incident to Sam. He actually seemed to believe it was the Rangers keeping them safe, that men like Lammons were the only reason they'd been able to live in peace.

She didn't think that was true at all. She thought the Indians left them alone because they'd kept to themselves, though she'd never have been able to convince Samuel of that. He didn't understand there was another way—the way of subterfuge—something she'd learned from Odysseus when she was just a girl.

She was free this day because of trickery, not carnage, and she was grateful she'd never stained her soul with blood. Her freedom came from determination and cunning.

But is that true? she wondered. It was the threat of violence that freed you, Sam cuffing that planter, Childers.

I might've gotten away eventually. Childers might've made any number of mistakes.

But that wasn't what happened. Sam struck him so hard it knocked all notions of mastery from his brain. You are free now because of fear.

And yet, if she hadn't run from Haverford; if she hadn't slipped out the window of that house in Natchez; if she hadn't escaped the cotton plantation or strolled out the front door of that grocer's home in Natchitoches she'd never have been sitting on that buggy next to Childers. Sam would never have been blocking the road with his big bay horse.

So it was will and cunning and cruelty, all three. And perhaps a hundred other things combined.

* * *

Sam had once slept soundly, though he'd committed many vicious acts in the Revolution with Lammons—Lammons whose face was etched by the violence he'd done the Mexicans, the Indians; that was another thing about that man: she'd never seen anyone so haunted. There was a time when she'd have thought Sam was exempt from all he'd done, that he was too simple a creature to be hounded by conscience. Was a mountain lion troubled when it pounced upon a deer?

So, wasn't it strange that, having laid aside his panther cap, that his sleep was troubled? Something was happening to him. He seemed to smell blood on the breeze, whereas she smelled nothing but cedarwood and sunlight, the clean scent of Robert's skin after she scrubbed him down. Sam worked dawn to dusk and then went to pacing around the cabin. Or he stepped outside to check the sky. Or he woke in the middle of the night and sat with door open, his rifle on his lap.

"Here," she said when he kept getting up one night, "come to me."

She thought he'd argue with her, but instead, he crossed the room, stepped over Robert on his pallet, and lay down. She stroked his hair, brushed her fingers through his beard, slid her hand down and put it on his chest.

He was a wild, sweet soul, the most beautiful man she'd ever seen. She loved him so hard she ached. He'd had to do many savage things to make it to this very moment, his head on her lap, heart beating under her hand, his blue eyes blazing up at her.

"What is it?" she said. "What is it you think will happen?"

He didn't say anything. He closed his eyes.

"Tell Suss, now. Or do you think it will scare me?"

He gave a slight shake of his head.

"Nothing's going to happen," she told him. "We're safe out here."

When he opened his eyes, she saw they were wet.

No, she thought. It is just the moonlight.

But a tear left the corner of one eye and streaked across his cheek. She leaned down and kissed it, tasting the salt on her lips. She'd never seen him cry and it frightened her so she never wanted to again.

He said, "We should have kept moving. Paw always said men were meant to hunt and move."

"We couldn't live like that," she said. "We wouldn't have a family."

"The Comanches have families. They raid and hunt and follow the buffalo. For a hundred years, they've done it. And the Apache before them."

"We do not have a hundred years, Samuel."

"That is true," he said.

We crossed the Rio north of Matamoros to find autumn waiting for us. On the American side of the river sat Fort Texas and here I bade farewell to Levi English, Uncle Ike, Joel Ramirez and the other fine boys who'd served under me, tendering my resignation to Colonel Hays himself.

For every year of service with the Rangers I'd been given a handwritten voucher, each representing a quarter-league of land. Having taken Noah's warning about property titles to heart, I'd traded most of those vouchers for horses or supplies, as did many rangers of that time—McClusky, for instance, handed several of his to ladies of the town, plying their avocation. Lord knew what they did with them.

Now, needing a place to hang my hat, and determined not to end up in a lawsuit, I had the adjutant general write me out an affidavit which I carried straight to the land office in Austin. It was a 350-mile ride and I made it in just under a week—hard riding, but I hardly seemed to notice. Something had happened to me down in Mexico: I felt twice as old and half as smart. Sometimes, a panic touched off in me like a cannon and I would feel precisely as I had that day on the cramped streets of Monterrey, Hirsh examining my pistol, and then his brains slapping the wall behind him, a new red mouth grinning at me on his cheek where the rifle ball had torn through.

As to when these spells would come over me, there was no timetable I could discover. I felt like a rabbit being chased through brambles; I'd turned to glance behind me, but no dogs were bearing down. I was hunted by my own thoughts, just as I'd once pursued Indians and other enemies of the Texan Republic. Now there was no Republic, just another state in the slave nation I'd fled twenty years before.

After scouting the country and hiring a surveyor, I was deeded 1,400 acres in Bastrop County just north of Sam's headrights and twenty miles south of the Smithwicks' claim up on Webber's Prairie. No coincidence, of course: it was the exact title I sought.

I didn't rest from my journey. I went out, located my acreage, and began to construct a little cabin. I had no great desire for a home, but meant to keep my thoughts from strangling me, and the busier I kept, the better my chances. Some days, Noah would leave his gun shop in his nephew's care and ride down to assist me.

I had time to reflect on my life. In fact, I did little else.

There were all these notions I'd developed that had become rather dear to me, precepts I'd held about the merits of hunting versus hoeing Mother Earth, about frontier-living versus city life, about the nation I'd been born in and run away from only to be engulfed by despite my best efforts. They were not just ideas to me: I'd stepped onto them like the planks of a bridge, following them step by step to this place where the planks fell away and a great chasm opened at my feet.

What I couldn't seem to decide was whether I'd formed these opinions before Pap suggested I clear out of Kentucky or afterwards—and it mattered quite a lot which it was. If the principles that had directed my course for the past twenty years had come to me naturally, that was one thing.

But if all my clever beliefs were merely things I'd told myself after Pap turned his back on me, they were simply a salve I'd applied to my conscience as a man might smear a poultice on a wound.

And for the life of me, I couldn't seem to settle the matter one way or another. I tackled my horse and rode down to Bastrop, went into Amos Alexander's store and bought several sheaves of paper and a brand-new inkwell. Evenings, I'd sit on the porch of my sad little cabin, scribbling down everything I could recall about my life in Kentucky, about my notions concerning civilization and society that had once seemed so important. Now they didn't. In truth, they seemed rather flimsy, rather frail. As a young man, I'd been so certain my beliefs were bedrock. Now they seemed like shifting sand.

The loneliness that descended on me was like a thousand of brick. I could feel the weight just as heavy as you might a saddle on your shoulder.

Mister Lammons, I told myself, if you keep on prodding at yourself like this, you'll end up putting one of those shiny pistols in your mouth some morning.

And so, I swallowed my pride and rode down to call on Sam.

When I rode up to the cabin, I heard little Bob wailing inside. I lighted and tied my horse, stepped to the open door, and saw Miss Suss kneeling beside a chair and airing her paunch into a bucket. Sam had Robert on his hip and the boy was bawling like he'd lost his best friend. Samuel was trying to calm the child and see to Cecelia both.

I knocked on the door to announce myself.

Sam turned and glanced at me and I saw, for the first time, an alarmed look in his bright, blue eyes.

I gestured to Cecelia. "Is she poorly?"

"Seems to be," he said, crossing the room to slap my shoulder, then nodding down to Bob. "Could you take him a moment?"

It wasn't a request I received very often. Fact, I'd never received it at all.

"Give him here," I said, and when he passed the boy to me,

Robert drew a deep breath and stared up at me with his tear-streaked little eyes.

"You're all right," I told him, and the novelty of my moustache seemed to provide a distraction. I stepped outside and sat down in the grass. I stood him there in front of me, made a face at him and got the hint of a smile.

His nose was running. I swiped at it with my sleeve.

"How old are you, little ranger?"

He didn't know what to say to that. He turned and looked at my horse. Then pointed at it and said, "Hoss!"

"Yessir," I said. "And a pretty good one. Would you like to sit on him?"

He scrunched his nose and looked at the ground and seemed to consider it.

"Hoss," he said, somewhat contemplatively.

"Well, come on," I told him, and picking him up, carried him over to where my mount was tied and set him on the saddle. Old Roger was an easygoing gelding, didn't mind a bit.

Robert's face lit up and the sulk he'd been in when I'd arrived was a hundred years ago. That tickled me some.

I said, "Well now, Bob, how about it?"

He said, "The hoss is ride!"

"Well, sir," I said, "that's a fact or I never heard one."

"The hoss is ride!" he squealed.

Directly, I was laughing along with him, and by the time Sam came out to check on us, Bob and myself were friends.

* * *

I was in Bastrop about a week later, visiting with Timothy Lynch at his hotel. John Berry walked over from his shop—he'd ridden in my company back in '38—and said, "You just missed them."

"Missed who?" I asked.

"Your man Felix and the Mexican. They come in wanting me to work on a rifle they'd dry-balled."

I listened for a moment or two before what he'd said sunk.

"Felix McClusky?" I said.

"Yeah," said John, "and his greaser friend."

"Juan Juarez?"

"That's him."

"He's not Mexican," I said. "He's Spanish."

Timothy laughed. "Well, there's a great distinction."

"Anyway," said John, "you'd have seen them yourself not half an hour ago."

"Were they looking for me?" I asked.

"Never mentioned you," said John. "I just know Felix had ridden with you, is all."

This was a troubling piece of blather, though I couldn't exactly say why. Perhaps the thought of running into Juan and Felix was a bit prickly for me, given how things had gone at the battle of Monterrey.

Of course, there was also the fact that Juan knew something about me other men didn't. I didn't believe he'd trumpet the knowledge, did not even think he'd tell Felix.

It was more him knowing in the first place that bothered me.

I bid Tim and John a good day and went to visit Sam.

CECELIA

—TEXAS, 1846—

Robert turned three that fall. The boy had his father's energy; he was into everything there was. Cecelia would get so exhausted she'd break down crying. Then she'd start to laugh.

"What is it?" Sam asked, coming inside one afternoon to find her wiping tears out of her eyes, chuckling to herself like a madwoman.

"Your son," she said. "He never stops."

Sam glanced over at Robert who, as if to spite her, was now napping on their bed.

He said, "Looks like he's stopped pretty good."

"Half an hour ago he had the sugar loaf down in the floor."

"I need to build another shelf," said Sam. "Move things up a little higher."

"It won't help," she told him.

There was something that did help, and that was Duncan Lammons. Robert developed a fondness for the man like she'd had never seen. Lammons would ride down for supper, and the moment he walked in the door, Robert would be in his arms. It might have embarrassed her, but she could tell Lammons enjoyed it. He'd sit there with Robert snoring against his chest.

"Here," she'd say, "let me take him."

"Leave him be," Lammons told her. "What's the Savior say? If a man sleeps, he does well."

Sam shook his head.

"Well," he said, "that fixes it: boy's got you playing nurse-maid and quoting scripture both."

Lammons patted Robert's back. "He's good, this one."

"He is," Sam said. "Wish he was a better judge of character, but you can't have everthing."

It moved Cecelia, watching the child with Lammons. Didn't make her trust him any better—he still stared at Sam with the same longing—but his skill with Robert certainly surprised her. She could tell it surprised him too.

To hear Sam tell it, Lammons was as ruthless an Indian fighter as ever walked the earth. Men feared him, and she knew it wasn't for no reason. She hadn't seen that side of Lammons, but she could tell it was there.

Robert saw another side. He'd be sitting on Lammons's lap, pawing the man's moustache with his fingers. You'd think it would annoy someone like Lammons, but it was just the opposite. The man's features would start to soften: his eyebrows arched and a light came into his face. She watched him become a grandfather before her eyes.

She thought it was so curious. Who were these people down inside us? Who did she have inside of her? She'd been a house servant, a field hand, a runaway. Then, unexpectedly, a frontier wife to a man who stumbled into her at a slave sale. Now she was a mother, and perhaps other things as well.

Who would she be next year?

Who would she be in years to come?

For years I'd barely drawn a sober breath, numbing myself to loneliness and the horrors of battle. I must've reckoned I was very brave, but once the grip of the demon rum had loosened from around my throat, I was like a raw nerve in the wind—the slightest breeze could overwhelm me.

I wish I could say that parting ways with liquor freed me of the stain of jealousy. But sometimes I'd see Sam glance across the supper table at his lovely helpmeet and envy would twist my innards like a rag. It is a shameful thing to admit. A man may rectify his behavior but changing the desires of your heart is another thing entirely.

It was Robert who salved this wound and kept my feelings from festering into resentment. I'd had no experience with children. I must've thought of them like a crop you tended. I hadn't the least notion that they tended you as well. The affection of a child can mend the raveled hem of your soul. They are such genuine creatures; there is no feigning or fakery with them, nothing counterfeit.

Robert made a place for me in that family—let me say that right out. Only my mother had ever given me such unearned approval. I'd carve him horses out of cedar, whittle little soldiers out of pine. I'd get down and wrassle him around the cabin floor, and the sound of his laughter chased away my sadness.

* * *

In those days, I was back and forth to Bastrop all the time, making forays for this or that. As I'd never set up a proper house, I was always needing provisions or tools or some blasted thing. I'd acquired thousands of acres in my years of service but ended up selling a good deal of it for operating capital. My ambition had been to maverick up a herd of cattle, but that proved considerably more work than I'd reckoned, and I had no talent for it. In truth, I just wanted something to keep me busy between visits to Sam's cabin.

At the time, Bastrop was a few dozen cedarwood stores and houses. Most of the streets were named after trees, others after the great men of our Revolution. I'd ride in to visit John Berry at his gunsmith shop or Timothy at the City Hotel.

I was in the general store talking with Amos Alexander late one evening when John Berry came in and clapped me on the shoulder.

I said, "Do you ever spend any time in your own shop or do you just wander about?"

"He wanders," said Amos. "Ask him how much coffee he drinks. He can't sit still."

John said, "Come visit with me 'fore you leave out."

"What is it?"

"Just come talk with me," he said. He looked over at Amos and said, "Get back to work, loafer."

"You get to work," Amos said.

John went back out and Amos shook his head.

"He's a secretive sumbitch, ain't he?"

"I guess so," I said, though *secretive* wasn't a word anyone ever laid at John Berry's door. If he ever heard a piece of news he didn't tell, I'm a senator's son.

Directly, I said my goodbyes to Amos, walked down to

Berry's shop, went in and found him standing by his furnace. His demeanor had stiffened some.

"They aim to take Sam's headrights," he said.

"Who's going to take them? Where'd you hear that?"

"Don't worry where I heard it. You just convince him to clear out."

"Clear out to where, John? That's his land."

"It was his land," he said. "Is it true he's took up with a nigra?"

Well, that raised my hackles. I said, "What's it to you who he's took up with?"

"Duncan," he said, "I wouldn't care if he married an alligator. I'm trying to tell you something, is all."

"Well, tell it."

"You never seen people so greedy for land. And Sam didn't help hisself, thumbing his nose at the Rangers, neither."

"He didn't thumb nothing," I said. "And come to think of it, I didn't see you signing back on."

"No, you didn't. But Mrs. Berry is a white woman, and there's no comparable gossip to help the land-jobbers swindle me out of my claim."

I stood there, staring at the fire. This low talk about Cecelia made me ashamed for my own ambition against her. How did I tell her it wasn't her skin I begrudged, but where she laid her head at night?

Then something occurred to me.

"Why didn't you tell him?" I said.

"How's that?"

"Sam. Why didn't you tell him they're moving on his claim?"

"I ain't never been out there," he said.

"Yeah, but that's not it, is it?" I saw how nervous he was acting, anxious to be associated with Sam in any way. His conscience gave him just enough courage to warn me what was coming.

"You're really something," I said. "You know that, John?"

"Dammit," he said, "you just make him understand. These folks are going to end up with that property. If he just moves along, it'd be a lot easier."

"There's nothing easy about somebody stealing your home from you."

"There's plenty worse things," he said. "You make him listen. I don't want to see something bad happen here."

"You really think folks in this town are going to stand by while a man who fought in the Revolution is run off his own property?"

"Duncan," he said, "you don't have no idea. It ain't that they're going to stand by for it. I know these people pretty good. If it comes to it, they'll pitch in and help."

CECELIA

—TEXAS, 1846–1847—

That winter, Samuel went to work on a cow pen. Mister Lammons rode down on the weekends and the two of them would spend the day cutting pine trees from a grove beside the river.

Then one morning the man turned up in the gray light of dawn and as soon as she opened the door, she knew something was wrong.

"Miss Suss," said Lammons, and the look on his face was grim.

She showed him inside, put a mug on the table, and set the kettle on to boil. Sam roused himself from bed and came in knuckling sleep from his eyes.

"Duncan," he said, and you could tell he was bewildered; they'd not been expecting him so early.

"You need to get to the land office," Lammons said. "They're going to contest your claim."

"Do what?" Sam asked.

"Your headrights," Lammons told him. "I'd not even wait for your coffee."

It was spitting snow when they rode for Austin, and it was dark and raining by the time they got back. Samuel came in and sat down at the table. He wouldn't look at her.

They'd woken Robert up. The boy got off his pallet, walked over and Lammons took him on his lap. Usually, Robert ran to greet the man, but even a child could read the atmosphere in the room.

She sat beside Samuel, waiting for him to speak, a steady patter of rain on the cedar shingles.

"They say there's a flaw in our title," Sam told her. "They say we have to buy it from them or lose our improvements."

"What title?" she said.

"Our property," Sam said. "This property right here."

She didn't understand what she was hearing. She said, "You got this land for your service."

Sam nodded. "Now they got witnesses saying it's an old Spanish grant, so it wasn't ever the Republic's to offer."

"That doesn't sound right," she said.

"It's not right," said Lammons, who up until now had been silent. "They manufactured this business about a Spanish grant. These witnesses of theirs are just men they bought off."

"Who's *they*?" she said. "Who's doing this?"

"Could be anybody," said Lammons. "Someone working in the land office, someone who's moved out from the States and has taken a shine to your property."

For the rest of the evening, she listened to Sam talk about the evils of annexation. Hadn't he told her these things would happen?

She had a cold feeling, very cold. She couldn't help but think it might even be Lammons himself working some scheme against them.

After the man left and she'd gotten Robert down, she went and knelt beside Sam.

She said, "Folks know Duncan socializes with you."

"Seems to me they know pretty much everything a body does," but before he could start ranting she said, "They're trying to scare us. They want to know if we'll spook. If Mister Lammons will take our part in it."

Lammons was back over a few days later and she told him of her suspicions. Or most of her suspicions. She certainly didn't mention her misgivings about him.

He listened to everything she had to say, stroking the whiskers on his chin, his gray eyes intent. When she was finished he looked at Sam and said, "I think she's right."

"About which?" Sam said.

"All of it," Lammons told him. "They want to see if you'll just fold. They're not sure how you'll come at them."

The three of them sat for several moments.

Then she turned to Lammons and said, "What should we do?"

Lammons scratched at his cheek. "Sam ought to go see Joel Ponton first thing tomorrow morning. He knows these titles inside and out."

"Lawyers," said Sam, shaking his head.

"Why us?" Cecelia said.

Lammons said, "Pardon?"

"Why'd they pick us to torment?"

"It's not just you," said Lammons. "A lot of folks are being done brown. They did the same thing to Noah Smithwick's mother-in-law. And her a widow with children."

"Is it just that Sam wouldn't ride to Mexico with them?"

"That is part of it," Lammons said.

"Part of it," she said. "And what is the rest?"

Lammons glanced down at the table and cleared his throat. she watched him. She didn't need him to say it.

Or actually, maybe she did.

"It's me," she said.

Lammons didn't say anything. He didn't look up.

"I saw how they looked at me and Robert when they came out here asking after Sam. They're going to keep at us and keep at us till we're gone."

Lammons shook his head. "It's shameful, Miss Suss. It's not everyone thinks that way."

"No," she said. "Not everyone."

* * *

The next day, Sam hired Joel Ponton to act as their agent. Ponton said he'd ride to Austin the first chance he got and see whether their title was truly flawed or if it was all just a swindle.

She was proud of Sam not going for his guns, though she knew that's exactly what he wanted.

And Lammons seemed worried it still might come to that. He showed up the following day to give Sam a pistol.

It was a beautiful, shining thing with walnut grips and an octagonal barrel. He said the weapon had come from Paterson, New Jersey. It would fire five times, quick as you could work the hammer.

Sam stared at the gun for several moments, then looked up at Lammons.

"I can't take your pistol," he said.

"You will take it," Lammons said. "You'll take it and you'll keep it handy."

"I've got a pistol," Sam said.

"You've got a one-shot hand musket that takes a minute to reload. You've got a rifle that's the same way. That's two shots, if you're quick. I know you don't count very good, but this here's an improvement."

That night, she lay in bed, trying to think it through. Everything seemed to be speeding up on them; everything was going very fast.

She rolled over and looked at Sam.

"Why don't we just leave?" she said. "Why not let them have it? We can find another piece of land."

"Let them have it," he said.

"I know how they are. They won't let up."

"I won't either," he said.

She put her palm on his chest. "I know who you are, Samuel Fisk. You don't need to prove yourself."

He stared at the ceiling. "I'm not going to give them our home."

She lay there, breathing. She'd known she wasn't going to convince him.

He drew her head to his shoulder. "Let's hear what Joel Ponton has to say."

She thought the next time Lammons visited, she'd pull him aside. Maybe the two of them could go to work on Sam together.

They were expecting him that weekend, but when she heard the sound of hooves coming up the trail and opened the door, it wasn't Mister Lammons's appaloosa she saw but the apron-faced sorrel with its four white stockings. On the horse's back was the Irishman with the milky eye. McClusky. She couldn't recall his Christian name.

It was evening. The weather was unusually warm. Riding next to the Irishman was a balding man in store-bought pants and an oilcloth coat. He sat a little steel-colored Welsh pony with gray splotches over its hips. The two men reined up several yards from the cabin, McClusky staring at her, the other man studying the ground.

She turned to call for Sam, but Sam was already there beside her. He walked a few paces out into the yard and she saw he had the pistol Lammons had given him tucked in his belt.

She thought immediately of Robert. She turned and saw him toddling up to see what was happening, and she shooed him back.

Sam stood there, watching the men on their horses.

"Evening," said the Irishman.

Sam told him good evening.

"I'm Felix McClusky."

"I remember you," Sam said.

"And you know Mr. Ponton."

She glanced at the man on the Welsh pony, and a tingling sensation went up the back of her neck.

Sam said, "How are you, Joel?"

Joel Ponton nodded hello. He still hadn't looked up.

McClusky sat there taking everything in. He turned to Ponton. "Tell him," he said.

Ponton cleared his throat, glanced at Sam.

"I don't think I can represent you," he said.

Sam said, "Change your mind?"

"I just don't think I can manage it."

"What'd they threaten you with?"

"Didn't threaten me," the man said sheepishly, but he was looking at the ground.

"What'd they pay you?" Sam said.

Ponton didn't say anything. She thought she saw his cheeks darken.

"Some men," said McClusky, "are leery to take a losing side, you see."

Yes, she saw how it was very clearly. Of course, this dead-eyed man had been involved in their difficulties. Of course.

Sam didn't seem surprised either. His shoulders were bunched up and that vein was standing out on his neck. She was aware like never before how the world in which she moved and mothered rested on those shoulders, how, if those shoulders collapsed, her world would tilt and slide into extinction.

She took a step forward.

If I can touch him, she thought, everything will be all right.

McClusky seemed to be enjoying himself. His good eye left Sam and fell on her. That pupil was so strange, like something had exploded in it.

"Well," he said, "this man's given you his answer."

"Seems like," Sam said.

"You let me know if you need anything else," McClusky told him. He lifted a hand and touched the brim of his hat.

He's brassy, she thought. You have got to give him that.

Sam stood there watching. Then something caught his attention, and he glanced down to his feet.

It was Robert. The boy was sitting on the ground beside him, legs crossed, playing quietly in the dirt. He had one of the little horses Duncan carved for him. How long had he been there? She didn't see how he'd gotten past her. She was reaching for him, when McClusky said something she didn't catch— one of the words sounded like *lark* or *dark*—and she could tell by the way the man was leering it had been some quip about her son. She was glad she hadn't heard.

But Sam seemed to've heard just fine.

"What's that?" he said, and the amused expression vanished from McClusky's face.

She hissed Sam's name, but that savage scent was in the air and he was already moving toward McClusky's horse. The sorrel took a step backward, bogging its head, but Sam was quicker. He brought his boot up and kicked the horse in the jaw.

The sorrel bucked, then bucked again. McClusky lost his seat and went sliding sideways, striking the earth with a hard, heavy sound. He rolled onto his back and lay wheezing, his good eye startled wide.

His horse took off trotting across the yard, tossing its head. Ponton was saying, "Mr. Fisk! Mr. Fisk!" his own mount starting to sidle.

Sam stepped up and stood over McClusky, then straddling him, sat down on his chest. He grabbed hold of the man and struck him with the heel of his hand. Once, twice, a third time. It didn't look like he was hitting him very hard, but McClusky's nose was already bleeding.

"Sam," she said, "that's enough," and then she was behind him, pulling at his shirt.

He let go of McClusky and the man collapsed. Sam stood and took several steps back, holding up his hands.

It should've felt good, their tormentor lying on his back, but she knew McClusky would recruit other men to his cause, folks he could goad, or bribe, or bully. Like she told Sam they'd just keep coming and coming.

And so, when Ponton managed to rouse McClusky and get him mounted back on his horse, it didn't surprise her that the man's face showed neither rage nor embarrassment. His nose ran bloody, and his hat was missing, but the corners of his mouth were twisted into a smile.

* * *

That night, they argued about Lammons a final time.

"That Irishman," she said. "He was with those men who tried to recruit you for Mexico. And aren't they the ones who rode with Mister Lammons?"

"A lot of men rode with Duncan," he told her. "I rode with him too."

"And you don't think it's awfully suspicious that they follow at each other's heels? Lammons and this McClusky?"

"Duncan left the Rangers," he said. "And he's the one who warned us about all this in the first place."

They went back and forth, but it was no use. He wouldn't listen to a bad word about Lammons and she wouldn't air her true suspicions and be accused of jealousy.

She woke at first light and lay for several minutes, watching Sam as he slept. There was still something of the boy in his features; that he hadn't lost. She wondered if he ever would.

She went to the fireplace, stirred the coals into bright flames, put a few kindlers on the fire and waited for them to catch. Robert was asleep on his pallet. She sat on her heels, watching the yellow light flicker across his face, sawing shadows back and forth. Lammons hadn't come the previous night, so he'd most certainly be here this morning. She was anxious for him to arrive. She'd already roasted coffee beans in the pan, tied them up in buckskin and beaten them to powder with her cooking stone, enough for several kettles. She took the bucket from the nail and went outside.

It was cold and clear. The sky in the east was the color of slate, stars still hanging in the west. She followed the path down to the stream and knelt on the bank filling the bucket, listening to the water running, plashing over the rocks. She was trying to remember how much sugar was left in the loaf. She'd been putting it in everything lately: their coffee and corncakes, their bacon and bread.

She could feel the weight of the past several weeks slipping from her. It was the time of morning that did it. Your thoughts were so clean and sharp. You could take an idea and turn it in your mind, hard and bright as a jewel.

You've never seen a jewel, she thought.

Some day.

She lifted the bucket. It was a little heavy, so she tipped some of the water out, then started back up the path.

She was walking through the cedars when she saw a dark form pass in the distance, backlit by the eastern sky.

Coyote, she thought, and here came another.

She reached the edge of the clearing and one more went trotting past.

But they weren't coyotes; they were horses. The hair stood up on the back of her neck. She could just make out the front of the cabin, firelight flickering in the windows.

"Sam," she said, then drew a breath and called his name.

Her voice sounded small and shrill in the air. It died away and everything went quiet.

Maybe they weren't horses, she thought.

Then a rider passed between her and the cabin, not fifty feet away. She dropped to a crouch and the water sloshed onto the ground. Her heart was kicking inside her chest. She couldn't see the rider very well, but she didn't need to see him to know who it was. She glanced over as another horseman rounded the far corner of the house.

How many were there?

She squatted there and counted three of them.

She counted four.

Birds had begun to chirp from the branches. The stars were fading. She was going to have to find a way around the riders, but they were between her and the cabin. She wondered if she could crawl past them, and then Sam stepped out the door and a gunshot boomed from somewhere in the woods.

Sam retreated inside. A few breathless moments passed. Then he came back out.

He won't know where I am, she thought, and then she was standing, but that didn't seem like the right thing to do, and she had the powerful sense that the horizon had tilted, and she couldn't quite keep her balance.

Sam was hunkered at one side of the door. She thought he had a pistol in hand, but she wasn't sure. One of the riders was moving toward him. Sam extended his arm and a flame burst from the tip of it. She saw him for half a second in the flash of his gun: hair wild, his eyes like black slits. The rider kept on coming, though his horse had slowed to a walk. The man fired a pistol of his own, but Sam side-stepped the horse, shoving the barrel of his weapon into the rider's ribs as he passed.

The shot lifted the man from the saddle. Or perhaps the horse had simply bucked. Sam fired three more times; it sounded like someone hammering a nail. Then she couldn't see the rider anymore and the horse was on the ground, screaming and kicking in the dirt.

The air smelled like pine trees and pitch. Sam had disappeared inside a cloud of gun smoke. The horse raised a screen of dust, but there was no wind to disperse it. The smoke slid lazily, bolstering the sensation she had that the world was listing to one side. She thought if she could just see Sam, it would right itself instantly.

Her thoughts were interrupted by another gunshot. She saw a man standing beside his horse with his feet planted; the pistol he'd just fired had issued an enormous plume of smoke. He began to fumble for the powder flask hanging around his neck and then a shot came from the drifting screen that obscured Samuel, sound and flash, like lightning inside a cloud bank. The man reloading his gun doubled over as if he'd been punched in the stomach, then turned and began to run.

Then everything was quiet several moments. A rider was dismounting a steel-colored horse out by the tree line. He had a rifle in hand. He was eighty, ninety feet away, but she could see him quite clearly—it was the Spaniard who'd visited them in the spring, trying to recruit Sam for their company. He went to his knee and she heard him cock the hammer, the sharp click of it like a branch snapping in the quiet air. She wondered if she'd feel the ball he'd send through her body. Maybe she wouldn't feel anything at all.

The rifle cracked, but the man hadn't been aiming at her. He knelt there, reloading. She glanced back to the front of the house where she'd last seen Sam. The dust rose and the smoke went gliding across the ground.

Then she saw him: Sam down on his hands and knees. Her breath caught in her throat. She felt the horizon tilt even farther, and now everything started to slide: the smoke, the dust, the reefs of rusted clouds.

And then that apron-faced sorrel. She didn't even hear the hoof beats; the horse seemed to hover. The Irishman with the milky-eye slid out of the saddle, slid across to Sam, a cocked pistol already in hand.

Sam, for his part, wasn't sliding at all. He just stayed there on his hands and knees like he was deciding whether to be an animal or a man. Blood dripped out of his shirt. McClusky lifted the pistol and put it to Samuel's head.

The world tilted over all the way. Sam raised his head and looked at her. Or she thought he was looking at her. Maybe he was looking into the barrel of the gun. His blue eyes were very bright. There was a loud boom and they flashed even brighter, two blue suns in the muzzle's flare.

DUNCAN LAMMONS

—TEXAS, 1847—

I had an anxious feeling in my belly when I started out that morning, and it got no better as I went along. I remember riding along the trail, glancing out through the cedar trees and seeing a pecan hiding back there in the brush, crawling with honey bees. I'd been coursing bees since I was just a boy, and had taken plenty of hives by myself, but I was almost forty that year and such tasks were above my bend. You really needed two or three folks to do it proper, and even then, it was an all-day affair: hacking down the tree, puncturing the comb, collecting the honey in a cased deer hide. A single skin would hold nearly two hundred pounds.

I thought I'd tell Sam about it, and maybe we'd rob the hive come spring, but my nerves were so bad, I forgot to mark the tree, and that should tell you a great deal.

I was fording the creek when I heard voices coming from up on the hill. It smelled like someone was making meat. Old Roger's nostrils flared and I knew he could smell it too.

I cleared the crest of the hill and came down at a lope. Sam's cabin was standing just as I'd left it, but there was a wagon backed up to the door, and half a dozen men were milling around the yard. I saw Moses Rousseau's boy. I saw Sampson Connell. A horse lay on the ground just where you didn't expect a horse to be, and it took me a few moments to realize the animal was dead.

Connell had seen me by this point. He glanced up at me,

then he looked away. The other men stopped talking. They all stood real quiet.

I slowed up and trotted my horse into the yard. It was like I'd entered one of those dreams where you can imagine a thing and it will appear for you. I found myself wishing for Noah or Levi or Uncle Ike Casner—any of the old rangers who'd ridden with me. I turned to ask Sampson what was going on, but it was like I had a mouthful of leaves.

That's when I saw the body. It was sprawled in the dirt and there were brains scattered in wet clumps across the grass. The body was faced away from me, but I knew who it was. I would've known him from the slope of his shoulders or the shape of his hands. I reached out to steady myself on the pommel.

You are just sleeping, I thought. You are just lying there.

I reined up beside the wagon. There were all kinds of tools in its bed: a bullet mold and a patch knife. A bone powder measure. A priming horn, a vent pick, a small horsehair brush. A fire-new adze and a wooden loading block. A buckskin bullet pouch. Pots and pans and pewter dishes. My eyes started to hurt; the sun seemed very bright.

Two men came walking out of the cabin. One carried Sam's rifle and a powder keg, the other a rolled haversack and a government-issue canteen—I had one just like it.

The two men looked at me. Then they looked away.

I glanced over and saw Rufus Helmsley. I saw Paul Wilkinson. I wondered if all the fine citizens of Bastrop were present and my hands started to shake.

A third man was coming out of the cabin. He had Sam's pistol tucked in his belt, the five-shot Colt I'd had given him the previous week. It was Felix McClusky. He squinted up at me with his good eye.

"Cap'n," he said.

A noise came from my mouth, a sound like a starved animal.

And then Juan Juarez walked out of the cabin and stood behind the Irishman. The blood was whining in my ears.

I looked at McClusky and said, "What the hell did you do?"

It wasn't real for me just yet. It felt like Sam could stand up and all of this would turn into something else.

McClusky said, "We were fired on, Cap'n. We just came here to talk to the man."

"You son of a bitch," I said.

"No need to curse me, now. Tom Joyce is laying over there cold as a wagon tire, and Dave Henry's gut-shot and might die yet."

"Where's Cecelia?" I asked. "Where is the boy?"

"They are no concern of yours," he said.

I considered drawing my pistol. I knew if I reached for it these men would blow me down, and that seemed a good deal preferable to this new life I'd stumbled into, which I knew wasn't really a life anymore.

I thought I heard a child crying. Then I was sure I did. I slid from the saddle and started for the cabin's door.

"Cap'n!" said McClusky, but I'd already stepped inside.

It looked like a storm had swept through: tables over-turned, bedding scattered. Crockery smashed on the floor, a skillet smoldering in the fireplace.

Clothes were strewn all over; the corn shuck mattress stood against the wall.

And there in the middle of it all sat Robert, his eyes red and his nose running.

But unharmed, I thought. Unharmed.

Robert went quiet and the two of us stared at each other. I can recall the exact look of his cheeks, his skin the color of creamed coffee.

When I stepped back outside, I was carrying him on my hip. I'd already decided to shoot anyone who tried to stop me.

I went over to my horse, but I couldn't mount up just yet. I turned and looked at each of the men in turn, naming them to myself: Jesse Rousseau, Rufus Helmsley, Samson Connell, Martin Sapp. Not a single one would meet my gaze.

Except for Juan and McClusky. Who just stood there, staring.

I was getting ready to question them about Cecelia, but I knew if I pushed the matter any further, neither me nor Robert would be going anywhere. I could leave my life in this place, or I could leave with Samuel's son. It was one or the other, and I had to choose.

* * *

I rode out with Sam's corpse bound to the horse like a bedroll and Robert bouncing in front of me on the saddle. The boy's feet barely reached the top of the fenders, and I kept one arm around him, hugging him close.

That afternoon, I dug a grave on the prairie while Robert sat on the ground crying.

"Shhhhh," I said, "hush now, son," but he had every reason to carry on, and after a while, I was bawling too. I couldn't look at Sam's face, his blond hair matted with blood.

It is a sickness in this world, I thought. A sickness to destroy beautiful things.

When I had Sam in the earth, I filled the hole in and packed the dirt until it was level, walking back and forth, stomping it flat. I felt like a madman; I didn't know how to feel.

I gathered a pile of brush and built a fire atop the grave. If you didn't, there was a smart chance the Indians would dig up the body and scalp it. This way, all they'd see was charred limbs and ash, assume it was a campfire, and move on.

And leave you out here, I thought. No coffin or cairn.

Yes. The world scranched beauty between its teeth and ground it into nothing.

I rode back to the cabin and got Robert fed—cold corn dodgers and a few pieces of pork—then sat there trying to figure out what to do. I didn't think the cowards would ride on me that night, but I knew men who didn't dare look at you in daylight might burn you alive come sundown. By dark, I'd packed my guns, a few tools and blankets, some cornmeal and dried venison, and with Robert sleeping in the saddle, I took a cattle trail north, leaving my property and this life I'd built behind.

* * *

We spent the next several months up on Brushy Creek, living in a dugout beside the river. Our only neighbors were Noah and his family. Noah's gun shop wasn't doing much business, but he'd scrounged up a herd of wild cattle and was making a go of it with his wife and his nephew, John Hubbard. I told him of Sam's death, and he took the news very hard.

"What was the cause of it?" he asked. "Was there a dispute?"

I was leery of naming Cecelia to him, and I did not mention that the boy sitting in the grass beside me was Samuel's son. I thought Noah would be of the same mind as I was, but I meant to protect Robert as best as I could.

"They wanted his headrights," I said. "They bogused an old Spanish grant and Sam wouldn't budge."

His face colored. He said, "They did the same thing to Mother Blakeley."

"I told Sam about it," I said.

"Did he have an agent?"

"He was supposed to've hired Joel Ponton."

"I know Joel," he said. "Did he not look into it?"

"I don't know if he looked or he didn't. Next time I saw Sam, he was lying there in the dirt."

Noah stood there. I don't know that I'd ever seen him so angry.

"You know who did for him?"

"I know."

"What do you aim to do?"

"I reckon I'm doing it," I said.

Which didn't seem to satisfy him at all. He glanced down at Robert and studied him for several moments, his brows furrowed up like caterpillars. Then his forehead relaxed. When he looked back up at me, he had a different expression on his face.

"Yes," he said. "Yes, I see."

"Not a word," I told him. "Not to anyone."

"No," said Noah. "Not a word."

* * *

Those first months were very hard. If I end up in hell, I'll feel cheated if I don't get credit for them.

Bob had been such a spirited little boy. Now he was careful and quiet.

I gave him all my attention. I wondered what he'd seen of Sam's murder and worried what he'd recall in years to come. I remembered Sam telling me about his own pap's knifing, and it seemed very cruel to think a man could pass on these calamities like a harelip or a stutter.

I'd fall into a brown study just thinking about it. Lying there at night, a rage would come up in my throat, and I'd have to go outside. I'd stand there staring at the bright tangle of stars. It seemed that God had retreated behind them. There was less and less of Him all the time.

And Miss Suss, I wondered. Was she alive to be tortured by these notions?

I didn't think she was. I wanted to, but I couldn't see how that was possible. She had been so kind to me.

"If You'd let it happen to that woman," I said, "it's not a soul safe amongst us."

After a while, I'd go back in and see Robert sleeping on his pallet, his thin little chest swelling up and sinking. That would settle me. Having someone to care for settled me. The fit would blow on through and I'd get clear inside myself, thinking, *He depends on you, Duncan. You best straighten up.*

I'd lay my head down and go to sleep.

Cecelia

—Texas, 1847—

She was jostled awake by a creaking rumble, the hard ground shuddering beneath her. It was very cold and the gray sky pressed against her face. Something was wrong; her skull was humming; pain lanced behind her eyes. The earth continued to tremble, the sky weighed down, and after a while she came to understand it wasn't ground or sky either one. She was lying under a screen of burlap in the bed of a wagon, and as her vision sharpened, she saw the earth passing below her through a gap in the boards and heard a horse's hooves striking dirt.

Her wrists were tied together, her ankles tied; she lay on her side with her knees to her chest, a grown child in a travelling womb. Lord, how her brain hurt! It was very hard to think, like startling from a dream and not recognizing the waking world, your body heavy with sleep. Part of her knew Sam was gone, and another part of her didn't see how that could be.

You are the one, she thought. You're the one that's gone.

That first day, she wept soundlessly, but it wasn't any kind of weeping she'd ever done. It was like watching herself weep—her eyes leaked and her body ached, but she was high up inside herself thinking, Look at you. You're the most miserable thing that ever lived. You are shaped for misery. You draw it like bugs to a fire.

Then her brain would begin to pulse and she couldn't think at all. Days passed, or she passed in and out. She wasn't always clear. There were images she couldn't fit together. She knew—

or thought she knew—that she'd been clubbed in the head; she saw it like a painting: a man walking up and striking her with the butt of his rifle.

But how could that be? You can't see yourself from the outside. What is wrong with you?

Then another thought like a slap: They killed my Sam.

And then Robert would flash in her mind and her entire body would be painful and panicked.

No, she told herself. You cannot do that now. Not if you ever want to see his face.

* * *

She'd decided there were several men driving the wagon, at least two, but when they stopped to make camp, it was only one: a young man, little more than a boy, with dark hair and big brown eyes. He made a fire, offered her beans and bread, but she would neither eat nor answer him.

He told her his name was Davy. He asked if she needed to relieve herself again, and she thought, Again?

What else had she done that she couldn't remember?

He asked her again after supper. He seemed quite worried about it. He was the most nervous man she'd ever been around and she wondered if she frightened him. Then she knew she did. Which was strange. It didn't seem possible he hadn't killed her yet, and she thought that if he kept her alive, there could only be one reason. A conversation spooled out in her thoughts: a circle of men standing round, after they'd knocked her senseless, discussing her fate. She couldn't believe she was just imagining it.

Maybe I'm not. Maybe part of me was awake and took it in. Maybe I heard without hearing.

What sense does that make? They must've clubbed you pretty hard.

Still, the voices were so clear:

And what're we supposed to do?
Do about what?
About her. You ask me, we're fools to let her live.
She's money. That's a hunk of money lying there.
That's a witness lying there. The clean thing would be to blow out her lamp.
You've an objection to feathering your nest?
My objection is to the noose.
Won't be a noose, the man said.

* * *

The following night, she lay in front of another campfire, thinking how, only a handful of days before, she been lying in bed next to Sam, begging him to let it go. She could close her eyes and picture him, and she thought maybe all of this was a dream; she'd open her eyes and this horrible new world would vanish and another more familiar one would take its place.

But when she opened her eyes, it was only Davy sitting on the other side of the fire, this timid young man carrying her to auction.

He glanced over and gestured with his chin.

"If you need to do your business," he said, "you got to let me know."

She stared at him. He'd undone her ankle bindings earlier, and now she raised her wrists toward him as well.

He nodded, stepped over, and helped her to her feet. She could smell the nerves on him. His eyelashes were long and black, faintly feminine.

He's afraid of me, she thought. Won't even look me in the eye.

Davy gave a soft tug on the knot between her hands.

"I take this off, you won't try and go nowhere, will you?"

She didn't want to answer him, but there was no other way: "Where would I go?"

He seemed to agree with the sense of this. He took her very gently by the arm and led her off into the cedars, then spent several minutes fighting with the knot, trying to untie it, squinting to see in the failing light. Finally, he pulled a knife from a sheath on his belt and severed her bindings.

"It wasn't me who tied that," he said, and there was something in his voice that asked her approval.

Then he nodded to her and turned to face the fire.

She took several steps backward, her legs shaky as a fawn's. She hiked her filthy dress and squatted.

I won't be able to do anything, she thought, but her stream came right away. She started to cry again; there was a kind of betrayal in all this; she wanted her body to rebel against Sam's murderers just like her mind.

But the body was only flesh; it manacled you roughly as men.

When she stood up, Davy still had his back turned to her, staring out toward the fire and the wagon and the horse on its picket line. It occurred to her right then what she would have to do. The sensation was so strong, it was like she'd already done it, and she thought, Yes, this is what the World has starved you down to, this is what you'll become.

* * *

They were on the road another three days, the same one she and Sam had taken on their way out from Natchitoches ten years before: *El Camino Real de Los Tejas*. The King's Highway.

"Old San Antonio Road," Davy called it.

The country bore little resemblance to the wilderness Sam had led her through; now there were farms and towns and settlements. And, my Lord, the plantations—cotton plantations like she'd only seen in Mississippi, the fields fallow now, waiting for spring. They'd travelled west while she'd slumbered in her dream of freedom, chasing her down: you no longer walked the earth; the earth moved beneath your feet, scrolling toward the sun.

Sam had been correct in everything he said: America had come flooding in from the east in a white, rising tide. And how could a body escape drowning?

It'd swept her whole life away, and now she thought of Robert; now it was impossible not to. Being separated from him was like someone hacking off a limb, only, there was nothing on her that would hurt so much to cut away. It ached and ached. Would they sell him? Would they injure him some way? She refused to believe he was dead, wouldn't even let the thought pass through her mind.

Instead, she thought of that traitor, Lammons. The thought of doing him violence felt like a sanctuary. She saw very clearly how it must have been him who'd set this madness in motion, wanting so badly to get Sam to himself that he'd unleashed these demons, destroying the very man he'd wished to claim. Likely, he'd meant for McClusky to kill *her*, but Sam did what he always did and forced a fight.

She felt sure that Lammons would know where Robert was being kept. If she made it back to the cabin Sam had built her, would she find Lammons living in it like a shrine? There was only one way to find out.

Each night, Davy would stop the wagon and she'd help him collect wood for their fire. He'd come to have a kind of trust for her, though always he took off his belt before lying down, rolling it around his big knife and slipping both inside the folded blanket he used for his pillow. So, he didn't trust her all the way. It was more like he couldn't stand for there to be any meanness between them or any silence either. He'd likely spent his childhood being mothered by house servants, black women who fed and pampered him, perhaps even chastened him with his mother's approval.

They developed a strange rapport. He never mentioned their destination and as she didn't plan on them reaching it, she never asked. The young man was another distraction from her grief. He was pretty as a girl, soft-featured. His brown eyes glittered in the firelight. She began to sit beside him on the wagon seat during the daytime, and as they went along, she'd think about what this boy might've been if he hadn't been raised among slavers.

One evening, they made camp along the banks of the Neches—he said it was the Neches. They ate their supper of bacon and bread, sitting across the fire from each other with blankets around their shoulders, talking about the constellations. The weather had turned cooler, but there wasn't a single cloud. She pointed out Orion, standing straight and tall in the southwestern sky.

"How do you know their names?" he asked.

"I read about them," she said. "I was lettered by my mistress in Virginia when I was just a girl. I read every book in that house."

Davy said, "I don't think I've read a whole book in my life. I read some Bible verses, but I was made to do it. How many books you think you read?"

It was a good question; she didn't exactly know.

She told him how they'd been like food to her, how once she'd lived inside them. She told him about Odysseus and the Poem.

"There was a time when I thought it was all I'd ever need. I thought as long as I had that book, everything would be all right."

"I wished I'd been thataway," he said. "Probably would've saved me some trouble."

"No," she said.

"How's that?"

"I don't think these books save you any trouble at all. If anything, they cause it."

That seemed to interest him; his head tilted to one side like a dog's.

"Because you're Negro?" he said.

"No. Not because I'm Negro. Because I wanted to be like the people in the stories I read. Maybe I thought I was *in* a story."

"Well," he said, "I reckon all of us are in some kind of story. Maybe not a book-story, but still."

"It's better not to be," she said.

"Not to be what?"

"In a story. From the time I was fifteen my life was one story after another. And then for ten years there was no story to it. Now, the story's back again."

"Like I say, I think that's the way with all of us."

"Not all," she said.

* * *

She opened her eyes to soft starlight. The sky was cold and clear and she lay watching her breath drift from her mouth like smoke.

There's a fire inside you, she thought. There has always been a fire.

She thought of Robert. It was painful to think of him, but it was the pain of longing, and she knew there was nothing she wouldn't do to get back to him, nothing in all the world. She glanced over at Davy, lying there asleep.

The campfire was down to crackling coals. She lay listening to Davy breathing. She sat up in her blankets, got onto her hands and knees, and started to crawl toward him, then knelt on the bed of dry leaves he'd made himself. He was on his left side and she watched his chest rise and fall the way she'd once watched Sam's. What she was about to do would be very hard, no turning back once it started. It wasn't that she doubted she could go through with it, only that she wasn't entirely sure who she'd be once it was done. She wanted to spend several more minutes as the woman Sam would recognize if he were still here.

But he's not still here, is he?

He's here inside me. Inside, he's here.

She didn't like the idea he was staring down from some ledge in the sky. She didn't want him watching what she was about to do. It was better she have him down in her breast where she could talk to him, but he couldn't see.

She moved her hand into the blankets under Davy's head, then placed the other on his shoulder and felt the heat of him.

"Davy," she whispered.

He slept on and she squeezed his shoulder.

Finally, his breath caught and he rolled onto his back. His eyelids opened a slit and he looked up at her.

"What?" he said. "What is it?"

She leaned in closer, feeling him go rigid under her hand, his breathing shallower. Had slave girls once come to him in the night? Had he gone to them?

She imagined him slipping inside a pinewood shack, bending over the sleeping form of a young woman the way she was now leaning over him, sliding her hand farther inside the blankets, farther and farther until she found the handle of his knife, then gripping it, drawing it from its sheath, from the folds of blankets, and before Davy's eyes could light on it, she'd passed the blade across his throat, drawing it toward her in the same motion she'd used to dress the deer and turkey Sam had brought in, pulling and pressing down.

Davy's eyes sprang wider and he sat up clutching his neck in both hands.

They stared at each other a moment, their breath mingling, fogging the air between them.

"Help me," he said, as if he couldn't believe she'd slashed him.

"You're all right," she said, then hacked at him with the knife, only cutting his fingers this time, thinking, That's wrong. You did it wrong.

Then Davy was on his feet, staggering away from her.

Don't let him get his rifle, she thought, but he didn't seem to grasp what had happened or even consider the weapon. She stood and followed him several steps. She had that strange sensation of watching herself again—as though all of this wasn't her doing; it was a silhouette woman cast by firelight against a wall.

Davy had begun to sputter and cough, bleeding through the seams of his fingers. He bent to spit blood from his mouth. She stepped up to cut at him again, but then a whistling noise came from his throat and the sound of it stopped her cold.

You could tell it shocked him as well. He pulled his hands from his neck and looked at them. The dark slit she'd carved into his windpipe wheezed. A bubble formed over it, blew big and popped. Davy's panicked eyes widened and he released a terrible scream.

Or tried to. That whistling noise came from the gash, much louder now, and then something she'd never have imagined: he took off running.

Then here she was chasing after him, running out through the cedars, the knife still in hand.

He was moving very fast for an injured thing. She could just see him up ahead, dodging limbs, a shadowed form jerking through the trees.

Don't let him go. Do not let him go. You can see him by the light of the moon. Bright, old moon. If it were darker you might not make him out, but it isn't darker. I am darker, dark

as the ring outside the nimbus—that is the word, *nimbus*—
your heart is cold as the moon and black as the sky around it.

When she caught up with him, he was sitting beneath the
spread of a live oak, holding his throat in both hands as if he'd
strangle himself, wheezing. He looked up and saw her and she
knew he'd have run again if he'd been able. His life was leaking out of him and he seemed to understand that he would die.

He began to shake his head.

"Don't," he said, "please don't." His voice sounded very
strange.

She came up and squatted a dozen feet away. Her ears were
stinging from the cold.

"Why'd you do that?" he said, and his voice was all hurt
and outrage, as if she'd betrayed him horribly.

She studied him a few moments. Then she said, "You
shouldn't have taken up with those men, Davy. They killed my
Sam."

"I didn't kill nobody," he said. He might have yelled it if
he'd had the strength. His voice was beginning to crack. He
spoke in a whisper.

"I'm not going to be a slave again. What would make you
think you can just cart me off this way?"

He began to tremble. He was terrified of her. She'd never
done this to anyone, and though she took no pleasure in it,
there was a puffed-up feeling in her breast. She felt herself
puffed up very high.

He said, "I'm going to die, ain't I?"

She didn't say anything.

"My mama won't even know what happened to me."

"I'm sorry," she said. And, in a way, she was. There just wasn't
anything she could do about it.

"It hurts to talk," he told her.

"Maybe you should be quiet," she said.

Then he said, "You're going to cut me again."

"I don't need to," she said.

She watched him think about that. He began to cry. After a few minutes he said, "I'm scared."

"Are you?"

He nodded. "I was raised in the church. I kindly got away from that when I left home. I always thought I'd take up with it again, but I never got the opportunity. You think the Lord's liable to put me in hell over it?"

"I don't know," she said. "I don't know what He's liable to do. There's some I'd like to see Him put in Hell, but I don't feel that way about you, Davy. I'm confident none of this turned out like you might've thought it would, but it hasn't turned out for me either."

He sat there weeping softly. He said, "I never for one minute thought you'd stab me like that."

"That's how I was able to," she said.

"It was almost like we were friends," he said, and the outrage was back in his voice, the disbelief.

"Almost," she said.

He sat with that a moment.

She said, "Are you sorry you took up with those men?"

"I'm sorry as I can be. I never wanted to be a part of no killing."

"I believe that, Davy."

They sat for a time. He was pressing around on his throat.

He said, "If I keep my finger like this, it doesn't make that sound."

"Then keep your finger there."

"Maybe I won't die after all?" he said, but it wasn't really a question, and she could tell he knew the answer.

Then he said, "Can you sing?"

"I haven't sung since I was a little girl," she said.

"Would you sing a hymn?"

"I don't know any, Davy. Do you want me to sing to you?"

"Mama used to sing hymns to me all the time. I keep trying to get a church feeling to where I can pray, but I can't do it. If you'd sing to me, maybe it'd be better."

She wondered what kind of woman slashed a man's throat and then sang songs to him. But then, a song formed on her lips. She hadn't thought of it in years and she was surprised to find she still knew the words. The first verse went:

The Spirit of God like a fire is burning.
The latter-day glory begins to come forth;
The visions and blessings of old are returning,
And angels are coming to visit the earth.

When she was done, she saw Davy was sitting there, eyes closed, mumbling his lips. She sat quietly until he finished.

Then he opened his eyes.

"Thank you," he said.

"You're welcome, Davy."

He leaned his head back against the trunk of the tree and watched her a few moments.

He said, "How much longer will it take?"

* * *

It took the rest of the night. He bled slow, but he bled steady. By dawn he was ashen and an hour later he was blue. She could see how she'd cut him now, a gash across his Adam's apple, no marks on the veins at either side of his neck. By good daylight, his pupils were the size of beetles, the round black beetles you see in the crevices of things.

She walked up and squatted there in front of him, then reached out, intending to brush his eyelids shut. But as soon as the tips of her fingers touched his brow, her hand recoiled. The smell of feces was strong and she realized he'd messed himself.

Yes, she thought. You may've been your mama's darling. But you are not mine.

She left his dead eyes staring at the sunrise and found her way back to the camp they'd made the previous evening. The horse was tied to a picket line. When she entered the clearing, the animal raised its head and looked at her.

She thought, I have a knife, a rifle, and a mount as well.

She was pilfering through the boy's belongings, deciding what to take, what to leave behind, when she stopped and glanced over at the gelding.

You can't just go riding down the road. That horse will get you caught. And you'll never be able to hide with it.

The rifle was a problem too. She knew how to fire it, but she wasn't sure she remembered how to load and fire again. Did the ball go in first or was it the powder?

She stood there holding it, trying to judge its weight. Twelve or thirteen pounds.

And what's it going to be like carrying it day in and out? Not just the gun, but the horn and pouch of lead?

She ended up leaving everything but the knife, a small slab of bacon, and a half-loaf of stale bread, carrying the food in the shot pouch and starting out across the country-side, the road somewhere north of her, off to her right. By dark she'd lost track of it altogether and focused only on moving west.

Which didn't sound so difficult, but it was incredibly so. Some days, she'd emerge from the pine trees to discover she'd been travelling south or southeast even, standing at the edge of the woods with the sun sinking toward the horizon, thinking, This can't be right. It should be over there.

She made the bread and bacon last the better part of a week—she thought it was a week; it was hard to keep track—and once it was gone, began to forage. She was very lucky that it was springtime: there were morels on the southern slopes of hillsides or clustered around dying trees. But there certainly wasn't much else. She thought she could find crawdads in the little streams she'd been stumbling on and she wished now she'd saved a few pieces of pork for bait.

One evening, scrambling along the bank of some nameless creek, searching for the little mudbugs, an image rose up like a painting on the inner wall of her skull: Davy sitting beneath that tree with both hands around his throat, blood pumping through his fingers, staring at her with his astonished eyes. It hardly even seemed like something she'd caused, had to be some other Cecelia who'd drawn the blade across the poor boy's throat.

Poor boy? You can't kill and pity him too.

And why not? Maybe that's how it's done.

She went over and squatted beside a pool where the creek flowed past, quiet as a thief. She glanced down and saw a crawfish in the water not a foot away and before she even had time to consider it, her hand had snatched it up. She pinched its head between her fingers and tore the tail away with her teeth, sharp legs wriggling against her tongue. It was like eating a slick, wet grasshopper. She crunched it down, then waddled over to where the water went over a short falls and scooped palmfuls of it to her mouth, rising out bits of flesh and shell.

She crouched around the pool till dark, seizing crawdads. Wasn't as easy as the first one had been. Sometimes she'd barely reach for one before they'd go jetting backward and she'd be left with her palm hovering above the clouded water. She learned to use both hands—one to grab the critters, the other as a kind of trap—and by nightfall she'd caught and eaten six of them and her belly was rumbling. She slept fitfully that night, worried she'd be sick and vomit, but she managed to keep it all down. When dawn came, she opened her eyes and stared at the branches overhead.

You can't live off crawdads forever. Mudbugs and mushrooms. Avoiding these plantations where slaves eat their corn and fatback.

She never thought she'd come to envy slaves their meager helpings, but she'd never been so hungry. Or if she had been, she couldn't recall it now.

Then something strange occurred to her. The idea was so sharp, a thrill of terror travelled up her spine and she knew in that instant precisely how she might feed herself and reach Bastrop in the bargain. The only problem was the problem of nerves: she didn't doubt it would work, but what would be left of her to confront Lammons at the journey's end?

What's left of me now? I have killed a boy.

She was on the verge of crying, but she couldn't afford the effort of it, and she said, "I don't know where you went, but I won't let you go from me. You hear? It's your son I'm trying to get to; he belongs to you as well. Throw your shadow over me. You had to kill in your life too, and now, so have I. And will again."

She stopped and lay there. She felt a swell of love enter her heart, faint, at first, and then stronger. She'd reached out to Sam in a kind of despair, but now she could feel him quite keenly.

She sat up and got to her feet. The sky in the east was the color of skin. She turned and started to walk.

DUNCAN LAMMONS

—TEXAS, 1847—

S undays, I'd get Bob dressed and walk him through the cedar trees to see Noah and his family. The Smithwicks had two little girls—the youngest, Robert's age—and these visits to their home were a great boon for me: though I had great affection for the lad, his energy was so different from mine that come evening each day, I'd be fagged completely out.

Thurza could tell what a troublous time I was having and on our Sunday visits she always made certain to make over Bob and give him attention. Robert soaked in every drop; you could see how badly he missed motherly affection. Lord knows what a poor surrogate I was.

Whenever we came on the Smithwick cabin and Noah's dogs began barking to herald our arrival, Thurza would walk out onto the porch and standing awaiting us.

No matter what mood Bob was in—whether he'd been fussy or fractious that morning—the sight of that dear woman would set him smiling. He'd sprint across the yard and scramble up the steps to her.

"There he is!" Thurza would say. "There's my little dumpling," by which time she'd already have him in her arms or wetting the hem of her dress and scrubbing soil from his cheeks.

"Do you ever clean him?" she'd ask me.

"It's a long defeat," I'd tell her. "The dirt's winning."

He'd tail her around long as she let him. Being in the presence of a woman did him considerable good.

One afternoon, I was sitting with Noah on the porch there, drinking coffee and discussing the latest rumors of General Scott's campaign down in Mexico or Fremont's out in California while the children chased each other round the yard, involved in some intricate game only they knew the rules of.

Noah was telling me of Stephen Kearny and the Battle of Rio San Gabriel when I realized the youngsters had gone quiet. I looked over and saw Bob and Nanna, Noah's youngest, were fussing at each other, though I couldn't make out what they were saying. Bob was holding a little ragdoll, Nanna a horse that I'd carved. Bob had the strangest look on his face. He reached for the horse, but Nanna jerked it away. He drew a deep breath and his cheeks went red. He looked so angry he would burst.

And then he did, releasing a loud, piercing wail that brought me to my feet. I set my coffee on the chair I'd risen from and started to make my way down the steps to fetch him. Thurza reached out and took hold of my shirt.

"Wait a minute, Mister Lammons."

I didn't see what I was waiting for. The Lord alone knew what He was doing when He put that tortured note in a child's shriek.

But Thurza had seen children scrimmage a time or two and as I stood there, trying to figure out how I'd extricate myself from her grip without giving offense, the elder Smithwick girl—Rachel—walked over, took the doll from Robert and handed it to Nanna. And that child, sensing a negotiation was under way, turned loose of the horse and allowed Rachel to pass it to Robert.

Well, this was a marvelous piece of diplomacy and no mistake about it. Robert went just as quiet as a rabbit. He and Nanna eyed each other a few moments, mumbled back and forth a few more. A minute later, they were running around the yard again, laughing with delight, the matter of the wooden horse and ragdoll laid aside.

I took up my coffee and sat back down, looking at Thurza like she was some wizard.

She just smiled at me.

"It is better," she said, "to let them work through it. If you settle matters for them, they will never learn."

I shook my head and chuckled. I nodded toward Rachel.

"Reckon we could sent her down to Mexico City? I'm sure General Scott and Santa Anna have need of such a politician."

CECELIA

—TEXAS, 1847—

That spring, a rumor traveled among the slaves of Houston County. They said a banshee had come to agonize the pine trees beyond the fields, some vengeful spirit that fed on shoats and stole grain from the corncribs. A haint of the timberlands. A terrible wraith.

Field hands would only speak of her in whispers:

> These pigs are a trick on us. Fact is, she lives off the blood of children, slips her tooth inside their throat.
>
> It ain't just them woods she stays in, neither—her home is underneath the ground. She tunnels through it like a mole.
>
> She's no spook at all, but an old, black witch. The blood she's knowed to drink turns her into dogs. You think it's dirt she lives in? She might be any mutt amongst us, that mangy bitch right there.

Hunger starves the sinews but feeds folks' imaginations. When Cecelia first heard these stories, she was too famished to grasp they were about her.

She'd been moving overland by day, stealing through the piney woods, searching for morels among the rotten stumps. Then slipping onto plantations in the eventide and down to the slave quarters, hoping for a handful of cornmeal and a dry place to sleep.

This never would've worked in autumn at picking time when hands labored well past dark, toting their baskets up to the steelyard where overseers would weigh and mark down each man's load in his ledger. But in the spring when slaves stooped to nestle cotton seeds inside the earth, the overseers only took headcount in the morning, calling the names of every man and woman and assigning each to a captain. And as no one expected to have more slaves at the end of the day than he had at dawn, she was able to use their math against them.

The first time she crept onto one of these plantations she was so frightful her teeth began to chatter. She sat in the tall pines at the edge of the field, watching as hands worked the mud with their hoes. It'd rained all morning and the laborers were so spattered with muck they looked like creatures made of soil.

Tonight, she thought. Tonight, I will try.

But when the hands slung their hoes on their shoulders and began marching up to their quarters, she couldn't even stand. The terror was like smoke inside her veins and she stayed right where she was.

She was back in the same spot the next evening. The sky was clear and the stars had begun to burn. She watched the slaves as one by one they shouldered their hoes and left the fields, travelling up along the earthen dike. She got to her feet, but the moment she did, her bowels churned, and she stag-gered a few steps before squatting to hike her dress, the fear rushing out of her hot and foul.

She covered her mess like a cat and then stood there sev-eral moments, thinking. She felt she might be able to do it now and she stole out of the woods, crossed the field and approached the pinewood shanties situated beside a muddy wagon trail.

Folks were gathered under the loblollies, eating and swap-ping stories, the men in rough pantaloons and the women in their threadbare calico.

She saw the problem right off—her gingham dress didn't

look like slave-cloth at all; didn't matter how frayed and filthy it was. She might have fled back into the woods if the eyes of these people weren't already on her.

Every one of them went quiet.

Fool! she thought. Now you are in for it.

She felt shame scald her cheeks and she lifted a hand to shield herself. She didn't want these folks looking at her; it had never occurred to her how out of practice you could get.

How long had it been since anyone had set eyes on her at all?

Davy was the last one, watching you as he passed.

She heard a high-pitched squeal and then two boys sprinted up from behind her. They were chasing a laughing girl of maybe six or seven, all three of them sleek as deer.

For a brief moment, they startled her out of her embarrassment.

My, but they are beautiful! Little angels running the earth!

But when the children turned to look at her, she had to cover her face.

Don't stare at me, she thought, hands over her eyes. Please do not stare.

She'd begun to tremble when she felt someone touch her arm. She spread her fingers and peeked out between them.

It was the little girl.

"Did you come to visit me?" she said.

Cecelia stood there, shaking. For weeks now, she'd planned out everything, how she'd sneak onto these plantations and seek sanctuary among the slaves. But this child had never occurred to her, this tiny hand on her arm, sixty pairs of watching eyes.

The girl stood on tiptoe; she reached and took Cecelia's hand.

"My name is Lily," she said.

Cecelia tried to swallow, but her throat caught. Lily's palm in hers was soft and warm.

Then the girl was leading her toward the people watching from under the pine trees. Several began to whisper, and then others were whispering, a rustling sound like wind in the leaves.

She felt eyes begin to fall away from her as the voices swelled and folks' attention turned back to their evening conversations. A pair of women came walking up to either side of her. She gripped tight to Lily's hand.

Don't leave me, she thought.

The taller of the two women had a face like an apple and just as round.

"Chile," she asked Cecelia, "where you run off from now?"

* * *

They didn't have much food to spare—a cold corn dodger and some chicken fixings—but they shared what they could and gave her a space to sleep.

She was up again before first light, moving westward through the pines, walking until evening found her in some wilderness or until she happened onto a plantation. Weeks of walking, one day mixing with another, one moon with another. Even the faces mixing, her own face mixed among them.

Their eyes seemed to say, *You belong to us. Your face is one of ours.*

One late spring night she made her way onto a plantation, but couldn't seem to find the slave quarters. Finally, she located a barn and crept inside it, crossing its bay in the dark, then climbing a ladder and bedding down in the loft.

She woke to a clacking sound and the low mumbling of voices. There were orange seams of sunlight coming through the planks, a scent of weathered pine. She'd meant to wake and be on her way before dawn, but her body had betrayed her. Weak ole body. I'd rather be a stone. She lay there very still, feeling the boards against her shoulder-blades.

I'm all edges, she thought. Hardly any flesh to me at all.

If they find you up here, you won't even be that.

She rolled over on her side; the boards creaked beneath her. The clacking noise was steady: *clack, clack, clack, clack, clack, clack, clack.* The men's voices were steady. She got onto her hands and knees and crawled to the end of the loft and looked down into the bay of the barn.

The big doors were open to the morning, golden sunlight slanting in. Black men bustled about below her; three of them stood at three low tables, turning the hand-cranks attached to three wooden boxes while others fed cotton into the hoppers and collected clean lint from the flues. She thought they were called flues. She realized she knew the names of the parts even though she'd never gone inside the cleaning house. She'd never actually seen a gin; it had been too dark when she'd crept inside the barn last night to see much of anything. The men at the cranks turned the rollers and the pale seeds dropped down into a pile. The engines went: *clack, clack, clack, clack, clack, clack, clack.*

She thought, It's springtime. Why are they cleaning cotton now?

On the plantation in Mississippi, they cleaned cotton right after picking. Or had she just assumed so?

She watched the men turn the cranks. Something about it frightened and fascinated her, like when Sam had first handed her the pistol in the woods outside of Natchitoches. The thrill of the little machine. The terror in it.

Her grandmammy had told her about that time before the cotton gin when you had to pick the seeds out by hand. It took hours just to clean a basket's worth, so the masters put you to work planting corn and tobacco and contented themselves with wearing wool.

But tobacco was hard on soil and folks said the soil was dying.

"And we thought that was very well," her grandmammy said, "for if the dirt took sick, what need would there be for slaves to work it? What need would there be for slaves at all?"

Then a man came along and built a cotton engine and what used to take hours and hours took several short minutes.

"The world sped along like a carriage on its wheels," said her grandmammy, "where before it was only walking." Now they could clean as much cotton as you could plant. Folks were like a mad dog in a meat house, starved for every scrap. Big factories sprang up in the North, hungry for Southern cotton.

"And weren't the Cotton Kings glad to feed them?" her grandmammy said. White folks no longer dressed in wool. They wanted cotton shirts, cotton britches. The planters stopped putting tobacco seeds in the ground; they had their slaves clear fields all the way to the Mississippi.

Because a man made a box to swipe the seeds from cotton quick as you could turn the crank.

She lay there, watching one of the men doing it, a big man with skin the color of clay. He wore a broad-brimmed hat and he'd sweated the crown completely through. He turned the hand-crank round and round, round and round, his expression blank as the sky, the emotion burned out of his face, his eyes looking at nothing. The machine had turned him into nothing. How long had he turned that handle? She wondered if he could even remember. And so, where did the machine stop and the man begin? Which was the engine and which the man who ran it?

She was still thinking about this the next morning when she climbed down the ladder, stole past the silent gins and out into the darkness. She was still thinking about it several days later, shaded up in a stand of pine trees, trying to find her way into sleep.

She thought, On that plantation I became an engine myself, a machine of blood and bone.

She sat up in the leaves. The cicadas stopped buzzing. She thought that before there were steamboats or the engines that made them run, before there were engines of any kind at all, there were people who stooped and picked and carried for those who would not stoop at all. These were the first machines.

Then came the man with a machine that needed more slaves to tend it, a machine to make machines of men.

It should have stood in for us, she thought. The slaves that picked the seeds from the cotton ought to have gone away, ought to have been freed by the new engine, but the engine only made more of us. There was a time before and a time after, before the engine and after. Her grandmammy spoke well of that before-time and ill of the after-time. She said, "The coming of a gin was a great evil."

But now Cecelia realized the truth of it. Men who made machines would make more machines; more and more men would become machines themselves. Even the masters.

And one day machines would become the masters. It wouldn't be cotton poured in the hopper, but men.

And where will be the hand to turn the crank?

There won't be a hand, she thought. The machine will turn itself, round and round and round, men spun up inside the rollers, our seeds swiped out. We'll come out the other side, just the lint of us, flat and clean and ready for the factory.

* * *

When she reached the outskirts of Bastrop, she stopped and stood there, swaying on her feet. She couldn't believe she'd come so far: it seemed that she'd passed an entire lifetime in the wilderness. And yet, just months before, she'd been living peacefully with Robert and Sam.

She spent the entire day finding a route that would take her around the town and then two more finding Sam's headrights. It did not seem possible she would discover their little cabin just as she left it, but she came up through the trees one evening and there it sat: smoke rising from chimney, the window glowing with golden light.

She watched for the better part of the night, peeping out from her nest among the cedars, making forays to the creek, making water farther back in the woods lest her scent carry on the breeze. She fell into a dreamless sleep for several hours, then woke and raised her head.

It was still night. The window had darkened.

She thought, You have to come out at some point, Mister Lammons. You can't hide away forever.

At dawn, she was sitting under the branches cleaning mud from underneath her toenails with a twig when the cabin door opened and a man stepped out into the morning sun, shirtless, barefoot, a length of rope over one shoulder—not Lammons as she'd expected, but the Spaniard who'd ridden out to visit them last spring with McClusky, the Spaniard who'd put a rifle ball in Sam. He was tall and thin, his hair completely white, his long beard the color of ash. He let the rope fall to the ground. She couldn't recall his name. A low animal groan escaped her lips and she clapped both hands over her mouth. Her chest went hot. Very slowly, she lowered herself to the forest floor, the leaves pricking her belly through her threadbare dress.

The man stood staring at the eastern sky, the pink skyline, the bright orange globe cresting the horizon. Or perhaps, none of these. Perhaps his eyes were closed and he just wanted to feel light on his face. What had the Poet called it? *Rosy-fingered dawn.* Like the sun could touch you with its hands.

His name reached out and swatted her—*Juan, his name is Juan*—and at that very moment he said something very loud, though not to her. It was like a song, but none she'd ever heard. He was singing to the sun. He lifted his hands as if he'd cup his ears, then bent and placed his palms on his thighs, singing.

Then standing up straight again. Then going down on his knees and touching his forehead to the earth. The sun cast his humped shadow across the ground and in its golden light she saw a latticework of thick scars covering his back from his shoulders to the base of his spine—old white scars and newer pink scars and red lash marks that looked quite fresh.

They are bad if I can see them from here, she thought. Like snakes have tunneled under his skin. She lifted her head to try and see better, but then he raised back up to sit on his heels and was just a dark shape against the sun, the silhouette of a kneeling man, edged in light.

He pressed his brow to the dirt again and then he stood. He raised his palms to the sky. He bowed to the sun, straightened up, bowed again, then went back down on his knees and rested his forehead on the ground. Still singing in his strange tongue.

When he sat up, he stayed like that for some time. His song broke off and he went very quiet. The crickets began to chirp. The sun rose higher. There was a scent of peace on the breeze. Then the man took the rope from over his shoulder and began to run it between his hands, almost like he'd measure it, limbering the rope which she saw was very stiff.

Once he'd done this, he gripped the rope at one end, coiling it twice around his hand, coiling it a third time.

Then he swung the rope over his right shoulder and lashed himself on the back.

The sound of fiber on flesh cracked through the clearing, an echo chasing it. The crickets went silent. He slung the rope over his left shoulder and struck himself on that side too.

She tried to swallow. She realized she was holding her breath. The Spaniard lashed his right side again, right and then left, right and left. It was a cool morning, but he'd broken out in a sweat, and the eighth or ninth time he struck himself, blood misted up in the sunlight.

He went on for some time, whipping himself till his back was good and bloody, opening new cuts as well as old, and when he'd suited himself, he stood up once more and ran the rope between the thumb and forefinger of one hand, squeezing the blood from it the way you'd wring water from a rag. Then he turned and went back inside the cabin.

When he reappeared he had a bucket in hand—the same bucket she'd used to gather water every morning for years. He went down the footpath toward the stable Sam had built.

She sat up. Her dress was sticking to her and she realized she was sweating. Her hands shook.

If Robert is in there, she thought, but she severed the line of that before her brain could string it any farther.

She sat there for a while keeping her mind shut up. Birds called to each other. Her blood made its rounds.

After a while, she got to her feet and stepped to the edge of the woods. She wondered when the Spaniard would come back. She needed to search the cabin, but if Juan came back and saw her, she'd be no help to Robert at all.

And then there the Spaniard was, coming up the trail with her bucket. He rounded the corner of the cabin, went inside and shut the door behind him.

She waited until the sun was down that evening and darkness fell like a shroud. The stars were bright and the moon at three-quarters, more light than she'd have liked, but what choice was there? She crept out of the cedars and stood for a while at the top of the hill. She began whispering to herself without really thinking what she said and it was a prayer she whispered: "Let him be untouched; let him be untouched; let him be untouched." She'd never been more frightened in all her life, picking her way down the hill, smelling chimney smoke on the breeze. The crickets would go quiet and she'd stop and stand there until they started back up.

Let him be untouched. No lash to his skin. Not a mark upon it.

Then she was standing in front of the cabin. She waited until the crickets began chirping, then stepped to the window.

The fireplace lit the room, but she barely recognized it. The shelves were gone; her cookware was gone. The table she and Sam had built was nowhere to be seen. The room was empty except for the Spaniard who lay facedown on the cedarwood floor, head pillowed on his crossed arms, firelight flickering over his bare back. He had managed to smear a salve over the lash marks. His skin glistened.

A rifle stood in one corner. A bundle of clothes beside it. The Spaniard's saddle. His pistol. A knife in its scabbard.

And no sign of Robert. She would have to make this man tell her where he was.

When she stepped away from the window, her body felt like it was floating. She went floating back up the hill, thinking of nothing, hearing nothing but her heart inside her ears, a river of blood pumping. She crouched in her nest with the knife in her hands, then sat cross-legged with her skirt stretched between her knees, the fabric catching the shavings of a branch she'd hacked off a cedar sapling. Her head felt as if it was rising toward the sky, getting higher and hotter as it went.

She was grateful for the moonlight now; she could see well enough to work. In an hour she'd carved two wedges from the cedar branch. She sat there staring at them, wondering if two would be enough. What if they were the wrong size? Or if only one of them was right? She began carving others, each different from the last.

Her lap was full of shavings. She took handfuls of these and made a pile beside her, tested the moisture of the ground with a palm, then sliced away a square of fabric from the hem of her dress, placed the cedar shavings atop it, then tied the corners to make a neat bundle. She sat there trying to remember everything Sam had shown her. Was it a softwood spindle on a hardwood board or the other way around?

She decided on a piece of dead pine for her fireboard and then began hunting around for a tree from which to make her spindle. The grove was mostly cedar and she wasn't certain that would work. Finally, she settled for a sapling with several straight branches about as big around as her forefinger. She stood on her tiptoes and cut the limb away from the sapling's trunk, then went back and sat in her nest, stripping away the bark with her knife. The wood underneath was damp. The branch was about two feet long and straight as a string, but she didn't like the moisture one bit.

To take her mind off it, she started to prepare her fireboard. Sam had said a lot depended on your fireboard. She gouged a shallow circle in it with her knife, then cut the notch like he'd shown her; she remembered his instructions about keeping it off the ground. She looked out into the dark, down the hill toward the cabin and then, spreading a pallet of leaves to work on, she positioned the fireboard between her knees, the heel of her left foot on its corner, pinning it down. She fit the tip of her spindle into the little bowl she'd carved, took the spindle between her palms and began to rub it back and forth, moving her hands down the branch as she worked, the wood sticky between her fingers. She went at it until her arms started to cramp, her forehead dripping sweat. When she lifted the spindle and felt the tip, it was warm, but that was about all.

A panic started to hum through her breast, but she slapped herself very hard across the cheek.

"Stop it," she hissed. "You just stop."

It's not dry enough. That's all it is.

She balanced the spindle atop the parcel of cedar shavings and lay down. She didn't see how she'd sleep with her heart going like this, thinking about Robert, where in the world he might be, the smooth slopes of his baby-fat cheeks and his calm green eyes—his father's eyes, though not the color, not the same color at all; she could always picture the exact shade of Sam's eyes so vividly; she might have painted them if she'd known how.

She started awake in the late morning light. Birds were calling to each other. The first thing she did was check the spindle, though she couldn't tell how damp it was; her hands were wet with sweat. She untied the pouch of cedar shavings, laid the spindle atop them and spread the square of fabric in a patch of sunlight. Maybe the sun would dry it faster.

Not fast enough, a voice inside her said, but it was cut off by a robin's song, up in a tree not a dozen yards away. She sat there watching the bird in its nest, its orange breast and bright blue cap. It occurred to her that there might be eggs in the nest. She waited several hours for the bird to fly away, and when it did, she sprang to her feet so quickly, specks swam before her eyes.

She shinnied a length of trunk until she could take hold of the lowest limb, then climbed branch to branch until there, like treasure, lay five green-blue eggs in the robin's nest. She carried them down in the woven bowl and then sat cracking the eggs over her open mouth like a bird herself, dripping the warm yolks onto the cup of her tongue. The last egg contained the body of an unhatched bird and this she swallowed whole, holding the nest in her lap, the taste so rich her eyes watered.

She spent the day shaping the cedarwood spindle, whittling it down with her knife, making it thinner, it needed to be much thinner. She set it in the sun to dry again and began making new notches in her fireboard.

Why didn't I practice this when he was here to help me? With him standing here to watch.

She hadn't realized just how skillful Sam was with fire—he

could get a coal anywhere, it seemed like; she'd seen him get a coal with drizzle falling and only the branches of an evergreen as cover, rubbing the spindle between his hands, the fireboard seeming to smoke almost instantly. The sickness of his death washed over her again: this man with his God-given genius for the working of things.

She carved the spindle to clear her head. The wood would feel dry and then she'd carve to find there was still moisture in it—what was the word: *resin*. The resin that made it such fine tinder. The resin that Sam worried about, seeping from the cedar logs of the cabin. She set it back in the sunlight and looked at the cabin down there, smoke trailing from the chimney. She wished she'd been able to hang onto Davy's rifle, but there was no help for it, and who knew if she'd have been able to hit anything with it anyway?

Another thing Sam might have taught her, if she'd known what was coming for them.

If course, if I'd known that, I'd have kept at him till he couldn't stand it and saved us from this hell.

She reached over, took the spindle, anchored the fireboard with her heel, and began rubbing the spindle between her palms, picturing Sam as she did, how his hands would start at the top of the shaft and work down. He did it so smoothly, as if there was no effort in it at all.

But when she did it, her palms got so raw. Her forearms burned from the effort. Or her shoulders. Or her back. The spindle-tip wouldn't stay in place, slipping out of the fireboard. It seemed to be the hardest thing she'd ever tried, and after an hour, her palms split and bled. She didn't mind the pain of it, but she feared the blood would dampen the wood. The stickiness made the task impossible. She worked all day without making anything but blisters, and when night came, she set the spindle aside and soon she was asleep.

* * *

She was in the cedars for what seemed like weeks, practicing with the spindle and fireboard, ranging deeper into the woods to forage. In addition to chaparral berries, she ate amaranth leaves. She found a clump of cattails down by the stream; she'd heard you could boil these somehow, but she couldn't boil anything. She cut several dry stalks to use as spindles and crept back to her perch.

The berries and plants were a blessing to her, but even so, she was starving. The best thing about her situation was the creek. She didn't lack for water. At least there was that.

One morning, she woke from her slumber to a pattering sound, and looking out from her perch, saw the sky was dark with clouds, darker in the west where sheets of rain raked the prairie. Drops of rain touched dry leaves here and there, and she started praying to the same God she often cursed these days, asking Him to steer the storm away from the cabin. If the rain soaked her kindlers, it would cost her several weeks of labor, and those were weeks she didn't have.

But the storm passed by, angling to the north. She watched it go, the clouds sweeping over the earth, blue sky behind. She knelt there on the ground and pressed her forehead to the dirt, giving thanks, weeping into the dead leaves, and when she raised her eyes she saw that Juan stood in front of the cabin with the bucket in hand. He was staring off to the north as well.

She spread a handful of dry leaves on the ground and placed the fireboard atop them. She took up the cattail spindle, fit the tip of it to the fireboard and began spinning it between her palms. The skin on the insides of her fingers was raw in places, calloused in others, but she set the pain aside and worked, thinking of how Sam had looked when he did this, how natural it had seemed.

All the things you take for granted, she thought. They come
back to visit you. They come again and again until what's left
isn't his beautiful face or his blue eyes burning, but all of what
you didn't stoop down and smother with kisses.

The smell of smoke drew a veil across her mind. Her heart
jumped up in her throat. There was the scent of smoke—it was
there and then gone—and she wondered if she'd only imagined it. She lifted the spindle and touched the tip of it and it
was so hot she jerked her finger away and put it in her mouth.
Her heart was humming. She tried to calm herself, fitting the
spindle back in place, taking it between her palms.

"Alright, now," she said.

She was able to get smoke twice more that evening, several
times the next day. She'd lie there sleeping, then wake, watch
the cabin a few minutes, then set up the spindle and board.
How much had Sam practiced this? she wondered. Did his
father teach him? Or was he just able to do it like he did everything else, having never been told he couldn't?

Her first coal came a few days later, sitting there one morning working the spindle between her calloused hands—one of
the spindles; she had several now, several fireboards too. The
smoke was rising steady and then she looked and saw a speck
of orange sitting atop the blackened dust in the fireboard's
notch. It smoldered a few moments, then turned to ash.

She sat there staring. She now knew she'd need to place
something under the notch to catch the next coal she got and
transfer it to the nest. A dry leaf would likely do. She'd have to
have everything just so.

She spent the rest of that day foraging for wild currant
berries, balled under the leaves of the little shrubs like drops
of bright blood. She ate the leaves of a linden tree and then the
buds. Then she stripped the bark and began to eat that too, as
Sam had once shown her.

He is feeding me even now, she thought, the sour-sweet

juice of the currant berries bursting between her teeth. She closed her eyes and thought of that day he'd brought in meat from the black bear and she missed him so badly.

When evening came, she was sitting there cross-legged with her fireboard and spindle, a currant leaf under the notch like a saucer, the nest of tinder she'd prepared at her knee, and a bundle of twigs and kindlers she'd tied together with a strip of cloth she'd torn from her dress. She waited till the first stars winked on. Then she set the tip of the spindle in place, positioned her hands and swallowed.

But she didn't start rubbing her palms. Not just yet. Instead, she prayed.

"Samuel," she said, "I'm lonely for you something awful.

"I don't know where Robert's gotten to. Whatever you have to give me, you best go ahead and give it. If you were still here, you'd do all this yourself, but now it's only me. If I'm fixing to join you, that's fine too."

Then she opened her eyes and began to work, rubbing the spindle between her hands, the scabbed-over blisters on her palms and the insides of her fingers covered in scabs, working down the shaft and when she reached the bottom, working her way back up, thinking the whole time of that first night outside Natchitoches, thinking, My hands are your hands; make my hands yours.

Something occurred to her she'd never considered and she bent down and rested her forehead on the spindle top, pressing it harder into the fireboard. She knew it wouldn't take long for the stalk of mullein to worry through her skin, but she didn't care about her skin. She closed her eyes against the pain, rubbing her hands together, the spindle hissing in its notch.

Her forehead had been bleeding several minutes when she smelled it. She opened her eyes and saw the tendrils of smoke rising, just the slightest twists of it, and she pressed harder and bore down, panting now, growling a little, the smoke coming thicker.

Do I pick the spindle up and look?

You do *not* pick up the spindle.

How will I see a coal if I don't? I'll have to pick it up.

She did. A few drops of blood spattered the fireboard and she bent closer and saw an ember, smoking. She put the spindle aside, removed the fireboard, and there was a coal atop a little pile of black dust. She picked up the leaf and tipped the coal into the nest of tinder, then closed the nest together in both hands like a prayer. For a moment she thought it had gone out and her breath escaped her mouth before she could catch it, but then a thin trail of smoke rose from the nest and she recalled Sam lifting his bundle of tinder and blowing into it. She lifted the nest as if it contained her life; maybe by this time it did—*maybe my entire world has become this spark in a poor bird's home*—blowing into it, smoke puffing out the other side. She inhaled deeply and blew again and the nest burst into yellow flame.

* * *

Later, she'd wonder what she must have looked like walking downhill toward the cabin that evening, a wasted woman in a worn-out dress with a burning tinder-nest in one hand and her bundles of wood in the other. She thought that if the Spaniard had been watching, he might have easily walked outside and put a pistol ball through her head.

But he wasn't watching. She steered for one corner of the cabin, setting the little fire she carried against its crook, then squatting and feeding it twigs and branches from her bundle. She still wasn't sure if the cabin would even catch. By the time she had a good fire going, she knew if she didn't see to the door, it wouldn't matter: he'd smell the smoke and come out and that would be that.

She took up the cedar wedges she had carved and fetched

around until she found a fist-sized stone. Her heart was kicking at the wall of her chest and her vision narrowed down. When she rounded the corner and approached the door she'd help Samuel hang, the insides of her thighs went wet and urine splashed the tops of her feet. She wasn't worried about that, just the dribbling sound it made. She didn't know how loud anything was with the blood pumping in her ears.

Then she was kneeling in front of the door. Everything came in flashes. There was still time for her to bolt. She heard a whippoorwill calling. She heard a crackling noise she realized was her fire. She drew a breath and began pushing the cedar wedges into the gap between the bottom of the door and the packed dirt, starting at one end and working her way down, pressing them with the heel of her hand as tight as she could get them. She sat there a moment. As soon as she started banging them in with the rock, there'd be no turning back.

Is this it? she asked Sam. Is this what I do?

Something told her to check the fire. She rose and walked around and saw it was going good; the logs were starting to blacken where the flames from her fire licked them, and she fed several more branches into it, then got down on her hands and knees and began blowing into it like she'd blown into the nest. Fire went trailing up the side of the cabin and she knew that it was time; this would either work or it wouldn't; there was no other way.

She walked back to the door, squatted, and began hammering at the wedges, driving them in her rock, and she'd barely gotten to the second one when she heard the Spaniard say, "Quien es?"

Her heart climbed up on the back of her tongue and there was no moisture in her mouth at all. She moved to the next wedge and hammered and then she hammered the one beside it. She was working at the last one when he first tried the door; it didn't budge. The second time he tried it, it only shivered.

She knew that soon he'd commence throwing himself against it. She went back around the corner to pitch the rest of her kindling into the fire, but there was no need: the entire eastern wall of the cabin was engulfed in flames. She stood there in wonderment, watching as the fire leapt toward the cedar shingle roof. She heard Juan lambasting the door with his fists. She began to back away from the cabin, watching the door shudder in its frame as the man hurled himself against it; or kicked it with his boots; or tried to shoulder it open. Her main worry had been that the wedges wouldn't hold, but it seemed that Juan's attempts to force the door only set them deeper.

And still she was backing away. Ten yards. Twenty. Even at the distance, she could already feel the heat on her face—the evening was lit up like a second sun. One goes down, another comes up. The roof was now smoking, flames dancing up the shingles, black smoke billowing toward the stars. The fire was roaring loud enough she couldn't hear Juan beating on the door, and then she realized the door no longer shuddered.

He is burnt up already, she thought.

Which was when she heard the sound of glass breaking and her eyes went to the window where a rifle butt had just burst through. Then it had vanished and was shattering another of the panes, sending bright shards scattering.

The stupidity of her error knocked the wind out of her.

For how many weeks have you sat in your perch staring at the same window you used to stare out yourself, and it never once occurred to you how easy it would be to crack and climb out of? Now you will die. He will come through it and shoot you and you'll never see Robert in this world.

She might have turned to run, but what was the point? She was so angry with herself she felt like she deserved her punishment. The glass was mostly out of the window, Juan was scraping the bottom of the sill with his rifle butt, smoothing away the sharp edges that jutted like broken teeth. He threw out the rifle, then placed his hands on the window sill to hoist himself over.

They've been right about you all along, she thought. You are a little fool.

Then something strange happened. The flames atop the roof leapt higher for a moment, then seemed to suck downward; a rush of smoke came pouring out the window just as Juan was climbing through it, followed by a huff of red fire. One moment, he was a man in filthy homespun and the next he was a screaming torch.

Like blowing on the nest, she thought.

The flames seemed to push Juan out into the yard, his clothes burning and his beard on fire. He struck the ground, rose and sprinted a dozen steps and then pitched onto his belly. He hadn't stopped wailing; he was gasping and howling all at once.

The smell hit her, like charcoal and copper.

Don't you turn away, she told herself. Don't you dare.

Juan struggled to his feet and lurched for her, but she sidestepped him. He looked like something out of the Poem, his beard burnt down to bare skin, the lower half of his face a black and bleeding mask. He fell again, rose again. She backed away. She wasn't even sure he could see her; the fire seemed to have damaged his eyes.

He went down on his hands and knees and began crawling like a beast, no longer howling; he seemed to be unable to catch his breath.

She stood several feet away, following him as he crept along the ground.

And wasn't Odysseus a murderer at the end of things? Hadn't he painted his own halls with blood?

Then the Poem spoke inside her, saying, *You dog! Not fearing my return, you have sheared my substance, headless of revenge. But death is on the wing for you. Death for everyone.*

The Spaniard's smell was terrible. He left bits of himself behind, clumps of fat and steaming flesh in the grass. He made it twenty feet or so before collapsing a final time.

She walked over and stood watching him a moment. She saw he was still breathing, his back going up and down, his wind coming in a ragged wheeze.

"My boy," she said, and her voice sounded like it belonged to someone else. "What've you done with him?"

Juan didn't answer, just lay there, hissing.

She looked around for a fallen branch. She located one, then came back over, worked it underneath his chest and levered him onto his back. When he rolled over, she saw that his bottom lip was dangling from his mouth; he'd bitten completely through it.

"Can you hear me?" she said.

He lay staring up at her, though he had no choice as his eyelids had burned away.

It's too much, she thought. You burned him too much.

She put the sole of her foot on his chest. The flesh was hot, like mud baking in the sun. She put some weight on it and the blackened skin slid under her foot, baring a strip of pink, steaming flesh.

He howled to the stars.

"My boy!" she shouted.

He was wheezing something in the midst of his gasps. She took her foot off him and squatted.

"What is it?" she said.

"Lounds," he hissed.

"I can't understand you."

"Lounds," he said.

She'd never thought about what a bottom lip could do, how a body sounded without it. She decided he was going to make himself understood to her, bottom lip or not and she picked up the branch again.

But it was too late: the Spaniard's body started bowing, his skin bursting as he stretched. Both his arms went rigid, his fingers clawing at the air. He began to shake so violently his clothing came to pieces.

She dropped the stick and stood there. The fire had reached its pitch. She watched the roof cave and embers swirl up into the stars.

* * *

She turned her back on the fire and went down toward the stable, following her feet. Not thinking, her brain a dead engine in its box of bone. She stumbled down the bare footpath, moving for much the same reason that water flowed along a thousand courses to the sea. She might as well have been water—her rag of a dress was soaked.

She undid the latch at the stable door and stepped into the dark, leaving the door open, the moon casting just enough light to see. She passed the first stall where Juan's horse stood sleeping and when she walked past the second, Honey raised her head above the gate and blinked her black, beautiful eyes.

Cecelia stood there breathing in the sweet scent. The smell blew her mind awake; the cogs spinning back to life. She tripped the latch on its nail and opened the gate, lifting her cupped palm to Honey's wet mouth and the horse nosed against her, breath hot as steam.

"Yes," she said, "you know Cecelia," and the little horse nuzzled her like a cat. She wasn't ready for this, wasn't prepared for this at all. She'd assumed the pony would have been taken by one of the men, sold or even shot, perhaps. Her chest started to break up and her eyes were leaking. She stroked Honey's neck, trying to contain herself, but that only made it worse.

"I don't know what they did with Robert," she told the horse. "They could have him anywhere for all I know."

A shout from up on the hill froze her in place. She wondered if she'd imagined it. Then it came again, someone up there carrying on. The first thought that came to mind was that Juan had risen to berate the moon, but she shook that away, stepped back over to the door, squatted and peered out.

The cabin was still aglow in the western sky and as she watched, a shadow passed, a scraggy silhouette against the blaze, then the silhouette of the horse the man led. He began shouting again and she could just make out the words.

"Hey, Juan!" he yelled. "You, Juan!"

Then the shadow vanished and the shadow of the horse behind him. A breeze caught the embers and sent them swirling down the wind, the fire leaping, yellow again for a moment, then sinking back to an orange glare.

She squatted there, watching, amazed at the destruction she'd created. How did she have it in her to do that? After all, it was the white man's place to steal and destroy, the negro's to press a cool cloth to the master's brow once his fit of violence had blown through, perhaps telling him, "You done good, Marse; you has burnt and kilt like your nature says to do," thinking all the while, *Where can I get to that these demons cannot? The Anglo will slash and slaughter, but I will preserve myself in righteousness that I may stand before the Lord and proclaim myself His servant.*

Servant, she thought. It doesn't please Him to make us servants here on earth; He'd have us bend the knee in Heaven too. Not enough to have us stoop in this sweating life; we'll bow and scrape in the next.

Not you, though. Not now. A murderess has no place in Heaven.

It hadn't occurred to her to call herself that, but that was the name, wasn't it? She'd murdered twice and was still no closer to finding Robert or killing Lammons, the man she desired to murder most of all, whose greed had set all of this in motion. So, if her luck held, she'd be a murderess thrice over. She'd be—

The man appeared again atop the hill, still leading the horse, but there was something in the saddle now, doubled over it, and he led the animal down to the road and started out along it. She watched him out of sight, knowing what this meant, what she'd have to do.

She worked quickly as she could, saddling Honey in the dark. She had hoped Sam's horse would be in its stall, but it was only hers and Juan's piebald gelding. She considered leaving it where it was, but what if no one came for it?

She stood a few moments, trying to think.

Then she said, "It's not your fault. You didn't pick your owner any more than I did Mister Haverford." She walked back and opened the door of the gelding's stall.

"All right," she told the animal. "Git."

* * *

It didn't take long to catch up with the man, on foot like he was, leading his horse. They were still on Sam's headrights, still in woods she knew. She stayed well back on the path, leaning down every few minutes to whisper in Honey's ear: "That's a good mare. Let's stay real quiet."

She worried what would happen when they left the property and reached the road to Bastrop, but they never went that far. In half an hour, the man she followed veered off onto a new trail, cut through the cedars, and after that, emerged into a clearing.

A cabin stood in the moonlight where there had been no cabin before: just trees and outcrops of stone. The man led his horse toward it. She slid from Honey's back, took the reins, and worked her way back into the woods. Tied to a low limb. Stroked the horse and whispered to her. Then crept back to the tree line to watch.

It wasn't just Juan who'd taken their land. This man seemed to have carved out an estate for himself too. How many other cabins were there on Sam's headrights now? And in which one was the traitor Lammons?

The man was now off to one side of his new cabin, digging. He didn't stop until first light. The sky brightened in the east, and he turned to lean on his shovel. When she saw who it was, she knelt down in the dirt and dug her fingernails into her scalp. Her entire body was trembling.

It was the man with the dead eye. The Irishman, McClusky.

He continued digging the Spaniard's grave. An hour or so passed and another man rode up—not Lammons, but one of the riders who'd been there the morning Sam was killed. This man spoke with McClusky, then climbed down from his horse and took up the shovel. He dug for a while, then passed the shovel back to the McClusky and they went on like this, spelling each other, until yet another rider approached.

Yes, she thought, I can see how it is.

They taken Sam's property and carved it up between them. It wasn't just Juan and McClusky who'd conspired against them. There was no telling how many men they'd recruited to get hold of Sam's claim.

And here now was another, a fourth rider trotting up. He climbed down from his horse and milled about, talking with the others.

She thought it was only a matter of time. Sooner or later, Lammons would come himself. He'd ride up to join this band of vultures and she'd have them in one place.

But that didn't happen. No one else came. They lifted Juan's body, carried it into the grave, then began to shovel dirt.

And once their comrade was buried, McClusky turned to

address the men. She was too far away to hear what he said—the screen of leaves that hid her dampened the sound as well.

When he'd concluded whatever he was saying, he went inside the cabin. The other men began to mount up and she thought that now they'd leave. Then she realized they were waiting for the Irishman, and when he came back out, he carried a rifle and there were pistols tucked in his belt.

It's me they are looking for, she thought. And I'm lying right here.

McClusky swung up into the saddle and, snapping the reins, he put his horse forward and the men fell in behind. In a few moments, all of them were gone.

She lay with her heart beating against the ground. She couldn't just wait until they came back, but where would she go?

You have to follow them, she thought.

Why would I follow them?

Maybe they'll go to Lammons. Maybe they'll lead you to him.

Then she imagined Robert. In one of these new cabins hereabouts. Crying for her.

Or maybe not crying.

Maybe in a grave himself.

* * *

When she went trailing after the riders, it was to keep this thought out of her head.

And when she caught up with them on a trail snaking through the woods, she saw just how foolish all of this was. If the rider at the rear of the little party happened to turn; if the men happened to hear her horse; if other riders came up behind her . . .

She kept Honey to a slow trot. She'd push up until she

caught sight of the men, then drop back, scared to lose them, scared to get too close, expecting it to go wrong at any moment; moment following moment as morning shifted to noon and the sun reached its zenith then began to cant toward the west.

Midday, the riders stopped at a creek to water their horses and she sat upwind of them, watching through the limbs.

At one point, McClusky's horse raised its head from the stream and looked back in her direction. Her blood sped up and she prepared to knee Honey into a gallop, but then the horse lowered its head and started drinking again.

By late afternoon, they'd traveled Lord knows how far. She was never good at judging distance. All she knew was that they were headed north and they'd traveled a number of miles. Ten or twelve. Maybe more.

Then the woods fell away and she saw a cabin in the distance. She steered Honey into the trees, tied the horse, and began walking.

When she reached the edge of the woods, she saw that a man had come out onto the front porch of the cabin. She'd assumed this would be another friend of McClusky's, but the way the man was standing told her he was no friend of the Irishman's at all. He was having some disagreement with McClusky and she thought she smelled violence on the breeze.

And don't I have a nose for it? she thought.

The man on the porch was a stubby figure with red hair and a bushy red beard. He had a dog beside him that would bark and go quiet. Bark and go quiet.

Do they think he burnt our cabin? she wondered. That he did for Juan?

She wished she could hear the conversation.

Then, just like that, McClusky mounted back up, turned his horse, and led the other men pounding out across the pasture, moving to the west.

By the time I make it back to Honey, they'll be long gone.

And so her plan to follow the riders had come to nothing.

She knelt there watching the red-headed man. He was star-ing across the prairie in the direction the men had gone, and after a while, a woman came out onto the porch to join him. They stood talking, then the man stepped inside the cabin, and when he reappeared he was carrying a rifle. The woman stopped him and he stood waiting on the porch while she went inside.

Several minutes passed. It would be evening soon.

Then the woman came back out and handed him a basket and something about that made Cecelia's skin tingle. She didn't understand exactly why, only the basket was curious. The bas-ket changed things considerably.

And so, when the man crossed the field and entered the woods, she rose to follow.

DUNCAN LAMMONS

—TEXAS, 1847—

That afternoon, I heard the sound of leaves rustling, stepped outside and saw Noah winding his way through the trees, his rifle in one hand and a grapevine basket in the other.

When he got up close I said, "Becoming such a big success has ruined your woodsmanship, Master Smithwick. I heard you kicking through the trees half a mile away."

His face was very grave. He handed me the basket and said, "Thurza sent you all some biscuits and chicken. Might be a pie in there, too."

"I thank you for them," I said. "You tell her I appreciate it."

"Where's Bob?" he asked.

I nodded over to the dugout.

He said, "You know a man named McClusky?"

"I know him," I said. "He rode in my ranging company." I didn't say what all else he'd done.

Noah said, "Well, him and three other ole boys come to the house this morning looking for you. And it wasn't a social call, neither. Some neighbor of theirs burnt up inside his cabin and they seemed to think you'd know about it."

"I been here with Bob," I said. "Only people I ever see are you and—"

He raised a hand and stopped me. "I know you didn't fire any cabin. I just come to tell you. I think you and Bob ought to light a shuck."

"To where?"

"I don't know, but these men are serious, Dunk. They figured I'd know where you were and when I told them I didn't they didn't seem any too convinced."

I stood there a moment, wondering if this story about a cabin fire was true. I'd often thought McClusky might come for me. Maybe he'd decided leaving witnesses to the murder of a white man was a bad idea after all. Maybe the fire was just an excuse.

Then something else occurred to me.

"How'd they know to talk to you?" I asked.

"What's that?"

"Trying to track me down brought them to your door— why'd they think to do that?"

"Well," he said, "we've made no mystery of our friendship. And folks from Bastrop are often in my shop. It would be more surprising if they didn't come to me at some point."

I supposed that was right, though I was having great difficulty thinking it all through.

"And what about this fire?" I said. "Do you reckon that's some shecoonery on their part?"

"No," he said. "Or, I don't know. It might could be. It makes no sense why they'd get up a posse on a Mexican's behalf."

"What Mexican?" I said.

"The man who burnt up. It was a Mexican name." His brow furrowed trying to recall it, but of course I already knew.

"Juan Juarez," I said.

"You know this man?"

A torrent began to pour out of me, all these things I'd kept dammed up, thinking it best for Robert's protection, telling how Juan had joined our company and of his injury in the Indian fight; our journey south to Monterrey. How Juan and McClusky had stepped out of Sam's cabin that terrible morning.

When I finished, Noah just stood there, blinking.

"These are the men who did for Sam," he said.

"These are the men."

He shook his head. "You and Bob aren't safe. Will you not consider leaving?"

"Where would we go?"

"Something very bad is going to happen. I don't like this one bit."

"No," I told him. "I'm not just real partial myself."

* * *

I was anxious all that day, near to jumping out of my skin. I kept going out to survey the woods, certain I was being watched. Noah had used the word *hunted*. It felt like that to me, though there was no evidence as yet, just the birds singing their evening songs, squirrels pausing on tree limbs to stare at me.

Come dark, I built a fire at the far end of the dugout, recognizing the attention it might draw if McClusky and his boys were indeed scouting these woods, but needing the light to raise my sagging spirits.

Robert and I ate the supper of chicken and cornbread that Thurza sent, and soon the boy was belly-up on his pallet, sleeping just as soundly as you please. The weight of our predicament slipped from my shoulders. I loved that boy considerably and I wondered how I could best protect him. Noah's advice was for us to put some more distance between ourselves and Bastrop, but it was all I could do to care for the child with the help of loyal friends like the Smithwicks: how would I manage on the run? And being hunted in the bargain?

It was a fretful evening, sitting there mulling everything, watching Bob sleep in the light of the flickering fire, his belly poking out the bottom of his little homespun shirt. I thought about Juan. Was it really as McClusky said? Or was the wild

358 · AARON GWYN

Irishman merely trying to gull us into an ambush? I did not know if anything at all had happened to Juan, and if it had, if he'd truly burned to death in that cabin, why was McClusky so certain murder was the culprit and not an untended fire?

For a while, I'd convince myself they were just trying to draw me and Robert out, rid the world of witnesses, and then I'd think, *No. There is a smell of truth to this. Juan has met his end and not by any accident.*

And yet, if McClusky's story was simon pure, who was Juan's assassin? It made more sense to lay his death at the door of raiding Indians, but signs of an Indian attack are easily spotted as McClusky well knew—I'd taught him to recognize these myself.

The longer I thought on it, the more my mind was at sixes and sevens; I hadn't the least notion what had happened. All I knew for certain was McClusky was hunting us. I climbed down on the pallet next to Robert, took my pistol out of my belt, checked that the nipples were capped, then wedged it down under my thigh, meaning to stand sentry over the boy. Or lie sentry, at least.

And then, just like those footsore peons at the San Jacinto who Santa Anna had kept up all night building his breastworks, I fell asleep.

* * *

When I woke, the fire was down to coals and there was no sound but Robert's breath beside me. No cicadas, no crickets. My right hand was lying across my chest. I reached for the pistol, but it wasn't there. My heart came up in my throat and then I felt the barrel of the gun against my temple and heard the click of the pawl as the hammer was cocked.

A woman's voice hissed into my ear: "I can use this," it said. "I have killed two men already. Move and I will kill a third."

She gave me such a start, I couldn't speak.

"Do you hear me?" she said.

I nodded that I did.

"You were supposed to be his friend," she said. "Were you all in league against us?"

She was pushing my head as she spoke, prodding it with the barrel of my gun. She shoved at it until my cheek was against my left shoulder. I cut my eyes over, trying to see her face.

"In league against who?" I said.

She pressed the gun harder into my flesh. "I knew you were false," she said. "I told him there was something false in you, but he wouldn't listen. He never listened to anything about you."

"If you aim to shoot me, I can't stop it. But there's no reason to hurt the child. There's a man whose cabin isn't more than a mile from here. He'll take the boy in."

"Boy?" she said, and I realized she'd not yet noticed Robert lying beside me in his blankets. The fire having burned down, there was little light to see by. And who would've expected a child in the company of a brute such as myself?

The woman was silent a moment. Then I heard her breath catch in her throat and the gun dropped away from my temple. When it returned, it was trembling, as was her voice.

"Don't you move," she said. "Don't you move a grain." She stepped over me and knelt beside Robert, one hand holding the pistol, the other passing over the boy's face, then fluttering over his body as if trying to touch every part of him at once, brushing along his cheeks and sweeping down his chest, stroking his little legs and the tops of his bare feet, left and right.

I saw her now quite clearly. It was Cecelia, Sam's helpmeet in a shredded, filthy dress, a rag tied around her head, her face very gaunt, eyes caverned back in their sockets. She would not take them off me long enough to bend down and put her lips to Robert's face, but she began to kiss the fingers of her free hand and lay it on his forehead, his chest, on one ear and then the next.

The boy didn't wake, just lay there dozing—he was the soundest sleeper I'd ever seen, and once out, you could sling him over your shoulder and cart him about like a sack of flour, and him with his mouth open, slumbering away.

"I don't understand," she mumbled.

"That is my daily prayer," I told her.

Her eyes flashed at me. She said, "Did you keep him to sell? Is that what this is?"

"I thought they'd killed you," I said, then nodded at Robert. "It's a miracle he wasn't."

She knelt there with the gun on me, still shaking her head, still brushing her fingers across Bob's cheeks.

"I never trusted you," she said.

"I know it," I said.

"You hated me. I could always tell."

"Yes," I said. "Maybe that is so."

"And for what? What offense did I give?"

"Certainly, none that you intended."

She just stared at me. You don't realize how full of nonsense you are until someone's ready to blow out your lamp.

I said, "He never once looked at me like he did you, Miss Suss. Never once."

"And for this you took vengeance on us?"

"Vengeance?" I said.

"Yes, vengeance." Her voice was hot with rage. "Why else would you help those who robbed Sam from me?"

Well, now it was my turn to be angry: "If you think I had aught to do with that, go ahead and pull the trigger. I didn't know it was McClusky trying to take your title until I was standing over Sam's body. If I could've traded my life for his, I'd have done it. Don't talk to me about robbery. I took your boy out of that cabin at hazard to my own skin. So, shoot me if you want, but you're firing into the wrong flock. One of the men who did for Sam's been burned to death. The others think I'm the culprit. They're hunting me over it. *Vengeance?* Somebody took vengeance for the both of us, I reckon."

She stared at me a moment. I realized she was no longer trembling.

"No, they didn't," she said.

"I just had word from a friend of mine. Someone's burned your cabin and a man who rode with me in my ranging company. A good part of what became of him you can lay at my door. He wasn't always—"

"I burned him," she said.

"*You* burnt him?"

"Yes," she said. "Though I was expecting you."

"Expecting to find me?"

"Yes."

"And then what?"

"And then I found Honey down in our stable—what used to be our stable—and that Irishman came riding up. Did you know he has his own cabin on our property now?"

"No."

"He does. And maybe other men besides him. He saw the fire and rode up and took the Spaniard's body and then other riders came and set out north. I followed them. They rode to another man's cabin; I thought they'd kill him, but they didn't. I had to decide whether to follow them or—"

"Smithwick," I said.

She nodded. "And when they cleared out, I followed this Smithwish and he came straight to you. So, let me ask you a question, Mister Lammons."

"Duncan," I said.

She laid her palm on Robert's forehead. "Why'd you take him?"

I lay there a moment.

Then I said: "I don't care a fig for my life anymore; it's brought me nothing but misery. So, if you put a ball through my brain, it's a smart chance you're doing me a favor. Taking Bob from that cabin was the only good thing I've ever done." I stopped and stared at her. "Do you think I'm lying to you?"

She watched me for a time.

"No," she said. "You're not lying."

"Well, then I will tell you another thing. We cannot stay here. The men hunting me won't stop. They are tracking me right now, McClusky and the yacks he rides with. You could take your son and ride north. If you're able to keep out of sight and avoid Indians, you might could cross into the Territory."

"I knew this man one time who told me there was a colony of runaways in Mexico," she said. "And he—"

Bob interrupted her with a loud sneeze. He opened his eyes and stared up at his mother. For a breathless moment, Cecelia and I waited to see what he would do.

Then he began to scream as only a young child can, a terrible sound that corkscrewed up your spine. He scrambled away from his mother like she was some goblin come to claim his bones and latched onto me, shrieking.

I sat up and took him in my arms, trying to shush him, kissing his little temple and saying, "There now; it's only your mama. It's all right. Hush now. It's only Suss."

I glanced over his shoulder and saw the expression of horror on her face, horror and hurt. She came up on her knees and reached to touch the boy, but Robert gave another squeal and commenced to clamber up me, trying to get away.

Cecelia was trembling all over. And though I could only guess at the terrors she'd endured, I could see this was the worst of them. It had never occurred to her she'd make it back to her child only to have him reject her and I watched something in her break.

"It's all right," I said, trying to console the boy and his mother too. "It's all right, now."

I said it over and over, but which of us believed it? We were three souls who feared nothing would ever be right again.

I closed my eyes and held onto Robert, hugging him to me, his heart hammering against my chest. I whispered things to him that might've only been sounds—I don't remember. I rocked him back and forth and stroked his head. My throat was thick; my entire life had coiled around it to squeeze the breath out of me. I clutched onto that boy until you wouldn't have known who was comforting who and the whole world was tight as a snare.

Then his heart began to slow; it tapped against me softer and softer. Softer and softer. His groans got calmer and his body went still and I felt the panic start to bleed out of him. His grip on me loosened. I rocked and shushed and whispered. He got very quiet. All three of us got quiet. I rocked him back and forth. I heard the coals crackle in the fire. Outside, the crickets began to chirp. The cicadas buzzed up. I felt Bob go slack in my arms and his breath started to sigh, his thin chest swelling and sinking.

CECELIA

—TEXAS, 1847—

And so she told him about coming to herself in the bed of the wagon, of the boy Davy and how she'd won his trust. How she'd knelt over him and drawn the blade across his throat—this blade right here. Of how, afterwards, she began moving west, going from plantation to plantation, running onto them for food and shelter—so different from how she'd once run away—using the plantations against the masters whose greed knew only one direction and so never suspected there could be another.

She told him of the cotton gin, how she'd watched slaves clean cotton and realized these machines would themselves become masters. How she'd reached Bastrop County expecting to find Duncan in her cabin and had found the Spaniard instead. Of the fire it had taken her weeks to build, and then her reunion with Honey—the horse's breath like a blessing.

Lastly, she told him of that terrible dawn that had set her on this journey, how that one-eyed reprobate had placed his pistol to Sam's head and scattered his soul.

Duncan said, "And McClusky. He's the one who killed Samuel? You're definite on that?"

"I saw it happen," she said, but what she didn't tell him was she could still see it. She could close her eyes and see it play out against the wall of her skull, the hard, little man gliding towards Sam, putting his pistol against that lovely face. Sam's eyes staring at her one last time.

Run, they seemed to say.

Lammons sat there, looking up at the rough ceiling of branches over their heads.

"And what is it you're wanting to do?" he said.

"About what?"

"McClusky. He and the men riding with him would enjoy to see both of us in the ground. Nothing would please them better."

"Then he should've done it the same day he murdered my Sam. That was his opportunity. He decided to sell me instead."

She glanced down at Robert. She looked back at Lammons and lowered her voice.

"Will you help me kill him?"

"McClusky?" Lammons said.

"Whatever he's called. You'll either help me or you won't."

Lammons said, "I have dreamed of that since the day I buried Sam. Those men riding with him will not just stand aside. I'd hate to see Bob get his mother back only to lose her again."

She said, "It is not tolerable that he lives and walks this earth while Sam is in the ground. It is not tolerable to me at all."

"No," said Lammons. "But wouldn't you rather see your child raised up to manhood? You'd rather have revenge on Felix?"

"I cannot stand knowing he's in the world and Sam isn't," she said.

"No," said Lammons. "Nor can I."

I t was still dark when we left out, Suss on her little chestnut pony and Robert riding in front of me on the saddle, two handfuls of my britches balled up in his fists. He'd yet to warm to his mother. Whenever she'd push up to ride alongside us, I could feel his entire body stiffen.

I wouldn't have guessed such a thing was possible, a child getting strange to his mama that way, and I thought, *Here is another thing we can thank you for, Felix. Wasn't enough for you to blow out his pap's lamp and try to sell Suss into bondage—you had to chock a wedge between a mother and her son.*

He'd certainly driven a few wedges into me: here we were heading north without a rock in our pocket or so much as a word to Noah. We'd never be able to return to Bastrop County and there was no promise we'd reach our destination, wherever that might be. When Noah came to the dugout and found it deserted he'd likely assume the worst. I know I would've. I'd left no note for him as I couldn't conceive a message that wouldn't alert McClusky to our intentions if he happened to stumble upon it, and so it was that I took leave of my oldest, dearest friend and went riding into exile, casting my soul into the maelstrom a final time.

* * *

A few days later we forded the Brazos at the falls by old Fort Milam—a frontier garrison which had been built before our Revolution and abandoned during the Runaway Scrape. It was reoccupied by Colonel Burleson's rangers for a time, then abandoned once again. That was in the summer of '37 when the enlistments of ranging companies began to expire. Now, a decade later, the fortress was a ruins, the blockhouse rotting and its roof caved in, the perimeter walls—tree trunks shorn of limbs and driven into the earth—leaning like saplings in a storm.

It put me in a dark frame of mind. So much of what I'd built had tumbled into wreckage and forty is rather late for a man to start constructing a future. What evidence was there that I might accomplish such a feat? Every attempt I'd made had ended up like Fort Milam; my entire life had rotted through. And although that was a rather grim thing to countenance, it did not hold a candle to knowing how I'd warped and withered the lives of those who'd loved me. Or whom I had loved.

This child I carried on the saddle, sleeping now against my breast; his mother riding a few paces behind us: there was no doubt they needed protection, and given the library of my failures, you couldn't have found a poorer choice than yours truly. The boy deserved better; Suss deserved better, and I can tell you right now, if the blue devils ever seize hold of you, do not look at a forsaken fort.

* * *

For the better part of a week we'd been moving up the Shawnee Trail which, back then, was just a muddy wagon trace, not the tributary it became—at the time, far more folks used it to enter Texas than travelled up it with a drove of cattle. It was long about sundown, a fair breeze blowing at our backs. We wound through a motte of blackjack and cedar, hunting a spot to bed down for the night. Old Roger lifted his head and his nostrils started working. Then the skin on the back of my neck prickled; the hairs on my arms stood up. I didn't say a word to Cecelia, just reached down and cheeked Old Roger, forcing his head toward his neck and turning him sharply left, then letting go of the cheek-strap and booting him off the trail, ducking to pass under the limbs. I looked back and saw Suss was right behind me and once we were deep enough in the woods that the road passed from view, I swung down from my seat, clutching Robert with one hand and taking my horse's bridle with the other. I stared at Cecelia and shook my head, begging her not to make a sound.

She read the gesture accurately, drawing rein and stopping her pony; then, sliding from the saddle, she dropped to the earth quietly as a cat. Soon as her feet touched the ground she sank into a squat, crouching there in a drift of oak leaves, motionless and silent, one arm hooked round the left front fetlock of her horse. It'd never occurred to me that you could immobilize a mount in this fashion.

You didn't waste your time with Sam, I thought. What else did he teach you?

My musings were interrupted by the calls of a whippoorwill. Another answered in the distance. I glanced up at the darkening sky between the branches; the breeze had set them swaying. Robert's heart was knocking away. The boy felt our alarm quite keenly and I was suddenly overwhelmed with terror at the thought he might start crying.

Then I heard hoofbeats on the road. The sound was hushed by leaf and limb, but growing louder. I stared at Suss and she stared back. If the riders were McClusky and his men; if they paused to study the tracks we'd left them; if they noticed how our sign led into the black oaks; if I was forced into a fight holding a four-year-old in one arm and nothing but trees for cover—

And now I caught voices, men speaking, none clear or loud enough for me to make out the words. I closed my eyes and tried.

There was the smell of bark and horse-flesh, the feel of my foot soles in these busted-out boots, of Robert's heart hammering against my chest. The birds calling. The muttering sound of men and the clop of the horses they rode.

Just keep going, I thought. Keep on going.

I caught the scent of tobacco on the breeze. I had never let my scouts smoke for just this reason.

Of course, I'd tutored McClusky in such matters, but if it was truly him up on the trail, he'd chosen to ignore this particular lesson. I feared that any moment I'd hear the crunch of leaves as the party entered the woods to flush us.

But the voices got quieter and the hoofbeats fainter and soon I smelled nothing but Bob's breath in my face. I opened my eyes and went to tell Cecelia to follow me back farther into the oak trees, but Cecelia wasn't there.

I cast around a moment before I located her, stealing from tree to tree, making her way back to the wagon road, a hunched and haggard figure that stalked soundlessly as a wraith. I watched how her feet found patches of bare ground or sandstone, never falling on a dry leaf or twig. She carried her naked knife in one hand and I knew exactly what she intended.

The panic hit me fresh and I felt sick at the stomach. I wanted to start after her, but I didn't dare upset Robert; that he hadn't already cried out was a miracle. I could not have even reached his mother without making a good deal of racket and though I'd always prided myself on how softly I stalked a deer, I had never been that silent.

And so I was forced to stand there sweating with Bob and the horses, watching Cecelia vanish into the gloaming.

There were a thousand things that might have gone wrong and every one of them played out in my mind. I could almost hear the sound of the gunshot that would touch off the fight, and I knew there'd be no way we'd survive it—or no way Robert and I would. I was of two minds about Cecelia and I thought maybe Bob was right to be scared of her. And if it was McClusky who'd just passed us by, he ought to've been as well.

Night was coming on. When I glanced up through the tree limbs, there were stars.

The sky dimmed down and the stars shone like nails. My horse blew and Cecelia's pony turned and looked back toward the road. I shifted Robert to my other hip and squinted into the trees and Cecelia seemed to float up to me out of the dark—no noise, just the shape of her getting closer until she was standing right there.

"Woman!" I hissed. "Good God Almighty."

"They're gone," she said.

I shook my head. My nerves were frayed down to nothing.

"Don't you ever do that again," I told her. "What would've happened had they seen you?"

She just stared at me. The whites of her eyes seemed to glow.

"They didn't see me," she said.

* * *

We couldn't risk a fire that night and had to content ourselves with a cold camp, sharing a few corn-dodgers between us, the last of the larder that Thurza Smithwick had sent me and Robert. I had no idea how we'd reprovision. If it hadn't been for the fear of being hunted, I would have taken my rifle out and barked a few squirrels, a doe if I was lucky, but as things stood, I didn't dare announce our presence.

Lord, how I wanted a drink! The ache for it kept me tossing all night, and come dawn, I left Cecelia and Bob in their bedrolls and went out to reconnoiter. It was daft of me to've ever taken us along the Shawnee Trail. Or up any thoroughfare, for that matter. Now I charted a new course for us, deciding to angle northwest across the prairieland. That was my notion, at least. It would be easier for McClusky to spot us on open ground, but not nearly as easy as spotting us on a wagon road. I knelt at the tree-line, staring out over the pastures, watching the stars fade.

I was moving back through the woods toward camp when I heard Robert screaming. The sound stopped me dead. Then the shock lifted and I took off sprinting, fast as my cracking knees could carry me.

The picture that presented itself when my companions came into view was a terrible one: Cecelia down on her knees in front of Robert, talking to the child, trying to settle him. For his part, the boy was backed up against a tree swatting at his mother, trying to fend her off.

And Cecelia—you ought to've seen her face. The night before, it'd been grim as a phantom's. But seeing her boy's terror, she looked haunted herself.

I rushed up and stepped between them; I might as well've gotten between a wildcat and her cub. A murderous rage filled Cecelia's eyes and I saw her hand disappear into a fold of her ragged dress. It occurred to me she might be reaching for her knife.

"Here, now," I said, "what's all this?"

She shook her head and pointed to Robert. "He woke and missed you. I was only trying to calm him."

"It doesn't seem to be working," I said. "Could you stand over yonder?"

"I'll not be told what to do," she said. The venom in her voice would've dropped an elephant.

I drew a breath and released it.

"I'm not telling you," I said. "I'm asking if you'll help me get him soothed a little."

Her eyes caught sunlight and flashed at me, but then she backed over to where the horses were picketed.

I turned to Robert. When I knelt to speak to him, he

clambered up into my arms and got a hold round my neck that liked to choked me. His cries cut off and he was just a trembling little body.

"There," I said, "Duncan is here." I laced my arms around him, palmed the back of his head and stood.

He slacked his grip on me enough to lean back and look me in the face. We eyed each other a few moments, his pupils very wide, green irises the color of jade.

"You're all right," I said. "There's a lad."

He drew back a hand and slapped my face.

Then he did it again. But before I could chasten him, he burst back into tears, hugging me with one arm, slapping at my shoulders with the other.

"You left!" he screamed. "No, no, no, no no!"

My eyes welled up and my throat thickened.

"You left!" he shouted, fussing at me the only way he knew, so angry that the skin under his fingernails had turned red; so glad to see me he couldn't help smiling. Like sunlight in a rainstorm.

What must he have thought, waking to find my empty bedroll beside him? Surely, that I'd forsaken him forever.

"Shhhhhh," I told him, "Duncan loves you. Duncan won't leave," saying it over and over like a spell.

The two of us clutched each other and wept like abandoned babes. And weren't we, though? Hadn't Sam deserted us both? No fault of his, but faults don't figure into feelings. All we knew was that if there was any family left, the two of us were it.

I turned and glanced at Cecelia over Bob's shoulder, expecting to see a look on her face that would've split my skull like a hatchet.

But the tears came down her face as well. She made no attempt to wipe them, just let them run.

For she was one of us too. All three of us had been forsaken. All three of us were lost.

CECELIA

—TEXAS, 1847—

A nd so she followed them out onto that broad, flat pasture where the wind sang constantly in your ears and the sky stretched from horizon to horizon—white and gray and bluest blue. The cedars fell away, there were hardly any trees at all, just a vast sea of grass that waved and rippled as an actual ocean must have done.

One cool morning, they forded a wide, muddy river, the horses stepping slowly, wading water that came to their fetlocks, their knees, their barrels. She thought that maybe the animals would have to swim. Could horses swim? Lord knew she couldn't. She called to Lammons, but the man didn't hear her over the sound of rushing water. He clutched Robert in one arm and held his reins and rifle in the other. He looked like something out of a dream: half-man, half-horse, the mists swirling around him, the entire surface of the river steaming.

She slipped her wet feet out of the stirrups and wrapped the reins around her hand. Honey blew two jets of vapor from her nostrils, thick as smoke.

Do not drown me, she thought, then felt the pony step on something solid and they began to climb. She gripped the reins tight; the horse stepped up and up. The two of them came out of the water and walked over to Lammons who was sitting his horse, dripping in the sun.

The man looked at her with gray, glittering eyes, the skin seamed like leather at their corners, his coal-black moustache

grown out over his lips and his lean face furred in silver. He
began to laugh.

She was still unsettled from the crossing, didn't see what
was funny.

Lammons picked Robert up, turned him around and sat the
boy on the saddle, facing him.

"How bout that?" he said.

Robert was giddy too, though he couldn't have understood
why the man was celebrating.

"Bird!" he squealed, and she glanced back and saw a heron
gliding over the river, skimming the surface on extended
wings, then coming to rest on its long legs beside the shore.

"Bird," she told Robert.

"Caw, caw," he said, mimicking a crow.

"Caw," she said, and that made him giggle. She began to
giggle too.

Then a great hunger possessed her and she had to touch
him. He wasn't an arm's length away.

She leaned over and put her hand on his knee, a little knob
covered in homespun. Just the feel of him would be a feast. She
could live on it.

But as soon as he felt her palm, he snatched his leg away.
The joy left his face.

Don't cry, she thought. Please don't do it.

He didn't, only cast her a scowl that cut right through her.

Lammons was already trying to catch the moment and steer it.
He said something cheerful to Bob, but she didn't hear what it
was. She'd already kneed Honey into a walk, turning her back on
Robert, not able to look at his face, not wanting him to see hers.

She trotted along the bright sand past the willows, birds
scattering from the branches and fury humming inside her
brain. Finally, she drew the reins, fetched up and sat the horse,
thinking, I only wanted to touch you, little monster. I just
wanted one touch.

Anger had such heat to it. She closed her eyes and felt its blood-light on her face.

But after a while, the feeling turned on her and twisted. The heat drained away and there was only the numbness of shame, shame like filth on her skin, cold and stuporous.

Davy's face flashed in her mind. She shook it away, but then there was the Spaniard, staring with his lidless eyes.

I won't take fault for them, she thought. I did what anyone would do, what they would've done to me. How is it any different?

She thought, It's not a bit different.

And then she thought, Neither are you.

* * *

When she got back to the river she saw Lammons had picketed his horse and was sitting in the red sand beside a clump of blackberry bushes. He had a little mound of the berries cupped in one hand and was feeding them to Robert.

Or rather, Robert was feeding himself. He'd reach over and take one out of the bowl of Lammons's hand and put it on his purple tongue. She didn't think she'd ever seen the boy so happy as he was this very moment, squatting next to Duncan Lammons, eating blackberries a stone's throw from America.

For they'd left that country now, or its States, anyway. The river they'd crossed separated Texas from these Indian territories and for the past few days that's all Lammons could talk about.

She sat her horse, glaring at the man.

I left America already, she thought, and it snuck up and surrounded us. What makes you think it won't happen again?

Maybe that was just the bitterness churning up in her, watching Robert eat from Lammons's hand.

To be separated from your own flesh. Like your arms ran off and left your body.

Lammons waved her up. She walked Honey over and slid from the saddle, letting the reins hang down.

"Get some of these," he said, offering her the berries.

She squatted beside him and took several. They were ripe and very sweet. She was surprised the crows hadn't already picked the bushes clean.

Robert stared at her. She saw that his teeth were stained and his tongue was nearly black. He reached for a berry and then she reached for one. Their hands touched, his tiny finger wiggling.

Warmth shuddered through her body, very different from the warmth of rage. She wanted to fetch him up and kiss him all over. She wanted to bite the chubby flesh of his arms.

They camped that night several miles north of the river, and when the stars came on, Robert was already asleep. She sat with Lammons while he stacked kindlers and then set them alight with his flint and steel.

The fire blazed up and the sun sank; she could feel herself sinking with it. Lammons was watching her through the flames. Very still. Very quiet. He reached to stir the coals and embers popped, sparks swirling up and dying.

All the bright things of this world swirled and died.

"Do you want to talk about it?" he said.

Why would I want to talk? What part of you could understand me? Never a slave nor widow nor mother.

She was silent for a long time, dropping lower inside herself.

Despair isn't just a word, she thought. It's a place you go like a crypt or cellar. A place within a place, tight as a coffin.

She said, "I've been running since I was just a girl. Did you know that?"

Lammons shook his head.

"My whole life has been running. I ran north; they caught and sold me. I ran south and they caught me there too. When I came west with Sam I thought my life had finally started; I thought those years we had were life. But even that was running. We might've stayed in one place, but it was only a rest."

Lammons watched her. He nodded after a time.

"When that boy they gave me to was carting me east, I told myself everything was over. All that was left was to get to him—"she nodded at Robert in his blankets—"just get back to him and smell his skin. It didn't even matter that they'd taken Sam from me because Robert came from him too. So, getting to him would be like getting to them both."

She paused, tonguing a blackberry seed from between her teeth.

"Now I don't have either one."

"How's that?" said Lammons.

She stared at the fire. It would burn down to ashes and the wind would scatter them and a rain would come and scour this place clean of any sign there'd been a fire at all.

"He won't let me touch him," she said.

"He's getting used to you."

"He's not getting used to me. Maybe he shouldn't. All my life there's been a beast inside me. I didn't even know. It took a lot of blood and suffering to peel the skin down to it, but it's peeled now and there's no covering it up." Her hands had started to tremble. She clenched them together to steady herself. "They wrecked me, Mister Lammons. Yes, they did."

She closed her eyes and tried to breathe. She heard Lammons stand up, shuffle around the fire and sit down beside her.

"Who wrecked you, Suss? It's no one wrecked you."

She shook her head. "They might as well've killed me."

"No, no," said Lammons. "You hush that."

"It's true," she said. "They started in on me from the time I

378 · AARON GWYN

was just a girl. And do you want to know the worst of it? I always told myself they were one thing and I was another. Can you believe I used to think that?"

"Think what?" Lammons said.

"That I was different," she told him. "That they were monsters and I was a person. That I wasn't a monster too."

"I don't believe that for a second," Lammons said.

She said: "I thought there were things I wouldn't do. When I was a girl I thought that. I think I thought that most my life. But do you know what? There isn't."

She felt Lammons's hand between her shoulders, rubbing her back. It felt so good, the touch of someone who wouldn't harm her.

And here's the proof of how I've been altered. Here is the proof.

Lammons said, "It seems to me that most of what people do comes from the situation they find theirselves in."

"Yes," she said, and something about the man's tone caused her throat to thicken. She felt herself getting blubbery.

Do not start crying, she told herself. Do not do that.

"And," Lammons continued, "I'd have to say that the situations you've found yourself in have got to be the worst I've ever heard of."

Then she did start to cry: the shame and anger turning wet. How she'd hated this man! She had comforted herself with thoughts of cutting out his heart, this man who now rubbed her back with his rough hand and said, "Shush, now. It's going to be all right. You're going to be all right."

"I'm sorry," she told him, but she couldn't explain what for. She was sorry to cry in front of him and sorry she'd wanted to carve on him with her knife and sorry her hatred had changed to something she didn't understand.

She opened her eyes, wiped at them, brushed the tattered sleeve of her dress under her nose.

And then she saw Robert.

The boy was sitting on his bedroll watching her and Duncan, a curious expression on his face, as if he was trying to decide whether he might be dreaming.

She and Duncan stared at him and the boy stared sleepily back. The three of them sat for a few breathless moments.

The fire crackled.

Robert blinked his eyes.

Then he lay back down. By and by his eyes closed and he was asleep.

* * *

A few nights later she dreamed of Sam.

She was alone in a vast forest with slave-hounds sniffing out her trail. It was eventide and night was coming on, the sun hissing into extinction in a dark ocean at the western rim of the world.

She stumbled through drifts of oak leaves and down into a dry hollow. She was young again and not. It was Virginia and it was not.

When she heard the hounds baying at her back, she knew they were not tracking her at the behest of some slave-catcher: they wanted her for their own. And if these dogs caught her they'd fill her with their seed and she'd have to bring forth a litter of beasts.

She was not going to lie with a pack of curs, but how would she prevent it if they surrounded her with their gnashing teeth? She considered climbing a tall cedar, but then she would have to live in that tree for all time, in this dark that would last forever now that the sun had drowned.

She went out across the hollow under the limbs of live oaks and beards of Spanish moss. She heard a cry behind her and turned to see the hounds cresting the hill: an enormous pack of mangy brutes with scabs and slavering mouths, popping their teeth and pawing the earth to get at her, beasts well-suited to the coming darkness, this perfect, eternal night.

She started to run, but it was like moving through molasses, and where did she think she'd get to?

Then a shape caught her eye, a magnificent gray wolf winding through the trees, blue eyes in its beautiful face. She knew immediately that it was him; the eyes were what told her, but she'd have known just by the way he moved: slowly, powerfully, stronger in death than he'd even been in life. Stronger and stranger.

The hounds saw him as well. They stopped like they'd struck a wall, or tried to stop, skidding through the leaves, their ears flattened and tails tucked, already scurrying for the brush.

The wolf came on. She saw now he was not entirely gray. He had golden markings on his ears, a strip of gold down his snout. His cheeks were white and there was white fur on his chest. As he came closer all her fear vanished. She knelt on the ground, waiting for him, and when he walked up and looked her in the eye, she seized hold of him and laid her cheek to his.

His nose was cold and wet, but his coat was very warm and she could feel the mighty boom of his heart. She stroked his head and spoke of all that'd befallen her and how changed she was.

When she'd finished, he yawned and licked his chops, then bent down and rested his chin atop his paws, staring up at her with his shining eyes. And then she was awake.

She lay there for a time, letting the dream wash over her, the glory of it. She expected that as soon as she opened her eyes her life would crash back in and sweep this feeling away—the sight of Sam, the sense of him.

So, she opened them slowly, expecting heartache to crush the breath out of her, bracing herself against it.

Robert was standing there, his feet at the very edge of her bedroll. Not touching it. Not touching her. Just standing there very quiet, staring down.

She lay still as she could with her heart jumping in her chest.

Do not frighten him. Do not so much as blink.

It was too dark to see his face; the stars above his head were like bright flowers, an endless field of them.

After several minutes, he squatted and bent closer. She could just make out the shape of his nose, the gleam of his green eyes. His nostrils flared. He held both hands to his chest as if shielding them from a fire.

Then he reached out and put his tiny palm to her face.

His hand was soft, a little cool, the touch of some woodland creature, his fingers light against her cheek.

Then, just as quietly as he'd come, he stood up and made his way back over to the pallet next to Duncan.

She lay there with the blood singing in her ears, speaking to Sam inside her head, blessing him, thanking him for coming back.

Yesterday, the Commonwealth of Virginia voted to take herself out of the American Union, following Texas, Louisiana, Georgia, Alabama, Florida, Mississippi, and South Carolina into madness.

The latter of these states was the first to declare her independence, thinking that by Mr. Lincoln's election she would lose her slaves and their masters might be required to perform an honest day's labor. Our new president is a Kentuckian, but it is feared the bluegrass state will secede as well. North Carolina and Tennessee will surely follow. As will Maryland. The capital will be cut off, surrounded by a sea of slavers. And soon, needing its cotton for her mills, Queen Victoria will come in on the side of Jeff Davis's Confederacy and the entire world will be at war.

What would Pap say had he lived to see all this? As I recall, he auspicated such a disaster would befall our country if we didn't atone for the crime of human bondage.

Perhaps he'd merely quote Brother Paul's letter to the Romans, as he often did to me: *the wages of sin are death.*

Let us hope it does not come to that—the demise of these once United States. Though I myself spent a good many years trying to get clear of America, now, seeing her torn in two, I shudder with terror. Is that not something? If the citizens of these rival republics commence to open fire—as they did in Charleston harbor last month—there will be red rivers running through the land. The confederate batteries that shelled Fort

Sumter on April 12th did so as a show of force; the only casualty was a hogbacked mare. LeRoy Walker of Alabama has said there will be no effusion of blood whatsoever, offering to wipe up any that is spilled with his own pocket handkerchief. Others take a similar line, most of them politicians who have never fired a rifle nor seen men ripped apart by bullets.

They are fools, every last one, having no idea what occurs when ranks of men open up on each other with rifled muskets. Ask the Mexicans what that weapon can do in the hands of a determined marksman. Many of our generals still believe you must close with your enemy and give him the bayonet—this in an age where men can easily kill at two hundred yards.

It will be butchery beyond what any of us can conceive.

* * *

I had a letter from Noah Smithwick some months back, just after Texas joined the Southern Confederacy.

His letter read:

> *Well, old friend, the thing is joined. Texas is too small to be a nation, and too large to be an insane asylum. Did you ever think to see such a day? I have sold my farmland for two thousand dollars, but this mill I built, I cannot unload at any price. I'm giving it outright to my nephew, who says he won't run from his own country. I hope the decision will not cost him, but he was never one to take on advisers.*
>
> *Mark my word—the South cannot win this war. Before news came that we'd thrown our hat in with the rebels, I took to the stump and told my neighbors as much, and now I am branded a traitor and might as well bear the mark of Cain. Can you imagine me making speeches? I gave it my best effort, but men I have known for thirty years seem to have changed in the twinkling of an eye.*

384 · AARON GWYN

Here is my suggestion: sell what you can, buy yourselves a wagon, and join our procession for the Golden State. Do not stay here among these bedlamites. California will be a fresh start, and a war will never touch us there.

Your Most Obedient Servant,

Noah Smithwick

I wrote back and told him I am too old for travel, but that is hardly the case. At fifty-three, I feel much as I did at forty. Some days, a good deal better.

The truth is I do not think the coming conflict can be escaped—not in California, not in the Yukon. It will place its bloody handprint on every heart and hearthstone.

* * *

We came to Lawrence in October of '56—Suss, Robert, and myself—just after Sheriff Samuel Jones and his pro-slavery ruffians had sacked the city and destroyed the offices of the *Kansas Free State* and the *Herald of Freedom*, smashing their presses and throwing their type into the river. Jones's men carried banners proclaiming SOUTHERN RIGHTS and SUPREMACY OF THE WHITE RACE. They went on to burn the Free State Hotel, Pomeroy's venerable establishment, and then set Mr. Robinson's home afire, the gentleman who would become our first governor.

Suss and I hadn't the least notion of any of this until the day of our arrival. Lawrence had been founded by Free Soilers from Massachusetts and what I knew of the town came from its papers, copies of which drifted down to me in the Territories where we'd been hiding for the past nine years, fearing McClusky might mount another search.

It had been frontier living all over again, the only difference being that the Indians I had once hunted in Texas now provided sanctuary for our strange, little family; without their kindness, we might well have starved.

The more I heard about Lawrence, the more convinced I was it had been founded especially for us: an abolitionist stronghold on the plains. And so, in the fall of '56, we packed our things and rode north.

The town still bore signs of the devastation that had been visited upon it four months prior, but the citizens received us with great cordiality. I took a job at the livery—an establishment I purchased two years later—and built us a rough cabin on Massachusetts Street. Robert was thirteen at the time and soon he was working alongside me at the stable, trimming hooves and salving set fasts. He's always had considerable affection for animals, and they for him, but I've never seen anyone so gifted with horses. That boy can calm a fractious colt or fork some highbinder who's never felt a saddle's touch. I saw him get aboard this one mockey bitch who'd thrown every man who'd tried to mount her, sitting her bareback like she was a lady-broke mare. He'll take some poor plug you wouldn't give a nickel for and in two weeks' time have her looking like an absolute topper. Where he learned all this, I've no idea.

The *Herald* sent their reporter round to do a story on him, knowing my special regard for their periodical and newspapers generally. There was a time when Mama couldn't get me to read newsprint with a hickory switch, but I've become a great supporter of the press in these latter days—or at least of Republican-operated papers. My allegiance to the Democrats faded with the Fugitive Slave Act and expired altogether with Justice Taney's Dred Scott decision—the party of Jackson has become the party of fire-eating slavers. From here on, it is Mr. Lincoln and the Republicans for me.

City life never sorted with my temperament, but here in Lawrence I am able to get my hands on both Greeley's *Tribune* and Garrison's *Liberator*, as well as half a dozen other journals.

Suss has wearied of all this politics and newspaper reading. She prefers her novels and books of poetry. When I go to read her an article about various goings on in the nation, she will clap palms to her ears and close her eyes.

"Tell me what good comes of fretting all of this," she says. "Can you do aught about it?"

Her eyes flicker behind her spectacles. She is grown softer in middle age. Her hair has silvered. She looks like the matron of some venerated institution that's not yet been conceived.

* * *

Since December, when word of secession started limping through the land, I sat down at the table and began to write everything I could recall of my life in and out of this country, wanting to put down a thorough record lest the world that used to be is burned to cinders. No doubt, there are more capable hands than mine, but I ask myself: just how many have seen the things I've seen? Most of the original Texan settlers have shuffled off this mortal coil. As have the men who rode in the first ranging companies. Captain Walker met his end down in Mexico. Uncle Ike died last year from bilious fever. Noah tells me that Levi English still survives—he was commissioner of Atascosa County for a time—but like most of the old rangers, Levi can neither read nor write.

If a history of the Rangers is ever written, it will likely be by men looking to smooth over our many defects and present us as unvarnished champions. Or perhaps by someone wishing to paint us with the brush of knavery, erasing any act of kindness we ever performed. This nation has no use for frail and fickle humans—it desires only tales of heroes and villains.

I write *nation*: it is difficult to remember that there are two Americas now. Perhaps that is the reason for my fascination with the papers; I can scarely believe the reality of what's happening from one day to the next. I keep waiting for the article which will tell me all of this has been some great misunderstanding. Or an elaborate prank.

Noah says the South cannot win this war, but I am less sanguine about the Union's chances of success. And if these new Confederate States draw Britain or France into an alliance—as they are sure to do—Mr. Lincoln will be forced to sue for peace.

What if the outcome is worse still? What if Jeff Davis manages to sack Washington as Sheriff Jones did to Lawrence? The North itself could be enslaved; the President hanged as a traitor to the white race; these western territories put under the iron yoke of Southern rule.

Those are the thoughts that startle sleep from my eyes and set me pacing.

* * *

This morning, Jim Colliers brought a stallion to the livery, looking to have it put down. He couldn't bear to shoot the horse himself nor could he sell the beast, knowing its viciousness.

I looked out to the corral where they'd managed to secure the creature. What a magnificent animal! A palomino with a shining golden tail, about sixteen hands, muscles rippling like waves beneath its golden coat.

"What all's wrong with him, Jim?"

"He bites," Jim said. "He bit Sarah in the back of the head, took out a hunk of hair the size of your fist."

I shook my head. There's very little you can do with a such a horse, and when Robert came back in that afternoon, I told him we might be forced to shoot it.

"What if I could get him gentled?" he said.

"Yes," I said. "And then maybe you could go to work on

some of these mountain lions that've been taking down folks' cattle."

I watched his brow furrow and his lips go tight. He is eighteen now, tall and thickly muscled, his hair cropped close, skin the color of tea.

"Did you clean the stalls this morning?" I asked.

"Not just yet."

"Well," I said, "see if you can gentle those."

He took a pitchfork and went to work. I walked over to Brigg's Hotel to pick up our supper.

When I got back, the stables were empty, the pitchfork leaning against the wall. I knew exactly where Robert had got to and I hustled on outside.

He stood there in the corral, staring up at the stallion which was now bridled with a saddle on its back.

"Bob," I called, "you come out of there!"

I'd no sooner said this than the horse went for him, rearing on its hind legs and then lunging forward, snapping its teeth in a way that recalled an alligator. If Bob wasn't so quick on his feet, the beast would've bitten into his face like an apple.

But Robert sidestepped the horse, reached over and snatched the reins. He slid up close and hoisted himself onto the stallion's back.

Well, the horse liked that about as much as you'd expect. It commenced to haul hell out of its shuck, bucking and turning at the same time. I was moving toward the corral fast as my legs would carry me. What did I think I'd accomplish once I got there?

The stallion turned and shot out its hind legs, released a loud scream and started kicking up clouds of dust like smoke from a brush fire. And Robert clutching the reins, perched high up on the saddle, the golden horse continuing to buck and spin. I expected Bob to be thrown at any moment and the odds of being trampled in such circumstances are very high indeed.

But he wasn't thrown or trampled either one. The stallion broke into a lope, circling the corral once, twice, then, on its third circuit, it slowed to a walk and bucked a final time. Then it stopped and stood there, quaking, slaver dripping from its furious mouth.

The sun was blazing down the western sky and the dust the stallion had raised drifted in the evening glare. The horse blew and tossed its head. Robert sat there, his back straight and his hands loose on the reins.

Then he turned and saw me. His green eyes flashed. He nodded and smiled just as Sam had once nodded and smiled. I knew in that moment that this little town could not contain him anymore than Arkansas Territory could've held onto his father. Someday he would make his way out across this beautiful, terrible land, pursuing his fortune as I'd set out at a similar age to hunt mine, passing out of the country and finding it in myself, passing out of myself to find love and heartache, mercy and terror.

I stood there watching him.

I had never been so frightened.

I had never had such hope.

Acknowledgements

I'd like to thank my agent Peter Straus and my editor Kent Carroll for their faith, guidance, and hard work on my behalf.

Thanks also to the wonderful folks at Rogers, Coleridge & White and the fine staff at Europa Editions—Raonaid Ryn, especially—for their tireless labor.

ABOUT THE AUTHOR

Aaron Gwyn is the author of three novels.
He is also the author of the collection *Dog on
the Cross*, a finalist of the New York Public
Library's Young Lions Fiction Award. His
short fiction has appeared in numerous mag-
azines and anthologies including *Esquire*,
McSweeney's, *Best of the West*, and *Every True
Pleasure: LGBTQ Tales of North Carolina*. He
teaches English at the University of North
Carolina-Charlotte.